THE KINGS OF LONDON

D0482190

RAWN

Also by William Shaw

She's Leaving Home

WITHDRAWN

THE KINGS OF LONDON

WILLIAM SHAW

MULHOLLAND BOOKS

LITTLE, BROWN AND COMPANY

NEW YORK BOSTON LONDON

The characters and events in this book are fictitious. Any similarity to real persons, living or dead, is coincidental and not intended by the author.

Copyright © 2014 by William Shaw

All rights reserved. In accordance with the U.S. Copyright Act of 1976, the scanning, uploading, and electronic sharing of any part of this book without the permission of the publisher constitute unlawful piracy and theft of the author's intellectual property. If you would like to use material from the book (other than for review purposes), prior written permission must be obtained by contacting the publisher at permissions@hbgusa.com. Thank you for your support of the author's rights.

Mulholland Books/Little, Brown and Company
Hachette Book Group
1290 Avenue of the Americas
New York, NY 10104
mulhollandbooks.com

First North American Edition: January 2015
Originally published in Great Britain as *A House of Knives* by Quercus, June 2014

Mulholland Books is an imprint of Little, Brown and Company, a division of Hachette Book Group, Inc. The Mulholland Books name and logo are trademarks of Hachette Book Group, Inc.

The publisher is not responsible for websites (or their content) that are not owned by the publisher.

The Hachette Speakers Bureau provides a wide range of authors for speaking events. To find out more, go to hachettespeakersbureau.com or call (866) 376-6591.

'Jennifer Eccles' words and music by Harold Clarke and Graham William Nash. Copyright © 1968 GRALTO MUSIC LTD. Copyright Renewed.
All Rights in the U.S. and Canada Controlled and Administered by UNIVERSAL— SONGS OF POLYGRAM INTERNATIONAL, INC.
All Rights Reserved. Used by Permission. Reprinted by Permission of Hal Leonard Corporation.

'Ballad of a Thin Man' by Bob Dylan. Copyright © 1965 by Warner Bros. Inc.; renewed 1993 by Special Rider Music. Reprinted by permission.

'Since You've Been Gone' by Aretha Franklin, reprinted by permission of Sony ATV.

Every attempt has been made to attain licenses to reprint lyrics from the following songs: 'Girls Can't Do What the Guys Do' by Willie Clark and Clarence Reid, Sony ATV; 'Young Girl' by Jerry Fuller, Sony ATV. Any omissions should be notified to the publishers, who would be happy to make amendments to future editions.

ISBN 978-0-316-24687-3

LCCN 2014947608

10 9 8 7 6 5 4 3 2 1

RRD-C

Printed in the United States of America

WITHDRAWN

For Lisa

WITHDRAWN

THE KINGS OF LONDON

WITHDRAWN

ONE

At the end of the summer a man takes his sick father to hospital.

The French have voted in de Gaulle again. Robert Kennedy has been shot. The Americans, stuck deep in Vietnam, are swinging behind the Republican, Richard Nixon, instead. The Soviets have just sent the tanks into Prague. It is autumn 1968. And London is always London and the rain that has been falling on it all summer is still falling.

The nurse behind the desk is plump and has a distracting moustache. She holds a gnawed biro in one hand and asks questions like, 'Any allergies?'

It is late night, or maybe early morning. The man is tired. It feels as if he has not slept for days. 'No.'

And, 'Next of kin?'

'Just me.' Because he's thinly built the man looks taller than he is. He is in his early thirties, from a generation that still dresses conventionally. A pale mackintosh. Cherry Blossom Light Tan shoes. A grey suit.

'Any other relations?' she asks him.

'No.'

'No one at all?'

The man shakes his head. The weariness shows in the dark skin beneath his eyes.

She takes her pencil and writes 'NONE' on the form.

It has been a long night. One of too many.

'Where can you be contacted in an emergency?'

'I'm a policeman,' says the man, as if that's an answer. And he gives the number of his local station in Marylebone.

'There's a waiting room at the end of the ward, if you like,' she says, pointing with her biro. Somewhere a radio plays an idiotic song by Alma Cogan.

'No. I'd better go now,' he says. 'I'll be back later to see how he is.'

The policeman is usually good with details but will remember little of this. Days of looking after his father between shifts has left him exhausted. Long disturbed nights after work. The dribbles of luke-warm soup around the old man's mouth. The bed baths and bedpans. Always the startled look in his father's pale eyes. Bringing his father to hospital today is a relief. He has had enough.

But he will regret that he did not stay longer. Really, there was no need to go straight back to work. He could have stayed just a few more hours. This is the cold black stone that will sit in his chest.

It has been a bad year. Right now he just wants to keep moving. To pause for too long would be to give in to the sadness of it.

As he goes to the stairwell to leave the building he is surprised to find that the world outside is still dark and quiet. He checks his watch. Ticka-ticka Timex. It is still only twenty minutes past five. The days have been so disorientating, so fractured. He had been inside the hospital so long he had imagined it would be daytime now, but it is still three hours before he needs to be at work. It would make sense to stay.

He pauses on the cold staircase. Not enough time to go back to the flat he shares with his father and sleep. And if he catches the bus to Marylebone, he will be much too early.

So he sets off walking. Out of the hospital, into the silent street.

He walks down through to Islington, down Caledonian Road, past torn posters advertising Judy Garland at the Talk of the Town, all the time cold wind at his back. The pavements are still empty, save for the occasional man returning from a night shift, or nurse waiting for the first bus.

It is six by the time the man reaches King's Cross and the sky is the colour of cigarette ash. The postmen are delivering letters. The milkmen are delivering milk. Men in pinstripes are starting to arrive from their suburban homes, leather briefcases swinging as they walk.

'They say it might be days yet,' he tells the office typist, who arrives at work forty minutes after him. She is young, wears a lot of hairspray and bright cardigans. She has smudged her mascara, he notices, but he doesn't tell her.

'You poor love,' she says.

'Don't worry about me,' he says, 'I'm fine.' He keeps his head down, hoping she'll get the message that he doesn't want to talk about it.

'I can get you something from the canteen, if you like?'

For an hour or so he sits at his desk, sharpening pencils, pretending to type reports.

And when the call comes in about some firemen discovering a body in a burned-out house in Carlton Vale he volunteers to be the officer at the scene without even thinking about his father. It will give him something to do.

He is down the stairs and out of the office and into the CID Wolesley in less than two minutes. An unexplained death is something to occupy the mind.

'Paddy. Message for you.'

He doesn't hear the voice, first time.

'Are you up there, Paddy?'

Or the second. The man is squatting, examining the remains of a room, concentrating on what he sees.

'Paddy!'

A room. A fireplace. A dull ooze on the floorboards.

'Paddy Breen!'

They have taken the body away earlier that morning. All that remains is this dark stickiness that had escaped from the roasting skin.

The detective sergeant is absorbing it all. An empty can of lighter fuel. Floorboards seared black. An old armchair burned back to the springs. He is taking it all in. He has seen worse. It would have been a quick death.

'Sergeant Breen!'

He hears this time: 'What?'

'Someone on the radio asking for you, sir.'

The house had been long derelict. One of a row bombed out during the war and still not pulled down. The walls bare, the plaster falling from the ceiling. Everything is uniformly black after the fire. He takes a last look around the room because so much depends on what you find in these first few hours. This is what he is good at.

'Coming,' he says quietly, picking up the empty can of fuel.

And he starts to make his way carefully down the charred stairs holding the empty can between finger and thumb. The black grease that coats walls after a house fire is everywhere. He already has it on his shoes but he's trying hard not to get it on his jacket.

At the bottom of the stairs, a man in a fireman's uniform says, 'Went up bloody quick, by the look of it,' and then hacks and gobs onto the bare floor.

'Right,' says Breen. He holds up the can. 'This what started it?'

'Got to be,' says the fireman. 'Too quick not to be petrol or something like it, poor stupid bugger.'

'Did it himself? By accident?'

'See it every now and then, yep.'

'Could this have caused such a big fire?'

The fireman stuck out his lower lip. 'Maybe,' he said.

Breen nods and steps outside.

'On the radio now, sir.'

Breen gets into the passenger seat and lays the can on the dashboard, then pulls out a handkerchief and wipes the smut off his hands.

'Delta Mike Five,' he says into the receiver. 'Breen here.'

★

And he should have called up the hospital then when the first message came through. Though it was probably already too late. The doctor will say it was a urinary infection that finally killed him, but his father had been dying for years, burning away slowly from the inside.

His father had almost killed himself in a fire six years ago, leaving the gas on under a pan. He had escaped with a bandaged arm. It was the first sign that he was unravelling. After the fire he had moved in to Breen's care.

So, Tomas Breen, builder, of Knocancuig, Tralee, dies alone that September afternoon. At the same moment as the nurse places the sheet over him, his son is staring hard at a different body, one as black as the room it was found in, in a white-tiled room in another hospital, half a dozen miles away. He stares at the dead man in the hope that something will start to make sense. An unidentified dead man in a cold room.

TWO

Breen kept the photos of the burnt body in his in-tray. Three black-and-whites. One of the man's disfigured face, teeth showing through burnt lips. One of the whole corpse, taken from the side. One of the whole room, showing the position of the body. Every now and again, as the weeks went past, they rose to the top. Sometimes the other officers in Marylebone CID caught him looking at them, peering closely.

Skin cracked like a spit-roast pig. Pale flesh and fat showing from below. Knees bent slightly.

Autumn turned to winter and the identity of the body remained a mystery. Other cases came and went. Nixon won.

Detective Sergeant Cathal Breen started to clear his father's belongings out from his flat, but never quite finished the job. He bought his first Beatles record, but only played it a few times. Music like that was for a younger generation. He thought about combing his hair differently and maybe growing his sideboards longer, but didn't. He was thirty-two. It would look ridiculous.

Precisely why the fire had started remained unexplained, officially at least, though Wellington, the police surgeon, said that a bottle had been found melted into the skin of the corpse. That and the empty can of lighter fuel meant it was probably an accident, and though Breen still questioned whether a single can could have created such an intense blaze, nobody else seemed that bothered by the fact. It was some drunken vagrant attempting to light a fire to keep himself warm in the wet weather, most likely. That was enough for Wellington.

Breen kept at the case longer than he knew he should. He returned to the white hospital room several more times to look at the charred corpse. Most of the skin on the man's face had been burned away, so it was hard to know what he would have looked like. There were no obvious signs of trauma on the flesh that was left. The longer he remained unidentified, the longer it seemed likely that he had been a dosser. Breen began to assume he had been one of the thousands of Irish labourers who were flooding into London now, desperate for work. Wellington confirmed this when he told Breen there were traces of concrete dust in the material on his trousers.

Breen wrote notes. He knocked on doors of boarding houses and asked if any of their tenants had done a bunk. He drew maps, marking out the locations of all the building sites in the area. He visited the Garryowen and the Palais on the weekend, where they danced to showbands playing 'Boolavogue' and 'Liverpool Lou' and other teary waltzes. In the Irish dance halls there were two or three men to every woman. Anyone know of a man who's gone missing? One less would give the rest of us a bloody chance.

At first other officers ignored his obsession. The man's father had died recently. He was not himself. Good man, Paddy Breen. Not one of the boys, exactly, but, you know, a good man.

But as time passed, Breen knew they were becoming irritated by him. This was not a real case for a CID man. Bloody Paddy Breen. Still wasting time on that no-hoper. Not pulling his weight.

There was other work to be done. Real people who had died in fights and robberies. Not alky immigrants whom nobody would miss anyway. Bloody Irish. Paddy excepted, of course. It was clearly just an accident so why was he so bothered about it?

'Don't waste your effort on jobs nobody's going to thank you for,' Sergeant Prosser had said, more than once. Breen noticed how it infuriated Sergeant Prosser that a fellow officer could waste so much time on a lost cause.

The inspector was kinder, letting Breen have his way at first. Once, in late November he caught Breen with the photos laid out on his desk. They were a little dog-eared now, yellowing already.

'For God's sake, Breen' he said. Very quietly. One man to another.

Inspector Bailey was an old-school policeman. Decent enough, but a stickler. He didn't like to see officers stepping out of line like this. Where would you be if coppers went around just investigating the cases that got under their skin? 'Still think he's a labourer of some sort, do you?' Inspector Bailey asked.

'Yes, sir.'

A pause. 'Your father was Irish, wasn't he, Sergeant?'

'Yes, sir.'

Bailey had nodded. Had given Breen an uncomfortable look. Other people in the room stopped their typing and listened. 'And he was a builder, I believe?' said Bailey. 'Your late father.'

'Yes, sir.'

'It's understandable that a man is upset when his father dies,' he said.

Breen didn't answer.

'Buck up, Paddy,' the inspector said, briefly laying his hand on Breen's shoulder before walking away, shutting himself in the small room that was his office.

And there was an embarrassed pause in the CID office. At the next desk Constable Jones, the youngest officer in CID, was staring, mouth open. Breen glared back at him until Jones looked down at his typewriter and pretended to be searching for a letter among the keys. The gentle hum and clatter of the office returned.

Breen knew what was going on in their heads. Paddy was not thinking straight. His obsession was nothing to do with the burnt man. This was about his father. It was like a penance.

Sometimes there was no answer. Sometimes things didn't work out. There was not a solution to every crime. People died alone and unloved. He had never really bothered to find out who his father was when he was alive. He had not been curious enough.

Even if he did find out all about who the burnt man was, it wouldn't change a thing. Breen knew that.

THREE

So, the night of Sergeant Michael Prosser's leaving drinks at the Princess Louise, Breen decided to let it go.

That was it. The case would not be solved. Some things were never mended.

He had to get on with life. He was picking himself up. The world were changing. After six years of looking after his sick father, going home straight after work, he had started to come alive. Last week he had taken a woman back to his flat and made love to her.

A mistake, probably.

She had been a little drunk. A WPC.

But it was the first time he had been with a woman in years. He had felt the blood pulse in his body again.

He would tidy up his flat. Finally sort out his father's belongings. It was almost December. Next year would be different. 1969. The future was here. He should start living in it.

So he got up early the next morning. Last night at the Louise, everyone else had been drunk. Breen was not like the other officers. He rarely drank much; he was out of practice.

The others had stayed, singing, buying rounds and punching each other on the arm. Sloshing pints onto the sodden pub carpet. Breen had slipped out without saying goodbye to anyone. They would not be in till later. He could have some time to himself. He had plans.

★

On the Circle Line on the way in, a jester walked into Breen's dirty old carriage. He was dressed in green and blue and was shaking a stick covered in bells.

'Morning, comrades,' he cried out.

The train was stationary at King's Cross. Men lifted their newspapers a little higher or stared harder at the adverts on the other side of the carriage: 'Give Capstan This Christmas'. Or at the wooden floor, ridges packed with old fag ends.

The people Breen travelled with relied on the morning journey to work to be soothingly dull. A nothingness before the grind of work.

'Good cheer to you all, good folk of London town!' A shake of bells.

The man's hair was long. He wore a string of wooden beads around his neck. There was a new word the British had started using: 'hippie'.

'Be merry! Free yourselves from the chains of oppression.'

A man in a pinstripe suit sitting opposite Breen rolled his eyes. 'Merciful God.'

In his gaudy costume, the jester began trying to hand out what looked like paper scrolls. Breen noticed he was wearing open sandals. And his feet were engrained with black dirt. A traveller sitting next to Breen took one of the pieces of paper, but when Breen held out his hand the jester ignored him.

'Don't I get one?' Breen asked. The new Cathal Breen. Ready to engage with the world again.

'Don't encourage him,' hissed pinstripe man.

The jester looked Breen up and down. 'Methinks you probably wouldn't like it,' he said, moving on.

Further up the carriage, he held out another roll of paper to two office girls sitting side by side. They were too shy and pretended he wasn't there, folding their arms tightly, looking down at their shoes and giggling.

'Have you got a licence to do that?' the pinstripe man called down the carriage.

The jester stopped and looked back. 'Have you got a licence to wear that suit?'

The office girls burst out laughing, open-mouthed, shocked. They were still trying to stifle their laughter when the train jerked into motion. The man in the suit said, 'I'll report you to the police.'

Breen wondered, Did you actually need a licence to hand out material on the Underground?

After the jester had passed on through the connecting door into the next carriage, the man next to Breen unfurled his small scroll, looked at it for a second then scrunched it up and dropped it on the floor.

Breen leaned down and picked up the paper. It was an advertisement of some kind. An old woodcut print of a head with the top of the skull removed, showing the undulations of the brain underneath. Below were the words: 'Alchemical Wedding, Royal Albert Hall, 18 December 1968'.

No other explanation. Breen chucked it into a litter bin on the way into work.

Inspector Bailey arrived just after half past eight; mackintosh, tweed hat and a rolled umbrella. He looked disappointedly around the almost empty office and at the three photographs laid out on Breen's desk and grunted, then closed his office door behind him, as he always did.

Sergeant Prosser's leaving party had been a big night. Longest serving officer in D Division, CID. Reputation for banging up hard ones. Liked to do things the old-fashioned way, avoiding paperwork.

Good riddance to bad rubbish, as far as Breen was concerned.

A voice said, 'Oh my God. I feel like crap. Does my mouth still smell of brandy?'

Marilyn, the office secretary, hair teased up with spray, was standing by her desk, hands cupped over her nose, trying to smell her own mouth. She reached in a drawer and pulled out a packet of Disprin. 'Want some, Paddy?'

'I'm OK.'

'There's going to be some heads, today,' she said.

Breen liked Marilyn. It wasn't easy to be a woman in this office, but she had arrived a couple of years ago and set about firmly organising the men, turning their unmethodical piles of paper into neat, alphabetically organised files. 'Should have seen the state of some of them, going home.'

She disappeared down the corridor into the kitchen and returned with a glass of water.

Prosser's resignation had been a surprise to most people in CID. A big crowd had turned out and stayed until the small hours drinking pints and brandies. Men huddled in corners. But why's he really going? He's a copper's copper. One of the best. Plus, Prosser's got a crippled kiddie to support. Loved the job. Makes no sense at all.

'How many tickets do you want for the Ball?' Marilyn said.

Breen groaned. 'God. Is it that time already?' D Div Christmas Ball. Dress suits, rum punch and Kenny Ball and his Jazzmen at the Cumberland Hotel. Breen said, 'I better take one, then.' All proceeds to the Orphan's Fund.

'Just one? Aww,' Marilyn said. 'No one you want to invite?' She was standing over him clutching a wad of pale tickets.

'One, please.'

Marilyn came closer again. Voice lowered. 'Not asking that WPC Tozer?' The woman he had slept with. One night only.

Breen looked at her. Did she know? It didn't take much for a rumour to do the rounds. 'Do you think I should?'

Marilyn said, 'God, no, sir. She's not your type.'

'Really?'

'Bit of a handful. Goes with a lot of men.'

Breen blinked. 'You shouldn't spread rumours.'

'Who says it's a rumour? There must be some girl, Paddy. Someone suitable. Nobody comes to the Christmas Ball on their own. Come with me if you like.'

'Thought you had a boyfriend already, Marilyn.' Danny Carr.

A short, Brylcreem-haired boy who sat around all day doing sweet Fanny Adams.

'Just pulling your leg, Paddy,' she said. 'Useless prannock was so drunk last night he chucked up in my handbag.'

Marilyn was always threatening to drop Danny, but never did. He'd been out of work since early summer.

'Marilyn, where do you keep the 728s?'

She lifted her handbag and sniffed at it. 'I cleaned it out with Vim twice when we got in and it still stinks. What do you want a 728 for?'

'Annual leave.'

Marilyn blinked. 'You're going on holiday?'

'Why not?'

'What? Proper holiday?'

'Yes.'

'You never go on holiday. Well-known fact.'

'That was before my dad died,' said Breen. 'Now I can. I decided last night. It would do me good, I think. Help me get on top of things again.'

Marilyn was still peering into her bag. 'Good for you, Paddy.'

Caring for his father had meant he had rarely gone out with other coppers in the evening and never left London for long.

'I was going to ask for the week starting December the ninth.'

She looked up from the handbag. 'Blimey, Paddy. You'll be lucky.'

'I'm due at least two weeks.'

'This time of year? What do you want to take a holiday in December for?'

Breen said, 'My dad left me some money. I thought I might use some of it to go and see where he grew up. Never been. I want to try something new.'

'No harm in asking, I suppose,' she said. 'Paddy. What's that smell? Is that your socks?'

'What smell?'

Marilyn sniffed the air. 'Can't you smell it?'

'It's your handbag, I expect.'

She tried her bag again. 'You hear the news this morning?' she said. 'Ruddy great gas explosion up in NW8. Blew a house to bits.'

She was right, though, thought Breen. Something did smell.

'Happening all the time now, isn't it? Gas leaks. Bloody Gas Board, you ask me. Bunch of useless . . .' Back in May the side of one of London's huge new tower blocks collapsed after a gas explosion on the eighteenth floor. In all the papers. Four people crushed to death. Marilyn dropped a piece of paper on his desk. 'Holiday form,' she said, with a wink. 'Might as well give it a try.'

He looked at it. A Roneo'd sheet of yellow paper. Length of leave requested. Special circumstances. He placed it into his in-tray.

The photographs of the dead man still lay on his desk. These people who come to London, build its homes and power its factories, and leave so little trace of themselves. His father had been one of them.

It had felt good to try, at least. But he knew he would get no further with this, so it was time to let it go.

He opened the bottom drawer to put the photographs away there once and for all. That's when the stench filled his nostrils.

'Jesus.'

Somebody had defecated in the draw of his desk. Not a cat or a dog. It was human excrement. The shit lay, a pale, moist curl, staining the pale-blue police manual it sat on. Someone must have squatted down, trousers around their ankles, drawer open.

Breen blinked a couple of times and slammed the door shut.

'What's up?' said Marilyn.

'Nothing,' said Breen. And instead of putting them away in the stink-filled drawer, he returned the photographs of the burnt man to his in-tray.

FOUR

Dust still hung over NW8. It had fallen molecule thin on the bonnets of cars and the leaves of shrubs. It lay palely on the tops of things, other surfaces dark. Dust shadows. It had fallen on the piles of brick and broken glass, on a pair of spectacles that sat on the lawn and on a pot of geraniums that stood by what had once been a front door.

A woman police constable walked carefully towards the ruined house. In each hand she held a mug of tea. Her flat shoes printed the dust with small, careful steps. Shreds of paper decorated the trees.

The streets around were quiet. Somewhere a radio sang:

> I love Jennifer Eccles,
> I know that she loves me.

A cold, dull London morning now the rain had stopped. A black cat padded across the street in front of her and stopped to look around, trying to figure out what was wrong, then slunk under an Austin.

> I know that she loves me.

The stink of burnt wood and plaster was stronger, the closer the policewoman walked. Two bored coppers stood at the door, watching her approach.

On the door, in fact. It had been blown flat, a scorched copy of *The Times* still poking through the letterbox. The two policemen perched on the wood, like a raft, to avoid getting their polished boots any dirtier.

'Plonk sighted. Six o'clock.'

'Uglier every year.'

'Don't bloody spill it, love. Won't be any left.'

''k sake, woman.'

But they didn't make a move towards her.

'You got sugar?'

She said nothing, but handed them the tea.

'What about biscuits?'

'Get lost.'

'Only asking.'

'God, I fancy a biscuit.'

'They find anyone in there?' she asked.

'You spilt half of it.'

'Go back for biscuits, will you? I been here an hour. I didn't have my breakfast 'cause of this.'

'Get them yourself. What do you think I am? Your mum?'

One face of the house had been blown completely away. Above, loose timbers jutted from the roof. It must have been a big house. Posh.

'Still a big crowd?'

'Only about fifty. Mostly just wanting to know when they can get back into their houses.'

They turned at the sound of a van, loud in the empty street. On its side: the words 'GAS SERVICE'.

The man behind the wheel looked pale and nervous. He shut off the engine, wound down the window and said, 'Are my fellows still in there?'

'How long before we can go in?'

'Not my department,' said the man from the Gas Board, getting out of the car. He wore black-rimmed glasses, a khaki warehouse coat and had a small Hitlerish moustache. Pipe bowl sticking out of the top of his coat pocket. He joined the two men and the woman on the door, looking into the remains of the house.

'Bloody Nora. Hell of a bang, weren't it?' said the Gas Board man, looking around him.

'Who's that?' asked the woman constable.

Halfway down the street was a man with long hair dressed in an army surplus store greatcoat, bending over a Hanimex, methodically taking photographs. How had he got there? People were getting panicky about their plumbing. People remembered the photographs of flats crumpled like cards in one of the brand-new blocks. And now this. Explosion Levels Maida Vale House.

'Oi! Do you have permission for that?'

It was so quiet in the street you could hear every snap of the shutter, even though he had to be twenty-five yards away. The thinner of the two coppers bent to put his tea down carefully on the edge of the door, then started to make his way through the rubble.

'The public ain't allowed . . .'

The photographer calmly took another frame, then another.

Past the rubble, the copper broke into a trot. Finally the photographer swept the long hair out of his eyes, turned and ran swiftly away down the street, disappearing around a corner back towards the barricades.

'Cheeky arse.'

'How come he got through?' said the gas man. 'I had a nightmare getting past your men. Your lot don't know what you're bloody doing, ask me.'

'No harm done,' said the woman. 'He's only taking photographs. Besides, there'll be a nice picture of you in tonight's papers.'

'We should have bloody nicked him.'

'Will there?' said the gas man, standing a little straighter. 'Do you reckon?'

One of the policemen tipped up the dregs of his cup and reached into his jacket pocket for a pack of ciggies.

'I hope you're not thinking of lighting that,' said the gas man.

The copper hesitated, then pulled a cigarette out of the packet. 'You'd smell if there was still gas.'

'Oh you would, would you?'

'Course you would,' said the constable, pulling out the Swan Vestas.

'Give me a minute to get to a safe distance then,' said the gas man. But he didn't move.

The copper pulled out a match. 'You're jokin' me?'

The man in the beige coat said, 'Wait till I'm two hundred yards away and then you're welcome to find out whether I am.'

The copper pursed his lips, sighed, put the fag back in the packet and said, 'I'm bloody gasping.'

'We shut off the valve at the top of the street, but a bang like that could have fractured the main. Happened all the time during the war.'

'But gas? You'd smell it.'

'Gets down in the ground. That's the trouble,' said the gas man.

From inside the ruined building came the sound of banging. One of the firemen, making the place safe before they could enter.

'My bloody boots will be wrecked,' said one of the bobbies.

There was a loud shout, followed by a rumble, then the sound of falling bricks. Another wave of dust blew out of the door.

'Fucking hell.'

Then a gust of laughter.

'You clumsy bloody divvy.'

The gas man was pale. 'What the hell are they playing at in there?'

'You're shaking. You should try a cigarette.'

'Listen,' said the policewoman.

'What?'

They listened. After the crash of falling masonry, the house had fallen silent again.

'They stopped laughing,' she said.

And they had. All at once the laughter and swearing from inside the house had ended.

A fireman emerged, the blue of his serge almost totally obliterated by dust. He looked at the two policemen. 'Something you should see,' he said. 'Something bloody . . . weird.'

The crow's feet on either side of his eyes cracked the dust on his face. The woman noticed his hands were trembling.

'You OK?' she asked.

He looked at her angrily. 'Course I am.'

'Christ sake, woman,' said one of the coppers, like it was her fault for asking.

FIVE

'You all right?' Sergeant Breen asked Temporary Detective Constable Tozer, shouting above the noise of the siren.

'Me? I'm fine,' she shouted back. They were in Delta Mike Five, the old Wolesley radio car whose gearbox crunched every time Breen put it into second.

He hesitated before saying, 'I meant to call you.'

'Course you did,' said Tozer.

'No. Really.'

She looked out of the window. Awkwardly thin, early twenties, in clothes that never seemed to fit quite right. Lank hair cut to a bob. 'I wasn't by the phone, waiting for it to ring, if that's what you were wondering.'

'Of course not.'

She dipped into her handbag. 'I suppose you told all the lads,' she said.

'What do you take me for?'

'That's something, anyway,' she said. 'Want a fag?'

He shook his head.

'Were you avoiding me?'

'No,' he said. 'Busy, that's all.'

'Fair enough,' she said. 'I been busy too. Getting ready to go home.'

Tozer had handed in her notice. She was leaving too. She had joined CID from the Women's Section as a probationer, hoping to do more than just interview women and children, or direct traffic, which was all you were supposed to do as a WPC. But it wasn't much different in CID either.

'I mean,' said Tozer. 'It was just a bit of fun, wasn't it, you and me?' Then, 'Christ. Must have rattled a few windows.'

Breen had pulled up outside the house on Marlborough Place. Or what was left of it. A grand, three-storey Victorian mansion, half of it completely blown away.

The Gas Board were still not allowing people back into their houses. They crowded behind the line of policemen, craning necks. A couple of press men with twin-lens reflex cameras complained about the way they were being treated. Breen recognised one from the local *Chronicle*. 'Oi, guv. What's going on? Get us in there, can't you?'

Things like this never happened around here. After the firemen had discovered the body news had spread fast.

'I was expecting to see you last night,' Breen said. 'At Prosser's leaving do.'

'Didn't fancy it much, be honest,' Tozer said. 'Don't even know why Prosser's leaving. Many there?'

'Everyone,' he said.

'Rats from the sinking ship,' she said.

Breen approached one of the three constables standing on the door. Two men, one woman. 'They found a body, they said. Where is it?'

'In the kitchen. What's left of it.'

A fireman came out of the building. 'Got a cigarette?' he asked, brushing down his sleeves.

'I said no bloody smoking,' said the gas man.

'Give it a rest. That guy's smoking over there. 'If he can, I can.' He pointed to a press man hovering at the front gate.

Tozer pulled a packet out of her handbag and offered him one. 'You a copper?' asked the fireman.

'Yes,' she said. 'For the next four weeks.' She wasn't cut out for the force, they said. Breen wanted to tell her that he'd miss her, but he hadn't found the right opportunity. Not yet, anyway.

'Why isn't you in uniform then?' asked the fireman.

'Didn't match my nail varnish,' Tozer said. The fireman looked down at her hand. She wasn't wearing any.

'Safe to go in?' asked Breen.

'Fire's all extinguished. But, ask me, whole lot could go any sec,' said the fireman. He took a long pull on the cigarette Tozer had given him.

'We need to see the body before they pull the place down,' said Breen.

'I could tell you all you need to know,' said the fireman. 'Some bastard sliced him up like a Sunday roast. Sorry, miss,' he said to Tozer.

'Who knows about that?' said Breen.

'Just us firemen.'

'Keep it to yourselves, OK? How do you know it wasn't just the blast?'

'During the war I seen all sorts of things happen in explosions. Never one skin a man, though.' The fireman turned to Tozer. 'What about after this, you and me and some of the lads—'

'Skinned?' said Breen.

'Like a ruddy banana. Not all of him, mind. What about a coffee bar or something, love?'

'Don't really think so,' Tozer said.

'Pardon me,' said the fireman. Then to Breen. 'Only asking out of politeness. She's got a face like bag of spanners, anyway.'

'You haven't been able to get the body out?'

'Not our job, mate. Too risky in the circumstances.'

Breen said, 'I want to see him for myself before anything else falls on him.'

'Only I'm not supposed to let anyone in,' said the fireman.

'I'm a policeman,' said Breen.

The fireman hesitated. 'Your funeral, mate. They're bringing a 'dozer to pull the lot down. It'll be here any minute.'

'Come on then,' said Tozer.

'Oi!' said the fireman. 'Go careful. Don't want to be hoicking out three bodies.'

'You don't have to come,' said Breen to Tozer.

'I know,' she said.

What he should have said was, 'You're not supposed to come.' If she got hurt there would be a stink. But it would be good to have her there with him.

Leaving the fireman, they went inside, walking through the empty door-frame into what was left of the hallway. An upright umbrella stand, unbothered by the debris; a large brass ceiling lamp lying on the hallway floor. They stepped past it, picking through lath and plaster. Air thick with the tang of brick powder and smoke. Breen caught his foot in something and looked down. His shoe had gone through the canvas of a painting. He tried to kick it off but stumbled, falling against the wall where the picture had hung. Plaster dust fell from the ceiling onto him. Tozer laughed.

'It's not funny,' said Breen.

She reached out a hand to him and he took it, bent down, and tugged the frame off his foot. There was a ripping sound. At first he thought it was the canvas, but looking down he saw a triangle of material hanging loose from his trousers.

'Blast,' he said.

'Come on. I'm sure Marilyn could mend it for you.'

'What?'

'Everyone knows she fancies you, Paddy.'

'Rubbish.'

'Soft spot for her, have you?'

'Don't be a cow.'

'As if.'

*

Towards the back the damage was worse. The rear of the house had caught fire after the explosion and still stank of smoke. The firemen had supported the door to the kitchen with a loose plank. Breen had to squeeze himself past, careful not to dislodge it.

'Well, she's certainly got a soft spot for you,' said Tozer.

'Stop it,' he said, looking down at his jacket. There was a long smear: that would need dry cleaning too.

The kitchen had taken the worst of the blast. An entire wall had been blown away on the right side. The ceiling from the room above had given way, so that a large twisted metal bed now lay in the centre of what had been the kitchen. The room still dripped with water from the fire hoses.

Scrambling over the rubble, Breen managed a glance at his brogues. If he wasn't careful they would be ruined.

Tozer was already next to the fallen bed. She stood on the sopping mattress, grabbing a brass bedpost to steady herself. Breen struggled his way around to join her.

The man lay awkwardly, legs trapped under a fallen beam. Propped against the remains of a chair, his head was leaning back, eyes wide open. His corneas were covered in an even sheen of dust that had continued to fall on him, long after the fire had been extinguished. It made him look blinder than he already was. Like one of those blank-eyed Roman busts in the British Museum.

The dusty body was like nothing Breen had ever seen. It was skeletal, bones poking through the skin, as if the man had been starved to death.

'You not going to be sick or anything?' said Tozer.

Breen approached the man, took a deep breath, then knelt down and tried to brush the dust from the side of the dead man's face. It was crusted on by the water poured over everything by the firemen.

Breen's squeamishness at death was a new thing; useless in his line of work. The skin had been gently fried by the heat of the fire, but not roasted, as his other body had been. But from his upper arms to his wrists the skin had been peeled away. Not carefully. Chunks of muscle had been torn off in the process, and the remains hung, loose and singed.

The dust brushed off the wounds easily. The blood underneath was dry. 'He was dead long before the explosion,' said Breen.

Even without the dust, his skin looked pale, his eyes sunken. Breen started picking the half-bricks and splinters off the man's body.

'God there. Poor bugger,' said Tozer. She knelt down and joined in removing the debris. He was propped up in the rubble at a jaunty angle, body already stiff from rigor mortis. He seemed to be completely naked.

'Arrogant twat,' said Tozer. 'It's not like he was any oil painting, exactly.'

'What?' said Breen, brushing the greyness off the man's face.

'That fireman,' said Tozer.

Breen hesitated. 'Jesus,' he said, flinching backwards.

'What?'

'Look at his throat.'

'God there,' said Tozer again.

Beneath the dead man's chin, a long dark line. His throat had been cut.

The two stared at him for a second. The man's legs were trapped under a charred wooden beam, but you could see the skin had been yanked off from his ankles to his knees. A young man. Handsome, possibly. It was hard to tell.

He tried to pull the beam away, but yanked his hand back instantly. The wood was still hot from the fire.

'Where's all the blood?' said Tozer. 'I mean, if somebody cut his throat you'd expect to see blood.'

Breen nodded. 'It's odd. Somebody cleaned him up. They must have,' he said.

Crouching awkwardly to inspect the body was giving Breen cramp. He straightened, realising he was trembling slightly. 'You're very calm, looking at all this.'

'Used to dead things, you know,' said Tozer. 'Seen as bad on the farm. It's not all that I mind. It's laughing boy outside. Glad I'm leaving the job,' she said. 'Be honest, I've had enough of it.' Temporary Detective Constable Tozer was going back to Devon to work on the family farm. Soon she would be done with the job; done with him.

The sound of bells and sirens. More police arriving outside.

'Know what? It's like he's been bled dry,' said Tozer. 'Like a ruddy pig.'

Breen gazed at the disorder surrounding him. 'Look for a knife. Whatever could have been used to skin him.'

'What? In all this?'

The roof creaked above them. A sudden trickle of broken brickwork poured down into the middle of the room. Dust filled the air.

'We should get out,' said Tozer. 'They said it's not stable.'

'Not yet.'

Breen looked around. At a crime scene you were supposed to look for the small things that seemed out of place. Here, everything was out of place. This was a bomb site, like the ones he had played on during the war. They had scrambled over bricks, finding reminders of of life among the ruins. A doll. A chequebook. A corkscrew. The children collected them greedily. Talismans of the impermanence of their parents' world. Evidence that when they were told that everything was going to be all right they were being lied to.

'You OK?' said Tozer again.

'Yes.'

Only the gas cooker seemed to have come out unscathed, knobs still twisted fully on.

'I'm not flipping dressed for this,' Tozer said, hair thick with dust, tights snagged. She carried on picking away bricks from around the dead man.

'You don't have to be in here.'

She didn't answer. In the remains of the study, a desk lay covered in debris. The drawers were half open, as if somebody had gone through them. He pulled out one that was full of correspondence. Taking out a pile of papers, he put it on top of the desk and looked around for something to put it on.

'Oi, copper!' called a voice from outside the building. 'You OK?'

'Fine,' said Breen.

'The boss says you should come out now. It's going to go.'

'In a minute.'

'I'll bloody catch it if you get squished.'

They would tear the building down. This crime scene would be gone. He had to see whatever he could, grab whatever he could.

He found another picture frame, face down, and picked it up. It would act as a tray. He placed the pile of papers on top of it and looked around some more, but it was hard to know where to start in the chaos.

'What about upstairs?' he said. They were running out of time.

'What's that you've got?' asked Tozer.

'Just some papers,' Breen said. 'If there's anything you think might give us information about him, grab it.'

'Right you are.'

Bedrooms could reveal things about a man. An unmade bed. Or a secret in a sock drawer.

When he reached the bottom of the stairs, Breen looked around for somewhere to put his pile of documents. The telephone table had been knocked on its side. He laid the picture frame across the fallen legs and went upstairs.

The late November light was thin. It was hard to make things out, but Breen could still see that the main bedroom was curiously undisturbed by the mayhem of the rest of the house and the street outside. The bed unslept in.

The bedroom itself was a surprise. An oriental fantasy. Moroccan lamps hung from the ceiling. Indian cotton drapes surrounded the bed. The bed showed no obvious signs of a crime of passion. On the dressing table sat statues of Indian gods, next to a cluster of cut-glass atomisers. On the walls, more paintings that looked familiar. Very modern. He thought he recognised the pale fleshy pink of one of the fashionable painters who got drunk in Soho. Others were less recognisable, but they seemed not to have been collected out of the usual sense of duty, or the urge to fill the walls with things that looked right. They had been chosen by someone who clearly loved each one and had positioned them with care.

He wondered about taking the paintings off the wall to save them. They would all be destroyed with the house. It seemed a waste. But there was no time.

He returned to the wreck of the kitchen, where Tozer was picking through the rubble.

Voices from outside: 'Oi! Coppers. Come out now.'

'Found anything?'

'Not really,' said Tozer. 'Paddy? Come on. We should go.'

'They're going to bulldoze it with the body still in here?'

'Reckon. It's not safe to start digging around.'

'What if we got one of the photographers outside to come in? Some sort of record, at least.'

'I don't know.'

He remembered the last time he had stayed too long in a burnt house.

'What about trying to move the beam?' he suggested.

'Bloody hell,' said Tozer. Then, 'OK.'

Breen found a ripped curtain to wrap around it. Crouching in the gloom they found one end and tried to lean against it. It was wedged over the dead man's thighs, crushing the empty skin.

No movement. They changed positions. Breen moved to the other side, ready to pull it towards him.

'After three,' said Tozer.

'One. Two . . .'

They never got to three.

'Is that gas?' said Breen.

Tozer let go of the beam and sniffed.

'I can't smell nothing.'

Breen breathed in again. 'Can't you smell that?'

Tozer shook her head.

'I'm sure I can smell something.'

'Bloody hell,' said Tozer, scrambling away.

Breen paused.

'What about the body?'

'Bugger that,' said Tozer. 'If you can smell gas . . . Jesus. Don't just stand there. We need to get out.'

His papers. Where were they?

'Leave it,' hissed Tozer.

'No,' said Breen, looking around, trying to remember where he had left them.

'Bloody leave it.'

She was right. The fire was doused but there could still be embers.

'Hurry.'

Reluctantly he followed her, stumbling out of the room, squeezing past the small space beside the wedged beam. He was just heading for the front door when he remembered: the papers were on the telephone table behind him.

Tozer looked back, holding her arm out towards him. He tried to follow her but couldn't. Something held him back. What? He looked down and saw he had snagged his jacket on a shattered piece of stud-work.

'Come on, Paddy,' Tozer shouted.

Twisting his body to yank the cloth off, Breen was suddenly free.

''Bout time,' said the fireman, as Breen reached the cold air outside.

'He smelt gas,' said Tozer.

'I thought I did,' said Breen. 'I might have been wrong.'

'Really?' said the man nervously. Breen paused to squat down and examine the fallen front door. The lock was intact. No sign of forced entry. But the killer could have smashed a window and there would be no evidence of it now.

'Don't believe us, go in and see for yourself,' Tozer was saying to the fireman. She picked up the handbag she'd left by the fallen door. 'Fag?'

The fireman almost took one, then pulled his hand back at the last second.

Breen laid his pile of documents on the back seat. Tozer looked him over. 'You OK? Your jacket's ruined.'

She was right. The trousers could be mended, but there was a six-inch tear that started from one of his pockets through which you could see the the material beneath.

'What's that?' said Tozer.

There was a sudden shout.

Breen stood up and looked. The coppers and the firemen were running down the path, away from the house.

'Fire!' At first Breen couldn't see what they were talking about, but then a jet of flame burst through the fallen rubble just beyond the kitchen where they had been. It burned about four feet into the winter air, so brightly it turned the sky around it dark.

'Blimey,' said Tozer.

Breen's heart started thumping. He felt sick.

They sat in the car for a while as the firemen ran around, shouting at each other and at the gas man.

'What if we were still in there?' Tozer said.

'We weren't.'

A rush of flame in the London air.

'Pretty, in't it?'

Breen nodded.

'Not going to be much evidence left now, though,' she said, watching the firemen working. 'I mean, why're they not using the hoses?'

'Gas fire,' said Breen. 'No point.' It would burn until they found some way of shutting off the gas.

Eventually Breen said, 'Want a lift back to section house so you can get cleaned up?'

'Suppose,' said Tozer. 'What if I drive?'

'Not on your life,' said Breen. Women police: not allowed behind the wheel. She rolled her eyes, stuck out her tongue at him, then looked away.

SIX

The drive back to the station took longer than it should have. The road was blocked with a queue of cement mixers. Even in the rain, the whole city seemed thick with concrete dust. They were building everywhere.

'Young, wasn't he?'

'Not that young. Maybe twenty-eight,' said Breen.

'I meant, to be so independent.'

'Family money, I'm guessing.'

Tozer tugged on the lever to tilt her seat back. 'Will you let me help out on this one?'

'Oh no,' said Breen. 'I'm not doing it.'

'Who says?'

'I was just the only one in when it came through. Everyone else was in late because of Prosser's party. I'm handing it on. I'm going on holiday.'

He looked at her. She was offering him a stick of chewing gum even though she must know by now that he never accepted it.

'What's so funny?' he asked.

'I mean, what are you going to do on holiday?' said Tozer, un-wrapping a Juicy Fruit for herself. 'Go fishing?'

'I don't like fishing.'

'That's what I mean. I'm picturing you in a pair of swimming trunks lying on the beach on the Costa del Sol.'

'I'm going to Ireland. To see where my father came from. I've never been.'

The laughing stopped. 'Right. Sorry.'

Cathal Breen's father had been a Kerryman who had eloped to England with the love of his life, a local schoolteacher. She died when Breen was only a few years old. A self-contained man, he had raised the boy alone, rarely talking about his home country. Breen had always been acutely aware of being Irish, being different, but his father never discussed his past. Only when he was old and losing his mind, the two of them alone together, did he start talking about Ireland again. Mostly gibberish. Names Breen didn't recognise. Snatches of Gaelic. By the time Breen had reached the age when he wanted to know about the place his parents had grown up, his father was no longer able to tell him.

'I'm glad,' said Tozer. 'It'll be good for you.'

'Tralee. It's where he was from. I'll hire a car. I was thinking of booking in to a hotel there for Christmas. Take a few walks, maybe.'

'On your own?'

'Yes.'

As long as he could remember, Christmas had been just him and his father, eating in silence. Ham usually. A chicken was too much for two to eat.

'Impossible,' said Inspector Bailey. 'No.'

'Sir?'

'No.'

Breen had borrowed a jacket from Constable Jones to replace the one he'd ripped in the escape from the building. A blazer with silver buttons. He was taller than Jones, so the jacket was too small; it made Breen feel like a music hall comedian.

'But, sir . . .'

Inspector Bailey's office was a small rectangular room carved out of the main office floor. 'In case you haven't noticed, we are down two men. Sergeant Carmichael has left us for the Drug Squad and Sergeant Prosser has resigned. For no apparent reason. No great loss, but it means we're short two men. Request refused.'

'I'm due almost three weeks, sir.'

Bailey's eye twitched. 'I have just been contacted by the Home Office. The victim at the site of the gas explosion was Francis Pugh. Had you established that yet?'

'No, sir.'

'Well, now you know. The son of Rhodri Pugh,' said Bailey. When Breen didn't respond, he added, 'Under-Secretary of State in the Home Department.'

'A minister?'

'Exactly.'

Breen's heart sank. 'What about compassionate leave, sir? With my father dying . . .'

'That was three months ago, Sergeant. No.'

'Two-and-a-half, sir . . .'

'On a case like this we'll be under a lot of scrutiny.'

Breen understood. The Home Office was in charge of the police. The dead man was the son of a senior politician.

'It's not my turn, sir.'

A small sniff. 'There are no such things as turns. This is not Monopoly, Sergeant. Constable Jones will assist you.'

Constable Jones. Secondary modern boy with just three Certificates of Secondary Education, a fondness for the royal family, and a pregnant wife.

'With Prosser and Carmichael gone, you are the longest serving officer here. I have contacted Rhodri Pugh's people. They will wish to meet you to ensure that the case is handled with the sensitivity it requires. I hope you haven't booked tickets or anything stupid like that?'

'No, sir.'

'Good. One more thing.' Bailey paused as if he had something difficult to say. He smoothed the sheet of blotting paper on top of his desk with the heel of his hand.

'It's my birthday on Tuesday,' he said.

Breen blinked. 'Congratulations, sir.'

'It happens to be my sixtieth,' said Bailey.

'Yes, sir,' said Breen.

A pause while Bailey pulled on his ear lobe. A slight tremble in his fingers. 'I know I'm not always the most popular officer with the younger men,' he said finally. 'Probably my fault. Always a bit formal, I expect.'

'I wouldn't say that, sir.'

'Don't fib, Paddy.'

Unlike the other men in D Div, CID, Breen actually liked Bailey. Secretly, at least. The way he put the photo of his wife and children on his desk. The way he collected rainwater to feed the African violets he kept on his windowsill. The way he stuck to the rules, irritating all the younger, more impulsive coppers.

'I don't like to be thought of as stand-offish. My wife was planning a dinner for me at home, but I suppose there'll be plenty of time for that when I've retired. So I thought maybe I should go out for a drink with my mates on the job.'

His mates on the job. The phrase sounded absurd in Bailey's mouth. He was one of those stiff-backed men. One of those who had fought in the war. One of those who believed conformity was a sign of trustworthiness.

'What do you think?' asked Bailey.

'Well, sir . . .'

'You think they'll want to come?'

'Of course they will,' said Breen.

'Splendid.' Bailey smiled. 'I shall look forward to that, then. Perhaps you could spread the word?'

Breen hesitated. 'Wouldn't it be better if the invite came from you, sir?'

'I don't think so. Nothing formal, you see. Just a jolly evening with the lads.'

'Right, sir.' Breen turned to go.

'I meant to ask,' said Bailey. 'Was there any talk last night about why Sergeant Prosser was leaving us?'

'No, sir,' said Breen. 'Not a thing.'

'I just wanted to get to the bottom of it, that's all. Sergeant Prosser was a lifer.' Breen turned to face the inspector again. 'He was in it for the full pension. He has a family to support. People like that just don't resign out of the blue unless something's going on. Something is up. I want you to be my eyes and ears, Paddy.'

'Sir?'

'To find out why he left us so suddenly. If there's any muck there, I need to know. Eyes and ears, Paddy.'

'Yes, sir,' said Breen.

'Don't look so glum, Sergeant. I wouldn't give this case to anyone. I hope you appreciate that. Do it well and it'll be good for you.'

Breen down looked at his shoes. The scratches in the leather. 'Thank you, sir.'

'What's wrong?' said Marilyn, standing up at her desk. 'What did Bailey want?'

Breen said nothing. He walked on straight past her to the shelves behind her desk.

'You in a bate about something, Paddy?'

He took two old box files. They had been emptied, but they still had the names of old cases written on them. Cases that had happened long before Breen's time here at Marylebone.

'Paddy?' said Marilyn again. 'Are you OK?'

The CID room was brightly lit by neon strips that flickered occasionally. He took the box files and dropped them on his desk. Sat down. Called up the travel agency he had been talking to about his holiday. 'What about if I went to Ireland in January instead?' he asked.

'After the New Year, the ferries stop sailing until Easter,' the woman said.

Marilyn padded alongside him after he'd finished the call.

'Anything I can do, Paddy?'

'No thank you, Marilyn,' he said, too loudly. 'And my name's not Paddy. It's never been Paddy. It's Cathal.'

And the room was silent for a minute. The neon buzzed a little more loudly. The thing about Marilyn was that everybody knew she was a pain sometimes, but she kept the office working. Without her there was chaos. And Breen, of all people, was never rude to her.

Finally Constable Jones said, 'Shock, I expect. From the explosion.'

'Jesus,' said Breen.

A pencil rolled off a desk and clattered onto the floor, unnaturally loudly.

'Well, I'm sorry,' said Marilyn eventually. 'Excuse me for trying to help you, Sergeant Cathal Breen.'

Breen concentrated on the pile of documents he had grabbed from Pugh's house. He divided them into two even piles and put each into one of the two box files.

When he snapped the clip shut on the first he looked up to see everyone in the office staring at him.

He realised he was shaking. Could they see that? He ignored them, picking up the picture he had used as a tray to carry the documents out of the house, turning it over for the first time.

It was a print, but modern. Very modern. Several perfectly round black dots on a white background. The dots were three different sizes. They were spaced as if in a pattern, but what the pattern was was not easy to discern. It had been mounted in a plain white frame a little more than two foot square.

Breen held it upright on his desk and looked at it, trying to work it out.

'What the hell's that?' said a voice behind him. Constable Jones.

'A picture I took from the house in Maida Vale.'

'Modern art?' said Jones. He held a comb in one hand.

'Yes.'

'I mean, who do they think they're kidding?' said Jones, tugging the comb through his thick hair to try to keep his side parting in place.

Breen nodded, still looking at the picture.

'I mean, a five-year-old could do that. Even I could do that.'

'Even you, Jonesy,' said Marilyn.

Jones had a cut on his face just below his left eye. A graze on the cheekbone where someone had thumped him. He'd been fighting last night. He often got into fights after a late night drinking. It was part of the fun.

Breen stared at the picture still. The dots were printed onto perspex. In the bottom left-hand corner, a signature had been etched, but Breen could not make it out. Below that a number: 14/75.

Marilyn joined them. She said. 'You sure it's meant to be that way up?'

Breen said, 'Sorry I was rude, Marilyn. I'm a bit out of sorts.'

Marilyn nodded. 'No holiday then?' she said.

Breen shook his head.

'That jacket would look OK on you if it was a couple of sizes bigger,' she said. 'Turn around.' And she started brushing flecks of lint from the cloth, tugging at it to smooth out the wrinkles.

The box files and the print sat awkwardly on his lap on the bus home. On Kingsland Road the bus stopped, and the conductor ordered all the passengers out because the bus had changed its route.

'Everybody off,' the conductor said. 'This bus don't go nowhere.'

The passengers refused to move at first. 'It said Stoke Newington on the front, you stupid coon.'

The West Indian just stood by the stairs, arms folded, metal ticket machine strapped to his stomach, a weary smile on his face. A wiry old man in a wool cap said, 'I ought to smash your ugly black face in.'

The black man said nothing, still smiling. The old man quivered with anger, but after a couple of seconds moved on and stepped off the bus.

When he'd gone, the black man spat out of the bus after him.

'Everybody off now,' he said.

An old lady in a hairnet was struggling to pull a shopping trolley out of the luggage compartment under the stairs. The conductor moved to help her but she elbowed him aside. 'I'll do it myself, thank you very much,' she said loudly, and carried on yanking at the trolley's walking-stick handle.

There were around fifty people already queueing for the next bus and at this time of day it would be full when it arrived, so Breen decided to walk the quarter-mile home, still using the picture to balance the boxes. He passed The Scala. A poster advertised a late-night showing of *The General*; though he didn't like modern pictures much, his father had once talked about seeing the Buster Keaton at the cinema in Killarney when he was a boy: 'Greatest film ever made.' Breen had never seen it.

His flat was a basement in Stoke Newington. He had moved in back when he was working at the local police station. It had given him somewhere to look after his father in the last years.

Tomas Breen had not approved of his son joining the police. He had wanted better for him. A schoolteacher like his dead mother, perhaps. Or a lawyer.

'What you do makes you who you are,' he had said. His father, who had dreamed of being a great writer but who had been a builder all his life.

'People who spend time in sewers end up smelling of excrement,' his father had said.

He placed the pile down on the steps and struggled with the lock for a minute before opening the door. He reached for the light switch, but the meter had run out.

Walking into a dark flat, he banged his shins on the boxes of his father's possessions.

When the lights were back on he took off his clothes and set them on hangers above the bath and put on his pyjamas and dressing gown.

There was a tin of sardines already open in the fridge. There wasn't much fresh veg on sale by this time of the year but he'd found some firm-looking tomatoes at the weekend. They weren't very ripe but he fried them with some mixed herbs and then crushed the sardines onto the toast and put the tomatoes on top, then settled down to eat them with a glass of milk.

He spent the evening in front of the television, leafing through Francis Pugh's documents. They were not in any particular order. A few bank statements. Some receipts. One or two letters. He owned shares that paid regular dividends. Sums of over £100 a month were paid in from an account named 'Pugh Trust'; the estate of some rich relation, he supposed.

Breen spent a while sorting the dead man's bank statements into their correct order. With gaps, there were just over two years' worth.

He took a sheet of cardboard he'd ripped from a used packet of Quaker porridge oats and started listing the payees, leaving out ordinary-looking payments: the GPO, the Gas and Water Boards and the Greater London Council. Stephens Brothers, Shirtmakers. Regent Shoes. Dougie Millings the tailor. Dolly's in Jermyn Street. Foale & Tuffin in Panton Street. Apple Tailoring. A shop called Hung On You. Another called Dandie Fashions.

It took almost three hours to list each payee, and by the time he'd finished, the back of the cardboard was completely covered. If Harold Wilson's Labour government were union men and grammar school intellectuals, the sons of miners and labourers, Francis Pugh didn't see himself as one of them. He was a dandy; one of the beautiful people.

Swinging London was just a small, exclusive part of the city. Francis Pugh had either been part of it, or had badly wanted to be.

★

Breen slept badly. He woke in a dream in which men jumped out at him with knives. 'I'll bloody cut you for what you bloody done.' After that, he could not get back to sleep again.

He had fallen out of the habit of sleeping through the night.

As his dementia had taken hold, his father had lost track of the hours. Breen would often wake to find all the lights on in the flat, his father sitting by the front door with a suitcase at the ready. 'Is it time yet?' he would ask.

'Not yet, no,' Breen would reply, and make a cup of warm milk for them both.

'I thought I heard them calling my name.'

'Just the wind.'

'Later then?'

'A lot later, yes.'

The proportions of things changed at night. The volume of the ticking travel clock. The lump in a mattress. The memory of a night with Helen Tozer, naked in this bed and the shape of her back against his.

Tonight he rose, switched on the light and began to search for something to do. The front room was tidy. He had replaced all the papers in their boxes. The plates from supper were washed up, dried and put back in the cupboard.

He took his brogues and carefully brushed wax into the leather, spitting on them occasionally. He added a second layer of wax, then a third, each time rubbing them shiny with the buffing brush. He was a man who polished his shoes.

He held them up to the light bulb. They shone, but he could still see the scuff marks left where he had stumbled amongst the debris. Then he looked around for something else to do.

The picture on which he had carried the pile of papers was still there, leaning face down against the wall. There was a gas fire in the fireplace. Above it, Breen had put a faded reproduction of a Cézanne he had bought in Petticoat Lane. He took down the old print and put up the black-and-white dots.

It looked bright and airy. Optimistic. Clean. New. And disturbingly meaningless. A void. Like the plain white cover of the new Beatles record he had bought a few weeks before.

It wasn't that the picture looked out of place amongst his belongings. More that it made the rest of his flat look out of place.

He considered taking it down again and replacing it with the dark print of two men in hats playing cards, but he didn't. Instead he sat looking at it for a while, waiting for it to say something to him.

SEVEN

'I had plans this weekend,' complained Jones. 'Bloody nobs, getting themselves killed.'

Jones was driving one-handed and fast. He wore a pale-blue long-sleeve hand-knitted cardigan. Breen wrinkled his nose. 'Are you wearing perfume?'

'What?' said Jones.

'It smells like perfume,' said Tozer who was sitting in the back.

''k off.'

London looked grey and dirty. At least it wasn't raining today.

Tozer sniffed again. 'It's not me, that's for sure.' She leaned forward towards Constable Jones. 'It *is* you. You're wearing perfume.'

'It's aftershave,' protested Jones.

'Aftershave?' said Breen.

'Whatever it is, it stinks.'

'My wife says she likes it. She says it's nice.' He was only twenty. His wife was a year older. Coppers married young; that way you got out of shared rooms in a police house into your own flat.

'It's all right for you two,' said Jones. 'You probably got nothing better to do. I had plans this weekend.'

'Thanks very much,' said Breen. 'What plans, anyway?'

'Decorating,' he said. 'Doing the kiddy's room. Dulux. No expense.'

'You looking forward to the baby?' asked Tozer.

'Course,' said Jones, looking away.

For a Saturday morning, the traffic was unusually slow. Jones

honked the horn and waved to get the attention of a pedestrian. 'Look,'
he said. 'Over there.'

Breen looked. Ahead, a woman in a black coat was yanking a boy of
about ten years old up the street. The boy's movements were clumsy,
uneven. One foot dragged.

'He looks like he's one of the bloody Flowerpot Men, don't he,
poor bugger?' Jones honked the horn again, but the woman didn't
seem to hear it.

'Who's that?' asked Tozer.

The boy appeared to wobble as he walked, as if his limbs were
beyond his control.

'That's Sergeant Prosser's boy, Charlie.'

They drew level, inching up Maida Vale. The woman was dark-
haired, thin-faced. A bit too skinny for her age, perhaps. She caught
sight of Jones in the car, smiled and waved. Her son stopped and stared
at the car and smiled too. 'Hi, Jonesy,' she called, waving.

'He's a spazz,' said Jones. 'Ask me, she should have put him in a
home.'

Breen watched her taking her son by the arm. 'A spastic?'

'I didn't expect her to look like that,' said Tozer, looking back at her
through the rear window.

'Like what?' said Jones.

'I don't know. Kind of, not exactly pretty, I suppose, but . . .'

'I'd give her one,' said Jones.

'You're pathetic, Jonesy,' said Tozer. 'Admit it, Prosser wasn't
exactly Steve McQueen.'

He drove on, up Hamilton Road towards Marlborough Place.

'I mean, imagine having a baby that turns out to be like that, though,'
said Jones. 'Christ.' A flicker of the eyes. Nerves, thought Breen.

Outside the flattened house, a paperboy was about to prop his bike
against the kerb.

'Oi!' Jones rolled down his window. 'Move that.'

The boy pulled the bike away, grumbling. In one hand, he held the morning's copy of *The Times*, unsure of what to do with it. The house he had been going to deliver it to wasn't there anymore.

A single copper stood marching on the spot to keep his feet warm in the November chill. A mother with a large black pram paused for a cigarette in front of the remains. 'Isn't it awful,' she said. 'Poor bugger.'

They started with a cigarette break on the pavement, blowing smoke into the still air, while the coppers gathered around them. They knew that Francis Pugh lived here alone; there was no immediate wife or family on hand to talk to.

'And no girlfriend or nothing?' said Tozer.

'I don't know.'

'Or boyfriend even?'

'What? A pansy?' said Jones.

'I don't know,' said Breen. Until he could talk to the family there was so little they knew about him. He listened to Jones trying to organise the coppers.

'Right,' said Jones. 'You lot take odd numbers.'

A groan. Breen stubbed out his first cigarette of the day on the pavement and walked up the narrow gravel path to the house next door, pushing past overgrown shrubs that invaded from either side. A man dressed in a cream jacket with a bright blue cravat stood at the door. 'I haven't slept,' he said. 'I kept thinking my house was going to fall down. Can you imagine?'

He was in his sixties, maybe older, thin and fragile. 'They said it's safe but I'm not terribly sure. Are you here to ask about the unpleasantness?' His hair was dyed an unlikely shade of black. He looked Breen up and down. 'I suppose you'd better come in.'

Breen waited in the living room while the man made a cup of tea, emerging from the kitchen finally with a porcelain cup and saucer that rattled as he walked. The man sat down at a small, ornate desk. Behind him, there was a thin crack in the striped wallpaper. Breen wondered if it was new.

'I never really liked being semi-detached anyway,' he said drily. 'Of course, the council have offered me one of their little flats, but can you imagine? I don't trust these skyscrapers. They're always falling down all over the place, aren't they? I'd rather be crushed under a pile of bricks, like poor Mr Pugh.'

'Did you know him?'

'Not in the slightest. He was really not my sort,' said the man with a twitch of the lips. He had the sort of papery voice the old have when they smoke too many cigarettes.

'Did he have a girlfriend?'

The man looked sour. 'Billions. Do you have a fag, by any chance?'

Breen noticed he had a packet of Park Drives on the coffee table in front of him. An effeminate brand of cigarette, Breen thought. He felt in his pocket for his own; he bought one packet of ten every other morning from the newsagent before he caught the bus and used them to divide up his day. He didn't like giving them away, but he handed one over. The man's fingers were stained with nicotine. He leaned forward to light it and sucked hard, pulling in his cheeks.

'Anyone regular? Anyone you'd recognise?'

The man made a face. 'I'm not a bloody snoop, if that's what you're suggesting,' he said, and blew smoke through his nose. 'Besides, the girls never lasted long,' he said. 'He discarded them. You'd often hear some dreadful floozie weeping by the door. For pity's sake. He wasn't that good-looking.'

'But no one you'd recognise?'

There was a patch of unshaved hair under his left nostril. 'As I said, I'm not interested in young girls.'

'But Mr Pugh was?'

The click of spittle in his mouth. 'Clearly.'

'There must have been someone who called regularly.'

The man turned his head away. 'The truth is, I'm half blind. Can't hardly see a thing. A bit of a handicap. I'd ask you to sit closer, but I'm not that keen on policemen either.'

'Did you hear anything unusual last night?'

The gas could have been on for hours, seeping down into the house's basement. It would have accumulated there slowly. The firemen had gone through the rubble looking for some kind of detonation mechanism. A match tied to an alarm clock striker, maybe, but they hadn't found anything yet in all the mess. Though the doctor had not yet completed his report, Breen reckoned the man would have been dead for a few hours before the explosion.

'Unusual?' said the man, stretching all four syllables of the word as far as they could go. 'Apart from a socking big bang?' He curled his lip.

'Before that, obviously.'

'No. I don't believe I did.'

'I can't see a car. Do you know if he had one?'

'I don't think Mr Pugh drove,' he said. 'He used taxis a lot. Used to keep them waiting outside for ages. Wasteful.'

'What sort of time of day? Was he going out in the daytime or the evening?'

'Never the morning. God, no. He didn't keep what you might call conventional hours. And he'd be back all times of night. Sometimes in the small hours. The taxis would wake me up. I never complained about it, mind you. Never complain.'

There was a framed photograph of a young man on the wall behind where he sat. It was a studio portrait. Stood in a circle of light, a young man with brilliantined dark hair, a touch of make-up on the eyes.

'Is that you?'

The same small smile.

'You were an actor?'

He turned his head slightly sideways, as if inviting Breen to recognise him. Breen didn't.

'Yes. I am an actor,' he said, after a pause. Emphasis on 'am'.

'Have you been in anything I'd have seen?'

The man scowled, tugged at an ear lobe. 'You're far too young to have seen me in anything. You haven't drunk your tea. Is there anything wrong with it?'

Breen said, 'You didn't like Mr Pugh very much, did you?'

'Is that part of Harold Wilson's new Britain? It's now compulsory to like your neighbour, is it? No. I didn't like him, as a matter of fact. Him and all his women. Sexual liberation. The permissive society. I don't approve of it, really.' He patted down his jacket pocket as if looking for something.

'May I have a quick look in your garden?'

'The young think they can have everything they bloody want these days. Why should they? If I couldn't have it, why should they?'

'The garden,' said Breen.

'If you must,' he said. 'I'm afraid I've neglected it rather.'

He let him out of the French window at the back of the living room. It was overgrown. The grass was long and dead-looking. Brambles were starting to creep across what had been a lawn. The beech hedge that surrounded his garden had become straggly. There were gaps where you could see the houses behind. They were big, three-storey Victorian homes, but much less grand than the mansions on Marlborough Place.

By the back door of what must have been his kitchen lay a pile of rusting tin cans that he must have tossed there. They were all the same. Campbell's Cream of Tomato Soup.

'There,' the man said when Breen came back inside, wiping his feet. 'Now, have you got enough?'

Outside Pugh's house, a group of kids gathered. One was snapping away with a camera.

'You a copper, mister?'

Breen ignored them.

'I heard he was sliced up by gangsters. They cut off his thingy.'

A girl with a big knitted scarf wound around her head giggled.

'That's what they said.'

'Who said?' said Breen.

'Everyone. Is it true?'

'No,' said Breen.

'You're a liar,' said the boy.

Breen pushed the gate open and walked around the rubble to the back garden of the dead man's house. A garden without a home. Broken glass and wood lay strewn on what had been a large gravel rectangle with a small Japanese-looking shrine, sitting in the middle. Maybe Indian. At the rear grew a line of bamboo, too tall to see over.

He could hear someone moving in the garden beyond.

Breen looked around. Seeing the wooden kitchen chair, he lifted it across the gravel and placed it next to the bamboo, then stood on it, parting the stiff green stems.

There was a woman, head tied up in a bright scarf. She was thin, boyish, with a long floral skirt, a white cotton blouse and a small waistcoat. She was pinning up a line of clothes. A line of greyish-white nappies, each one clipped to the next.

Behind her, a makeshift vegetable garden, a row of beans blackened from the frosts.

He watched the woman for a while. It was November and the air was cold, but she wore nothing on her feet. She picked each nappy from a large wicker basket, then took another pin from a cloth bag tied around her waist.

As she leaned towards the basket, Breen saw the outline of a breast, pale, smooth and soft. A dark nipple. Under her white cotton blouse, she was bra-less. The glimpse of her breast was gone in a second. She stood and pinned another half-dozen terry cloths to the line. He stayed a little too long, watching.

Pale skin under white cotton.

'What you looking at?'

It was Jones.

How long had he been standing there, watching her? He flushed and the woman looked up, startled at the sound of voices. Breen jumped down from the chair, ashamed of himself.

'I was trying to figure out if anyone could have seen into the house.'

'Let me have a look,' said Jones, standing on the chair.

Breen stood there, wondering if he was watching the young woman too.

'I don't think so. This stuff is far too thick to see through properly,' he said.

EIGHT

Monday was wet. Rain swilled rubbish down the gutters to block the drains. It was a mistake catching the bus this morning instead of the Underground. Roads flooded. Traffic crawled down Hackney Road.

The weekend had turned up nothing much. Most people in the street knew Francis Pugh by sight. Not one of them knew him in person. The Chief Inspector had visited his father; Bailey had been given an appointment to discuss the case with him later today.

A team of policemen had spent Sunday picking through the rubble, making a small pile of possessions. Records, a nail-clipper, a set of croquet mallets, some saucepans. Breen asked if they had found an address book, or anything that might tell them who Pugh's friends were, but nothing useful had been retrieved. Now the rain was turning the site to mud.

Nobody seemed to know who the victim's friends had been. Nobody had come forward to offer any useful information at all. Breen was in the dark.

When he finally got off a bus on Wigmore Street, a paving stone rocked under his feet, sending a spray of water across his legs and into the shoes of a pretty girl in a lime-green miniskirt. She glared at him before strutting off eastwards.

Breen ducked into the doorway of a Radio Rentals shop for shelter. The sign in the window said: 'Watch both channels every evening. And in COLOUR.'

By the time he made it into the CID office he was dripping and late. His bones felt cold.

'Hello, Paddy. Someone don't like you,' said Constable Jones. He was there with Constable Tozer who was gnawing on a Chelsea bun.

'What?'

'A little love letter.' Jones nodded towards Breen's typewriter. There was a piece of paper in it.

'Read it,' said Tozer, watching him closely. 'It's not very pretty.'

Breen shook the rain from his hair and walked towards his desk. Typed in capitals:

YOU ARE A DEAD MAN YOU CUNT

Breen looked at it for a second, then pulled it out of the machine. The letters had been thumped into the paper. 'Who saw this?'

'Marilyn. When she came in,' said Jones. 'She told me about it.'

Breen looked at the typewriter. The caps lock was still on. 'She tell anyone else?' he asked.

'Dunno,' said Jones. His navy tie, sticking out of his knitted jumper, was stained with that morning's egg. He was wearing an 'I'm Backing Britain' badge.

'Can I ask you a favour?'

'Course.'

'Don't mention this to anyone, OK?'

Jones frowned. 'But . . .'

Breen asked, 'Can you do that?' It was not easy asking favours of Jones. Breen didn't like him: his cockiness, his eagerness to get into fights, his ill-matched clothes.

Tozer looked cautiously at Breen. Jones smiled, embarrassed. 'I mean, no one likes you that much. But I don't know no one who could be bothered to actually hate you,' he said.

'It's just a joke, I expect.'

'Funny joke,' said Tozer.

Breen said, 'All I'm saying is, can we not talk about it?'

'I don't mind,' said Jones, and went and sat at his desk.

Breen opened his drawer and picked out a brown envelope and added it to the last one he'd received:

ILL BLOODY CUT YOU FOR WHAT YOU BLOODY DONE

'Christ,' said Tozer, quietly. 'When did you get that?'

'Shh,' said Breen. Inspector Bailey was making one of his rare forays outside his office. He looked at Tozer, paused, raised an eyebrow.

'My car's outside,' he said to Breen. 'Downstairs in five minutes.'

Breen placed the letters back in the drawer together and closed it, then called the police surgeon to ask when the post-mortem on the victim would be completed.

Breen sat in the back of Bailey's Cortina. A uniformed copper who looked even older than the inspector was driving.

'I have met Rhodri Pugh on occasion' Bailey said. 'He is on the Home Affairs Select Committee. A decent enough fellow, considering . . .'

Considering.

'It is advisable for the police not to become too involved in politics, whatever we may think privately. We are public servants.'

Considering he was a Labour politician, he meant. Bailey was from Harold Macmillan's generation. The straight-backed men. To them, Harold Wilson and his Party were a conniving bunch of Bolsheviks. But he would do whatever they required.

'However, this lot seem to be behind the police. At least the working classes understand the need for law and order.'

'Is he aware the body was mutilated?' Breen asked him.

'I believe so. He identified his son's body on Saturday after they'd pulled it out of the building, and he had a meeting with the Chief Inspector yesterday. I understand it was distressing. The body was a bit of a mess. And incinerated, I believe. I was briefed by the Inspector earlier this morning. He stressed how important this case was. That we should above all respect the wishes of the family.'

Breen understood. The police were not natural Labour fans, but the new Home Secretary was a populist. In the year he'd been in office he had been eager to show himself a law-and-order man, pushing through anti-immigration legislation, toughening his department's stance on cannabis and other drugs. Law-and-order men were always popular with the top brass. He was one of us.

'The wishes of the family?' said Breen, smiling slightly.

'His mother died of cancer two years ago. No brothers or sisters.'

'So the minister is the family?'

'In a manner of speaking, yes.'

'I see.'

Bailey sighed. 'Don't pretend you're somehow above all this, Paddy. Cynicism is not a sign of intelligence. They are our masters. We are there to serve them.'

They pulled up outside an office in Petty France. 'Thirty minutes,' Bailey told the driver, who grunted and reached for a packed lunch, wrapped in brown paper. A uniformed officer gave Bailey a little salute as they walked in through the door.

They waited in the lobby of the government office, sitting in straight-backed leather chairs as men in suits came and went. Young civil servants with Eton accents talked loudly and importantly as they marched through the lobby, bundles of paper under their arms.

After about twenty minutes a tall man in a pinstriped suit with wide lapels appeared. 'Inspector Bailey?' he said.

Bailey said, 'And you are?'

'My name is Tarpey. I am a colleague of Mr Pugh's. As this is a personal matter, Mr Pugh thinks it best that we meet somewhere . . . less formal.'

And before either of them had a chance to answer, he marched out of the building. Bailey and Breen followed behind.

★

The restaurant was a short walk away, on the corner of Buckingham Gate. The minister, a round-faced man with wire glasses, was sitting in a booth with a coffee pot and a toast rack in front of him, next to a pile of ministerial documents he was looking at.

'Inspector Bailey,' announced Tarpey.

The man looked up from his papers. 'Ah,' he said. 'Inspector. Please, sit down.' He spoke in a Welsh accent.

'I'm very sorry for your loss, sir,' said Bailey, taking the seat opposite. Breen was not offered a chair. He wondered if he should pull one up from another table.

Apart from Rhodri Pugh, the restaurant was empty, tables all set for lunch. The minister looked pale and tired. 'I thought it best I should contact you to offer my full cooperation with the investigation,' he said.

Breen recognised him vaguely from the news, but he seemed older in real life. His eyes were rheumy, perhaps from tears. His son was dead, but he was back at work. Things must go on.

'Very thoughtful, sir,' said Bailey. 'We will do all in our power to apprehend the responsible person. Or persons.'

'Persons?' said Pugh. 'More than one, you think?'

'Too early to say, sir.'

'Right.'

The restaurant was dark, lit by lamps around the walls. 'Coffee?' he offered.

'Thank you,' said Bailey.

Tarpey, who had sat next to Pugh in the booth, now leaned forward and poured Bailey a cup. The milk jug looked tiny in his big, bony hands.

Rhodri Pugh cleared his throat and said, 'See, I was not very close to my son.' He talked in a quiet voice; a man who was used to silencing a room by whispering rather than shouting.

'My son . . .' he said. His eyes teared up a little. 'He was a bright boy. I think we probably failed him.'

'Sir?' said Bailey.

Tarpey remained palely expressionless. Breen wondered if he was a civil servant of some kind. Or a Party worker. As the minister talked, the man glanced at Breen, still standing, looked him in the eye, gave him a small smile.

'A bit of a black sheep, really,' Pugh was saying. 'Somewhat of a disappointment, I suppose. When I was younger I worked as an electrician. You had to have a trade. My son had nothing like that to give him the discipline one needs. My fault, I suppose. Had it too easy.'

A 'disappointment', thought Breen. A hard thing to say about your own son.

'Did he work?' asked Bailey.

'Not real work. He had an allowance. His mother arranged it before she died. He got by on that, mostly.'

'A man of independent means,' said Bailey.

'Poisoned chalice,' said the minister. 'I wish she'd never given him money. He'd have had to work then. A man should work. If he doesn't work, he's nothing.'

'You said he was a disappointment,' interrupted Breen. 'In what way?'

Bailey turned to Breen and frowned, then turned back to Rhodri Pugh. 'Can I introduce Sergeant Breen, sir? He is in charge of the day-to-day details of the inquiry.'

The man looked up at Breen for the first time. 'The Chief Inspector said you were in charge of the inquiry, Inspector Bailey,' he said.

'Yes, sir,' said Bailey. 'Sergeant Breen is an experienced investigating officer, however. He will be handling operational matters.'

A pause. 'I see.' The minister looked back at Breen. 'Our party has fought to give every man the right to work. I am a man that understands the value of hard work and honesty. But perhaps I got it wrong. I was too dedicated to my own work to spare the time to pass on those values to him. As a result, he became a bohemian. 'A spender rather than an honest earner.'

'You weren't close to him?'

'Hardly knew him at all this last two or three years, if truth be told.' He looked down at his rack of untouched toast. 'We fell out when his mother became ill, I'm afraid. I saw him at the funeral. That was the last time.'

'I'm sorry.'

'You understand, however, Sergeant, I would not want any of this discussed in the newspapers?'

'Of course, sir,' said Bailey. 'I have explained that to Sergeant Breen.'

The Welshman nodded sadly. 'Good. It would be better that way.'

'Why are you concerned about that?' asked Breen.

Bailey turned and glowered again.

But the minister smiled sadly. 'With a violent death there is always risk of prurient interest,' he said. 'I am aware of my son's condition when you found him. I was shocked . . .' He petered out. For a while there was silence. Bailey lowered his head so as not to look the man in the eye if he began to cry.

Tarpey said, 'Perhaps I could fetch you a glass of water, sir?'

Tarpey's accent was Welsh too, Breen realised. Not a civil servant then; another Labour Party man. Someone from back home. A fixer.

Finding his voice again, the minister ignored him. 'See, there are people who would be very happy to damage this government and wouldn't care about facts. I am anxious that a personal matter should not be allowed to undermine the foundations of authority. You see that, don't you, Sergeant?'

'Yes, sir,' Breen.

'Thank you.' Pugh pulled a packet of cigarettes from his jacket pocket. Bailey reached for a matchbox and struck one. Pugh leaned forward and let him light the cigarette.

'Could you perhaps give the names of anyone who knew him?' said Breen, digging in his jacket for a notebook.

The minister closed his eyes and sighed. 'As I was saying, we didn't know him at all, really, his mother and myself. Not for a few years. He didn't like us much, I think. We're working-class people. Proud of it. My son grew up here in London, for the most part. He didn't even have a Welsh accent. Spoke like an Englishman.'

There was silence. A clattering of cutlery from the kitchen. The minister puffed on his cigarette a couple of times, then said, 'Of course we will do what we can to help catch the maniac who did this. I have asked my colleague, Mr Tarpey, to prepare a list.'

'Very good of you, sir,' said Bailey.

'Very eager to help.' He turned to Tarpey. 'Tarpey's a good man. Please contact him at any time of day or night if you have any questions at all.'

Tarpey gave a slight nod.

'I need to know what Francis was like, growing up. His friends. What he liked to do.'

'Why would you need to know that?' said the minister.

'He may have known his killer.'

The minister looked at his watch. 'I wouldn't have thought that was very likely,' he said.

'I need to know what kind of person he was.'

'Just a normal boy, at first.'

The Labour Party was full of self-made men. Trade unionists and Party men who had been born into working-class families, who had made the most of what the war had offered them. Breen wondered what it had been like to be the child of one of these high achievers, men who had crossed the English class lines.

'When did the family move to London?'

Pugh pushed his hair back over his scalp impatiently. 'When I first became a shadow minister in 1960. Tarpey can tell you all of this.'

Breen persisted. 'Did your son like it?'

The minister frowned. Breen could tell he was weighing up whether to answer or not.

'His mother said he was a sensitive boy. I wouldn't know what that means, myself. Our generation never had the luxury of being sensitive. But Francis hated it here at first. There was some bullying at school on account of his accent. So he lost that, quick enough. But by the time he left school I'd almost say he liked it too much. No inclination to go home.'

'And university?'

The minister picked up his pen and said, 'He went to study architecture. Dropped out in his first year. My fault too, maybe. His mother thought so. I persuaded him he should do something practical.'

'And do you have a photograph?'

'Tarpey has one for you. Is that all? I need to get on with my work now.' He looked as if he were on the verge of tears. 'And you will keep us informed?'

'Naturally, sir,' said Bailey, standing.

'Thank you.'

Tarpey stood too. He pulled two business cards from his suit pocket, handing one to each of them. Oliver Tarpey. A phone number and an address in Hampstead.

'Mr Pugh asked me to offer my full assistance,' he said to Breen, as they walked through the empty tables to the front of the restaurant.

'In what capacity?'

'I'm a friend. And Party member. I have done my best to assist Rhodri since he first stood for election back home.'

Breen nodded. 'What would be useful at this stage is a list of contacts,' he said. 'His doctor. Any associates at all. Mr Pugh's belongings were destroyed in the fire. We don't have a lot to go on.'

'Friends are not so easy,' said Tarpey. 'He had his own set.'

'You must have some idea.'

Tarpey smiled. 'We're very eager to help, of course. I will do what I can.'

'Of course,' said Breen. 'In a case like this, where we don't know all the facts, we usually work with the newspapers and put out requests for friends and acquaintances to come forward.'

Bailey hovered by the door, a short distance away.

'I understand your methods. But I think it's best to keep the fuss to a minimum right now, as the minister suggested. Don't you think?' said Tarpey.

'The first days after a murder are crucial. It's important to talk to as many people as we can as soon as we are able.'

'I'm sure that's what you will be doing. However, talking to the papers would not be in the minister's interest. Or the government's.'

'And what about Mr Francis Pugh's interest?'

'Frankie is dead,' said Tarpey. 'He doesn't really have interests, per se.'

Breen paused. 'He is a minister's son. There will be speculation about his death even if we don't talk to the newspapers.'

'You're right, of course. But please leave us to deal with that, Sergeant. Mr Pugh has some influence there.' Tarpey sucked on his lower lip. He lowered his voice. 'There's one acquaintance of Mr Pugh junior that his father is unlikely to be aware of. If I was to put you in touch with her, I would expect you to respect her privacy.'

Breen looked down at his shoes. Then he looked up again and said, 'Yes, of course.'

'What if there were some minor illegality involved? I'd want an assurance that you would not act on it.'

'It depends how minor,' said Breen.

'Without that assurance I can't do this,' said Tarpey quietly.

'You know, of course, that it's an offence to withhold evidence.'

Bailey was still waiting, checking his watch impatiently. 'Oh come, come,' said Tarpey. 'The Home Office withholds evidence all the time. Imagine the trouble if they didn't. But I'm just asking you as a favour. You'll understand why when you meet her.'

'OK,' said Breen.

Tarpey opened his briefcase and pulled out two folded sheets of paper and an envelope. The envelope contained a photograph of

Francis Pugh. A studio portrait of a handsome fresh-faced young man, hair uncombed, scowling slightly, as if he had not wanted his photograph taken at all.

'That's a private photograph. From the family. Not for public consumption.'

Breen unfolded the first piece of paper. The name and addresses of Francis Pugh's bank, which Breen already knew from the papers he'd picked up at the house, his doctor and his solicitor.

The second piece had a woman's name and address typed on it.

'Just one name?'

'Mr Pugh had lots of girlfriends. I'm sure you know that already. I have no idea who they were. The only time I was ever introduced to one was when he got one of them into trouble. He asked me to help her. I did. That's her name.'

'Did you tell his father about this?'

Tarpey shook his head. 'No. Rhodri Pugh is a very busy man. He had a great deal to worry about without adding Frankie's misdemeanours to the pile. I do my best to keep that kind of fuss away from him.'

'An abortion?'

Again, Tarpey nodded.

'You were a party to an illegal medical procedure?'

'I'm a religious man, Mr Breen. It was not work that I enjoyed. However, I take my job extremely seriously. I'm sure you do too. But Mr Pugh's reputation is important to the work that must be done.'

Bailey called from the door, 'Will you make your own way back, Breen, or do you want to come in the car?'

'One minute, sir,' said Breen.

'Francis contacted me just the once. In January this year before the new abortion law came into being. On a personal level, I don't particularly like our government making abortion legal. But we are a progressive government. I understand the reasons. And at least Frankie no longer had any reason to ask me to arrange anything like this with any of his other women. I wouldn't be surprised if there had been more. He slept around.'

Breen had been fixed on Tarpey's Adam's apple bobbing up and down as he spoke. He said, 'You disapprove of abortion, but you were happy to arrange it for Mr Pugh?'

'I never said I was happy,' said Tarpey. 'I have told her to expect a call from you. I have also assured her she will be treated with tact.'

'Thanks for your cooperation.'

'And you for yours,' replied Tarpey, holding out his hand, to shake.

The driver was fast asleep when they got back to the car. Bailey had to shake him by the shoulder to wake him.

'Where to now, guv?' he asked, blinking.

'Back to the station.' Bailey was not the sort of policeman to ever use the word 'nick'.

The traffic had thickened. They sat without moving on Old Portland Street for ten minutes. Breen turned to Bailey. 'Can I ask, sir, why is this investigation not being carried out by Scotland Yard?'

'Rhodri Pugh requested that this be treated like any other murder,' said Bailey. 'I expect it is because he is a socialist,' he added, as if this were explanation enough.

'And because he wants to keep everything quiet?'

'He's a minister. That's understandable.'

'He wasn't offering his cooperation at all. He just wanted to make sure we keep it out of the papers.'

'Enough, Sergeant,' said Bailey wearily. 'I am sure Mr Pugh is just as keen as finding out who killed his son as you are. Please bear in mind, he is a man of considerable importance. We are fortunate that the Home Secretary is a strong supporter of the police force. I am not a socialist myself, but the one thing I admire about them is that for all their talk of revolution, when push comes to shove, they understand the need for the rule of law. We should do our utmost to ensure his department is not inconvenienced by any of this.'

Breen looked out of the window. A motorbike and sidecar had broken down in the middle of the oncoming traffic and cars were trying to squeeze past it. 'I felt a little like a schoolboy called to the headmaster's study,' he said.

'You have never understood the way things are done, Paddy. If you don't understand that, all the good intentions in the world are worth nothing.'

The car pulled up finally at the back of the police station. Bailey got out. 'Do as he says, please. Give Rhodri Pugh's assistant regular updates on the case.'

'Even though he's probably getting them already from his boss's department?'

But Bailey didn't appear to hear. He was already halfway into the building.

NINE

The police surgeon, Wellington, was in a foul mood.

'How in buggering blasted hell can I be expected to work like this?'

They were redecorating his office. A man in blue overalls was painting the wall behind him, cigarette perched on his lip.

'Not my fault,' said the painter.

Wellington wore a dark worsted waistcoat and a bright-yellow cravat and smoked Dunhill Mixture in a briar pipe. A fan of light opera, he had once invited Breen to come and see him perform in *The Mikado* with his amateur operatic society in Guildford. Breen had used his sick father as an excuse to miss the second act.

'I was perfectly happy with this office the way it was. This obsession with painting everywhere . . .' But the painter ignored him, dipping his brush into the off-white and returning again to the wall. 'Why have you brought that woman with you?' he said, even though Tozer was only a few feet away. 'There's no reason for a woman to be on this murder investigation. Mind you, I seem to remember it's you who now habitually throws up when you see dead bodies, Breen.'

'Tell us about the body that was recovered from Marlborough Place. Is it here?'

'The body's been sent to the Home Office pathologist. Burnt to buggery, unfortunately. I had a good root around though.'

'And? Could you still see the mutilations?'

'Fascinating.' Wellington grinned. 'All *post mortem*, far as I could see. Hacked about like nobody's business. I don't suppose they found a bucket of blood anywhere?'

'Blood?'

'Whoever killed him strung him up by his ankles and bled him.'

'Like a pig,' said Tozer again.

'Exactly.'

'Why, do you think?'

'I'll get to that.'

'But after he was killed, not before?' Tozer persisted.

'Precisely. Not terribly effective after the heart's stopped, but there must have been quite a lot of blood all the same.'

'So how was he killed?'

Wellington smiled. 'Hard to say. Skull was all smashed in but that might have been the house collapsing. There were signs of pulmonary oedema in the lungs, apparently,' he said. 'And an eyeball survived. It was moderately bloodshot. I'd guess suffocation. But that's just a guess. See what the pathologist says.'

Tozer said, 'You think he was tortured?'

Wellington leaned across the desk and said, 'Paddy, old chum. Are you the investigating officer on this case, or is this bloody woman in charge?'

'Sorry,' said Tozer.

'Like I said, the skin wounds on the legs and arms are *post mortem*, as were the incisions on the wrists and neck, so it's hard to know if it was torture or not.'

Breen asked, 'Had he been tied up?'

Wellington said, 'You'll have to wait for the pathology investigation. Bit of a corker, this one. Never really see this sort of thing. Looks like somebody got a kick from carving him up after he was dead, though we can't be totally sure yet that all the wounds were *post mortem*.'

Tozer said, 'So you think this was some loony?'

'I would have thought so. Not even the dear old Kray gang do this kind of thing. Whoever it was had a whale of a time with the poor bugger.'

'What about the knife?' asked Breen. 'The one they used to remove his skin.'

'All in good time. Wait for the analysis. It was sharp, that's for sure.'

Tozer delved in her handbag and pulled out a packet of cigarettes. 'Want one?' she asked, offering them round.

'Horrible things,' said Wellington. Breen shook his head. The painter, though, placed his brush across the top of his paint kettle, took one from her and stuck it behind behind his ear for later. 'Ta.'

Wellington said, 'Did I hear that you're leaving the police, young lady? What a terrible loss to the service.'

Breen was thinking about the skin. After digging out the body, policemen had been told to search through the bricks for any trace of any missing body parts. Nothing had been found. 'Why would someone steal skin?' he asked.

'And the blood,' said Tozer.

'There's an interesting case come in recently from America,' said Wellington. 'A man who stole the skin from people he killed to make himself a bodysuit from the parts of dead women. He dug some up from the graveyard and when he didn't have enough he killed a few more. I can show you photographs, if you like. They're quite something.'

'No thank you,' said Breen.

'Do you think that's what's going on here?' asked Tozer.

'We're obsessed with copying every other silly American fashion,' said Wellington. 'Like pizza restaurants. God save us. Nothing would surprise me.'

Crossing Marylebone Road, Tozer said, 'He gets his kicks from all that, doesn't he?'

'He's just doing his job.'

She walked ahead, dodging a taxi which blared its horn.

'Wish Bailey would let us put a radio on. It's so bloody quiet in here,' complained Marilyn. 'It's like a morgue.'

'Minus prat in the cravat,' muttered Tozer.

'For God's sake,' said Breen.

It was true. Breen had never known the office like this. There were two empty desks now. It wasn't just Prosser. Sergeant Carmichael had gone to the Drug Squad in Scotland Yard too. Breen missed him. They had been school friends together; Breen had followed him into the police, then into CID. The Drug Squad was still recruiting. Carmichael wanted Breen to follow him into it. But they were a loud team, brash and confident. Always getting in the papers. Not only were they fighting a whole new type of criminal, but the ones they were arresting were usually far more glamorous than the usual CID fare. Breen felt more at home where he was.

He unfolded a piece of paper and called the number on it. A young woman answered. 'The Hemmings residence.' A housemaid's voice.

When Mrs Hemmings came to the phone, Breen said, 'Oliver Tarpey gave me your number.'

'I've been expecting your call.'

'Could I come and speak to you?'

The woman lowered her voice, 'Not here,' she said. 'It wouldn't be ... convenient.' A deep voice. Public school. Posh. Not the sort for the son of a working-class Labour man to be hanging around with. They arranged to meet on Wednesday in Battersea Park.

Jones crossed the office and put a list of all the known and convicted burglars in the NW8 area on Breen's desk. The two of them sat, going through them.

Jones said, 'Thing is, we don't really know if anything was stolen, even. If we knew that, we might be able to narrow it down a bit. What about other murders? Anything like this?'

Two burnt men. Breen thought about the body in the fire: the man who had died the night his father went into hospital. But that was different. He had been drunk. The fire had killed him. This man was dead before someone had tried to obliterate the evidence.

Breen looked up from the list and said, 'Are you coming to Bailey's drinks tomorrow?'

'Do I have to?' said Jones.

'Give him a break. He'll be retiring soon.'

'Not soon enough,' said Jones.

'You'll have a baby any sec,' said Tozer. 'Take the chance to live it up while you can.'

Breen said, 'When is it due, Jones?'

Jones blushed. 'May. So the wife tells me.'

'So come on. You won't be able to go out so much, after.'

'Who said having a baby's going to stop me?' said Jones with a grin. 'Never stopped my dad.'

'Boozer, was he?'

'Is,' said Jones. 'Bloody alky, more or less.'

'Language,' said Marilyn.

'Gin. Cider. Anything. He'd spend his life in the boozer if they didn't shut.' And Breen noticed how he started methodically flicking his biro in the air when he started to talk about his father.

Breen said, 'You know we saw Prosser's girl on Saturday. You're friends with her, aren't you?'

'Shirley? Don't see much of her since she ran out on Prosser.'

'Do you have her address?'

The biro went up a few more times before he asked, 'What do you want that for?'

Breen looked back down at the list. 'I just thought I should see if she's doing all right.'

Jones said, 'You didn't even like Prosser.'

'Just wanted to know she was OK, that's all.'

Jones paused, then said, 'A flat above a record shop on Edgware Road. That's where she went when she left him. Maybe I should come too?'

'It's all right,' said Breen. 'Any idea what it was called?'

'Something daft. I don't know.'

'Jumbo Records,' said Tozer.

'That's it,' said Jones. 'Sells a load of jigaboo music. Not real jazz or anything.'

Tozer was looking at Breen with a puzzled expression, but she didn't say anything.

The next morning he took the picture off his wall, wrapped it, tucked it under his arm, and carried it on the bus back to the police station.

It was Tuesday. The Bond Street art galleries would be open. With Tozer, he caught the bus to Piccadilly Circus and walked down Piccadilly, reassuringly plain in the drizzle. A street of shops selling Norfolk jackets, bowler hats and umbrellas. Grey stone facades and tea at Fortnum's.

'Are you going to Bailey's drinks tonight?' he asked her.

'Suppose,' she said. 'You want me to?'

'It's not up to me,' said Breen. 'Is it?'

The first couple of galleries they went into sold oil paintings of horses and pastoral landscapes. 'Modern nonsense,' a lady in pearls said after a single glance in the first one they visited. A man in a yellow waistcoat in the second gallery said, 'Try that place in Mason's Yard. Can't remember its name. It's more their kind of thing. If it's still going.'

'How can anyone afford this stuff?' said Tozer. 'Those prices are loopy.'

Mason's Yard was a couple of streets away. The gallery was called Indica, according to the big sign over the window, but it seemed empty. A young woman with dirty blonde hair came to the door and said, 'Who are you?'

'Is this an art gallery?'

'Who are you?'

'We're police,' he said.

She smiled. 'Is this a raid? Only there's nothing left here any more. The gallery's closed.' She wore a suede miniskirt and large patent leather boots.

'I've only come to ask about a picture.' Breen took the print out of the brown paper he'd been carrying it in and held it up towards her.

The young woman frowned. She looked from Tozer to Breen. 'What about it?'

'Do you recognise it?'

'Bridget Riley, of course. Is it stolen?'

He examined the small etched signature. He hadn't been able to make the name out before, but she was right. He should have recognised it. She was famous for those black-and-white geometric paintings that made you dizzy to look at.

'Who in their right mind would nick a Bridget Riley, anyway? Op Art is finished,' she said. 'It's inarticulate.'

'We just want to know who might have sold it,' said Breen.

'Ask Bob Fraser,' she said. 'He used to sell stuff like that. Not any more.'

'Who?'

'Robert Fraser Gallery. Only he doesn't really like the police much.'

'Why not?'

She rolled her eyes. 'Don't you actually read the papers? Because a bunch of your lot busted him for drugs last year. There was a fuss.'

'What sort of fuss?'

'He went to jail. Clink. Loved it, apparently.'

'Oh,' said Tozer. '*That* Robert Fraser.'

The Robert Fraser Gallery was just off Grosvenor Square, close by. They walked there, but it was empty as well; no art visible through the windows. Breen rang the bell for a few minutes, but nobody answered.

Striding back up towards Piccadilly, Tozer said, 'You fancied her, didn't you?'

'Who?'

'That girl who told you about the painting.'

Breen said, 'Don't be ridiculous.'

'Posh girl. Nice hair. I saw you peeking at her legs. Not surprised really. She was very pretty.'

'I was not looking at her legs,' said Breen. 'I was observing.'

'Observing,' said Tozer.

'It's my job. Why? You jealous?'

'God sake,' she said. 'Why would I be jealous?'

Breen put the collar up on his raincoat and walked faster.

Back in the office, Breen was drawing on a large sheet he had made by sticking two pieces of typing paper together.

'What is it?' asked Jones.

'It's a graph.'

'A graph?' He sniggered.

'I hated maths,' said Tozer, holding up a powder compact in one hand and a stick of lipstick in the other. 'I was always rubbish at it at school.'

'Me too,' said Jones. He stared at Tozer trying to put lipstick on. 'You don't need maths anymore, anyway. They're going to make calculators you can do it all on, so why bother?' He turned back to Breen. 'Why do girls always make faces when they're putting on make-up?'

'You try doing it without,' said Tozer, holding the lipstick towards him.

'Bog off,' he said, recoiling. 'You're not supposed to wear lipstick on duty. ''Sides, I don't think you should be allowed to do that in the CID room, anyway.'

'You don't have to look,' said Tozer.

Breen had bought a packet of ten coloured crayons from W.H. Smith's and now he took the sheets of paper and placed them on the floor. With a ruler he started drawing lines, half an inch apart.

'Did you know your tongue sticks out when you concentrate?' asked Tozer.

When he'd finished drawing the grid, Breen started plotting points on the big sheet of paper using the crayons.

Jones said, 'What's it supposed to show?'

Francis Pugh had banked at Lloyds in Holborn Circus. Breen had requested all Pugh's bank statements, filling in the gaps. He had spent the afternoon looking at them, breaking the payments down into different categories. Now he was plotting his notes onto the graph.

Tozer said, 'Are you going to be long? Jonesy and I can see you in the pub if you like?'

'Has Bailey gone already?' said Jones. 'Don't want to miss the free round.'

Breen didn't answer. He was concentrating on joining the small green crosses he had drawn on the paper. The floor was old and uneven. The worn grain of the wood showed through in the unevenness of his lines.

'Free round?' said Tozer.

'There's always a free round if it's someone's birthday. Besides, how else is Bailey going to get anyone coming?'

Breen stood up and looked at the line he'd made. Then picked up the red crayon and started joining the red crosses.

'I don't mind waiting, mind,' said Jones. He was watching Breen's careful hand. 'Imagine what Prosser would have said if he'd seen you doing that.'

When he'd finished the red line, Breen stood up. He stared at the graph.

'What's it mean?' said Jones.

Breen looked at the graph. 'I'm not sure,' he said.

Tozer joined them now, make-up back in her bag.

'What's the green line?' she asked.

'All the sums of money he spent on clothes since March 1967.'

'And the red one?'

'Cheques made out to cash.'

The green line started high and descended as time progressed. Over the few weeks before Pugh's death it bumped along the bottom of the X-axis. The red line did the almost exact opposite. Starting low, it began to rise in around March of this year. In the last few weeks it had risen steeply upwards.

'I don't understand it,' said Jones.

'Maybe he was buying clothes with cash, instead of cheques,' said Tozer.

'Maybe,' said Breen. The two lines crossed in mid-June. He stood there staring at the graph, sure that there was some meaning to it, but not able to figure out what it was.

'I'm dying for a drink. Aren't you?' said Jones.

TEN

The Louise was for drinking and little else: lit too brightly, no jukebox, just stools and benches in the public bar. The floor was always thick with cigarette butts and wet from spilt beer. A police pub. There were only three women in the place, including Tozer and Marilyn.

'Ah, Paddy. Wondered where you were. Let me get you a drink.' Bailey greeted Breen a little too eagerly. 'What are you having?' Bailey's wife had patched the sleeves of his tweed jacket with leather ovals.

'Thank you sir. Lager.'

Other officers smirked. 'Oooh. Teacher's pet,' someone muttered.

'Another one, Jones?'

'Go on then, sir.'

'I was hoping there would be a few more in,' said Bailey. 'But I suppose people are busy.'

'Yes, sir.'

Breen had tried his best, but there weren't many in the pub. Inspector Bailey had grown less popular. The Met was going to hell, as far as he was concerned. He didn't trust the younger officers with their new ways of doing things, especially when it came to the way they bent the rules. He would be gone soon anyway.

Breen took his drink and sat with his boss. Jones was on Bailey's other side.

'Any progress with the Pugh case?' asked Bailey, offering around a packet of Senior Service. Old-man fags. No one took one.

'I thought this was supposed to be a birthday drink, sir,' said Jones. 'No shop talk.'

'I hear your wife is expecting, Constable Jones. Congratulations are in order.'

'Thank you, sir,' murmured Jones.

'Best thing that happens to a man,' said Bailey.

'Yes, sir.'

'I should do this more often. Take you lot out for a drink.'

Conversation dried.

Until Breen said, 'Are we recruiting new officers, sir? To make up for the shortfall?'

Bailey said, 'I thought this was supposed to be a birthday drink.'

'Good one, sir.' Though nobody laughed.

'I don't know,' said Bailey. 'It seems as if we're not the most popular department.'

'I mean,' somebody was saying, 'I knew why Carmichael wanted to go to the Drug Squad, he was always a flashy git, but I thought Prosser would be carried out of here in a coffin.'

'Mind if I join you, sir?' Constable Tozer was standing there with a rum and blackcurrant.

Breen shuffled down the bench to make space for her.

'You bringing Mrs Bailey to the Christmas party, sir? They got Kenny Ball. Lovely stuff,' said Jones.

Bailey smiled politely, then turned to Tozer. 'I hear you are leaving the police too, Miss Tozer?'

'Yes, sir. Going back to Devon.'

'She's going back to the farm. We're too fast for her up here,' said someone. 'Ain't we, Helen?'

'My father's not well,' said Tozer. She looked at Breen as she did so.

They had never discussed it: looking after sick parents. He'd just finished that; she was about to begin. Not the kind of thing you talked about.

'Acker Bilk, Chris Barber, Monty Sunshine. Proper music. None of this pop rubbish,' Jones was saying.

'Police life is not for everyone,' Bailey said, sipping on his pint. 'It's better to discover that earlier rather than later.'

'Shame you didn't discover that earlier,' someone muttered.

Bailey didn't seem to hear or pretended he hadn't. Another drink, lads?' he said.

Officers smirked. 'Lads': sounded ridiculous, coming from Bailey.

A voice said loudly, 'Don't mind if I do.' Everybody looked round. Marilyn's shortarse boyfriend Danny had arrived. Check shirt and rockabilly quiff.

'He didn't mean you, you prat,' said Marilyn. He leaned over and gave her a kiss.

'Of course I did,' said Bailey. 'Daniel, isn't it?'

'Lager and black then,' said Danny with a smile.

Jones gulped down the pint Bailey had just bought him and banged the empty glass on the table. 'Go on, sir. I'll have another.'

The inspector stood, trying to get into the role, 'Righto. Drinks all round,' he said, leaving Breen, Tozer and Jones sitting together.

'You like that Bob Dylan feller, don't you, Tozer?' Jones was saying. 'That's not singing, is it? It's torture.'

'He's OK,' said Tozer.

'You wait,' Jones was saying. 'Couple of years and nobody will remember any of that. It's the classics they're going to remember. Real music. I didn't know your dad was sick, mind you.'

Tozer nodded, sipped her rum.

'Sorry to hear that,' said Jones.

Tozer nodded again. 'Thanks,' she said.

'You get on with him?'

Tozer nodded.

'I hate my dad,' said Jones.

'Will you shut up about your bloody dad, Jonesy.' Marilyn joined them on the bench. 'That true, Helen? You don't like police life?'

Tozer said, 'Just the company you have to keep, that's all.'

People laughed, thinking she was joking. Tozer said, 'I heard Prosser had gone because someone had rumbled he was bent.'

'Don't talk bollocks,' said Jones. 'You don't know anything.'

Older coppers glared at her. Jones added, 'Best copper we ever had on CID, Prosser.'

'What about Paddy?' said Marilyn, scooching up next to him.

Jones didn't answer.

Bailey came back with a tray. 'One for the road, eh, chums?' he said, sitting down next to Breen. 'Chin-chin.'

Marilyn leaned round Breen and said to Bailey, 'I think Paddy's great, don't you, sir? He's lovely.'

'He's a good man,' said Bailey uncomfortably.

'I feel sorry for him, living on his own,' continued Marilyn. 'If you ever want me to come around and cook you a meal, Paddy. Do some laundry. Anything like that.'

'Stupid woman,' said Danny, standing across the table from them. 'You're drunk.'

Breen stood and went to the toilet. Jones joined him at the urinal. The toilets in the Louise stank of piss. Fag ends blocked the drain.

'Thing is,' said Jones. 'Sometimes I wish I could talk to women. Properly. Like you do.'

Breen was doing up his flies. 'Me? Are you having me on?'

'Marilyn and Tozer. They talk to you.'

Jones was splashing noisily against the porcelain.

'Why do you want to talk to women anyway? You're married.'

'My wife is making me sleep on the sofa,' Jones said, urine still splattering.

Breen was about to go and wash his hands. Jones never talked like this. Not to him, anyway. Breen turned to him and asked, 'Why?'

'We row a bit. That's all. They go a bit funny when they got a baby, I think. I don't know how to talk to her. So I just go out. You know. Walking. Or to the pub. She don't like pubs much.'

Breen said, 'I don't know. You just talk, that's all.'

'I'm just scared I'll do something wrong,' said Jones.

Breen moved to the sink and started washing his hands.

'Like what?'

Jones turned and did up his flies, not answering. There were splashes on his trousers.

Breen looked for the towel. It was lying on the floor, grey with grease and dirt. He wiped his hands on his trousers instead.

Jones said, 'My dad used to whack my mum. Fucking bastard.'

The door barged open. A copper, still in uniform, lurched in. 'Jonesy!' he shouted.

'What about you? Have you hit your wife?'

Jones ignored the newcomer. 'God, no. I would never do that.'

'But you're frightened you will?'

Jones's eyes seemed to lose their focus for a second. 'Frightened? I'm not frightened of bloody anything.' And he pushed out of the door, ahead of Breen, without washing his hands.

Breen sat down between Marilyn and Bailey. 'Are you getting the cooperation you need from Rhodri Pugh's men?' Bailey asked.

Breen looked across the table. Jones was sitting next to Danny, shouting something in his ear, as if their conversation in the toilets had never happened. He turned back to Bailey and said, 'The trouble is, we still know almost nothing about the man. I've tried everything. All the people I can find, which isn't many. But nobody's seen anything of him these last few months. It's as if he had already disappeared.'

'Keep at it,' said Bailey. 'You'll find something.'

'I'm not drunk,' Marilyn was saying. 'Just saying what I think.'

Bailey took a sip from his pint of beer. Breen tried to remember if he had ever seen Bailey drunk.

'What are you two conniving about?' Tozer barged in next to Breen with a rum and black in her hand, pushing Marilyn to one side.

Marilyn protested, 'Hey. I was sitting next to Paddy.'

'Want another?' Jones said, holding up his empty glass.

'Don't mind,' said Danny.

'Steady on, Jonesy.'

When he'd gone, Breen said to Marilyn, 'He ever talk to you about his dad?'

'Oh God. Jones? Was he talking about his dad?' She was holding her glass, heavily smudged with lipstick.

'Yes. Just now, in the toilet.'

Marilyn scowled. 'Never shut him up now. He does it every time he's on the sauce. Starts talking about his dad. Gets all wound up.'

'What's up with his dad?'

'Jonesy fucking hates him, that's all.'

'Language, please.'

Tozer said, 'His dad put his mother in hospital a few times. Gets drunk. Comes home. You know how it goes. Had a go at Jonesy a few times when he was a nipper too, I think.'

'He told you that?' said Breen.

'More or less.'

Marilyn said, 'I reckon it's why he's so shit scared of having a kid himself.'

'Is he?' said Breen.

'Oh, Paddy! Can't you tell? Poor lad goes white every time anyone mentions the baby.'

Jones was coming back from the bar, pints in hand. Tozer changed the subject quickly by saying to Bailey, 'So, sir. Happy Birthday. You planning your retirement?'

Conversation faltered. People turned to Inspector Bailey to hear what he would say. And though Bailey was laughing at her question, there was such a look of sadness in his eyes that Breen felt like giving Tozer a sharp kick under the table. What do people like Bailey do when they retire? They die, mostly. Or start gardening.

And London was surrounded by a belt of semis with gardens that spoke of the horror of it.

★

Breen couldn't sleep.

Beer and remorse. He was not good with alcohol.

After Bailey had left, and full of more lager than he was used to, he had realised how soon Tozer would be gone. Then he had asked her if she wanted to come home with him after the pub. Like they had done last time.

'I don't think that's a good idea,' she'd said, placing her hand on his.

She had probably been right, but he was annoyed all the same about the way her hand had lain on top of his. It wasn't her sympathy he wanted.

There were plenty of other girls. She had said that too.

'Try asking someone else out. Go on. I dare you.'

He could have said he didn't want to ask just anyone. Instead he'd said, 'I just don't meet them.'

It was true. Years of looking after his dad meant he had fallen out of the habit of meeting women.

'Try harder,' she'd said.

He needed new habits. New places to go to. He was a man who seemed easier to hate than to love, as the growing pile of death threats in his drawer showed.

Now he was awake and it was two o'clock in the morning, so he made mint tea and drank it and put on one of his father's records, enjoying the simple misery of Kathleen Ferrier's 'When I Am Laid in Earth'. The swell of her voice. The crackle of the needle. His father had listened to music with a seriousness that Breen had never understood, sitting in an armchair, head on hands, only listening, never doing anything else. It was never a background for him. He was never a man for the carelessly played radio. Or the carelessly played anything else, for that matter.

Breen sat in that same armchair his father had sat in, writing notes. Making two piles. Two bodies, both in destroyed houses. One had been silent for two months, because he was a man of no importance. The other was equally silent so far, but for different reasons.

Francis Pugh must have had friends of some kind. But Breen had yet to meet them.

Bailey had laughed the previous night when Tozer had talked of retirement. He was not laughing the next morning.

He was furious, hands quivering, a flicker of spittle on his lips.

'Who did this?' the man who barely ever raised his voice shouted at the men in the CID room. Blood pulsed at the vein in his neck.

They sat at their desks. Nobody answered.

'Marilyn, Constable Tozer,' said Bailey. 'Leave the room please.' The women filed out silently, Tozer looking backwards over her shoulder as she left.

'Jones? What have you got to say?'

Jones had a packet of aspirin in one hand. 'Nothing, sir. He must have fallen over in the cell.'

Bailey closed his eyes. 'Your name is on the arrest sheet, Jones. I'm holding you personally responsible.'

Bailey had left to catch the last train home at ten o'clock. Jones was trying to persuade everyone to play a drinking game called Fuzzy Duck when Breen said he was going home too.

'We came across him outside the pub, sir. He was drunk. A woman said he had been molesting her. We thought it would be safer for him to spend a night inside, that's all, sir.'

'That's what you say, Jones.'

'Yes, sir.'

Bailey said, 'You were sober though?'

Jones cocked his head to one side. 'No, sir, not exactly.'

'But you felt sober enough to lock a man up for being drunk.'

'He was assaulting a woman, sir.'

'And you have her witness statement?'

'Not exactly, sir. She went off while we were pulling him in. He was drunk, sir. We thought he needed to sleep it off.'

'And gave him a couple of whacks to make sure he learned his lesson?'

'He was fine when we locked him up. Swear to God.'

Breen watched the veins on the inspector's neck pulse. 'The man has a broken rib and he may lose the sight in one eye. I've ordered Wellington to examine him, Constable Jones. If he finds injuries that are not consistent with your explanation I shall kick you off the team.'

Jones said evenly, 'Ask the duty sergeant, sir. He'll back us up. He was fine when I brought him in. Just a bit tipsy, that's all.' Wellington was on the coppers' side. He wouldn't rock the boat.

Bailey stood there glaring at Jones for a second longer, then said, 'You don't fool me. I know what goes on.' And he walked to his office and pulled the door to.

'Stupid twat,' said Jones, a little too loudly. 'Sooner he goes . . .'

A couple of minutes later Marilyn was at the door. 'Safe to come back in?' she asked.

'Storm's over,' said Jones. 'I thought the boss was going to blow a gasket. I mean it was just a bit of argy-bargy. We didn't really hurt him.'

Breen said, 'So what happened?'

Jones said, 'And don't you bloody start.'

'Who was it beat him up?'

Jones thumped his desk hard and said, 'Paddy. Don't bloody start. Christ sake. Whose bloody side are you on?'

ELEVEN

'It doesn't really make sense, though, does it?' Tozer was saying as they walked across Battersea Park.

'Women are better at looking after children.'

'Says who?' says Tozer. 'I'm OK with kids. But I can do other stuff too. In the police, men get to do all the proper work and women constables are only supposed to talk to children. Or women. It's as if that's too embarrassing for the men. It's daft.'

'Because you're better at it,' said Breen again.

'What? And you're better at talking to men?' she snorted. It was a cold day. The park was deserted. Breen wanted to find a way to apologise for asking her back to his place last night, though if he tried she'd probably only find some new way to take offence. Instead he said, 'I'm not sticking up for how it is. I didn't make the world.'

Tozer said, 'Besides, you go green whenever you see dead bodies.'

The woman whose name Tarpey had given him had insisted they meet at Battersea Funfair rather than at her house. Mrs Hemmings did not want to have to explain to her husband why the police were visiting her. She was waiting on the steps by the entrance with her two boys, the older dressed in a grey flannel school uniform, the younger yanking on her arm. The coloured lights on the first letter above the turnstiles were not working so the sign read: 'UNFAIR'.

She looked around twenty-five and was very pretty, in a classy, moneyed kind of way.

Breen and Tozer walked across the tarmac to meet her. 'There you go,' said Tozer. 'I thought you said you never got to meet any women.'

'She's married,' said Breen.

'Didn't stop her before. You could be in with a chance, Paddy.'

'Shut up. She'll hear you.'

Mrs Hemmings wore a dark-green dress and Jackie Kennedy dark glasses even though the sun was already losing its strength. 'You're late,' she said when Breen held out his hand to shake.

'Sorry.'

'Mr Tarpey promised you would keep this confidential.'

Breen said, 'Did he?'

'I wouldn't be here unless he had,' she said.

Breen paid for the tickets and led them through the turnstile into the park. On a winter weekday the funfair looked bleakly empty. Half the rides were shut.

'Can we have candyfloss?' said the youngest of the boys.

'Go with this nice lady,' said Mrs Hemmings. 'So I can have a good chat with this gentleman.'

'I don't want to,' said the little one. 'She doesn't look nice.'

Tozer glared briefly at Breen, then put on as much of a smile as she could manage and looked down at the two children. 'Do you want to go on a roundabout?'

'I won't give you any sweets if you don't,' said Mrs Hemmings.

'Don't care. Don't want none.'

'Don't be common,' said Mrs Hemmings. '"I don't want *any*." Run along now.'

Tozer pulled the younger one away and the older boy, knees red below his grey shorts, followed.

'You know why I want to talk to you?' said Breen.

'About poor Frankie. Mr Tarpey warned me,' said Mrs Hemmings. The sign on the Dolphinarium read 'Closed until March'.

'When did you last see him?' Breen asked.

They walked ten yards behind Tozer, who now had a child clinging on to each arm and was walking towards the the queue for the merry-go-round.

'I hadn't seen him since December last year. It was a fling, that's all. No harm done.' They were by the fruit machines. She reached into her handbag and pulled out her purse.

'How long did your affair last, Mrs Hemmings?'

'Call me Laura. I hate being called Mrs. Two, three months. Tarpey tells me that was about average. I was offended by that. Nobody wants to be average, do they? Not that I minded. It was fun. He was fun.'

'When did you meet him?'

She delved in her purse, pulled out a silver coin and placed it into a one-armed bandit.

'It was at a party. He was there with another girl. No, I don't re-member her name, if that's what you're thinking. I'd hope she wouldn't remember mine, either.'

The merry-go-round had stopped. Both children ran towards the horses and Tozer followed, lifting them both onto the ride.

'He had loads of girls. He was single. And lovely, really. Loved life. I was just one of the unlucky ones who got pregnant.'

'Others got pregnant too?'

'I wouldn't be surprised.'

'Did he dump you after he found out?'

She pulled the handle. The reels spun.

'Yes. But he always said he would dump me. That was part of the attraction. No commitments. I wasn't the only one. He always had two or three of us on the go.'

The reels stopped. Cherry, Lemon, Bell. She tugged the handle again.

'He was completely harmless.' Apple, Cherry, Bar. 'And he was very entertaining in bed. He knew exactly what buttons to press. Am I embarrassing you, Sergeant?'

'Are you trying to?'

She laughed and tugged the handle again.

'The thing about Frankie was you never really knew him, really. He never let you in. Sometimes I used to think the poor boy just needs a good cuddle, but he doesn't know how to do that. Quite cold at heart, really. But you took him on his own terms. He drank, of course. But doesn't everyone? Oscar!' she suddenly shouted. 'Don't try and get off. It's still going around. What is that idiotic woman doing?'

Breen looked. The older child was trying to get off the merry-go-round and Tozer was yelling something at him. A bell rang and the merry-go-round slowed.

'She's not very good, is she?' Mrs Hemmings looked back at the fruit machine. Orange, Cherry, Orange. Then turned back to the roundabout. It had finally stopped. The younger child was getting off. He was crying.

Breen said, 'Did you meet any of his friends?'

The rollercoaster hurtled past. His question was drowned out by the sound of rattling wood.

'What?' she shouted.

He repeated it.

'He knew lots of people. Loads of artists. He was very passionate about art. Dreadful bores, most of them. But I don't think he had friends, exactly.' She watched Tozer trying to guide the two children to another ride. 'He was a bit lonely, I think, really. No one really kept pace with him, do you know what I mean?'

The two kids were dragging Tozer towards another ride: 'JET FIGHTERS'.

'What about places? Was there anywhere special he took you?'

She gave a little laugh. 'Hotel rooms, mostly. He liked checking into hotels in the middle of the day with no baggage. He used to enjoy it that people thought I must be some smart whore he'd picked up. He found that kind of thing funny.'

'Did he use prostitutes, do you think?'

'Perhaps. I doubt it though.'

Breen stepped around a large muddy puddle full of litter. His brogues needed cleaning again. 'Were any of them jealous?'

'Jealous enough to kill him?'

'Yes.' The rollercoaster rumbled round again. 'Almost certainly. I mean, he always said he wasn't interested in anything more than a roll in the hay, but it wouldn't surprise me at all. People get their feelings hurt.'

'What about when you found you were pregnant?'

'He wasn't interested in children either. And neither was I, of course.' Her eyes flicked towards her sons. 'He had moved on by then. He did it very graciously. Afterwards he sent me a Get Well Soon card. That was a nice touch, I thought.'

Breen said, 'You didn't see any more of Frankie? Or hear anything?'

'He stopped turning up to parties. He used to be at all the best ones. But he just wasn't there anymore. Bored, I expect. I can't say I blame him. London is becoming very dull and self-righteous these days.'

'Whose parties?'

'God. You know. Just parties. Let me think. The last one was a party at Annabel's. You know, the nightclub? Super place. My husband refuses to go. He's so dull.'

'Who were his friends? I need names.'

'Like I said. He didn't really have friends, exactly. There was a wall around him.'

'His circle, then.'

'I suppose so. As long as you didn't say you got them from me.' She dug in her handbag and pulled out a small address book. Flicking through it she read two or three names. Breen noted them down.

'Robert Fraser,' she said eventually. 'He admired him a lot. I didn't like him much.'

'Fraser. He runs an art gallery?'

'Yes,' she said. 'Selling pretentious rubbish. Frankie fell for all that stuff. I was surprised, really. But he was terribly modern.' She said the word as if it were an insult, then laughed.

'Do you have a number for him?'

'Probably.'

'Can you try and find one? Let him know I'd like to speak to him. Was there anyone else?'

She shook her head. 'I was only with him for a short time, you understand.'

'But you stopped seeing him around?'

'The scene has been so dull. I'm not really interested any more. I blame that awful woman Vanessa Redgrave and all her communist pals. Everything is so bloody worthy now. If they care so much about the starving children in Africa, why don't they go there and bloody feed them?'

'What about his father? Did you ever meet him?'

'God, no. I always found it rather amusing that I was sleeping with the son of a minister, but Frankie never talked about him. I don't think they had much to do with each other, really.'

The children came running up. 'The lady won't let us go on the Jet Fighter,' complained the older boy.

'I didn't have a proper go on the merry-go-round because Oscar got off his horse and the man stopped it,' said the younger boy.

'It was boring,' said his brother. 'Merry-go-rounds are for girls.'

'It's not fair,' said the little one. UNFAIR, thought Breen.

'I miss him,' said Mrs Hemmings. 'He was fun. But rather like a comet whizzing past, you know.'

'Can we have candyfloss? Please, Mummy, please?'

'Your husband doesn't know about . . .' Breen paused. 'The procedure?'

She shook her head. 'I said I was visiting my sister in Cornwall for a couple of days. What you don't know can't hurt you,' she said. 'There's no need for him to know, is there?'

Breen shook his head.

Afterwards, walking back to the car with Tozer, Breen said, 'She said she didn't mind he slept with other women.'

'Why's that so strange? It would be a little hypocritical of her, wouldn't it?' said Tozer. 'So did you ask her out, then?'

'What do you think I am?'

'I bet she'd have said yes. You could have been her bit of rough on the side.'

'Lay off. For a start, she's a suspect, in theory.'

Battersea Bridge looked rusty and tired. It could do with a lick of paint.

'Her?' said Tozer. 'I don't know. Doesn't look like a woman did it, to me.'

Breen asked, 'Why?'

'I don't know. Just because.'

She had her own way of thinking, Breen knew. She had had more reason than most to think about what sort of person it took to kill another. Her sixteen-year-old sister had been raped, and stabbed to death. Left under a pile of twigs and leaves.

'I thought you said you were good with children.'

'They weren't kids. They were nightmares. I'm OK with most kids. Spoilt little brats. "Please, Mummy, please." ' They were at the car now. Tozer kicked at the rear wheel a couple of times, like a child herself.

They met Jones back up at Marlborough Place. The door-to-doors were proving a waste of time. People in houses with large gardens made a point of not knowing each other's business.

He walked with Jones and Tozer round to Abbey Gardens, the houses that backed on to Marlborough Place. 'Nothing here, neither,' said Jones. 'I tried already. No point.'

'I'll just take a look.'

'Don't you trust me?'

Breen said, 'It's just worth looking again, sometimes. That's all.' Jones was like a puppy, always wanting reassurance.

There were two girls in school uniform sitting on a wall halfway down the road. Breen recognised the uniform as St Marylebone's. They had their white shirts untucked and wore their ties fat. 'Why aren't they in school?' asked Jones after they'd passed them.

'Why not ask them?' said Tozer.

'That's your job,' said Jones.

'Go on,' said Breen.

'God's sake,' muttered Tozer, turning back. She got out her cigarettes and went to offer the girls one.

Abbey Gardens was a terrace of four-storey Victorian houses. It was
less well-to-do than the houses on Marlborough Place. Most had been
divided into flats. Because it was an unbroken terrace it was hard to
judge which house backed on to the dead man's garden, but Jones said
he reckoned it was the squat.

'Squat?' said Breen.

'There,' said Jones. 'Bunch of funny buggers.'

It was a house like all the others, except that the small front garden
was overgrown and the white paint on the stone around the windows
was peeling. The ground-floor window had been boarded up; the
boards were painted with large imaginary flowers and vines to make
it look like a Rousseau jungle. The curtains of the window above
the front door were a Chinese communist flag that must have been
nailed to the top of the frame. On the door somebody had painted
in big, bubbly letters, 'The Paradise Hotel'. At the bottom of the
door in yellow paint: 'Marylebone Arts Lab. Volunteers wanted. Free
yourself.'

'Nice,' said Breen.

'Scum,' said Jones. 'See what I mean?'

Breen pressed the front doorbell, but it made no sound. He waited
a few seconds, then thumped on the large wooden door with the side
of his fist.

Nobody came. 'They won't let you in, even if they do answer.
Called me a pig. Come outside and I'd teach them a lesson.'

'Like you did to that guy in the cells, other night?'

'Jesus,' said Jones. 'That was his own fault. He was picking on a
woman.'

'A bit like your dad?'

Jones looked at him, a sneer on his lips. 'What you on about? You trying to play the big psychologist?'

Breen stood back, and as he did so the red flag twitched. Somebody was watching them. He knocked on the door again, then knelt down to call through the letterbox, but the flap was nailed shut.

'Police,' he cried.

A sash above them rattled open. 'Morning,' said a voice. A bearded face emerged from the window, peering down at them. 'Back again?' His long dark hair hung down like a curtain around his head.

Breen craned his head upwards. 'We'd like to talk to you about a murder.'

'Go on then,' said the man.

Breen knew it was going to be like this. 'Can we come in?' he asked.

The man pretended to think for a moment. 'Er . . .' He frowned, pursed his lips, then said brightly, 'No.' Breen could hear people tittering behind him.

'See what I mean?' said Jones. Then shouted up, 'Let us in, or we'll arrest you.'

'What for?'

'Obstructing the police.'

'Who's in charge?' said Breen.

'We're all in charge,' said the man quietly.

'Profound,' said Jones. 'Let us in, or else.'

'Or else what?' muttered Breen quietly. 'We'll call the police?'

'Or else,' replied Jones.

'I don't think so,' said the man, before pulling his head back in and closing the window.

'Bastard,' said Jones. 'Want me to bash in the door? I don't mind.'

'What's your name?' shouted Breen.

'What's yours?' The same head reappeared.

'I'm Detective Sergeant Cathal Breen.'

'I'm Jayakrishna.'

'See?' said Jones. 'They don't even tell you their proper names. Just made-up crap.'

'Would you at least come to the door and talk, Mr Jaya . . .'

'. . . Krishna,' said the man. 'I'm fine here, thanks.' A woman squeezed her head through the window next to the man and peered down at them.

Breen said, 'I want to ask about last Thursday night. The night of the explosion.'

'And?' said the man who called himself Jayakrishna.

'Did you see or hear anything suspicious that night?'

'A bloody big bang.'

The woman giggled. It wasn't the one Breen had looked at from Pugh's garden. This woman had shorter, darker hair.

'Mind your language,' said Jones.

'I mind your language,' said the man.

Another giggle.

Breen said, 'Did you know the man who lived there?'

'I know he has moved on to a different existence.'

Breen looked down at his shoes. His neck was aching from looking upwards. He sighed and looked up again. Jayakrishna was smiling back down at him. 'Before that,' Breen said.

'No. Is that all?'

Later, as they were walking away back to Marlborough Place with Tozer, Breen said, 'It's this tiresome assumption that they're enlightened, and everything from our generation is still in the Dark Ages.'

'Maybe it is,' said Tozer. 'Looks like it from my point of view.'

Breen looked at her briefly, but her expression didn't change. For a woman who wore miniskirts, got drunk and kissed coppers, she had a bleak view of the world. Not surprisingly.

Jones said, 'Enlightened, my bum. I should come back here when it's dark. They'd see who was enlightened then. I mean, how can they live like that? You can smell the damp in the place. We're building all these new homes and they chose to live in a slum.'

'What about the schoolgirls?' Breen asked Tozer.

'They said they had a free period at school. Only they changed their mind sharp enough when I said I was going to call their school to check. Know what they said? They said a body had been found in the house in Marlborough Place with its knob cut off.' Tozer offered Jones a cigarette. Breen shook his head. 'Only saying what they said. They heard it had been cut off and stuffed up his bum.'

'Charming,' said Breen. 'Where did they hear that?'

'Outside EMI studios. That's what all the girls who hang around outside were saying.'

'So much for avoiding scandal,' said Breen.

'What?' said Jones. 'Did they really cut off his prick?'

'No,' said Breen. 'Didn't you read the report?'

Jones shook his head.

The longer it took to solve this, Breen thought, the more likely it was to blow up in their faces.

Tozer stopped at the corner. 'Maybe if I go back there on my own?'

'Go back where?'

'To the squat. They'd probably let me in, wouldn't they? On my own?'

'Worth a try,' said Breen.

'You're bloody joking, aren't you?' said Jones. Breen stopped and knelt to do up a shoelace. When Tozer was a few yards ahead, Jones hissed, 'She can't do undercover.'

'It wouldn't be undercover. She'd just be taking a look.'

'She's a plonk, God's sake, Paddy.'

'Which means they probably think she's just as much of a joke as you do,' said Breen. 'So maybe they'll actually talk to her.'

'Don't think I didn't hear that,' said Tozer.

When they arrived back at the office Oliver Tarpey was sitting at Breen's desk. Breen raised his eyebrows at Marilyn, but she was on a phone call. She cupped her hand over the receiver and said, 'I told him he could wait downstairs but he said you wouldn't mind. And I've got a caller for you. She won't give her name.'

Breen strode across the office and picked up the phone on his desk. Tarpey didn't stand, so Breen had to stand by the desk with the phone by his ear. It was Mrs Hemmings. 'I spoke to Robert Fraser. He's not happy, but he'll agree to meet you. This evening.' She gave the address of a restaurant called Seed.

'Seed?'

'Yes. As in Onan.'

'What?' said Breen.

'In the Bible. The poor fellow who was killed for spilling his seed on the ground. Quite appropriate, in Robert's case.' Mrs Hemmings hung on to the phone a little longer. Eventually she said, 'I want you to understand. I'm only doing this because it was Frankie. Whatever it was that happened, he didn't deserve it. I know you don't think I'm very nice. But *he* was.' And then she put the phone down on him.

'Afternoon,' said Tarpey, not getting up.

One of the constables was one-finger typing in the corner. Nobody had taken down Carmichael's pictures of Lee Marvin that were Sellotaped to the wall. The dust lay thick on top of a row of reference books and manuals. Marilyn was chattering on the phone. Through an outsider's eyes, Breen saw, the CID room might not look impressive.

'Do you have somewhere private we could talk?' asked Tarpey.

Breen looked into Bailey's small office. It was empty. Breen guessed Bailey wouldn't mind. He opened the door. 'Can you make a cup of tea, Marilyn?'

She had picked up the phone again. She mouthed, 'I'm on a call.'

'Never mind,' said Tarpey. He picked up a pigskin briefcase and followed Breen into the small room. Tarpey looked around. 'Violets,' he said. 'My mum used to keep them.' He picked up a small metal watering can and dribbled a little water into one of the pots. 'Well?' he said. 'Jealous husband or a woman spurned?'

'We don't know,' said Breen.

'But it is a possibility?'

'Of course. Will you be expecting updates like this regularly?'

'If they're no trouble,' said Tarpey. He took a potted plant and sat in Bailey's chair with it. 'We'd really like to know.'

'*We?*'

'Mr Breen. I know you think I'm interfering, but Rhodri Pugh is a very decent man who clawed his way up from nothing. Absolutely nothing.' He put the plant pot on the desk and slowly turned it around. 'You're a Londoner. I don't suppose you've been to Wales much, have you?'

Breen shook his head. 'Never.'

'We're very proud,' said Tarpey. 'We are proud our Member of Parliament holds office. We need people like him. He represents the legitimate aspirations of the ordinary working man. Like myself. Like you, as well, Mr Breen. Politically, we Welsh are a progressive people. In other ways we are quite traditional. Or rather, we are men of principle. Frankie was a handful. He was a Londoner, not a Welshman. Like so many of today's younger men, he didn't share his father's values. He was only interested in himself, not in the greater good. I always found that very sad. That's a personal matter, however. But, if it were to affect Mr Pugh's reputation, especially back home, I would be concerned.' He turned and replaced the plant on Bailey's windowsill.

Breen sat down in the chair opposite Tarpey. 'We're not sure how he was killed. Suffocated, possibly. The skin was then peeled from his arms and legs. His body was then bled.'

Tarpey frowned. 'Definitely after he died?'

'Yes.'

He touched the tips of his long fingers together. 'Sounds like the work of a lunatic.'

Breen said, 'That's what the police surgeon thinks. Some sort of ritual mutilation.' He looked at Tarpey. A well-groomed sort. A well-cut suit for a Labour Party man. 'All I know is they removed the skin and the blood for a reason. I don't know what reason.'

'Because they were insane, presumably?'

'Why did they leave the gas on? I think they were assuming that the explosion would mutilate Mr Pugh's body enough so that it wouldn't be obvious what they had done to him. So what happened to his arms and legs is important. It's not just a random act.'

'But that's just a guess?'

'If you want to put it that way,' said Breen. 'You realise that the longer we take to solve this, the more likely there are to be rumours about the death? They're already starting. And in the absence of information about who he mixed with, there's no guarantee we can make headway.'

Tarpey sighed. 'I understand your argument. But shining a spotlight on Frankie's . . . style of life. It's a risk we can't take.'

Breen tugged at the knee of his trousers, then looked Tarpey in the eye. 'If you are holding back any information about Francis because you think it might harm his father's reputation, you're only making it more likely that this whole thing will blow up in his face.'

'Believe me, we want this wrapped up as much as you do.'

'I've spoken to his solicitor and his doctor,' said Breen. 'They were helpful but told me nothing that I couldn't have guessed already.'

His doctor had been a Harley Street man. Vague, hand-wringingly sincere, uninformative. He had only been Francis Pugh's doctor for a few months. 'Frightfully sorry . . . Barely knew the man . . .' Another blank.

Breen said, 'We just don't know enough about Francis Pugh. We have no idea of his movements in the week up to his death. None at all. We don't know who his friends were. He was paying for everything in cash so we have no idea of where he was and who he was visiting. It's extremely frustrating. At this stage, we have no idea why. The simplest thing for us would be for the case to be in the papers. That would give the people who knew him, who cared about him, the chance to come forward.'

Tarpey said, 'As his father said, that's a very last resort. We really don't want that to happen. We are happy to put you in touch with anyone we can. And of course I will be in regular contact myself.' He stood, holding his hand out for Breen to shake.

'Is that it?' said Breen.

'Would you like me to stay longer?' replied Tarpey, eyebrows raised.

After Tarpey had left, Marilyn knocked on Bailey's door. 'You look like you swallowed a lemon. 'Who was that woman calling earlier who wouldn't give her name, anyway?'

Breen looked up from the notes he'd been making.

'Just a friend of Francis Pugh's.'

She smiled. 'And there was I, thinking you'd got yourself a girl-friend,' she said.

TWELVE

It was in the basement of an old hotel on Westbourne Terrace. Under the restaurant's name, hand-painted, the words 'Organic & Macrobiotic'. Breen stood looking at it for a second or two, puzzled.

He descended the stone steps and peered into the room. He could see by the light of paper lanterns that it was already half full of young people. He looked around. Nobody appeared old enough to be a gallery owner.

'Is there a Mr Fraser here?' he asked the young man in jeans who seemed to be in charge.

'How would I know?'

'A table for two, then.'

'Sit where you like . . .' The man gestured. 'We don't book tables.'

The tables were giant cable-reels, lying on their side. Around them were arranged giant cushions covered in Indian cloths on which the diners sat, cross-legged.

There was only one of the tables left without any diners round it, so Breen lowered himself onto one of the cushions and scanned the menu. It was less of a list of what you could buy, more of a manifesto:

We eat vulgar foods. The coarse, unleavened bread, seaweed, unhusked rice. But if you prefer fish and chips we understand. There will be more for the rest of us.

The sneer of the new generation. Everything you know is wrong.

'I'll order when my guest is here,' Breen said.

A young couple appeared and were about to sit themselves on the cushions opposite him.

'I'm expecting someone to join me,' said Breen.

'Fine,' said the young man, sitting down on crossed legs opposite him. The girl wore a crocheted waistcoat and sat clutching his arm. She picked up the menu, chewed her lip and said, 'What's buckwheat?'

There was Indian music playing softly in the background, all twangs and swoops.

The girl opposite whispered, loud enough for Breen to hear, 'Look. It's John.'

Her companion turned round.

'Don't stare,' she hissed.

'Where?'

'Just coming in.'

'That's not him.'

'It is. John Lennon comes in here all the time.'

'Yeah, but it's not him. It looks nothing like him.'

Breen looked. He had seen John Lennon once, close to after he'd been arrested for drugs. The man was right. It looked nothing like him.

Breen was hungry and wanted to eat. Sitting on the cushions, his foot had gone to sleep. He had to shift to ease the pins and needles. He looked at his watch. The couple opposite him were being served something brown and nondescript in earthenware bowls.

'Delicious,' the boy said to the girl, 'isn't it?'

Something about the food's lifelessness reminded him of the meals of boiled cabbage and potato his father used to make before his son took over the cooking. Widowed when Breen was only five, his father had never felt at home in the kitchen.

'Do they have salt here?' the girl said, looking around.

'You shouldn't have salt with it,' the boy answered.

'But it's kind of boring, to be honest.'

'You need to rebalance your taste,' said the boy. 'You're just too used to the taste of salt. You need to taste the food instead.'

'I just prefer it saltier,' she said.

'Anyway, you shouldn't add salt after it's cooked,' he said. 'It's not digestible until it's cooked.'

'Really?' she said. 'What about pepper?' She looked at Breen and winked.

The boy didn't answer.

Breen smiled back at her, sucked down his tea and looked at his watch again, then looked around to see if he'd somehow missed Fraser coming in. Despite the hair-shirtness of the food, the restaurant was popular with the young and the beautiful.

He noticed a tall, dark-haired man in a pale-pink suit arrive. He came straight over to Breen.

'You must be the policeman,' he said.

'That obvious?' said Breen, struggling to his feet to shake his hand.

'I k-kept you waiting deliberately,' he said, stuttering slightly. 'To make you feel uncomfortable.' He wore the suit without a tie; when he undid the buttons of his jacket, Breen caught a flash of a sky-blue lining. 'You understand, I only agreed to come because of what happened to Frankie,' he added unsmilingly. 'Normally, I don't much like the company of policemen. My experience of them has not been good.'

'So I hear.'

He sat down on a cushion. From a distance Breen had taken him for another one of the young and beautiful. He was surprised to discover, close to, that he wasn't so young at all. He was in his mid-thirties, Breen guessed, older than he was himself. And yet he seemed not only at ease in this place, but somehow above it. People stared.

'Was it you who put a p-policeman outside my flat?' he said. Breen noticed how Fraser's eyebrows went up with each stutter.

'That was not me. Plain clothes or uniform?'

'Plain clothes,' he said, labouring over the words. 'But as easy to spot as a nun in a whorehouse. They should give policemen lessons in how to dress. Who is it, then?'

'I don't know.'

'Bloody Drug Squad, I expect.'

'Hi, Robert,' the waiter who had served Breen called out with a smile.

Fraser turned to the waiter and said, 'A Heavy Special, please.'

'Make that two,' said Breen.

'Are you sure, Sergeant Breen?' asked Fraser.

'I'll tell you later,' said Breen.

'Good for you. Do you know about macrobiotic food?'

'Do I look like a man who knows about macrobiotic food?'

'Not in the slightest,' said Fraser, grinning for the first time. 'As I said, you look like a policeman. It's a diet based on ancient sacred principles. The most ancient food is whole grains, you know. Avoid processed grains and sugars.'

'About Francis Pugh . . .' said Breen.

'You're not interested in food, then? Or the spiritual life?'

'I'm working, right now,' said Breen.

'I understand you are an art collector,' said Fraser.

Breen frowned. 'Who told you that?'

'A little birdie told me you'd been showing around a Bridget Riley of Frankie's. How did you come by it?'

The woman from the gallery must have told him. 'I found the picture in the remains of his house.'

'Was it wrecked? He had a lot of good stuff, Frankie.'

'Actually right now it's hanging on the wall in my flat.'

Fraser laughed. 'You're an art thief? How superb. There's hope after all.'

'Did you sell it to him?'

'I probably did, as a matter of fact,' said Fraser. 'I used to do a lot of Bridget's work. Do you like it?'

A waiter appeared with steaming earthenware bowls. They seemed to be full of a thin brown soup of some kind. 'I don't think I do, I'm afraid,' said Breen.

Fraser sighed. 'Please don't tell me you're from the I-know-what-I-like school of British taste.'

Breen looked him in the eye, then shook his head. 'The opposite. These days I don't know what I like, at all. I used to think I did. But, no, I don't much like it.'

Fraser nodded, smiled, lifted the soup bowl to his lips, took a gulp and then put it down again. He wiped his chin with a paper napkin. 'Shame you saved the wrong picture, then. Frankie had one of the best Hockneys I've ever sold. And a Jim Dine that was amazing. I'm pretty sure he took a Patrick Caulfield off me, though I don't think he ever paid. But you leave all the paintings and save a lousy print. And I heard they just bulldozed the rest. Sad, really. Are you keeping it?'

'Keeping it?'

'I mean, I would if I were you. I doubt the family would ask for it back,' said Fraser. 'His dad couldn't care less, I don't expect. You wouldn't be the first copper on the take and at least you'd be taking something half decent, even if you didn't know what it was.'

'Is that why you like art? So you can feel superior?'

'You miss the point. I don't have to like art to do that.'

Breen said, 'It's what the English middle classes do, isn't it? Use culture to look down their noses at other people.'

'How d-dare you. I'm not remotely middle class,' said Fraser. 'I went to Eton. Your trouble is the same as all of the English. Seriously. You think people like me are snobs and that art is a trick that's being played on you. And so you can never enjoy it for what it is, which is a shame. The British are afraid to feel anything at all. We are living in a golden age of art and music but most people in this country are too small-minded to notice.' Fraser looked around him, then lit a cigarette. 'The only trouble with vegetarian restaurants is they don't serve wine. Why is that? I mean, wine is vegetarian, isn't it?'

The rest of the food arrived. More earthenware bowls full of brownish rice and another of dark mush.

Breen eyed it. He stuck a fork in and tasted a little. The woman opposite had been right. It needed salt. 'So was Francis Pugh's collection worth a great deal?' said Breen.

'In money terms? Or art terms?'

'Either.'

'Frankie had a good eye,' he said.

'Which means?'

'He got it.'

'Got what?' said Breen.

'It, of course. It.' Fraser took a mouthful of brown rice and held it on the fork in front of him. 'Money-wise, I think if he'd lived he'd have quadrupled what he'd paid for those paintings in ten years.' He popped the rice into his mouth and chewed slowly. 'More, probably. But right now, none of them are worth that much.'

'Really?'

'But who cares? I don't think Frankie cared that much about the value of things. Do you like the food, Sergeant?'

Breen prodded his fork into the bowl and pulled out something pale and rubbery.

'What is it?'

'Tofu,' he said. 'Fermented bean curd. A lot of this stuff comes from Japan. We have a lot to learn from them.'

Breen nibbled on the pale white rectangle that seemed to taste of nothing. 'Did Pugh buy anything off you in the last couple of months?' he asked.

'No, Frankie hadn't bought anything off me for months. Broke, I expect.'

'Or anyone else, that you know of?'

Fraser lifted another a forkful of rice into his mouth and shook his head.

'When did you last see Francis?' asked Breen.

Fraser said, 'I expect you know the answer to this already, don't you? The policeman outside has probably told you.'

'That's nothing to do with me.'

'I last saw Frankie about three weeks ago. He came to my flat. Longer probably. Four weeks.'

That was something, at least. No one else Breen had spoken to had met him so recently. He laid down his fork. His jaw ached from chewing. 'What was he doing at your house?'

'He just dropped in. We had a drink.'

'What did you talk about?'

'God. What does anyone talk about?'

Breen said, 'The man is dead. I need to know who he is and what he does.'

'Art, if you want to know. I'm pretty sure I told him about two artists from St Martin's that I met. I am planning to show their work at the gallery later this month and I was probably trying to persuade him to buy something from them. He argued the work was sensationalist. I agreed, basically. Tell me something, Mr Policeman. These artists want to put the words "Shit" and "Cunt" in my gallery window. Just for a day. It's a kind of happening. Do you think I'll get away with it?'

'If you don't tell the police first,' said Breen.

'Exactly.' Fraser laughed. 'But is it art?'

Breen thought for a second. 'If it's on a toilet wall it's an obscenity. If it's in an art gallery window, then it's art.'

'Bingo,' said Fraser with a smile. 'You're not quite as bad as you look.'

'And did you speak to him on the phone or anything after that?'

Fraser thought for a second, then shook his head.

'You sure?'

'Yes. I liked him. But he'd fallen off the radar a bit, if I'm honest.'

So far, Fraser was the only person who had seen Pugh, or talked to him, in the last weeks of his life, but that was still weeks away from his murder.

'Why?' said Breen.

'I haven't the foggiest, I'm afraid.'

'And you can confirm where you were on the evening of the twenty-eighth of November?'

Fraser put down his fork too, now. 'I was wondering when you'd get to that. I have house guests. Too many, as it happens. They can confirm I didn't go out and kill Frankie, if that's what you mean.'

What little Breen had eaten sat heavily on his stomach. 'How well would you say you knew him?'

Fraser sucked his lower lip for a second, then said, 'I suppose I knew him as well as anybody. Not that Frankie was the kind of person who let anyone get close to him.'

'Shy?'

'Not really. Just p-private. The p-people who have to invent themselves often are, I find.'

His stutter had returned, Breen noticed. 'What do you mean?' he asked.

'We got on because we were the same thing. P-people who are escaping what England demands they should be. From other ends of the class spectrum, p-perhaps. But though class is clearly important to you, it's not important to me.'

The restaurant was thinning out a little. The couple opposite them stood and left.

'So why do you think somebody killed him?'

Fraser looked Breen in the eye and said, 'I don't know. I honestly don't. The thing about Frankie is that nobody disliked him. Apart from his daddy, of course. Why don't you look there? Nothing would surprise me.'

'Did you know any of his girlfriends?'

Fraser shook his head. 'I didn't really think much of his camp followers, to be honest. He liked married women. That way he knew they wouldn't try and run away with him.'

'Jealous husbands?'

'Possibly. He was young. And very, very good-looking. And there was no chance of him wanting to become involved. Women liked that.'

'Really?'

'You sound surprised. You think it's just men who want to fuck a lot?'

Growing up in a woman-less house, his understanding of women was limited to what his father had told him about them. It turned out to have been not always accurate.

'I could swear you're blushing, Sergeant.'

Breen said, 'Were there any women in particular?'

Fraser smiled. 'Like I said. His women didn't interest me. He knew better than to turn up at my flat with them.' He looked around. 'Are we finished here? I could do with a drink.' He looked at his watch. 'There's an opening at Kasmin's. Free wine. Want to come, Sergeant? As you're an art collector now.'

He stood, leaving Breen to pay the bill.

'Well?'

'What?'

'Do you like these?' asked Fraser.

The gallery was painted white – the walls, the ceiling and the floor – and full of people clutching glasses of free wine. Fraser clearly got a kick from introducing Breen as a policeman.

'He's been questioning me about a murder,' he said.

'How fascinating,' they cooed.

The artist was a young American with thick glasses and a bush of dark hair who talked intensely to a circle of people who surrounded him, nodding occasionally.

The paintings consisted of strong geometric curves painted in bright colours. Interlocking rainbows of pink, purple, blue and yellow. Breen peered forward, trying to imagine how they were created, they looked so meticulous. They were standing next to a young woman called Suzi who wore denim and who Fraser said was a revolutionary.

'Yes,' Breen said. 'I do like them.'

Fraser wrinkled his nose. 'Really?'

The revolutionary said, 'This is a time for revolution, not post-abstract expressionism.'

'I don't know what you mean,' said Breen.

'Neither does she,' said Fraser. 'Get us some more wine, dear,' he said, and handed her his glass. Breen watched her go and wondered if she was a model, or some glamorous pop star's girlfriend. She had straw-blonde hair and high European cheekbones, and her jeans fitted tightly around her behind.

'What about this one?' said Fraser.

'It's not like I prefer one over the other. I just like them. I find them joyful.'

'I suppose they are,' said Fraser.

'You don't like the exhibition?' asked Breen.

'I'll be honest. I think most of this stuff is a dead duck. But you like it. That's all that matters.'

'Thing is,' said Breen, 'I've hardly seen any art like this. I'm probably naive.'

'B-bully for you,' said Fraser, smiling. 'It's something no one here would admit to.'

A youngish woman in a fox-fur stole holding an ashtray in one hand approached and grabbed Fraser's hand. 'Dear Robert. How lovely to see you. Do you know Harry Cox?' she said. 'He's a collector. Very keen,' she said, in a stage whisper. 'I haven't seen you in so long. Are you having another exhibition soon? Please say you are.'

The man she was with was short, bald, and wore a gold chain around his neck. He held out his hand for Fraser to shake.

'Robert does Peter Blake, Harry,' said the fur-stole woman. 'You adore his stuff, don't you, Harry? Harry's frightfully rich.'

The man called Harry smiled. He liked being called rich.

The woman steamrollered on. 'Are you doing a new exhibition

soon, Robert? We do so miss your shows. Robert is the most thrilling gallerist in London,' she whispered to Harry.

'I've heard all about you,' said the short, bald man. 'Do you rate this artist? I was thinking of buying something.'

'Were you?' said Fraser.

'Do you think I should?'

The woman was still grasping Fraser by the hand. He turned to her and said, 'I was just telling my policeman friend here, I'm planning a show called "Shit and C-cunt",' stuttering on the 'c'-word. 'One day only.'

'Really?' said the woman, face abruptly fixed in a smile.

'Do you know Cathal?' said Fraser. 'He's an art thief. And an excellent critic too. Cathal finds this work joyful, Mr Cox. I'd take his advice on it, if I were you.'

'How delightful,' said the woman, looking less sure of herself. 'And what about you, Robert? Are you well? Have you recovered from your brush with the law?'

'You think this work is good, do you?' the fat art collector asked, turning to Breen.

'Well . . . I like it.'

The man nodded. 'You'd recommend me buying it?'

The man was looking at him eagerly, as if his opinion counted for something.

'Cathal has a talent for finding a real steal,' said Fraser, ignoring the woman who was still trying to get him to talk about life in prison.

'Are you really a policeman?' said the fat art collector.

'Yes,' said Breen.

'Met?'

Breen nodded, looking around the room.

'Never met a policeman who was up in art. What division?'

Breen looked back at the man. He was older than Breen, fat but muscular with it. 'D,' said Breen.

'You must know Jack Creamer. Old friend of mine.' The man took a gulp from his wine.

'Inspector Creamer? Works out of the Maida Vale station.'

The man nodded, grinning. 'Excellent man. You in Maida Vale?'

Breen shook his head. 'Marylebone.' He looked the man up and down. In a check suit and two-tone shoes, he was too flamboyantly dressed to be a copper himself.

The man frowned. 'Marylebone? That's where Sergeant Michael Prosser works, isn't it? Know him?'

Breen took a sip from his wine. 'Not anymore. He's left the force.

The man's mouth opened. 'Really? You sure about that?'

'Harry –' the woman tugged at the round man's sleeve – 'you should meet John. He's got a couple of Barnett Newmans you might be interested in.'

Breen asked, 'Are you a friend of Michael Prosser's?'

The man shook his head. 'No. Not at all. Just met him a couple of times.'

Breen noticed a gold signet ring on the man's finger. The ring was engraved with the symbol of a square and a pair of compasses. Breen asked, 'What line are you in that you know coppers?'

The man's laugh was squeaky, high-pitched. 'Me? Rugby.'

Breen must have looked puzzled.

'Big supporter. Metropolitan Police Rugby Club. Great men. You a rugby man?'

Breen shook his head. His friend Carmichael had tried to persuade Breen to play when they first joined up, but Breen didn't have the physique for it.

'I'll send you tickets to one of the games, if you like. There's one on Saturday. You like the art, then?' asked Harry.

Breen looked around the small room again. 'Well, yes,' said Breen. 'It's very fresh.' The wine was going to his head.

'Know what? I think I do too,' said Harry, slapping him on the back. He pulled a silver tin from his inside jacket pocket and handed

Breen a business card from it. 'Get in touch,' he said. 'I'd like to thank you some time for your advice.'

Breen left them alone to look at the paintings again. The crowd was young, rich and confident. Conversations were loud. Bursts of laughter. There was a sense that if you were here, you were uniquely privileged. You had arrived at a special place, at a special time, before anyone else. A sense of breaking out of Britain's predictable greys and browns into something bigger and stranger.

Between the laughter, Breen heard the young artist saying, 'Brush-strokes are a, uh, layer that lies between the painting and the audience. I feel that flatness is just an absolute necessity for modernist painting.'

The revolutionary returned, holding three glasses of white wine carefully in both hands. 'Where's Robert?' she said.

Breen looked around. He couldn't see him anywhere.

'Did he tell you he was a homosexual?' said the revolutionary.

'I guessed,' said Breen. He lifted his wine glass.

'He said he thought you were very good-looking. He said he wanted to fuck you.'

Breen coughed, almost spilling what was left in the glass. Afterwards he gasped for air. She hit him on the back and said, 'Are you OK?'

'Fine.'

'Are you interested in men?' she asked, 'Or women?'

Breen was wiping wine from his jacket and didn't answer.

'When I was younger I used to love openings. I hate them now,' she went on. 'They're so ridiculous. I'd blow up the lot of them. I think Robert's gone, you know? He does that sometimes. Just leaves if he's bored. I think he's really quite rude.'

Breen looked at the crowd around him. Harry Cox was buying one of the paintings, leaning over a desk with his chequebook out, a crowd of people around him.

Two glasses of wine had made Breen feel bolder than he would normally. He turned to the pretty revolutionary and said, 'Maybe we could go somewhere else for a drink?'

The woman paused for a second, looking surprised. 'No,' she said. 'I don't think so.' He watched the gallerist's assistant take the cheque with a distant look on her face, as if she were doing the bald man a favour by accepting it. The gallerist was shaking his hand, smiling. When Breen looked back, the revolutionary was not there. He looked around the gallery, but she must have slipped away too, leaving him here on his own.

THIRTEEN

On Thursday morning, Breen picked Tozer up from the women's section house in Pembridge Square at 8.30. Most of the women in D Division lived here, sharing rooms in a pair of huge old Regency houses that had been knocked together. No men were allowed beyond the sitting room.

Tozer came clattering down the steps, cardigan half on.

'Here I am. All ready,' she said, tugging a brush through her hair as she got into the passenger seat of Breen's car. 'The walking joke of D Div.'

'What are you on about?' said Breen.

'You said I was a joke. In front of Jones. I heard you.'

Breen crunched the gears, pulling out into the Bayswater Road. 'No I didn't. I said those squatters would take you as a joke. That way you'd get a better chance of talking to them than by trying to break down the door.'

'Super,' she said. 'Thanks.'

'Why are you in such a bad mood all the time?'

Tozer didn't answer.

Bayswater Road was stationary, so he U-turned, intending to cut through Westbourne Grove.

'Look out,' said Tozer.

'What?'

'Didn't you see that kid on a bike?' she said, looking back over her shoulder.

'Of course I did,' said Breen.

They crawled northwards. 'You should have stayed on Bayswater Road,' Tozer said.

'We'll be fine.' He swung the car left again to cut up to Royal Oak but the traffic was backed up here, too, cabbies honking their horns and swearing.

'This is horrible,' she said.

Breen could see what had happened. A lorry had got stuck trying to reverse into a building site ahead. It had taken the turn too sharply and was now grinding against the metal gatepost.

Breen pulled the car over and got out.

'What are you doing?' said Tozer.

'John!' Breen shouted. 'John Nolan.'

A big man in a frayed tweed jacket who was attempting to direct the lorry driver turned. He wore blue workmen's trousers and black boots with the steel toecaps showing through.

'It's me,' said Breen.

'Well there. Cathal Breen.' The Irishman put out his big red hand. 'How you been?' he asked in an accent exactly like Breen's father's. 'Good to see you.' If he closed his eyes, he could be standing in front of his dad.

'What's going on?' said Tozer.

'Give me a minute,' said Breen.

'Bunch of bloody idiots,' said Nolan. 'Will you look at that?' The lorry continued to move backwards and forwards, trying to get clear of the gate as the queue of cars got longer.

It wasn't until the age of twelve or thirteen that he had realised his father even had an Irish accent. A strong one at that. It had come as a surprise when his school friends said they couldn't understand what his father said.

By eighteen he had become so embarrassed by the way Tomas Breen spoke that he had found excuses to avoid inviting his girlfriend home, a cheery seventeen-year-old redhead who had let him fondle her breasts but no more.

It wasn't just the way his father had spoken. It had been everything about him.

Listening to Nolan now, he was shocked to realise how much he missed the sound of his father's voice.

'I've been OK,' said Breen. 'Do you have a minute?'

'For the son of Tomas Breen I have more than a minute. I've an office just around the corner.' Nolan had known Breen's father as a younger man. He had been one of the many struggling to find a job in London who were given work on the building sites by his father.

Tozer was out of the car and standing next to him now. 'Is anything wrong?'

'This is an old friend of my father's,' said Breen. 'John Nolan.'

Tozer held her hand out to him.

'That's right,' said Nolan, glancing down at Tozer's thin legs, then up to her chest and then, finally, to her face.

'Why don't you wait in the car?' said Breen.

'I'm OK. I can wait.'

'It's just I wanted to ask Mr Nolan something,' said Breen.

'I don't mind,' she said.

Breen was about to insist but Nolan said, 'Come and join us for a cup of tea.'

'OK,' Tozer said with a grin.

The building site was just on the far side of Lord Hill's Bridge. They followed Nolan down the path next to the concrete foundations dug ten feet down into London's crust, shored up by thick planks of wood.

'What are you building?'

'That road,' said Nolan. 'You know. The big road on legs. The West Cross Route.'

They had been smashing down houses right the way from Shepherds Bush to Paddington for months. Beautiful old rows that had survived the German bombs. A clear line curving from the west. There had been protests from locals, whose communities were being cut in half, and bricks thrown at the bulldozers in Notting Hill, but mostly people wanted the roads.

'It's going to join to a highway that will run right around London, they say,' said Nolan. 'And then three more "ringways" outside that. It'll be better than Los Angeles, they reckon. Bloody cars zipping everywhere.'

'Plenty of work for you?' said Breen.

'Loads of money and work for those who know how to make it, sure. You have to feel sorry for the poor buggers in the way, if you'll excuse my language.'

'I love the idea of driving above the city,' said Tozer. 'It'll be like flying.'

'I would say I prefer to be a little closer to the earth,' said Nolan, stepping over bare dirt.

A man standing on the back of a lorry whistled at Tozer as she walked past.

'You want to watch that,' called Nolan. 'This girl's a copper.' He was smiling though.

'She can bang me up any time,' said the man.

'What did he say?' said Tozer.

'I had the priest say a Mass for your father,' said Nolan as he passed them. 'Hope you don't mind.'

'My father would have hated that you did it,' said Breen. 'But if there's a God he'll have been proved wrong and if there isn't he's past caring.'

Nolan laughed and led them to a small caravan with a box outside for a front doorstep. He entered first and was still trying to conceal the calendar advertising Mahony's Skip Hire, with its picture of a bare-bosomed woman holding a wheelbarrow, when Tozer entered.

'Don't mind me,' she said.

Nolan put the calendar into a file drawer and slammed it shut. The caravan was heated by paraffin. Condensation streamed down the walls. There was a small palm crucifix hanging on a nail on the wall, left over from Easter. Nolan plugged in the kettle, which sparked and fizzed. 'There now,' he said. 'My office. Take a seat.'

Nolan scooped up the plans which lay on the small dining table and Breen and Tozer shuffled onto the bench seat alongside it.

'The thing is, I've got some holiday coming up,' said Breen, 'I was thinking of going to Tralee,' he said.

'Is that right?'

'I've never been to Ireland,' he said. 'It never entered my head until my father died.'

'He never went back?' said Nolan.

'Never.'

Nolan poured a little water into a huge brown pot to warm it, opened the door of the caravan and emptied it outside. He said, 'Some of the young men . . . they never go back either. It's like it's lost to them. Maybe they're ashamed. They leave home boasting they're going to make their fortunes and they end up working on some shitty job like this, 'scuse my language.'

'My father was too proud to go, I suppose,' said Breen.

'I would say,' said Nolan.

Tozer offered Nolan a cigarette. Breen shook his head. Nolan lit hers first with a silver lighter, then tore the filter off his and lit the broken end, scraps of smouldering tobacco falling onto the floor, then burst out coughing, thumping his chest.

Breen said, 'And now I wish I'd asked him to take me. I would like him to have shown me around.'

Nolan nodded solemnly. 'I understand,' he said and took another long pull from his cigarette. 'It's always home, whether you're born there or not.'

With the cigarette hanging from his lip, Nolan spooned tea into the pot and poured on the water. 'You must go and see my cousins when you are there. I will tell them to show you the place.'

'That's what I wanted to ask. I won't know anybody there.'

Tozer said, 'Don't you have any aunts and uncles?'

Breen said, 'I don't know. My father never talked about anybody.'

'Sure, there must be relations there. You'll have cousins. Everybody has cousins.'

If there were, Breen's father had never mentioned them.

The tea steamed in the teacups. Nolan added sugar without asking. 'It is true,' he said. 'He set himself apart from the place. He was a disappointed man.' Nolan distributed the cups, then sat at the table, pulled out a sheet of paper and started writing a list of names and addresses for Breen.

Tozer said, 'I think they should bulldoze the rest of London and start again. It's an ugly, dirty old place, far as I'm concerned.'

Nolan asked, 'What about that dead man you were asking about last month?'

'No luck,' said Breen. 'Sometimes you never find out.'

'It must take it out of you,' said Nolan, and he erupted into coughing again. He wrote slowly and carefully, adding a telephone number when he had one. Tozer looked at her watch, drank her tea, said nothing. When he'd finally finished the list he handed it over to Breen. 'You tell them I sent you. You'd be made most welcome. If you go, will you take some packages from me?'

Afterwards, walking back across the mud to the car, Breen looked up and tried to visualise a road above his head, cars roaring along it, heading west. Buildings had already been pushed aside; a giant parting combed through the city.

Tozer said, 'I didn't understand a ruddy word that man said. His accent was so strong,' she said.

'Speak for yourself,' he said.

'I mean, I may talk in a Devon accent, but at least that's ruddy English.'

They drove to Abbey Gardens and pulled up on the other side of the road to the squat. The street was quiet. The curtains of the building

were all closed. Since they were last here, somebody had written a sign
in big letters and stuck it on the inside of one of the windows:

Admit it. You're frightened aren't you????

'Sorry I'm in a bad mood,' said Tozer, looking away from him. 'It's
just I don't really want to go and live back on the farm. I like it here.
Only I have to. You know what it's like.'

Breen nodded. He looked at the squat. On the front step, a tabby cat
sat waiting to be let in. 'You don't have to do this,' he said. 'Like Jonesy
said, really. You're not supposed to do anything like this.'

'I'm not supposed to do nothing,' said Tozer. 'That's the problem.'

She finished a cigarette and stubbed it out in the ashtray. 'I just go
and knock on the door, then?'

'They won't know you're there if you don't,' said Breen.

Breen wound down the window and watched her knocking on
the big front door with the side of her fist. Again, the window above
opened and a bearded man with long hair appeared. Breen could see
Tozer looking up, talking to him, but he was too far away to hear
anything.

The conversation went on for at least a minute before the door
finally opened. In the dark of the doorway Breen caught a glimpse
of the young woman he'd seen in the garden, now talking to Tozer
at the door. Pale, slender and slightly Pre-Raphaelite in a long cotton
dress. Then the front door closed behind Tozer. Breen waited for ten
minutes but she didn't come back out.

She would be OK.

He would be in big trouble with the women's division if she wasn't.

He turned the engine on, put the car into gear, and drove away back
south towards Westminster.

The shiny new sign was stuck: a big triangular metal stand with
silver letters reading 'New Scotland Yard'. It had only been outside

the new building for a few weeks. It was supposed to turn round and round, symbolising how the Metropolitan Police were taking care of the whole city. Or as Carmichael had said, 'How we're always going around in circles'.

Two men were up a ladder trying to get it revolving again. Breen watched them struggling with it for a while until one of them finally pulled out a hammer and started thumping something inside the sign.

The giant building was so new it smelt like the inside of a plastic bag. The new lifts weren't working, either, so Breen had to walk up four flights of stairs to find Carmichael's office.

Big John Carmichael's sideboards were even longer than last time Breen had seen them. Breen watched him for a minute, one finger typing, until he spotted Breen, stood and roared, 'Paddy, you bugger! How's things in D? What about that yokel bird you're knobbing? Bailey still driving everyone crazy?'

'I'm not knobbing anyone,' said Breen.

'Can't have that, Paddy. You'll waste away.'

Compared to the dark, high-windowed room where the two of them had worked together at Marylebone, this place was modern and light. There were orange plastic chairs. New green plastic telephones. Neat Olivetti typewriters. The future.

'I want to hear everything. Come to the canteen. I'll buy you a coffee. It's crap, mind.'

Carmichael was wearing a blue-and-yellow checked blazer that made him look even larger than he was. He grabbed Breen's arm and started pulling him through swing doors and down corridors.

Breen had never been to the canteen here before. It was huge. People clutched wooden trays and queued for chips and sandwiches served by a line of serving women in pale nylon pinnies.

'So?' Carmichael said, sitting down opposite Breen at a long table.

From up here, Breen could see right across the Thames towards Nine Elms. He asked, 'Do the Drug Squad do much surveillance of suspects?'

'You know we do.'

'I'm trying to find out about a man called Robert Fraser. All I know is he was arrested last year for drugs and sentenced to six months. He thinks your lot are still keeping an eye on him.'

'Probably are, then,' said Carmichael. 'Name rings a bell. Big case. They pulled in Mick Jagger too, remember?'

Breen tried. The last two years were an exhausted blur of bed baths and hospital visits. Breen took a gulp of coffee. Drainwater.

'What do you want to know?' asked Carmichael.

'A murder case I'm on.' He was wary about telling Carmichael more.

'And you think this Fraser was involved?'

'I don't know. I'm crashing around in the dark, to be honest.'

'I thought you were on holiday, anyway.'

There was an odd burst of light as the sun broke through the London cloud. The grey streets outside looked suddenly brighter.

'Bailey didn't let me go. Because we're short-handed. Because people like you have jumped ship.'

'Don't blame me. You should have come here too. Marylebone CID is a dead duck. Bailey's stuck in the past. Longer he stays there, the worse it'll be. This is where it's going on.' He gestured around at the dozens of coppers sitting in the canteen. The future looked more like a bank headquarters than a police station.

Breen pushed the coffee away from him. Even the smell was making him nauseous.

'This is where we are,' Carmichael was saying. 'Ten years ago you could have listed the names of pretty much every heroin addict in London. There were – what? – two, three hundred in the whole of the city. Since the beatniks and the pop stars, drugs are everywhere. That's why the Home Office are trying to put the lid on it. They've changed their tune. Now they want us to put them away.'

'I'm just interested in what you have on Fraser.'

'It's the Frankie Pugh murder you're on, isn't it?'

'Who told you?'

'Everybody knows. Why haven't I read anything about this in the papers? You'd have thought they'd be all over it.'

'Francis Pugh is Rhodri Pugh's son,' said Breen. 'One of Harold Wilson's men. Until we know why he's been killed, he's keeping the lid on it. It's like there's an unofficial D Notice on the whole thing.'

'Ah,' said Carmichael. 'Right. And Bailey is all for the hush-hush, I suppose?'

'You know him. I'm reporting back to Rhodri Pugh's people.'

Carmichael laughed. 'See? Everyone thinks England is swinging, everybody thinks there's a revolution going on, but your place is stuck in the Middle Ages, far as I can see.'

'I'm being expected to work in the dark. I'm not allowed to make an appeal in the papers. They're controlling who I interview.'

Carmichael said, 'Either the whole thing will backfire and the press will get wind of it, or you'll get nowhere at all. The Home Office will demand heads. Either way you're being set up to take the blame for it.'

Breen said, 'Is Fraser still on drugs?'

'I don't know.'

'How would you know someone was on drugs? It's not as if they carry a sign.'

'Do you think Pugh was on drugs?' Carmichael said.

Breen didn't answer. Go carefully. The Drug Squad were notorious for liking headlines. If they started nosing around, the story would end up in the press in no time. So he said nothing.

'So it's good here, then?'

'I'm still finding my feet. But least it's not Bailey.'

Once he would have told Carmichael everything. They were mates. He would have told him about the death threats. They would have laughed, maybe. But now he kept things to himself, wondering whether someone was lurking behind corners, waiting for him.

There was a loud bang behind them, then a burst of laughter and clapping. A young constable had dropped his tray on the floor, spraying cottage pie over the lino. 'Nice one!'

'And half the bloody rock stars are buying big houses in the countryside and driving around in white Rolls-Royces. Some bloody revolution if you ask me. Know what? They gave us all a reefer to smoke last week. So we could recognise it. You should have seen me. Afterwards they asked me what was so funny. And I couldn't even remember.'

A young woman in a nylon coat and white cap elbowed the young policeman out of the way and started cleaning up the mess.

'Leave it with me. I'll see what I can find out.'

Breen watched the woman on her knees, patiently sweeping up the spilt food into a tin dustpan.

'Look at the bum on that,' said Carmichael. 'Not bad, eh?'

The sign was still not working when Breen left the building. The workmen had abandoned it.

Carmichael was right. If he was not careful he'd end up taking the flak for anything that went wrong.

A gust of wind funnelled by the tall building caught Breen's raincoat. It flapped suddenly upwards, obscuring his vision. He was heading back to the older building in Marylebone. To the comfort of worn floorboards and ancient dirty windows.

Breen's stomach lurched when he saw the paper stuck into his typewriter. Another threat? What this time? It was starting to wear him down, make him jumpy.

Nobody seemed to have noticed it.

But when he looked it was just a note from Marilyn, written in her neat round hand: 'Harry Cocks (?) called. Has tickets for rugby on Sat. 01 723 9567.' Breen screwed up the note and put it in the bin.

Tozer arrived back at the office just before lunch. She was carrying a slightly battered guitar.

'Bloody hell,' said Jones. 'What is that?'

'It's a hairdryer,' said Tozer. She leaned the guitar against her desk while she put down her handbag and sat down, then picked it up again and laid it across her lap.

'Not what I meant,' said Jones, but Tozer ignored him.

'You have a nail-clipper, Marilyn?' she asked. 'I think I should cut them. You can't play guitar with long nails. Mind you, I bite them anyway.'

Marilyn ignored her. One of the strip lights was flickering again. It was giving Breen a headache. He asked, 'How was it?'

'This bloke in the squat's going to teach me guitar,' said Tozer.

'Jesus,' said Jones to Marilyn. 'I'll be glad when she's gone. At least things will be normal again.'

'I always fancied it. Being honest, I only thought lads played guitar,' she said.

'You got into the squat, then?' said Breen.

'I should have guessed,' said Jones.

Tozer nodded. She was holding the guitar on her lap, awkwardly trying to get her hand around the neck.

'She's a bloody woman, for pig's sake! 'Sides, that's not proper police work.'

'Did they see anything?' asked Breen.

Tozer shook her head. 'They said you can't see into their place anyway. I checked. They're right. The angle's wrong. You can just about see into the garden, but that's all.'

She cradled the guitar onto her lap and struggled to arrange her fingers on the fretboard.

'It's a commune,' she said. 'Free love and everything. They asked me to join.'

'Free love?' said Jones, sounding interested now.

Marilyn sneered at Tozer. 'I expect you'd like that. Free love.'

'What do you mean by that?' demanded Tozer.

'Free love?' said Jones again. 'She couldn't even give it away.'

Tozer pretended not to hear him. 'Cow,' she muttered.

'How many people live there?' asked Breen.

'Six or seven. Two women.'

'One of them has long fair hair?' asked Breen.

She nodded and looked up from the guitar. 'You noticed her, then?'

Breen said, 'Just saw her for a second, that's all.'

'She's called Hibou — so she says, anyway. It's "owl" in French, apparently.'

'She a frog?'

'French? No. It's just a name.'

'What about that man, Jaya . . .'

'Jayakrishna.'

'What the heck kind of wog name is that?' said Marilyn.

'It's Indian. I think it's nice,' said Tozer. 'The other girl's called Padma, only her real name's Emily.'

'That's bloody weird. They all change their names.'

'Jayakrishna says you need to leave your self behind.'

'Leave your marbles behind, more like. What's your new name going to be?'

'What about the owl girl. What's her real name?' asked Breen.

'She wouldn't tell me,' said Tozer. And she dropped her fingers across the nylon strings. 'That's a D, that is,' said Tozer. 'I'm not sure it's in tune though.'

'Don't care if it's A-flat minor. It's horrible. You going to change your name to Hiawatha or something?'

'Not that kind of Indian,' said Tozer.

'Higher purchase,' said Marilyn.

'Higher than a bloody kite, I expect,' said Jones.

'Had they seen anything at all?' said Breen.

'Nothing,' she said. 'I was thinking of going back tomorrow, Paddy. Is that OK?' She strummed the strings again.

'Why?' demanded Breen.

'What?' said Jones. 'So you can learn another bloody chord?'

'Maybe,' said Tozer.

Jones said, 'Right. It's five to one. Lunch break. Who's coming down the Louise for a pint?'

Marilyn had her powder compact out already and was putting lipstick on.

Breen watched Tozer concentrating on keeping her fingers on the fretboard while trying to pluck the strings one by one.

Bailey emerged from his office and paused open-mouthed at his door, looking at Tozer, sitting at her desk in the CID room, a big guitar across her scrawny lap. Breen put the phone down.

'Off to the pub for lunch, sir,' said Jones. 'You coming?'

Bailey closed the door again.

FOURTEEN

For the third night in a row, Breen slept fitfully, waking with a full bladder, banging his ankle on a chair as he groped his way to the toilet in the dark. He stood in front of the toilet bowl, relieving himself as he listened to the sound of cats fighting in the yards behind the houses.

Back in bed, he fell asleep again and dreamed his father was in the kitchen, cooking a giant bird of some kind. The bird flapped its wings occasionally, but his father kept saying, 'It looks dead to me.'

In his dream, Breen was not surprised when the bird burst into flames. The scorched creature blundered around the room, keening in distress. His father had once set fire to his own kitchen, Breen remembered. It was the reason why he now lived with Breen. Only, Breen considered thickly, his father was dead now.

The shock of the thought woke him.

Breen smelt the fumes as he surfaced into the real world. Smoke. Not dream smoke. Real smoke. Breen had got into the habit of leaving his bedroom door open to listen out for his father. A grey cloud was now drifting in through the open doorway.

He jumped out of bed and went into the living room. Thicker smoke was already curling below the ceiling.

It took him another second to register that his front door was alight. On fire. Flames were licking up it, already two or three feet high. He stood there, dimly wondering how a front door could catch fire, before the horror of the situation struck him. Though he could escape to the small yard at the back of the house, and the flat above him was empty, he would be trapped.

He lurched towards the kitchen, yanking out pans, placing two into the sink and turning on both taps. He found it hard to think, head still in the dream.

By the time he returned to the living room the flames were higher, crawling up towards the top of the door.

He hurled both pans at the flame. The wood hissed and the flames shortened for a second, then sprang back alight.

The sense of being in a dream wouldn't leave him. This was the same fire that had burned his father six years ago; the same that had killed the man in the empty house. He had to wake up. Think what to do.

He ran back to the kitchen and refilled the pans, coughing from the smoke. As a copper on the beat he had seen the after-effect of fires. He probably only had a few minutes in which to escape.

The blackened man on the slab in the white room.

He ran to the back door and shouted 'Fire!' as loudly as he could, then returned to the front room with the pans. By now the flames had fully regained their strength. And more. At the top of the door, the paint was starting to bubble. The water he had in his pans would not be enough to stop the fire now, but he threw their contents onto the flames anyway. The water was swallowed whole, this time having no effect at all.

A sudden wave of heat stung his face and he sucked in air from the shock of it. His lungs exploded into coughing and he dropped to his knees as if knocked down by a punch. His chest felt as if it had been raked by broken glass.

In the fire's light he saw the print from Francis Pugh's house hanging on the wall, the white turning pink from the light of the flames.

This is how you die. This is how you wind up on a slab in Wellington's hospital. He wished his life had not been so solitary.

And then he heard the fire engine's bell over the crackle of the fire.

★

They gave him breakfast at Stoke Newington police station. It was the first station he'd worked at after he left Hendon, an austere but familiar three-storey Victorian block standing out like the last good tooth in a rotten mouth of broken buildings close to the cul-de-sac where he still lived.

As the morning shift arrived, everyone seemed to have heard about the fire.

'We'll get the bastard,' the desk sergeant had said. 'We'll fry his bollocks and see if he likes it. I promise you that, Paddy.' All the policemen, whether they were faces he recognised from when he worked here or newcomers to the station, tutted and sympathised. That it should happen on their turf. That someone should try and kill one of them.

The breakfast was large and oily on a big, cracked white plate. Four slices of fried bread, double eggs, three rashers of bacon and two pale-looking sausages. He could only manage a little of it, people patting him on the back and wanting to know what had gone on. Breen thanked them but couldn't wait to get away, back to his flat.

'Jesus, Paddy. Who did you piss off?'

When he returned to the cul-de-sac, a man from the council was fixing his wrecked door.

'You were bloody lucky,' the chippie said, a nail dangling from his lips. 'What woke you up?'

'My father,' said Breen. There was a little smoke damage on the outside of the house, but not that much. Yes, he had been lucky.

'Was he in there an' all?'

The firemen had said it was probably paraffin or meths. Petrol would have gone up quicker. A crude burning rag shoved through the door. The local police had knocked on doors already, but no one had seen anything.

'Oi, Breen!' called a voice. 'Your boss is at the station. He wants to see you.'

'Inspector Bailey? He's here?'

'Thin bloke,' said a uniformed constable at the end of the street. 'Bit of a misery.'

'That's him.'

Breen walked back out into the high street. From twenty yards away he could see Bailey standing on the pavement outside the station, talking to the local head of CID.

'I've been telling Inspector Bailey that we're going to throw everything we've got at this, Paddy,' he said.

Bailey looked at Breen and said, 'In that case, perhaps you better tell the inspector what Constable Tozer told me when she heard the news. It'll save him an awful lot of work.'

'Sir?' said Breen.

'Apparently Sergeant Breen has been getting death threats. He didn't think to mention them to me.'

'That right?' said the inspector.

'And Constable Tozer says she thinks you have a pretty good idea of who you've been getting them from.'

Breen coughed up smoke.

'Well?'

'Yes. I do.'

Bailey pursed his lips, looked towards his left and said, 'I'm extremely disappointed, Paddy.'

Breen said, 'I may know who did this.'

'Who?' asked the Stoke Newington man.

'I think we should go inside,' said Bailey.

When they were inside an office with a closed door, the inspector said, 'Well?'

'It's a copper,' said Breen.

'Oh, Christ.'

Sergeant Michael Prosser, late of Marylebone CID, was bent. Or had been bent, at least. From day one at CID Prosser had never trusted

Breen, or liked him. He'd liked him even less after Breen had forced him to quit the job he loved.

Prosser had been running a coat-hanger job. At Marylebone they kept spare sets of keys to a few of the local businesses. To raise extra cash for his spastic boy, Prosser had been making copies and selling them on to a gang of thieves. He wasn't the first copper to have done it. Nor the last. Back in September, Breen had stumbled onto the scam.

Breen had used the knowledge to force Prosser off the job. If he didn't leave, Breen would expose him. He would lose his pension and be sent to prison. If he resigned, Breen would tell no one. It would be their secret.

With a spastic child to pay the bills for, Prosser had had no choice.

'Michael Prosser?'

Like Marylebone, the Stoke Newington CID room was lit by long neon strips, but it was much less tidy. There were piles of paper and folders on every desk. They didn't have a Marilyn to keep the place in order.

'Early forties. Been in the police all his life,' said Bailey.

'Shocking,' said the policeman.

'I wish you'd told me this,' said Bailey. They were talking in lowered voices. 'You were wrong to think you could protect him.'

'Where does he live?' asked the Stoke Newington man.

'I don't know,' said Breen. 'He split from his wife in the summer. She's in a flat somewhere with the boy.'

The officer said, 'This won't do us any good if it gets out. The papers would have a bloody field day.'

'Agreed,' said Bailey. 'And there were several death threats before this, Constable Tozer said.'

'Yes, sir.'

'Oh dear God,' said Bailey. 'Why would you stick up for a man like that?'

'It wasn't him I was doing it for. He will lose his pension. He has a wife and a crippled child.'

The Stoke Newington inspector shook his head and looked at Breen. 'What a bloody mess,' he said. He turned to Bailey. 'Can we be clear that this happened on our territory and it's our investigation? Sergeant Breen is a witness. Nothing more.'

'Absolutely,' said Bailey.

'We don't want this getting out of hand,' said the inspector. 'The less your force knows about it, the less chance it'll get out into the open.'

Bailey nodded. He liked it when clear lines were drawn.

In the Zephyr on the way back to the station Bailey said little.

On the Pentonville Road he spoke just once. ' You probably thought what you did was noble. But it wasn't. It was obstructive and you were an idiot. You should have told me what was going on.'

'His pension will be stopped now,' said Breen.

'Of course it will,' said Bailey. 'That's his own stupid fault.'

Tozer looked up at them as they entered the Marylebone office. A downward flutter of the eyes. She was embarrassed.

Marilyn said, 'How awful. I can't believe it.'

'I'm fine,' said Breen. 'A bit shaky, to be honest.'

Jones said, 'I mean, you sure it's Prosser? I know he didn't like you much, but—'

'Are you in love with Prosser or something, you pouf?' said Marilyn. 'He tried to kill a fellow copper. The man's mental.'

'Grow up, Jonesy,' said Tozer.

'Bloody hell,' said Jones. 'I was only saying.'

Tozer said, 'Sorry, Paddy, only I had to tell Bailey. I know you told us not to say anything about the notes, but that was before he went psycho.'

Breen said, 'I wish you'd talked to me first, that's all.'

Marilyn was punching holes in sheets of paper. She paused, turned to Tozer and said, 'Paddy'd asked us specifically not to tell no one about the notes.'

'I realise that, thank you,' said Tozer. 'But he tried to ruddy kill you, Paddy. I don't care who knows about it. He's nuts.'

Breen looked at Tozer, then at Marilyn. 'As it happens, Bailey said we should keep this to ourselves too.'

'Why?' said Tozer.

'Because if it gets out that Prosser was bent it'll be bad for our reputation.'

Tozer blew air from between her lips and said, 'Don't spoil our reputation? Bit late for that.'

'I'll be glad when she's gone,' muttered Marilyn, thumping another pair of holes into a pile of paper. 'Won't you?'

'Well, maybe it's the reputation we bloody deserve,' said Tozer.

Breen said, 'If people don't respect the police then we won't be able to do our jobs. That's all Bailey means.'

Tozer raised her voice and said, 'It's like bloody everything in this crappy country. Keep it all quiet. Don't rock the boat.'

'What's got into her?' asked Marilyn.

'I'm not a her,' said Tozer.

Bailey yanked open his door and said quietly, 'Constable Tozer. I can hear your opinions in my office. I would rather you kept them to yourself.'

'Yes, sir,' said Tozer, looking down at her desk.

'And get rid of that . . . musical instrument. It has no place in this office.'

'See?' Tozer said, more quietly, after the inspector had closed the door.

Breen's hands were shaking, he realised. A gentle tremble. Delayed shock, he supposed. He went to the toilet and vomited up the breakfast they had given him at Stoke Newington. When he had finished retching he went to the sink and poured cold water into his hands, splashing it onto his hot face.

His lungs felt heavy. He spat in the sink. There was still grey smut in his saliva.

A fat sergeant Breen knew vaguely came out of another cubicle, yanking his belt tight and tucking in his shirt. He paused to inspect himself in the mirror.

'Sounded rough. Out on the town last night, was you?'

Back in the office, Marilyn placed carbon paper between two sheets and ratcheted them into her typewriter. 'But what if he tries it again? I mean, we know he's been getting in here,' she said, and looked over her shoulder towards the door, as if she expected him to walk in at any second.

'Exactly,' said Tozer.

Breen's phone rang. 'Mount Street,' a voice said. It was Carmichael. 'Number 23.'

'What?'

'Where that fancy art dealer lives. You know. Guy who sells a piece of wood with a nail in it. That'll be five hundred quid please.'

'Robert Fraser?'

'Yes. Robert Fraser. Runs the Robert Fraser Gallery in Duke Street.'

'That's him,' said Breen.

'You were right. We've been keeping an eye on him on and off. Only, West Sussex Constabulary barged in and did him for heroin last year. Big party. Pop stars. Naked birds. Some girl naked with a Mars bar up her fanny. Remember? It was all over the papers. Rolling Stones. The lot. Fraser was sent down for six months last year after that raid. Wormwood Scrubs. Our lot was furious that everyone else got a slap on the wrist. Bloody pop stars. They're like royalty.'

'So he's still on drugs?' Breen asked.

'They all are,' said Carmichael. 'We picked up Georgie Fame the other day. Used to like him. And Tubby Hayes. He looked like a sack of shit. It's everywhere.'

The line buzzed and popped.

'Something else. Someone tried to kill me last night,' said Breen.

From down the crackling line: 'What?'

'Someone pushed a burning rag through my letterbox. Around four in the morning.'

'Bloody hell.'

'I've been getting death threats as well. At my desk. Typed notes. I've had four.'

'Fuck my boots,' said Carmichael quietly. 'Prosser?'

'I'm pretty sure,' he said. Carmichael was one of the only colleagues Breen had told about Prosser being bent.

'He never liked you, but . . .' said Carmichael.

'Has Prosser been in touch with you at all since leaving the job?'

'Me? No. Any idea where he is?'

'No.'

'And he's not been in touch with anyone else?'

'No. Keep it quiet though. Bailey doesn't want anyone to know.'

'Bloody Bailey,' said Carmichael. 'OK then.'

From the other side of the room Marilyn was chewing on a Cadbury's bar. 'Want some, Paddy?' she called after he'd put the phone down.

'I'll have a bit,' said Tozer.

'I wasn't offering it you,' said Marilyn. 'I was offering it to Paddy. Sugar's good for shock.'

Breen shook his head.

Marilyn took another square herself. 'I shouldn't myself, really. It's not good for my figure. What do you think, Paddy?'

Tozer stood up and said, 'I'll go and buy my own then.'

'You sure you're going to be all right staying by yourself, Paddy?' she was saying. 'I mean, what if he comes back? I'd say you should come over to mine and stay there for a bit, but Danny would go doolally if he heard I'd had you over. I mean, you could if you wanted, but . . .'

Breen wasn't listening. He was unfolding the graph he'd made on Tuesday afternoon, staring at it again.

FIFTEEN

On Friday night he piled blankets onto the armchair in the front room, listening for every noise outside in the cul-de-sac. The weather was freezing. He placed a one-bar electric fire by his feet. At four in the morning the meter ran out and he woke, shivering in the cold.

On Saturday he went to the local police station and asked the sergeant if he'd heard whether anybody had made any progress on his case.

The sergeant said, 'You'd have to ask CID. Not heard anything though.'

He took a bus heading west, changed at King's Cross and then walked from Piccadilly Circus to Mount Street, the address Carmichael had given him for Robert Fraser, and pressed the bell.

It was 9.30 in the morning. Mount Street was a long, smart Victorian parade of shops that seemed to sell either posh women's wear or equestrian paintings. He stood outside the large mansion house and looked upwards. A street cleaner was pushing a broom along the pavement, sweeping up dead leaves and rubbish. No one answered the door so he kept his finger on the brass bell.

Eventually a man with a gaberdine mac and wearing a handlebar moustache came out, and Breen stuck his foot in the door to stop it closing.

'I say . . .' objected the man.

'Police,' said Breen.

'Good Lord,' said the man, and scuttled off down the street.

There was a small lift with a diamond-grid gate, but Breen took the carpeted stairs. Fraser's flat was on the second floor.

He banged on the large door, but nobody answered. A window looked out on the street below. People were pulling up the shutters on the shops, opening doors and taking in pints of milk.

He banged again.

This time he could hear someone moving behind the door. 'Who is it?'

'Cathal Breen.'

'Who?' A tentative voice.

'I want to speak to Robert Fraser.'

Breen pressed his ear to the door. He could hear at least two voices.

'Tell him he isn't here.' A woman's voice?

Breen said, 'I know he's in there.'

Another round of whispering.

'Who is it?'

'I'm Detective Sergeant Breen.'

Distinctly, from behind the door: 'Shit. Fuzz. Wake Robert up.'

'I'm alone,' said Breen. 'I just want to talk to Mr Fraser. This is not a raid.'

On the floor above, Breen heard a door open.

'What's going on?'

'That bloody flat downstairs again,' an elderly voice grumbled.

The door to Fraser's opened. Robert Fraser was standing there, unshaven, in a maroon silk dressing gown. 'You again,' he said. He looked Breen up and down. 'Bit early.'

'Can I come in?'

'Why?'

'I just need to talk to you about Francis.'

Fraser sighed and held the door open for Breen.

The man who had been behind the door when Breen had knocked was more bohemian. In his mid-twenties, he had thick dark hair that straggled below his ears and large silver rings on his fingers. One was in the shape of a skull, with deep black eyes on it. Unshaven, he was dressed in a djellaba, a cigarette dangling from his lips. 'Hi,' he mumbled quietly.

There was a young woman too. Ash-blonde hair and mascara smudges around her eyes. She was dressed in a short cotton dressing gown and stood next to him.

'He's cool,' said Fraser, as Breen entered the room. 'Go back to bed.'

Obediently, the young man padded away. The woman said, 'I'll make some coffee. I've got to be on set in an hour anyway.' She had a European tinge to her accent.

'Had a party?' asked Breen.

'We just don't keep the same hours as you lot,' said Robert opening a drawer and pulling out a fresh packet of cigarettes. He yawned and undid the cellophane. 'You look pale, Mister Policeman. Having a rough time?'

'Actually, yes,' said Breen. 'Pretty rough.'

'I hope you're not ill,' he said, not sympathetic.

There was a chaise longue in the middle of the room surrounded by cushions, with a more modern sofa next to it. Old and new, modern and antique, all jumbled up together in a big, light airy room. Without being asked, Breen sat on the sofa, in front of a blue sculpture of a headless angel. An elaborate antique hookah pipe sat beside him.

'Coffee?' said the woman.

'Please,' said Breen.

'Me too,' said Fraser.

She had the husky voice of someone who'd smoked too much the night before.

Fraser sat on the sofa opposite him. Breen said, 'That's a Matisse, isn't it?' A large painting on the wall.

'Not m-mine,' Fraser said. 'Just between owners.' As his dressing gown rode up, Breen noticed scars and long scabs on his legs. Lines under the skin as if there were worms burrowing beneath the surface.

'That sounds good,' said Breen. 'To have this kind of thing but not to have the responsibility of owning it.'

Fraser laughed.

'You can just wake up in the morning and say, "Oh, look. That's a Matisse." That's a . . .' Breen pointed at another one. A silhouette of a jug: plain black lines on a blue canvas.

'It's by a friend of mine. Can I interest you in it?'

'I couldn't afford it.' He kept looking down at the marks on Fraser's legs.

Fraser said, 'From what I hear there are plenty of members of the Metropolitan Police who rake in more than I'll ever earn.'

The woman brought two coffees in large French cups. Real coffee.

'Did you know Francis Pugh as well?' Breen asked her.

'Don't think so,' said the woman.

'Frankie,' said Fraser. 'You remember him. He was here when we had that party for Dennis Hopper. Quite quiet. Asked you to go to bed with him.'

She shook her head. 'Most men ask to go to bed with me. I don't remember.'

'Well?' said Fraser. He sat on the chaise longue. 'Say what you have to say. I want to go back to bed.' To Fraser, Breen was a man in pressed trousers and polished shoes. An amusing figure they would probably joke about when he had gone.

Breen leaned forward a little and asked, 'Did Francis Pugh take drugs?'

'Oh God. I knew it would come back to bloody drugs. It's all you lot are interested in these days.' He looked away.

Breen fixed a smile on his face. 'Did he?'

'What makes you say that?'

'In the last couple of months he was just drawing out cash. I think he may have been spending it on drugs.'

Fraser took a gulp from the coffee. 'A lot of people do these days.'

'Did you take drugs with him?'

'Got any sugar, darling?' he called. 'As you know, I no longer take drugs. I learned my lesson.'

Breen looked around the room for a second, then spoke. 'Please don't treat me like an idiot,' he said quietly. 'I'm not interested in arresting you or any of your friends for what they do. I just want to know about Francis. Please. Otherwise I'll have to talk to my friends in the Drug Squad.'

'You're like a bunch of playground bullies, you lot.' Fraser smiled again. 'OK,' he said. 'Yes. Frankie took drugs. And?'

'Who did he take drugs with? You?'

Fraser shrugged. 'As you know, I no longer take drugs. They're illegal. And much as I enjoyed my stay in the Scrubs, I prefer to come and go as I please.'

'Was he an addict?'

Fraser said, 'We're all addicted to something. Booze. Coffee. An orderly society.'

'Please answer the question.'

The woman came back with a bowl of sugar. 'I'm going to have a shower,' she said. 'If the car comes to pick me up, tell them to wait.'

Was the woman an actress? Breen didn't recognise her, though that didn't mean a great deal.

Fraser said, 'I wouldn't say he was an addict, as much as an enthusiast. He was enthusiastic about most things.'

'Where did he get them from? From you?'

Fraser shook his head. 'The drugs? God, no. I sell art, not drugs.'

Breen said, 'Who?'

Fraser paused and said, 'Tell you what. If I help you, will you get your chums in the Drug Squad off my back?'

Breen paused. He had not intended to come here to strike a bargain with a convicted man. 'I can tell them you've been helpful,' he said.

Fraser reconsidered. 'You have to understand how this works. In the scene, you never talk about your connections. For obvious reasons.'

'Heroin?'

Fraser said, 'Why would I know?'

'Because you take heroin yourself.'

'Took. Past tense.' Noticing Breen looking at his legs, Fraser pulled them up beneath him and tucked them under his dressing gown. 'You hear things, obviously. Frankie liked a bit of heroin, it's true.'

'So where would he have got it from?'

'Have you asked his doctor? They always have the good stuff.'

The sound of a shower coming on down the hallway. From another room, a guitar strumming.

'What's it like out there? The weather?' said Fraser.

'Cold and wet,' said Breen.

'I've had enough of this bloody country. Is that all?' said Fraser. 'I want to go back to bed.'

Breen had almost finished his coffee. Delicious black sludge at the bottom of a cup. He asked, 'Did you ever meet a man called Oliver Tarpey?'

'Tarpey? Thin man? Looks like a toilet brush in a suit,' said Fraser.

'You met him with Frankie?'

'His father's minder. I met him once. He didn't like me. Told me to stay away from Frankie. Thought I was a corrupting influence.'

'What did you make of him?'

'He called me a fraud. He said, "You pretend to like this art rubbish and they fall for it." Typical of the English at their most venal. They only understand money. They don't understand what's happening in the world. That everything is changing. That people are waking up. Everywhere apart from England.'

Breen said, 'What's it like, taking heroin?'

'Try it and see,' said Fraser.

'Do you lose interest in women? When you're on drugs.'

Fraser said, 'I've never really had that much interest in women.'

'In sex then?'

Fraser suddenly looked sad. 'Maybe that's the real attraction. Sex is everywhere, these days, isn't it? The permissive society means sex is a chore, almost. I wonder if that's one of the things that makes dope so attractive. It makes sex less important.'

Breen said, 'I thought you take drugs to feel more.'

Fraser laughed. 'Lots of people think that. Even the people who take drugs. Doors of perception and all that. That's why everybody's so interested. But it turns out they're quite wrong. I thought so myself for a while. I'm sad to say it's precisely the opposite.'

The man was still strumming away on the guitar, the same riffs over and over again.

'Your hands are shaking,' said Fraser.

Breen looked down at his hands. He was right.

'You should see a doctor about that,' he said.

Breen placed his hands firmly on his thighs so that Fraser wouldn't be able to see them move.

Afterwards, Breen walked northwards. There was a small delicatessen open in Duke Street. Smoked mackerel hung in the window, shiny and orange. Since the fire he had not been eating properly. His appetite had gone. He went in and bought one for his supper, walked out with it wrapped in paper.

Back at home he took a ten-pound note from the tin cash box and bought a fire extinguisher and asked for the change in florins. He fed these into the electric meter.

That night he slept in the armchair again. He woke, covered in sweat, imagining that the place was burning again. It was just the heat from the electric fire.

On Sunday morning he spent three hours alone in the CID room going through notes from the door-to-doors. He used the phone in the office to call up Stoke Newington CID, but no one picked up.

In the afternoon he was back home, sponging the soot off the ceiling with turpentine when Tozer called up. 'I was just speaking to my mother. She was asking after you. She wanted to know, are you OK? You know, with the fire and everything.'

'So it's not you asking. It's your mother?'

'Of course I'm asking too,' she said.

'I'm OK. I'm cleaning the place up a bit. What are you doing?'

The line was silent for a while, then she said. 'I've been practising the guitar. I should come over and give you a concert of my one good chord.'

Breen stretched the phone cord over to his father's old chair and sat down. 'The place stinks,' he said. 'I've been cleaning the smoke off the ceiling. I'd say come and give me a hand, but I'm almost finished.'

'I was going to go back to the squat this evening to ask for some tips, anyway. They do a thing they called an Arts Lab there on Sundays.'

Breen said, 'What is it you are after in that place?'

'Guitar lessons,' she said.

'Is that all?'

'Maybe I fancy men with long hair and beards.'

Another pause. 'I think I should go and see Shirley Prosser,' said Breen. 'Find out if she knows what's going on.'

'Shouldn't you leave that to Stoke Newington?' she said.

'You think I should just sit here and wait for Prosser to try it again? Will you come with me?'

She was calling from the women's section house phone. Breen could hear the sound of someone in the background saying, 'How long you going to be, Hel?' It was Sunday. There would be a queue for the phone.

'See you Monday then, Paddy.'

And he went back to sponging off the dark, thick residue left by the fire. A curiously satisfying, mindless occupation.

He woke at three in the morning, thinking he had heard someone outside the front door. Heart banging, he went to the kitchen, took a meat knife from the drawer and went back to the front door, the knife in his right hand.

Quietly he slid back the bolt, then yanked the new door open.

Blackness and silence. A prickling of stars. Nobody there.

Just his imagination.

SIXTEEN

The door to the flats above the record shop was to the right of the glass. There was no name on either of the two bells so Breen rang them both. No one answered.

'Damn,' he said.

'Why don't we go and ask in the record shop?' said Tozer.

There was a young man with long sideboards working behind the counter at Jumbo Records. Button-down shirt. Behind him were three turntables. 'Shirley and the boy? They should be back any minute. She takes him out for a walk round this time.'

'We can wait,' said Tozer.

She started leafing through the records. The man was playing singles; black music mostly. 'Girls, you can't do what the guys do, no, and still be a lady,' sang Tozer along to the record.

There were two listening booths at the back of the shop. Through the glass in the door Breen could see a young woman nodding her head along to a different rhythm, cigarette hanging from her lips.

'You friends of Shirl's?' said the man, as he slipped a single back inside its sleeve.

'No,' said Tozer.

'Yes,' said Breen simultaneously.

The man looked from one to the other suspiciously. 'Oh. You police again?'

'Yes,' said Breen.

'Again?' said Tozer.

'Stoke Newington would have been here,' said Breen.

The man chewed his lower lip thoughtfully. 'She doesn't know where he is, you know? She told you lot that already last time. She just wants you to leave her alone. She's not having a good time.'

'We know,' said Tozer. 'It's OK. We want to help.'

'She doesn't know where he is, you said. Her husband, you mean?' said Breen.

The man didn't answer.

'Does he ever come here?' asked Breen.

'I'm not saying nothing else. Not my business to say.'

He put on another record and shook his head to the music. It was loud and rhythmic and was giving Breen a headache. Another black woman singing over the top of brass and a piano.

'Who's this you're playing?' Tozer asked the man. He gave a woman's name. Breen had never heard of her.

The record shop owner wiped another record with a cloth. 'You like it?'

Tozer smiled. 'It's all right.'

The man shrugged again.

'Got any Canned Heat?'

'I bet you're more rock than soul, aren't you?'

Tozer nodded.

The young man shrugged and smiled at her. 'Thought so.' He pointed towards a record rack. 'Under C. I prefer soul, mostly.'

Breen followed Tozer across the shop. 'You know that man Robert Fraser?' he asked as she flipped through the racks.

'The Robert Fraser Gallery?' said Tozer.

'Yes,' said Breen.

'God, yeah. He's part of the inner circle. One of the groovy people.'

'Groovy? He's my age.'

'Still groovy, in spite of even that. Knows everybody. The Beatles and the Stones. Anita Pallenberg. Peter Blake. Yoko Ono. Richard Hamilton. He's like the cool art god.'

Sometimes she sounded like a teenager. 'Really?' said Breen.

Carmichael had sounded contemptuous when he talked about him. Tozer sounded awestruck.

'I went for dinner with him the other night,' said Breen. 'We went to a macrobiotic restaurant. Went to his flat at the weekend.'

Tozer said, 'You're pulling my leg, aren't you?'

'Me knowing Robert Fraser?'

'No. You going to a macrobiotic restaurant.'

Breen waded through the 33s filed under T. There were no records, just the sleeves. Bands' names were becoming more strange and poetic. Ten Years After, Them, Tomorrow, Traffic, Tyrannosaurus Rex. Looking at them all made him feel like a man cast overboard, the ship sailing on away from him. He picked up a record at random. *Turn Around, Look at Me* by the Vogues.

'Is this any good?' he asked.

The man wrinkled his nose. 'You might like it.'

'He means no,' said Tozer.

The boy laughed, grinned at Tozer. She smiled back.

'What about this?' Breen picked up another sleeve. A picture of a yellow banana and the name Andy Warhol.

'You wouldn't like that either,' said Tozer.

'How do you know?' said Breen.

Tozer shrugged. 'I just know.'

It was as if they were both in on the same joke. Breen hesitated. He was thinking maybe he should buy it just to prove them wrong. That's when he noticed the record shop man looking up at the window outside.

Breen turned and followed his gaze. Shirley Prosser was there in the same black coat they'd seen her in that last time, on the previous Saturday. Holding the boy's hand, she gave the man behind the counter a little wave and a smile, then started delving in her handbag for her front-door key.

Breen put the disc sleeve back in the rack and made for the front door. 'Mrs Prosser?' he called.

The boy leaned against the shop's glass. His legs were crooked. His left knee pointed inwards and he seemed to walk on the toe of his shoe. The left hand too was twisted inwards. He smiled lopsidedly at the record shop man who waved back at him.

'Yes?' she said, frowning. The thin lines on Shirley Prosser's face didn't stop her from looking surprisingly young. He had expected her to be older.

'I'm Cathal Breen. I used to work with your husband,' he said. 'Can we have a word?'

'Breen? Paddy Breen?'

He stopped himself from correcting his name.

Tozer emerged from the shop. Mrs Prosser looked from one to the other.

'What is it about? I've already talked to the other lot.'

Breen said, 'I'm worried about him. Can we talk inside?'

The boy said something. The consonants were not clear. To Breen's ears the sound was as much animal as human. 'It's OK, Charlie. You go on up.'

Again, the boy spoke. A long-drawn-out sound that was almost a wail.

'It's OK. I'll be up in a second and make lunch. Go on.' She twisted the Yale in the lock and the boy stumbled past, swinging his bad leg around in an arc as he walked. She watched him lurch along the corridor and then walk up the stairs, one at a time.

'Well?' she said when he was out of earshot.

'Maybe we should come in?' said Breen.

She looked at the ground a second, then said, 'Charlie understands everything you say, you know?'

Breen said, 'I thought . . .'

'Just because you may not be able to understand him doesn't mean he can't hear you. He wanted to know why you're worried about his father.'

Breen said, 'I'm sorry. I didn't think . . .'

'Hi. I'm Helen,' said Tozer. 'You want me to go upstairs and look after him while you chat?'

'I don't want to chat,' said Mrs Prosser. 'I want you to go away. I don't want any of this. I just want to be left on my own.'

'Do you know where he is, Shirley?' asked Breen.

'He's got a bedsit, I think. I'm not sure where. You're the one who got him sacked, aren't you?'

Breen said, 'He wasn't sacked. He resigned.'

She wrinkled her forehead. 'Same difference.'

'I think your husband tried to kill me last week,' Breen said. He watched her eyes grow big.

'Oh, Christ,' she said.

'Did the policemen from Stoke Newington not tell you why they were looking for him?'

'No. I just thought . . . I assumed they were looking for him, because . . .' She stopped, looked around nervously.

'I need to know where he is, Shirley. I think he'll try it again.'

'Maybe you should come up,' she said.

Charlie was lying crookedly on the floor with a pile of Matchbox toys. A small metal plane in one hand, he eyed Breen as he walked in the living room.

'Is that a Spitfire?' asked Tozer.

The boy smiled a big toothy smile at her and said something.

'A Hurricane?'

The boy shook his head again.

'That's the only planes I know.'

''Bish,' he said. Or something close to it.

'I know,' said Tozer. 'I am rubbish.'

'Come into the kitchen,' said Mrs Prosser. 'I'm just making you some beans.'

'I like beans,' said the boy. Breen heard it clearly this time.

She closed the door behind them and said, 'Why do you think it was him?' she said. 'He wouldn't be that stupid.'

'Because I've been receiving death threats at work. It has to be somebody who knows where I work. Because he hates my guts.'

She looked shocked. He shouldn't have told her, he thought. It was unprofessional to share what he couldn't prove, and besides, she probably had enough to worry about already. Shirley Prosser shook her head, turned the electric hob on and and waited for it to be warm enough for her to light a cigarette on. 'They just said they wanted to talk to him.'

'Didn't you wonder why they were so interested?'

'Why would I know?' she said, still looking at the cooker.

Breen asked, 'So, what did you tell them?'

'Like I'm saying to you. I said I didn't know where he was. Which is the truth. I don't want to, either. He moved last week. He didn't give me his new address.' She took a cotton hanky from her handbag and wiped her nose.

'Why not?'

'Why? Why? Why?' she said, suddenly loud. 'I don't know. Why would he not tell me where he lives? I'm the mother of his child. Maybe because I wouldn't tell him where I lived. I didn't want him to know. He had a temper. You know that.' She smiled lopsidedly.

Breen nodded. 'He hurt you?'

She shook her head. 'Not really,' she said, unpacking a nylon shopping bag. He found himself looking at the curve of her calves as she stretched to put a bag of flour on a high shelf. There was a small ladder in her black tights.

He looked away quickly as she turned and asked, 'So you don't have any idea where he is?'

She was at least ten years younger than Prosser, he realised. A little bit younger than Breen maybe. Tiredness made her look older, but there was a softness to her face still. Big dark eyes and thin lips.

'He sends me a postal order every week. Not once a month, though.'

She laughed and wiped her nose a second time. 'That would make it too easy. If I had a month's money I could rent somewhere decent.'

The kitchen was small. A small cooker. A Formica table. There was a high-backed chair with a cushion tied to one arm with a scarf and another strapped to the back with a belt, positioned where Charlie's head would be when he sat down to eat.

'He's just lost the job he loved. He's never been anything other than a copper.' She leaned down to the hob, cigarette in mouth. Hair flopped down in front of her eyes. She swept the fringe out of her eyes and picked a can of beans from a cupboard. 'He never liked you much, I remember. He talked about you all the time. He thought you weren't up to the job.'

Breen said, 'You said the police had come looking for him, but you didn't ask why.'

She shook her head.

'So it wasn't a surprise that they might be wanting to question him?'

She shook her head. 'Nope. He never told me what he was up to.'

She started pulling open drawers, clattering cutlery. 'Bloody can opener. I can never find it.'

She found it in the sink and dug it into the can.

'Tell me about the money he sends you.'

'He's been doing it since we broke up. A bit here and there. I'm never sure it's because he cares for Charlie or he's trying to impress me.'

'Where did you imagine the money was coming from?' Breen asked.

She slipped with the can opener and the half-opened can tumbled onto the floor. They both leaned quickly to pick it up, almost banging heads. He grabbed it first and handed it to her, hands touching briefly. A few beans had spilt onto the floor.

'His wages. Stuff like that. You say he tried to kill you? How?'

'A burning rag through my letterbox.'

'God. That's mad.' She frowned.

'Did you tell the other policemen about the money?'

She shook her head and said, 'Will you have to tell them?'

'At some point, yes.'

When she poured the beans into a small enamel pan, Breen saw her hands trembling and the shake of the end of her cigarette that sent small grey specs into the pan of beans. 'I mean,' she said. 'What if it wasn't just wages?'

'Do you think it was more than just his wages?'

'God. Will I have to pay it back?'

'It depends where the money was coming from.'

'Christ.'

She moved to the cupboard and pulled out a loaf of bread. 'I can't give it back. I need it for Charlie.' She picked up the loaf and started carving it, the knife passing slowly back and forth.

'Why did you leave him?'

'I was young when I married him. Nineteen. I'll be honest with you. The only person holding us together was Charlie. That wasn't enough.'

'Did Prosser mistreat you badly?'

'Mistreat?' The smile stayed on her face.

'Physically, I mean.'

She turned her back again to stir the pan. 'He used to call you the Bloody Paddy. Of all people, then, you ought to know what Prossie's like when he doesn't get his way.'

'He did, then?'

'That wasn't why I left him.'

'And Charlie?'

'No. Never Charlie. Mike isn't like that.' She picked out some beans on a spoon and put them in her mouth to see how hot they were. 'I always used to wonder what you were like, Mike used to go on about you that much,' she said. 'He hated you.' She smiled down at the pan of beans. Then the smile went. 'I don't want them to take Charlie away,' she said.

Breen nodded.

'Lunchtime, Charlie. It'll get cold.'

'The toast is burning,' said Breen.

'Bugger,' she said, yanking it out from under the grill. 'I hate this cooker. I've had so much bad luck.'

'Did you ever think that he had more money than a policeman should have?'

She laughed. 'How much money should a policeman have? He was just trying to get back with me. Get back with Charlie.'

'Why won't he give you his address?'

She scraped the burnt bits off the toast and ladled beans onto it. 'I don't know. Maybe if he's the person who attacked you, he wants to hide.'

'And you don't have any idea where he could be?'

Tozer appeared in the doorway with Charlie.

'Y'OK?' Charlie mumbled.

Shirley said quietly, 'Before I knew him he lived in Elephant. That's where his family's from. You could try there.'

She helped Charlie into his chair, tying a scarf loosely around his head so he could keep it steady while she fed him. Even so, when he began eating noisily, beans flew from his chin as his head jerked from side to side as he chewed.

'Well?' said Tozer. 'Told you I was OK with kids. Just the posh ones I can't stick.' She strode ahead towards the car, reaching into her coat pocket for her packet of gum. 'Anyway. So?' she said.

'I'm not sure.'

They got into the car. 'You look rubbish, Paddy. Have you been sleeping OK? Are you eating?'

'Did the boy say anything?'

'I asked if he'd seen his daddy. He said he took him to the zoo.'

'You can understand what he's saying?'

'Some. Mostly.'

Breen said, 'What day of the week was that?'

'He wasn't sure. About a week ago I think. She's taken Charlie out of school, you know? She's looking after him all on her own.' She rolled the gum between her finger and thumb until it was like a small swiss roll, then popped it into her mouth and started chewing slowly. 'She's quite a woman. Doing that on her own.'

Breen thought for a minute. 'Yes, she is.'

'You should hear what all the police wives call her.'

'I can imagine.'

'I bet half of them would love to do the same. Leave their husbands.'

'Wait here,' he said, getting out of the car.

'What are you doing?'

'I forgot to ask her something.'

Shirley Prosser stood at the top of the stairs. 'What now?' she said.

'I was thinking. It must be tough here, stuck on your own.'

She folded her arms. 'And?'

Breen wondered how stupid this was going to sound. Very stupid probably. 'I was wondering if you wanted to come out for dinner.'

The first thing Shirley Prosser did was laugh. Then she clapped one hand over her mouth. 'Sorry. I didn't mean to do that.'

'No. Forget it. I shouldn't have asked.'

Charlie was behind her now, propping himself up against the wall.

'No. I was just surprised, that's all. I'm not used to anyone asking me. Why do you want to do a thing like that?'

Breen hesitated. 'I just thought you'd like it. A chance to get out. Have a bite to eat.'

She smiled. 'Thanks. But I don't think so. I'd have to bring Charlie. I can't leave him on his own.'

'Right,' said Breen. Was that an excuse? Trying not to be rude. He turned to go. Then paused. 'I could ask Helen to look after him, if you like?'

Shirley's smile disappeared.

'It's OK. It was just an idea,' Breen said.

'I could do tomorrow,' she said.

Back in the car, Tozer said, 'What was all that about?'

'What are you doing tomorrow night?' asked Breen.

'Are you trying to ask me out again?'

'No. The opposite.' He put his hands on the ignition key. 'I just asked Shirley out.'

Her mouth fell open. 'You never?'

'I did. Yes.'

She frowned. 'But I mean. She's married.'

'For God's sake,' said Breen, starting the engine.

'To a man who is probably trying to kill you.'

'I just felt sorry for her. Besides, maybe I can find out about Prosser. If we talk.'

Tozer snorted.

'It was you who said that I should start asking women out,' said Breen.

'I know, I know. But I didn't actually mean her,' she said. 'God's sake, Paddy. Did she turn you down flat?'

He smiled. 'No, actually.'

She looked at him. 'Oh,' she said. 'Really?'

'Tuesday.'

'Serious?'

'Don't act so surprised.' When he had pulled out into traffic, he said, 'Actually, I was thinking you could look after Charlie while I was out.'

'You did what?' she said.

They paused at traffic lights.

'No bloody way,' said Tozer.

Leaning against a wall, a thin old man squeezing lush, rich, gypsy music out of a red accordion. Streams of notes full of swell and emotion. People walked past his open instrument case without stopping.

'Come on. Who else is there?'

The lights changed and the music was gone.

'I should babysit so you can go out with another woman?'

'What? Are you jealous?'

She said, 'Don't be bloody ridiculous.'

'Please,' he said.

'If you think I'm going to spend one of my last nights in London looking after that boy, you've another think coming.'

SEVENTEEN

The doctor was fat. He was wedged into his chair. Flesh rolled over his shirt collar and he wore trousers tailored to arrive above his belly. He had the look of someone seen in a fairground mirror.

His surgery was thick with cigarette smoke. 'I don't discuss my patients with the police,' he said. 'Even my former patients.'

'Francis Pugh is dead,' said Breen.

'My duty of confidentiality is still alive and kicking, however.' A smile. 'Is that all?'

Breen had tracked down Dr Milwall through Francis Pugh's bank statements. Breen had noticed that there had been payments to a second doctor which had stopped earlier in the year.

Breen tried a different approach. 'I suppose Mr Tarpey ordered you not to speak to me.'

'I don't take orders from Mr bloody Tarpey,' said the doctor.

'Really?' said Breen.

'Certainly bloody not.'

'But he did tell you not to.'

Dr Milwall broke into a big grin. 'He may have tried.' He giggled like a naughty schoolboy. 'Jumped-up twerp,' he said. 'Awful little Welsh grammar school boy. Thinks he can tell everyone what to do just because he's pals with the minister.' Another smile. 'Right. One question. Then out.'

Just the mention of Tarpey had done it; a common enemy.

'Tell me about when you prescribed heroin to Francis Pugh.'

'I beg your pardon?' Smile vanished. Jaw clenched.

'You prescribed him heroin, I presume. You were his doctor.'

'I did no such bloody thing,' said Milwall loudly. 'I don't know what you're trying to suggest.'

'Didn't you?'

'Absolutely bloody not. And if you so much as suggest I did I'll bloody sue you.'

'But you knew he was a heroin addict?'

The doctor said, 'You're trying to trick me, now.' The outline of a chin was in there somewhere, beneath the flesh.

Breen sat down in the chair opposite the doctor. 'I just want to know why he died. Don't you?' He tried another tack. 'Why's Tarpey so worried about you talking to me, anyway?'

'There you go, you see?'

'Skeletons in the closet?'

'Of course.' He pressed a bell on his desk and asked his secretary to bring Pugh's notes. A brittle, thin woman who offered tea and looked offended when Breen said no.

'Francis came to me in . . .' He looked at the notes. 'In January this year, it was, and asked me to prescribe diamorphine to him. He said he had picked up a habit, as if it was something you caught, like a common cold. Sad, really. Always liked Frankie, but always a bit of a rascal. And now he's gone. Got mixed up in something. But heigh-ho.' There was a stuffed pug sitting on a walnut sideboard. It seemed to be looking directly at Breen.

'But you never supplied him with . . . diamorphine?'

'Heroin. No. Absolutely not. Like I said. I told Frankie I don't do that kind of thing. God. This isn't some opium den. This is a respectable practice.'

Unsettled by the pug's glassy stare, Breen said, 'I thought doctors could prescribe heroin.'

'Since April we're not allowed to any more. The law's changed. You'll know all about that. Good man, Jim Callaghan. New laws to keep out all the wogs and now another to lock up all the hopheads.

Now all registered addicts are supposed to go to the special clinics. Best place for them.'

'Why didn't you prescribe him heroin, then?'

'Learned my lesson there yonks ago. Let one addict have heroin and they tell all their junkie chums. In no time everyone thinks you're a drug doctor. They'll all come running to you. Scares the horses, having that sort in the waiting room. No good for the reputation. It was different ten years ago. Then, addicts were usually sweet little housewives who'd got a little too used to taking something for their nerves. Now it's all beatniks and Yankee draft dodgers.'

Milwall opened his desk, picked up a toothpick and started to dig around in his mouth. He paused, pulled out the pick and examined it.

'If you want to know, I was rather upset Frankie had got mixed up with that lot, but it was his own choice.'

Breen looked behind the doctor, out past his dirty window at the houses opposite. 'Was Francis upset when you told him you wouldn't prescribe it for him?'

The doctor shrugged. 'Not in the slightest. I gave him the name of a lady doctor who would accommodate him. And that was the last time he came to see me. It's a well-known fact that there are half a dozen practitioners in London who have been dishing out the stuff as if it's sherbert. However, she would have only been able to do so for a few weeks. Then the law changed.'

The doctor took a packet of cigarettes out of his desk and lit one.

'So you can no longer get heroin from GPs?'

'Only from GPs at the new drug treatment clinics. They wean the addicts off the drugs with substitutes. It's the only way to stop this ridiculous epidemic. Cut off supply. Monitor the addicts. Bring them off drugs.' The doctor looked at his gold watch and thrummed the fingers of his right hand on the desk. 'Mark my words, this way, in a year or so this whole addiction problem will be over and we can concentrate on sick people.'

'Did he tell you about how he'd become addicted?' asked Breen.

'He was the experimental type, if you know what I mean. Very Rive Gauche. Ridiculous, of course, but these things happen.'

'They've never happened to me,' said Breen.

Milwall sighed. 'Well, you know what I mean.'

A red light came on on his desk.

'Is that all?' He lit his cigarette.

'He wasn't registered as a drug addict at any time?'

'Well, it would have been a little embarrassing if he was, really, wouldn't it? His father being on the Home Office Committee on Drug Dependence.'

Breen said nothing.

'Didn't you know?' Milwall laughed.

'So if no other doctor was supplying him with heroin he must have been buying his drugs elsewhere?'

'I have no idea,' said the doctor impatiently. 'That's your department now. Drugs are no longer a medical issue. They are a criminal matter.'

'Tell me,' said Breen, still firmly in his chair. 'Does taking heroin leave you with sores on your arms and legs?'

'Injecting anything repeatedly will leave marks, especially if you don't do it hygienically. Abcesses can develop.'

'You inject heroin in your legs? Why would you do that?'

'Presumably after you have used up all the veins in your arms, yes.'

'Used up?'

'The veins collapse. Simple as that. Frightful business.'

'So you would have to be a serious addict for that to happen.'

'I would imagine. No sympathy at all for them from this quarter. Have you finished, Sergeant?'

'And people die after taking drugs?'

'Apparently, sometimes.'

'What would the signs be?'

'I'm not a pathologist, Sergeant. I'm a general practitioner. I've given you enough time, now, Sergeant.'

'So plenty of other drug addicts will probably be doing the same now, buying drugs from dealers?'

'As I say, that it is no longer a problem for the medical profession. It's a problem for you bloody lot,' he said, squeezing himself out of his chair and waddling to to the door. 'And of course, I have full confidence in the police to make sure that the problem is eliminated, yes?'

From the angle Breen was at as he looked back to close the door, the glass-eyed pug on the sideboard seemed to be grinning at him.

Chink, chink, chink. Chink, chink, chink. Outside the College Hospital, a man dressed as Santa Claus was shaking a collecting box for Dogs for the Blind. Breen noticed that under his red Santa cloak his trousers ended an inch above his shoes and that his socks were odd.

Grief hid in doorways, leaping out at Breen when he least expected. Odd socks. The sight of the elderly man's mismatched legs. Like his father's, he thought.

When Breen pushed open the door into Wellington's office it banged into something. A chair. A group of students sat around Wellington's desk, exercise books open on their laps. They were sitting on metal chairs, so crammed into the room that they were blocking the doorway.

'Busy, Sergeant,' called Wellington. 'Come back in half an hour.'

The room smelt of new paint.

'Just a quick question,' said Breen through the crack in the door. 'Have you had the pathology report back yet?'

Wellington looked over the top of his glasses at Breen. There was large glass jar on his desk with a long piece of flesh floating around in it. 'Can't you see I'm teaching now?'

'Tell me,' said Breen. 'Then I'll leave.'

'No. I'll chase it.'

'How does a heroin overdose kill someone?'

'Class?' A well-if-I-must voice. 'Overdose of opiates. Speculate on what condition would cause death.'

A young man in a pair of jeans and a denim jacket raised his hand and said, 'Heart attack.'

'Ridiculous,' said Wellington. 'Diamorphine is used to treat pain from heart attacks. Why would it cause them? Next?'

The boy looked stung. 'Hypotension,' said another.

'Don't be dim,' said Wellington.

The students were all in their early teens and twenties; apart from a single girl sitting at the far corner of the room, they were all boys. They were medical students training to follow in Wellington's footsteps. Some had ashtrays balanced precariously on their knees.

'You,' said Wellington, pointing at a young man in a brown cardigan.

'Um. Respiratory failure?' he said.

'Good.'

The boy beamed.

'Why?' said Wellington.

'Diamorphine can suppress the lung function.'

'Excellent. Will that be all, Sergeant?'

All eyes were on Breen. 'And how would you know? I mean, how would you know someone had respiratory failure?'

Wellington sighed. 'Anyone?'

The same boy raised his hand. 'Yes?'

'Carbon dioxide in the blood?'

Another student: 'Can I guess? Bloodshot eyes?'

'Not a bad guess,' said Wellington.

Breen said, 'The same as Francis Pugh?'

'Exactly. Now, boys,' he said, 'We were dealing with the putrefaction of wounds.'

'What if Francis Pugh overdosed?'

Wellington frowned. 'Possibly. Not likely though.'

'Why not?'

'Well . . . context is crucial. He's a minister's son, for God's sake. And there were no signs of drug abuse. Whoever killed him was clearly obsessive. When we get the results we'll know.'

'Francis Pugh was a heroin addict.'

'Oh.'

'People who use heroin have scars on their arms and legs. The skin had been stripped from his arms and legs. And they drained his blood. Could it have been that someone wanted to disguise that he had died from a heroin overdose?'

Wellington opened and closed his mouth.

'So it could?'

There was murmuring in the class.

'Silence!' shouted Wellington. 'Well, nobody bloody told me he was a heroin addict,' he said. 'If they had, then I would have obviously suggested that. And any result will obviously show up in the toxicology analysis. Is that all?'

The chattering stopped. A biro rolled off the edge of one of the chairs and clattered onto the floor. A student tittered.

'I am teaching a class right now, Sergeant. I will gladly discuss your theories when I am finished. Please let me continue.'

Breen shut the door behind him and left.

Santa Claus was still shaking his tin. Breen moved to the edge of the pavement to avoid him.

In the last years Breen had found it hard to keep up with the laundry. Sometimes he had knelt at his father's pale feet, struggling to dress him.

'But they're all wrong,' his father had complained once, crossly. A rare sentence for a man who was leaving language behind.

Breen had stopped caring if his father's socks matched any longer. He never went out anyway. Why should he bother? But it had still made Breen's father angry when he looked at his legs and noticed he was wearing odd socks. And it had made Breen angry at the time too. Why did the old man have to be so unpredictable? So difficult?

Breen crossed the road and walked slowly to the police station. It was almost lunchtime. The cold made him feel hungry. He could go to a cafe and have lunch. Maybe Tozer would be free.

Jones was coming out of the toilets on the ground floor as he arrived at the station. 'Tell me' said Breen. 'Has Prosser been in touch with you at all since his leaving party?'

'What are you talking about?'

'Has he?'

Jones blushed. 'Why would he?'

'Because he was your friend.'

'He was friends with loads of people.'

'You don't have any idea where he's living now, do you? Shirley says she thinks he may be in Elephant and Castle somewhere.'

Jones said, 'You talked to Shirl?'

'Has he called you?' said Breen.

Jones narrowed his eyes. 'How come you talked to Shirl? You shouldn't be doing this, Paddy. You should be leaving it to the other coppers. If Bailey found out he'd flip his wig.'

Breen nodded. 'And you think they're doing a good job, do you, these other coppers?'

'Keep your hair on, mate.'

'Just tell me.'

'What are you saying, Paddy?'

Breen looked straight at him. 'Has he been in touch?'

'No,' said Jones. 'He hasn't. OK? You should take a pill, Paddy. You need to bloody calm down a bit.'

Breen's phone was ringing as he reached his desk. He snatched it up. 'Tarpey here,' said a voice. 'I've had a phone call from Dr Milwall.'

'That was quick,' said Breen.

'What has been going on? Why were you speaking to Milwall?'

'Why didn't you mention Dr Milwall when I spoke to you before?'

'Sorry.'

'Was it because Milwall knew that Francis Pugh was a heroin addict?'

'He told you that?'

'I think that whoever removed the skin from his arms was just trying to disguise the fact that Francis Pugh was a heroin addict who died of an overdose.'

There was silence on the line.

'So you think it wasn't murder, after all?'

Not the work of a madman, collecting skin and blood. Or a torture scene with women's tights. 'I'm fairly sure it was not murder,' Breen was saying. 'But it was a conspiracy to deliberately mislead the police. Either to cover up who was selling the drugs. Or because it would be embarrassing for a Home Office minister's son to be discovered to be a drug addict. Have you had anything from the pathologist? I'm sure you'll be the first to know if I'm right. After all, they work for your minister, don't they?'

There was a pause. But only a brief one. 'Well I suppose the bright side of this is that your investigation can be closed now. You can move on to more useful work.'

'We still need to know who mutilated his body and then tried to destroy the evidence,' Breen said. 'We need to know who sold him his drugs.'

'There's no need,' said Tarpey. 'Death by misadventure would not be your department anymore, would it? While it would be nice to find out whoever did this, given the damage it would do if the truth came out, it's not really a priority, is it?'

'It's not your job to decide what is my priority or not,' said Breen.

A pause. 'You're absolutely right,' said Tarpey. 'It's not my job. I'll contact the Home Office and let them know.'

Breen was left holding the phone.

Marilyn's phone rang within a minute. 'Inspector Bailey? I'll put you through now, sir,' she was saying.

His father's socks. Pale, vein-circled legs. Spidery hairs poking over the top.

And a couple of minutes later, Bailey's door opened. 'Sergeant Breen.' He stood with a rigid smile on his face. A bearer of bad news.

'A minute of your time, if you please.'

EIGHTEEN

And that was that. The End.

Fin.

An incomplete trajectory. A moon rocket blasted upwards, failing to return to earth. It was just an imperfect job. There had been dozens like this before. So why was Breen so angry about it?

When Wellington called at around three o'clock to let them know that the pathologist had confirmed Pugh's blood showed traces of the drug the end was official. The lid was being firmly screwed down. The investigation now centred on an individual or individuals causing an explosion likely to endanger life or cause damage to property.

Bailey was apologetic as he told Breen he would be transferring the case. Slightly embarrassed. The English establishment closing ranks.

'It's not like it's a murder case now, anyway.'

'Yes, sir.'

'You did well, Paddy. You should be pleased.'

'Only they probably won't bother much because Rhodri Pugh doesn't want them to dig up anything that will damage his reputation.'

'Well,' said Bailey with a nod. 'That's probably true. But the good reputation of our leaders is important.'

Breen said, 'Of course it is.'

'Don't be arch, Paddy,' said Bailey. 'It doesn't suit you.'

'Don't you want to know why someone went to such extraordinary lengths to cover up why he died? They stripped the skin from his arms and legs.'

Bailey picked up a pencil and stuck it into a pencil sharpener mounted on the edge of his desk. 'Of course I do. I'm every bit as curious as you. But it's not our job anymore.'

Bailey twisted the handle of his sharpener a few times, scritch, scritch, scritch, pulled the pencil out and touched the sharp point.

'Please, Paddy. Don't look so downhearted. You can have your holiday leave now, if you like.'

Breen closed the door behind him.

Jones was already packing up the thin pile of notes he had, preparing to hand them over to whichever copper took on the case now.

An hour of one-finger typing reports in triplicate that would be filed away and forgotten.

'Where you going?' said Marilyn as he put on his scarf and buttoned up his raincoat.

Breen didn't answer.

'Paddy?'

Breen yanked the door shut behind him and leaned against it.

'Oooh,' he heard Jones saying. 'I think Paddy's in a bate.'

Cases rarely ended simply. There were always loose ends. Or the wrong person getting off too lightly. He should not take it so personally.

As Breen stamped down the stairs, Tozer came clattering after him, folder under one arm, cigarette in the other hand. She called, 'Hey, Paddy. Slow down. Where you going?'

'Home.'

'You can't go home. You're seeing Shirley tonight. Don't say you'd forgotten.'

Breen paused. 'No. Well, yes. I had.'

She took a quick puff and blew out a thin line of smoke. 'You bloody gonk. I gave up my ticket to see that new Yardbirds group tonight so you could have a chance to meet a woman. Against my better judgement.'

'I don't know if I feel like it.'

Tozer snorted. 'You invited her out. You can't just not turn up. And maybe it's not such a bad idea.'

'Why?'

'She needs friends. Almost as much as you do.'

'Thanks a bunch,' he said.

'Don't mention it.'

'I'll miss you,' he said.

'What?'

'Nothing,' he said.

'Six o'clock. Edgware Road.' She turned and went back up.

'Right,' said Breen. 'See you outside.'

He walked.

The slow route, passing time, winding through the back streets north of the Marylebone Road, past the chipped iron railings of Dorset Square and westwards, against the stream of head-down commuters pouring towards Marylebone station.

He still arrived outside Jumbo Records half an hour early. There was nowhere to wait; the cafes were closed and the pubs weren't open for another hour and a half, so he walked up and down the road, keeping warm. By six, he was standing outside the record shop waiting for Tozer.

This was a mistake.

Tozer arrived in a police car, tires skidding to a halt outside. Three young bobbies inside, Tozer's age, waving, laughing. 'See you, Helen.'

'Thanks, boys,' shouted Tozer, waving back as they drove away.

Tozer had gone back to the section house and changed. She was out of the frumpy suit she wore to work and had a miniskirt and a denim jacket on.

She looked at him and said, 'Didn't you get any flowers?'

'What?'

'God's sake, Paddy. I brought some Opal Fruits for Charlie at least.'

'I mean it's not like it's a date,' said Breen.

They rang the bell.

Shirley Prosser wore heels, had her hair in a headband and wore pink lipstick. 'God. You look fab,' said Tozer.

Shirley Prosser glared at Tozer for just a second. Younger girl. Shorter skirt. Smoother skin. Then broke into a smile. 'Thank you,' she said. 'Come on up. I'll talk you through what Charlie needs.'

Breen waited by the front door at the bottom of the stairs, hands in his pockets. If only he hadn't told Tarpey anything about his suspicions that Pugh's death wasn't a murder . . . Men who keep secrets should not be trusted.

Shirley returned again. 'There,' she said. 'Will she be OK with Charlie?'

'She'll be fine. She's good with children. Shall we get a taxi?'

'If you like,' Shirley answered.

So they stood for a while by the kerb and Breen tried to hail a taxi, but the only ones passing had their yellow lights off.

'Maybe we should walk a bit,' he said. 'Down to Marble Arch.'

And Breen marched off southwards, occasionally looking backwards over his shoulder for a taxi.

'Can you go a bit slower?' said Shirley after a while.

'Sorry,' he said. Still no taxi. Usually they'd be bumper to bumper.

'Please,' she said, 'I can't keep up.'

Breen held his arm up at a cab travelling the other way and whistled, fingers in his mouth, but it ignored them, roaring on northwards.

'You want to rest?'

'No. Just walk a bit slower, that's all, can you?'

Breen hadn't realised he was walking so quickly. He was about to apologise, explain that he was in a filthy mood, suggest they call the whole thing off and go home when a taxi finally arrived, pulling up next to them.

★

The restaurant in Frith Street was downstairs in a basement. The place was crammed, but Jimmy, the short, round Cypriot who owned it, beckoned Breen in and led them to a tiny table at the back. 'Who's this beautiful lady, Cathal?' he asked, but didn't wait for an answer, hurrying away to the door where another couple were already waiting.

'What did he call you?'

'Cathal. It's my name.'

'Everyone always calls you Paddy,' said Shirley.

'Everyone always calls him Jimmy,' said Breen. 'His real name's Dimitri.'

There were a couple of damp menus on the table. Breen ordered a bottle of the Greek red, poured them both a glass and then drank his too fast. It was thick and vinegary.

She said, 'I've not been to a Greek restaurant before.'

Breen was regretting coming here. He liked Jimmy's and used to come here often on his own, but had never realised what a dive it must look to Shirley. A white-painted cellar, full of taxi drivers stocking up between rides, or the drunken artists who lived around here, after a cheap meal. Paper tablecloths and greasy cutlery. The two girls on the table next to them were almost certainly prostitutes, taking a break before the pubs kicked out and the customers started arriving. He should have taken her somewhere nicer. Somewhere classier.

She scanned the menu.

'They do English food too,' he said.

'Don't you think I'm adventurous enough to want to try Greek food?'

Jimmy's wife appeared at table with a notepad. Shirley ordered stifado, giggling at the name. He ordered lamb kleftiko.

Shirley sat looking around the restaurant until the food arrived about twenty minutes later.

'It's nice,' she said, after a first mouthful. 'Is yours?'

'Yes.'

'Quite sure?'

'It's OK.'

She put down her knife and fork. 'Paddy. Tell me something. Why the hell did you ask me out?'

Breen had a mouthful of lamb. He swallowed and said, 'Sorry?'

'You've hardly said a single bloody word to me since we got here. You have barely looked at me. You're staring into the distance like I'm boring you to death. What did you ask me out for? Did someone put you up to this?'

Breen frowned. 'I just thought you might like a break.'

She pushed her plate away. 'You felt sorry for me.'

'No,' he said. 'It was nothing like that. Honestly.'

'What? Single woman. Going through hard times. Easy to lay?'

One of the tarts snorted suddenly, holding a red-nailed hand across her mouth.

'Is that what it's about, Paddy? You got Michael the sack and now you want to get his wife in bed?'

Breen looked at her and said, 'I liked you. I hadn't expected to, I'll be honest. I admire you, what you're doing for Charlie. I just thought it would be nice to get to know you. I don't think we're that different. I promise you that's all.'

Shirley put her napkin down on her plate. 'Well, you have a bloody funny way of showing it.'

Breen said, 'To be honest I didn't have a very good day. Maybe we should go home.'

She glared at him a second longer, then seemed to change her mind. She lifted up the bottle, poured wine into both of their glasses and said, 'OK. Why don't you talk about it, then?'

Breen looked up at the ceiling with the rickety fan hanging from it. 'Somebody just took away a case from me. I was getting somewhere, and then I was told to stop. That's all.'

He took the glass of wine and gulped some down.

'What case?' she said.

'I know I should be making conversation, but I don't really want to talk about it,' he said. 'Can we talk about something else?'

'Great,' said Shirley. She looked at her watch. 'What do you want to talk about then?'

'What about you?' Breen said.

'Me?' She looked down at her barely touched plate for a second, then looked up and said, 'You sure about that?'

'Yes.'

'OK.' She sucked on her lower lip for a second, then said, 'I got up today. Put ointment onto Charlie's sores. He wears a calliper and it chafes sometimes. I had to clean his sheets because he sometimes makes a mess of the bed. He doesn't mean to. He has to wear a nappy, which he hates, and sometimes he has accidents. The local launderette won't let me use their machines because they don't like me washing my stinky stuff in their machines. He's not exactly a baby any more. So I have to walk about a half mile with it to a Chinese launderctte. Charlie has to come with me which is a bit of a struggle for him. And then we have to take the laundry back home. Charlie has to take pills for the pain he gets in his guts, and we're running low. I wanted to get to the chemist to get some more, but by the time I did, what with the laundry taking all day, it was already shut.'

Shirley was staring right at Breen as this poured out of her. He didn't dare look away.

'Charlie gets bored because he's just like any boy really. He loves Scrabble so I play it with him, but today he knocked the board over by mistake and upset the tiles all over the floor, then got really angry with me about it. Then got angry with himself. And it took me so long to calm him down that I got behind with his dinner.'

She paused, took a gulp of wine, but before he could think of anything to say, she continued. 'And then I spent too long trying to get ready for this and he was angry with me again for not having time to help him with a puzzle he's been doing. And we were just getting over that when you rang on the doorbell. And I don't know why I bothered to dress up anyway. OK?'

A pause. The clatter of cutlery from the kitchen somewhere. Something shouted in Greek by a waiter.

'It must be very hard,' he said.

She laughed. 'So I'm sorry. But I couldn't give a damn that you had a bad day.'

'You're right,' said Breen. 'It's not important.'

She finally broke his gaze and looked down at her plate. She relaxed. 'I didn't mean to do that. It's not fair.'

'No. I had no idea.'

She picked up a toothpick and broke it in two. 'Michael never talked about Charlie, did he?'

Breen shook his head.

'We should drink this wine. It'll stop me from being such a bitch.'

She filled his glass again, even though he hadn't drunk much. He reached out and took a mouthful to keep her company.

'You're not a bitch. It's hard.'

'Thing is, Michael's not a bad father. But me and Charlie were never right for the police life. And that's what it is, isn't it? It's a life. Michael was just like you. If something bad happened at work he would be angry. Just like you are. It can last days sometimes.'

She looked at him. He had never liked Michael Prosser. Now she was pointing out how like him he was.

'Angry?' said Breen.

'Not so much with Charlie,' she said. 'But they were all like that in the section houses. The wives all learned to shut up about it. We just accepted it. That's what it was like, being married to a policeman. That's why I hated it so much.'

'Aren't you eating any more?' said Breen.

She shook her head, pulled out a packet of Embassy Regals, tapped the cigarette on the outside of the packet a few times and then put it in her lips and lit it without offering him one.

'I hated it in the police flats,' she said. 'I didn't like all the other women. They were evil bitches. Having a cripple for a son was like I'd let the side down.' She smiled. 'All of them with their healthy, fit boys and girls. And then I just had enough of it. Of him.'

She sighed. Blew out smoke. 'What about you?'

Breen picked up his glass and told her about how he'd moved out of a section house over six years ago to look after his father. Maybe it was the wine. He didn't talk so easily about it, usually.

Now he found himself telling her about looking after his father as his dementia had taken hold. About how he'd had to juggle life in the police with coming home to feed and change a man who didn't know him anymore.

She watched him, a softness in her face that hadn't been there before.

When he finally ran out of steam, she nodded. 'I'm sorry,' she said. 'We deserve better, don't we?'

'I suppose we do,' he said.

'I'm sorry,' she said again.

'What for?'

She looked away, chewed on her tongue for a second and said, 'For what you've been through, of course. Can we get some more wine? I never get the chance, normally.'

They ordered baklavas for dessert, though neither of them had ever had them before. Breen didn't like the honeyed sweetness, but Shirley scraped the plate with her spoon.

When she was finished, she smiled. There was a picture of a small village by the sea on the wall. A slightly faded photograph of whitewashed buildings in a rocky bay.

'I'd like to go there,' said Shirley. 'Greece. Somewhere on the Mediterranean. Far away. Blue skies. White buildings. Rocks and sand. I've never been. I could imagine me and Charlie, living by a beach somewhere. He loves to swim. He doesn't feel so clumsy when he's in the water. It's like he's free then.'

*

She kissed him on the cheek when the taxi stopped outside her flat. She smelt of perfume and brandy.

'Thank you, Paddy,' she said, opening the taxi door. 'That was better than I expected.'

'You didn't expect much, then?'

'Not really. I've given up on policemen.'

'Can we do it again?' he asked.

'Maybe,' she said, and leaned in to kiss him again. Soft skin against his cheek.

Upstairs, she sent Tozer down so Breen could drop her at Pembridge House.

'You're late,' Tozer complained. 'It's almost one.'

'I'm sorry. We went for a walk after the restaurant.'

'Where?'

'Just here and there. Around Soho. Across to Covent Garden.'

They had had drinks in one of the pubs that stayed open late by the market. They talked. She told him about how she'd wanted to be a film star before she was married. He told her about the holiday he was planning. They had both drunk enough not to be self-conscious.

'Sounds super,' Tozer said. Breen wondered if she was angry because they'd kept her up late or because he had gone out for a date with Shirley.

'Well?' Tozer said, staring out of the taxi window. 'And?'

'And it was a nice evening,' said Breen. 'She's had a hard life.'

'Are you drunk?'

'Maybe.'

'Nice?' she said, still looking away. 'Jesus Christ, Paddy Breen. I hope it was better than that. I just gave up one of my free last evenings in London for you.'

On Wednesday morning Cathal Breen had a hangover. So he called in sick. Why shouldn't he? Everyone else called in sick. Everyone apart from Bailey. All he would be doing today was putting pieces of paper away. And he could not face doing that. Two failed cases to pack up. Two deaths, assumed to be by misadventure. He got drunk so rarely, once would not hurt.

And he *was* sick, afer all. Everything hurt. Even his teeth seemed to ache. It was an unfamiliar feeling and he hated it. His body was not used to drink.

'Aw,' said Marilyn, fuzzy and distant on the phone. 'Is it a bug?'

He went to shave, but didn't feel up to it. In the mirror, stubble seemed to be growing out of his skin as he stared at himself, face pale, eyes red. He cleaned his teeth twice, took two aspirin, went back to bed and lay looking at the cracks in the bedroom ceiling, wondering if Shirley had thought him a bore, talking about his father so much.

But despite the aching head he felt surprisingly good. Tozer had been right. It was good to ask a woman out, to walk and laugh and talk. And now it felt good to turn his back on work, for a day at least. He dozed in bed, feeling like a schoolboy, bunking off school. The fog was lifting a little.

And then the doorbell rang. And rang again. And again.

He ignored it at first. It would go away. But the doorbell sounded again. This time a long ring. A finger pressed hard against the bell.

At the door, when he opened it, a uniformed copper and a plain clothes man looked him slowly up and down.

'Detective Sergeant Cathal Breen?'

NINETEEN

Breen didn't recognise either of them. It was freezing outside and the winter light seemed too bright right now.

'What?'

'Detective Sergeant Breen?' they asked, breath moistening air. They were looking at a man, unshaven, still in his dressing gown and pyjamas. They would be thinking, Are we at the right house? Does this man look like one of us?

'What's the problem?' Breen asked.

'Sergeant Michael Prosser, formerly of Marylebone CID, was found dead last night. We would like to ask you a few questions.'

Cold air caught in Breen's chest. He started coughing. 'Christ,' he said. His skin started to prickle. Last night's poison sloshed back into his brain, tilting the world a little.

'May we, ah, come in?'

Handing the two policemen tea, Breen looked down and noticed scrambled egg on his dressing gown. Had he eaten eggs today, or had that been another day?

'I mean,' said Breen. 'What happened?'

'Why aren't you at work today, Sergeant?'

They were both from Scotland Yard. This is what it must feel like, he thought, for other people.

'I called in sick,' he said.

The two policemen exchanged a look.

'What with?' asked the CID man.

Breen handed them a bowl of sugar. 'I'll be honest, I got a little drunk last night. I'm not used to drinking. I'm feeling a bit under the weather. Have you . . . have you told his wife yet?'

The CID man had fair hair that was matted across his forehead and fingers stained from nicotine. He asked, 'Any special celebration?'

'No,' said Breen. 'I mean, I was angry about being taken off an investigation, so maybe that's why I drank more than I usually do.'

'Angry?' said the constable. They were sitting on his couch, side by side. The constable was one of the older ones. He had taken his helmet off and it was sitting on the cushion beside him. The detective had unbuttoned his sheepskin coat.

'About being taken off the case,' said Breen.

'You were acquainted with former Detective Sergeant Prosser?' He pulled out a packet of No. 6's.

'Yes.'

The CID man offered Breen a cigarette, but not the constable sitting next to him. Breen shook his head. He couldn't face a cigarette right now. 'And Mr Prosser was responsible for an arson attack on this property?'

Breen nodded. 'He's a suspect.' Was Shirley OK? The father of her child was dead. He wanted to call her, but he realised he didn't even have a phone number for the record shop to get a message to her.

The CID man asked, 'Is there any evidence in particular to link Mr Prosser directly to the fire you had here?'

Breen shook his head. 'You'd have to ask Stoke Newington. It's their case. I'm obviously not the investigating officer for that.'

'And why would Mr Prosser want to burn down your house?'

Breen rubbed his unshaven face. 'Sergeant Prosser was involved with a local gang, helping them burgle shops. I caught him out. I threatened to expose him. That's why he left the police. He wasn't very happy about it. What happened? Have you informed Shirley Prosser yet?' he asked again, though he knew they would not answer. They wouldn't want to let him know what they knew. Standard stuff if you were a subject in the investigation.

Which he would be.

'What did you stand to gain by blackmailing him in this way?'

'I wasn't blackmailing him,' Breen protested. 'It wasn't like that.'

The CID man's name was Deason. He looked at the pages of his notebook, then straight at Breen. 'There is no record of him being involved in any illegal activity while he was an officer with the Metropolitan Police,' he said. 'Only that he resigned.'

Breen sighed. 'It's complicated,' he said.

'Isn't it?' said Deason. 'We spoke to Constable Jones. He said you have been asking him where Michael Prosser lived.'

'Yes,' said Breen. 'I wanted to talk to him. He didn't know.'

'You're a detective. I'm sure you have ways of finding out.'

'I didn't though.'

'No?'

The detective stood and peered at the print on Breen's wall. 'That's very . . . modern,' he said. 'What is it supposed to mean?'

'I don't really know,' said Breen. 'I don't think it's about meaning.'

Deason frowned at the painting, then said, 'Do you own a gun, Sergeant?'

'No. Of course I don't. Prosser was shot then?'

The detective wrinkled his nose, then moved across the room and into the kitchen. There were five notebooks sitting on his kitchen table. The moment he saw the detective's eyes on them, Breen wished he had put them somewhere safe. But the detective picked them up, slipped the rubber band off the first, and started turning over the pages.

'We'll be taking these,' said Deason.

Breen nodded and said, 'You'll want to know where I was last night?'

'You know the drill,' said Deason.

'At what time in particular?'

The man turned. Beneath the man's even smile teeth pointed

in all directions. 'Let's just say between 9 p.m. and midnight for now.'

'I was having dinner with Michael Prosser's wife, Shirley Prosser.'

The man whistled. 'Oh.'

'We were in Jimmy's in Frith Street. Ask Dimitri. He's the manager.'

'Until midnight?'

Breen shook his head. 'No. We went for a walk.'

'At what time?'

'I don't know. I think we left the restaurant at around nine.'

'A walk?'

'Just around and about,' said Breen.

'Around and about?'

'We'd had a meal. We went for a walk.' He tried to remember the name of the pub they'd been to, but his mind was blank.

Deason nodded. He went and sat on sofa again and made a few notes in his own book. Then he looked up and said, 'Are you and Mrs Prosser having relations?'

'Relations?'

'Sex,' said Deason.

'No.' Breen shook his head. 'It's nothing like that.'

Deason raised eyebrows and wrote in his notebook again.

'Perhaps you can tell me what it is like then?'

The sergeant on the front desk stared at him as he came in.

'What are you looking at?' said Breen.

'Nothing,' said the copper.

Marilyn's desk was alive with colour. Someone had put a huge bunch of flowers on it. Sitting in a clear waterless glass jug, they were artificial, but they were flowers, at least. Red roses and yellow daffodils, clashing.

'Bloody hell, Paddy' said Marilyn. 'You came in then?'

Breen looked at his desk. The drawers were all open. All his paperwork had been removed. 'They've been here already then?'

Now they had all his notebooks. His crime scene photographs. The pictures of the burnt man. He was trying to remember what else was in the drawers.

'They were in at 8.30. They found the notes. All them threats. I had no idea you'd had so many of them. Christ, Paddy. How long has that been going on?'

'What happened?'

'Well . . .' Marilyn smoothed down her cardigan. 'They asked where you were. They wanted to know what you'd been like these last few weeks.'

Breen said, 'Not that. I meant, what happened to Prosser?' Too loudly.

Marilyn flinched. 'Nobody's saying. Just that he's dead. I had to say you called in sick, Paddy. Was that OK?'

Breen said, 'Well I *was* sick, wasn't I?'

'Were you?'

'Yes I was,' said Breen. Too loud again.

'Sorry,' said Marilyn quietly. 'I mean, I didn't even like him much. But it's horrible, isn't it?'

'Did they say where he died?'

'Elephant and Castle. He was living in some bedsit. I don't know anything else. I promise.'

Breen looked around the room. It was quiet. Neither Tozer nor Jones was there. He asked, 'Who are all the flowers from, Marilyn?'

'From Danny. They're only plastic, but they're quite nice, aren't they? I like them anyway.'

'Your boyfriend?'

'He's never bought me flowers before,' she said. 'Not once. I don't suppose he could find fresh, this time of year.'

'A guilty conscience,' said Breen. He walked to the cupboard, looking for a new notebook. All his were gone. All his notes on the Pugh case. All his notes on the body in the fire.

'Why would he have a guilty conscience?'

'I thought you weren't bothered with him anymore, anyway?'

'Well maybe I am bothered with him, as no one else seems to be interested in me anyway.' Then: 'Get your own damned stationery, Paddy, and leave my cupboards alone.' She snatched the pad out of his hands, put it back inside the cupboard and slammed the door. 'I'm sick of it here,' she said. 'What's wrong with him buying me something for a change? Who else is going to? Why does there have to be something bad behind it all the time?'

Breen watched her, open-mouthed. He still had a headache and she was making it worse.

'Ah. Breen.'

Bailey must have heard the shouting. 'Marilyn said you were off sick,' he said. He had one hand on the door handle, head only slightly out of the door, as if he didn't want to emerge any further than necessary.

'I heard the news,' said Breen.

'Terrible,' said Bailey.

'What happened?'

'You'd better come in,' said Bailey.

Michael Prosser had been murdered in a bedsitter in Elliotts Row in Lambeth at around ten the previous night. A five-minute walk from Elephant and Castle.

A simple room with a Baby Belling cooker and a single metal bed and a paraffin heater. He had been shot twice. A first bullet had hit him in the abdomen, not far above his groin. It knocked him to the floor but failed to kill him. A blood trail showed that he had made it across the room towards the door of the small room where the second shot had been fired. He would have been looking up at his killer as it hit him in the top of the head.

'I shouldn't be telling you this. Officially at least, you are a suspect,' said Bailey. A stickler for the rules in normal circumstances.

Other tenants in the block denied seeing anyone. It was that kind of building. Full of vagrants and West Indians.

Breen nodded. 'It doesn't sound like someone who knew what they were doing. Or maybe it was an argument. Two shots, like that.'

'Please be clear. This is not your case. You are to do nothing at all. Phone no one. Talk to no one. Do nothing.'

Again, Breen nodded.

Bailey sighed. 'They know you didn't like Sergeant Prosser. He didn't like you. You were the reason he was forced to resign from the police. They know you received death threats from him and that he was a suspect in a murder attempt on you.'

'Yes,' said Breen.

'And Constable Jones told the officers from Scotland Yard you were asking him yesterday if he knew where Prosser lived.'

'Yes,' said Breen. 'I did.'

'And he told you Elephant and Castle.'

'That's right.'

Bailey pulled out a pipe and banged the bowl a couple of times into his ashtray. 'You know what has to happen now, don't you?'

'I suppose so,' said Breen.

'You are suspended from duty until further notice. On pay, obviously. I'm sure this will only be for a couple of days. We'll get to the bottom of this and then everything will be back to normal.' He pulled out a pipe knife. 'You have an alibi, I hope?'

'Yes.'

'Good.'

'Not a very good one,' said Breen. 'As it happens.'

Bailey sighed. 'If there's anything you want to tell me, you should tell me it now,' he said.

Breen remained silent. Bailey frowned and started scraping at the bowl of his pipe.

★

Breen was sitting at his empty desk wondering if he should call Jumbo Records to try to speak to Shirley Prosser when Constable Helen Tozer strode in, all lanky limbs and lack of grace.

'God there,' Tozer said. 'I can't believe it. You must be mighty relieved though, Paddy. He was a nutter, wasn't he?'

Marilyn said, 'Have some bloody respect.'

Tozer said, 'He tried to kill Paddy, Christ sake, in case you hadn't noticed.'

'I'm a suspect.'

'But it's only a formality, isn't it?' said Tozer. 'I mean, it's got to be.'

'Christ, Paddy,' said Marilyn. 'I'm so sorry.'

He said, 'Well, I wanted a holiday, didn't I?'

Marilyn stood up and said to Breen, 'What are you going to do?'

'They'll ask you about me. The Scotland Yard men. About last night. And when we got back.'

Tozer nodded. 'Right,' she said.

Marilyn said, 'You'll be fine, Paddy.'

'Who do you think it was?' said Tozer.

Breen said quietly, 'I don't know. He was bent. Maybe there was something going on we didn't know about.'

'I mean,' said Tozer. 'Bloody hell.'

'They'll want to ask about me and Shirley Prosser,' he told Tozer.

'What about him and Shirley Prosser?' said Marilyn. Breen looked at his watch. It was one already. Jumbo Records would be shut by now. It was a Wednesday; half-day closing. The only way to get in touch with her would be to go there.

'Who bought you those, Marilyn?' said Tozer, suddenly louder, fingering the plastic flowers.

'My boyfriend,' said Marilyn.

'I thought you were chucking him,' said Tozer.

Marilyn wrinkled her nose. 'I never quite got around to it. What about Shirley Prosser?'

'I really like plastic flowers,' said Tozer. Bright yellows, greens and reds.

'You don't think they're a bit tacky?'

'They're pop art, really, aren't they? Why'd he give them to you?' asked Tozer.

'Don't you start,' said Marilyn.

TWENTY

The Bridget Riley print wasn't his, but it wasn't anybody else's, Breen reasoned, so even though he didn't really like it much, it remained hanging on the wall in his living room, opposite the front door. He should have handed it over to Tarpey, but Rhodri Pugh wouldn't have been interested in it. And Tarpey just wanted to see the whole thing tidied away.

Keeping it was a petty act of rebellion. Black dots on a white background. Unconnected events in a plain landscape. He stared at them for so long they started to play tricks on him, the shapes imprinting themselves on his eyeballs, seeming to move as he watched them, set free from the whiteness.

It was Thursday morning. Normally he would be going to work now.

He changed his sheets. He cleaned the kitchen cupboards, wiping the bottoms of jars and tins. He took out the boxes from under his father's bed and started throwing out rubbish from them. There were dozens of tobacco tins he'd kept. One was full of neatly folded bills from a grocer he'd had an account with. Another was rusted shut. He put the bills into the dustbin outside in the cul-de-sac. The weather was getting even colder.

After that, finally, it was breakfast time. He boiled water for coffee, poached an egg and ate it on a piece of toast with a thin layer of butter on, then washed the plate and pan.

Around nine o'clock he cleaned the bathroom, then went out and bought *The Times* and the *Daily Telegraph* and looked through them.

The *Telegraph* had a small piece about the murder of a man in south London, but it didn't mention his name, or that he was a policeman.

For a while he tried sketching, assembling a still life of utensils from the kitchen on a table, but had lost interest by ten. He couldn't concentrate.

At 10.15 he called up Tozer. 'Is there any news?'

'Paddy? What are you doing?' There was a buzzing on the line. He could barely hear her voice.

'I'm not used to staying at home,' he said. 'What are you working on?'

'Woman raped up at the running track by the Regent's Canal. St John's Wood are taking me along to talk to her. I've got to go, right now.'

'Have they interviewed you yet?'

She said something he couldn't hear above the buzzing.

'I can't hear,' he said. 'This line's making a racket.'

'They wanted to know about you. Whether you'd been acting strange or anything.'

'Who was it? Sergeant Deason?'

'Yes. And wanted to know everywhere you'd been.'

'What about Shirley?'

A pause. 'Her too. What time you came back on Tuesday. They wanted to know if you were having it off with her.'

'What did you say?'

'I told them no. You didn't, did you? Have it off?'

'For God's sake. We just went for a walk, Helen. Did they let slip anything about her? How she was?'

'No. Deason plays his cards very close to his chest.'

A plodder, thought Breen. A one-step-at-a-time man. Sometimes that made for a good detective. Other times it made for nothing getting done. 'I was thinking, could you get in touch with Shirley for me? Tell her I'm sorry. Tell her I'll be in touch in a couple of days.'

'How will I do that? She's not on the phone.'

'You could go there.'

'I've got to go now, Paddy. Why don't you do it?'

'I shouldn't. We'll both be suspects. Who do you think would want to kill Prosser?' said Breen.

'Apart from you?'

'That's not funny. What if you come with me and talk to her again. At least you'd be there too. She might tell us stuff she's not telling Deason.'

A pause. 'Sure it's not just because you want to see her?'

'I feel sorry for her.'

She was whispering so he could hardly make her out now. 'I've got to go, Paddy. They're waiting for me.'

He heard a male voice asking. 'Who are you talking to, Constable Tozer?'

'My mum,' she said. 'My dad's not well.'

'I can't talk to you now, Mum,' she said. 'I'm at work. I'll call you after.'

'When?'

But she'd put down the phone.

At around midday Breen heard a van pulling up outside in the cul-de-sac. When he went out to Kingsland High Street to buy some supplies for lunch he noticed a blue Pickfords van unloading.

The flat above him had been empty for weeks. Breen watched as two men hoicked furniture into it. When he came back from the Jewish shop with lox and herring for lunch they were trying to squeeze a huge, very modern white fibreglass armchair into the front door. Bachelor? he wondered. Youngish.

He ate his lunch listening to the scraping and banging of furniture on the floor above. In a long damp season the day had turned out to be a bright one. If he hadn't been waiting for Tozer's call he would have gone out for a walk in Clissold Park.

At three he called the office. Marilyn answered. 'How are you, Paddy? It's quiet here without you. Maybe I'll come around to visit you this evening. What do you think?'

'Is Tozer back?' The buzzing was still on the line.

'What do you want her for?'

'There's just something I wanted to ask her, that's all.'

'Them police asked me about you. I told them you'd never hurt a fly.'

'Thanks,' he said. 'I appreciate that.'

'What about if I come round, then?'

'Not tonight, Marilyn. I'm not in a very good mood.'

'Suit yourself,' she said. 'Only a suggestion. Thought it might cheer you up a bit.'

Breen noticed a dark shape parking outside his window. Because his flat was on the lower ground floor, his living room was half submerged underground, down a few concrete steps. He could only see the bottom half of the black car.

'What about tomorrow? A few of us are meeting up for a drink after work. Just because you're suspended don't mean you can't come out for a drink with us. It would be fun.'

'I'll think about it.'

'You know. Just for laughs.'

He emerged out of the front door just as a young man with shoulder-length hair was pulling a leather suitcase out of the boot. He'd been right.

'Hello,' said Breen. 'Are you moving in upstairs?'

The man looked him up and down.

'Only I'd really appreciate it if you didn't leave your car there. It blocks my light,' he said, pointing to a sign fixed to the railings which said 'No Parking'.

The Pickfords lorry was taking up most of the cul-de-sac. The car was an old black MG Magnette.

'Your light?' said the man.

'Yes.'

'Do you own the light?' the man asked, suitcase in hand.

The phone was ringing, so Breen ran down the stairs into his flat. It was Tozer.

'What? Marilyn said you wanted me.'

Breen said, 'Can you make tomorrow? To see Shirley?'

A pause. 'OK. I'll try,' she said.

Loud music suddenly started booming from above.

'Hell,' said Breen.

'What's that noise?'

'New neighbours,' he said.

The man must have just connected up his hi-fi. Long repetitive bass notes shaking Breen's ceiling. A drone of electric guitars.

'I've got to go,' said Breen.

He looked around for a broom to bang the ceiling with, but then decided he should just go and ring the doorbell.

The same man answered. He had a screwdriver in one hand and a cigarette in the other. 'Oh. It's you again.'

'The music's very loud.'

'Not particularly,' said the man.

'It's a matter of opinion,' said Breen.

'I agree.'

'So I'd appreciate it if you could turn it down a little,' said Breen.

The man stared at him for a little while and then said, 'OK.'

But when Breen went downstairs again, the music seemed just as loud, if not louder.

The music carried on late. Breen switched on the TV. It was sport on ITV so he switched on to *24 Hours* on the BBC. The usual panel of men was discussing current events. It took a few minutes before he realised the one speaking was Rhodri Pugh, though he had to turn up the volume so he could hear what he was saying.

Something about Ulster. There was talk of rioting in Northern

Ireland. Civil war, even. Someone or other had resigned in protest. A bishop said, 'Of course, if you make concessions to extremists, that only tempts them to become more extreme.'

Rhodri Pugh said, 'The Home Office has not made concessions. We have simply made the necessary reforms to ensure that the government are acting in the interests of all the citizens of Ulster, not just the majority.'

The men around him nodded slowly.

Breen usually saved his last cigarette for this time of night. Five a day. Never more. He took out a cigarette but didn't light it.

The men talked about the Soviet Union, then they went on to talk about drugs, and about whether the new drug clinics were working. Somebody was saying that since they had stopped doctors dispensing drugs, the gangs were moving into the black market. 'Prohibition never works,' he said. The others tutted and shook their heads.

The bishop was talking again now. 'People tell me that drug-taking is an indication of a desire for a spiritual experience. I don't believe that for a second. Drug-taking is merely the result of an inability to come to terms with the real world.'

The music thumped down from above.

'It is an aftermath of war. Parents are determined that nothing should be too good for the children of peace. They grow up in a world in which nothing is denied them, fed on the cretinous optimism of consumerdom.' The bishop smiled, a line of white teeth above his neat dog-collar. 'It's such a deathly diet of good intentions . . .'

The camera cut to Rhodri Pugh. A man whose son had been a heroin addict, whom Breen had discovered had died because of his addiction. Who refused to let anyone know about what had happened to his son in case his reputation was damaged.

Rhodri Pugh's face was blank. Utterly expressionless.

TWENTY-ONE

The young shopkeeper was hanging up record sleeves in the window with clothes pegs. Breen watched him for a second. Huey 'Piano' Smith, *Rockin' Pneumonia*; Ramsey Lewis, *Maiden Voyage*; Sly and the Family Stone, *A Whole New Thing*. Carefully clipping each sleeve to the next, he didn't even see Breen and Tozer standing there.

'Maybe it takes a while, with the boy,' said Tozer, stepping back to look up at the flat's windows.

Breen rang again and they waited, but no one came to the door.

'I shouldn't be doing this,' she said.

Breen took his finger off the bell.

'Let's ask him in the record shop,' said Tozer.

When they opened the door music flooded out onto the street.

> Since you've been gone – why'd you do it?
> Why'd you have to do it?

The owner smiled at Tozer. She gave him a little wave.

'Have you seen Mrs Prosser?' Breen shouted above the noise.

'What?' he said. 'Hold on.' And he left the shop window and made his way past the record racks to the turntables at the back.

'That's better,' said Breen when the man had turned down the volume.

'Aretha Franklin?' said Tozer.

The man nodded. 'The best,' he said. 'You after Shirley and the kid again?'

'Yes.'

'They've gone,' he said.

'Gone out?'

'Gone. Skedaddled.' Breen and Tozer exchanged looks. 'Some time in the night, it must have been,' the record shop owner said.

The 45 he had been playing finished and the needle clunked back into the stand leaving the shop in sudden silence.

'I usually pop in to say hello and see if she needs anything. Charlie likes to come down and have a little dance in the shop before the customers start coming in.'

'He dances?' said Breen.

'He's crazy. Falls over sometimes, but he loves it. You should see him. It's super fab.'

'Is he more rock than soul too?' said Tozer.

'Other way round,' said the record shop man. 'He loves James Brown. I was teaching him to do The Monkey.'

'Never,' said Tozer.

'Go on,' Breen interrupted.

'So I went upstairs and the door was wide open. And they'd gone. She must have gone in a hurry 'cause she's left loads of clothes in the wardrobe. And all the tins. Charlie is mad about baked beans. The cupboard is full of them. But she'd put a note on the kitchen table for me.'

'What did it say?'

'Just that she'd gone.'

'Have you got it?' asked Breen.

He had folded the note and put it in the back pocket of his drainpipes. He fished it out. Written on the back of a brown envelope was a message written in pencil.

SORRY GOT TO GO EMERGENCY HERE'S £6/10
I OWE IN RENT PLEASE GIVE IT TO LANDLORD
HE ALREADY HAS £12 DEPOSIT SO WERE SETTLED UP

CHARLIE SAYS KEEP ON GETTING DOWN
HE'LL MISS YOU SORRY FOR MESS X

'The other police came yesterday?'

'That's right,' he said. 'A few of them. They stayed for about an hour, talking to her. They weren't as pretty as you,' he said to Tozer.

Tozer rolled her eyes. 'God's sake. Give over.'

'Can we see the flat?'

'Help yourself. It's open.' There was a side door into the shop from behind the counter. They walked up the narrow staircase.

It was just as he'd said. There were skirts and dresses still neatly folded in the chest of drawers, but the toothbrushes were gone. There was a copy of the *The Virgin Soldiers*, a Dennis Wheatley novel and a children's storybook on the bookshelf. Charlie had slept on a mattress on the floor next to his mother. She had not had time to even take the sheets. Above his head on the wall there was a drawing of Mowgli from *The Jungle Book*, carefully copied from the Disney cartoon.

'Why did she scarper?' asked Tozer. 'The police yesterday?'

'They would have told her her husband was dead.' They would have asked her about Breen too. How long had they known each other. About the meal. About how long they'd walked for after. Each other's alibis would have checked out, but didn't mean that they were both in the clear. A wife who hated her husband and a colleague who had forced the dead man out of the police, giving alibis for each other on the night of the murder.

'And she was definitely with you all that time?' said Tozer. 'Only that's one reason I can think of she'd want to run.'

'What are you saying? Shirley killed him? She was with me all evening.'

'Jesus. Keep your hair on. Just thinking out loud.'

'No. She's frightened of something else.'

'She didn't say anything when she was out with you?' said Tozer. 'About what?'

'I mean . . . Do you think she was scared that whoever killed her husband would come after her too?'

'Maybe.'

There was a dressing table in the bedroom. Alongside a hairbrush and a Yardley lipstick was a small blue address book. Breen flicked through it. There were only a few entries. He slipped it into his pocket.

'Christ. I mean . . . You think we should tell Bailey about this now?'

They went back downstairs into the record shop. There were still no customers. 'No forwarding address?'

The man with the sideboards was nodding his head along to the music. 'Nothing. Maybe the landlord has one, but I doubt it. I mean, it must have been some time real late they legged it, because I was in here stocktaking till gone nine.'

The man picked out another record, slid it out of its paper sleeve and placed it on the turntable.

'Did she have any regular visitors?' Breen asked. 'Anybody you'd recognise?'

The man shook his head. 'Not really. I felt sorry for her, being honest. It was just her and the kid.' He took a cloth and carefully wiped the black disc, following the curve of the vinyl. 'Is she in some kind of trouble?' he asked.

'I hope not,' said Breen.

'You said not really. So maybe a couple of people?' said Tozer.

Breen pulled out a picture of Michael Prosser. 'What about him?'

The man shook his head. 'That's her husband, isn't it?'

Breen nodded.

'Never him.' The man paused. 'One bloke. Came in here asking for her same as you.'

'What was he like?'

'Wore a hat.'

'A hat?'

'Just a cap, really. But he was only in once. Fairly big man. Yes, and a nice car. A Bristol. Don't see so many of those, do you? Rest of the time I didn't see nobody.'

Breen thanked him.

'Tell her hello if you see her,' said the man. 'She was a nice lady. Nice lad too. Real cool.' And he turned to play the record.

'Friday the thirteenth,' said Tozer. 'Bad luck.'

'What?' said Breen.

'Today. It's the thirteenth of December,' she said. 'Typical, hey? Shirley Prosser gone.'

'You don't really believe in that stuff, do you?'

'No. Just saying, that's all. Course I don't believe it. Like horoscopes. Rubbish, isn't it?'

'He was flirting with you, that man.'

'He was kind of nice-looking.'

Breen grunted. 'Teaching a cripple how to dance. It's not exactly a responsible thing to do, is it?'

'Why not?'

'Because it's only encouraging people to take the mickey.'

'What if they do?'

They were walking away from the record shop, down Edgware Road. The shop window for Woolworths was full of tinsel and cotton-wool snow.

Tozer paused to look into the window. 'You bought all your presents yet?'

'Not yet.' He didn't say that he had only ever bought Christmas presents for his father.

'I was thinking of getting my dad a camera. Look at that,' she said. In the shop window were piles of a game called Twister. The box showed a cartoon of an American man and woman, each on their hands and knees, grinning. The game that ties you up in knots. 'I don't think I'll be getting that for Mum and Dad,' she said.

'After work, some of them are meeting up,' she continued. 'John Carmichael asked me out.'

'Carmichael?'

'No need to look like that. We're meeting up in the Louise with all the rest of them. I've not much time left in London. I want to have some fun, for Christ sake. You know what it's going to be like for me when I go back down to the farm. Look –' she pointed to the board game again – 'I can't see that catching on in England, can you? Honestly, though? A game where you actually have to touch each other to play it.'

'I suppose I could come tonight', Breen said.

'Poor Paddy. Without your job, you're like a puppy looking for his stick.'

They sat at a table at the front of the Louise.

'I just didn't think you were interested in him,' said Breen.

The pub was busy. The landlord had put some crêpe-paper streamers over the bar and had written a notice in felt-tip pen that said 'HAPPY CHRISTMAS 1968'. It was the best they could manage in the Louise.

'I'm not,' she said. 'He's just a mate. Look. You and me. We just had sex once, that's all. We're not married or anything. It's just a laugh. He's a laugh. He's not a miserable old arse.'

'Did you have sex with Carmichael?'

'None of your business if I did.'

Breen held up his hands. 'I'm just surprised, that's all. I didn't think he was your sort.'

'I thought he was your best friend. Don't act so weird, Paddy.'

'I'm not acting weird.'

'I know things are hard on you right now.' She rummaged in her handbag and brought out her purse. 'I was thinking. What if you and me went out another night? Last chance before I go.'

'I'll have to check my diary,' said Breen. 'What with work and everything.'

She pulled out two tickets and handed him one. Breen looked at it:

ROYAL ALBERT HALL.
18 December.
Celebration in December.
20/-

'What is it?' Breen asked.

'It's this thing. The Alchemical Wedding. It's kind of a happening.'

He remembered a jester on a train. 'What's a happening?'

'I got the tickets from the squat. Jayakrishna and all of them are doing something there. Want to come?'

'You've been back there?'

'Yes. A few times.'

Breen frowned, looking at the ticket. 'I don't think it's really me,' he said.

'Oh, come on. Leonard Cohen's going to be there. And the Beatles. All sorts.'

Breen said, 'I don't know.'

'Call it research,' she said. 'You'll be helping me out.'

'With what?'

A drunken man came barging past. He spotted Tozer and started singing, top of his voice. 'Young girl, get out of my mind. My love for you is—'

'Go away,' said Tozer.

'Better run, girl. I'll touch your bum, girl . . .'

'Research into what?'

'Get lost,' shouted Tozer to the drunken copper. She was still holding the ticket out to Breen. 'Come on. What else are you bloody doing? Please? I want you to be there.'

'Why are you so interested in the squat?'

'I'm just curious. That's all,' she said.

Breen looked at her and said, 'I'll go if you come to Johnny Knight's house with me this weekend.'

'Who's Johnny Knight?'

'Shirley Prosser's brother. He lives in Borehamwood.' He pulled the notebook he'd found at her flat out of his pocket.

'This is Shirley Prosser's address book?'

Breen nodded. 'Her maiden name was Knight.'

She took the book and flicked through it. 'You should hand this over to Scotland Yard.'

'There's only a few numbers in the book. His is one of them. I've been trying to call Johnny Knight since yesterday, to see if he knows where she might have gone. But there's no answer. I was thinking of catching a train out there on Sunday.'

'Where's Boring Wood?' she asked.

'About forty minutes away by train,' he said.

'I don't know,' she said.

Carmichael came back holding a pint of lager and a rum and black. 'Did I interrupt something?' he said, trying to slide the glasses onto the table, spilling lager onto his twill trousers. 'Bugger,' he said.

'I'm sure you can afford the dry cleaning now you're on Drug Squad,' said Tozer.

'What's that supposed to mean?'

'Everyone knows you get a better class of bung on Drug Squad,' she said.

'Shut up. Why does everyone always accuse us of being bent?' said Carmichael. Breen noticed Carmichael had put on weight since he'd left D Division CID. Sitting down, Carmichael's stomach bulged over the top of his trousers.

'Just wanted to say, I'm sorry to hear about what happened, Paddy,' said Carmichael. 'It's a bloody shame. I'm sure it'll all be cleared up in a day or so.'

'He said he needed a holiday, didn't he?' said Tozer. 'Well now he's bloody got one.'

Coppers were wandering over to shake Breen's hand. 'We're rooting for you, chum,' and, 'Bloody disgrace,' they said. 'Ridiculous.' Even if a lot of them had liked Prosser, nobody liked to see a policeman suspended.

'Good luck, mate,' they said. Breen thought he saw a wariness in their eyes, though. As if they didn't quite trust him anymore.

Carmichael said, 'They pulled you off the Pugh thing as well, didn't they?'

'What I never figured out was where Pugh was getting his drugs from,' said Breen. 'I was thinking . . . Do you keep a list of suspected dealers?' he asked Carmichael.

'Yes. Kind of.'

'What do you mean?'

'I don't think we know the half of it. It's getting mad out there. They're bringing in heroin from Hong Kong now. We have no idea.'

Tozer said, 'God's sake. For months you've been singing the praises of the Drug Squad. Now you've joined them—'

'No,' said Carmichael. 'It's great.'

'Only what?' said Breen.

'If they spent more time tracking down the real dealers instead of doing all these raids on pop stars we might be getting somewhere.'

'You had a row with Pilcher?' Breen guessed.

'Thing is,' said Carmichael, 'there's just as much gear out there now as there was before. More, maybe.'

'Gear?' said Breen.

Carmichael ignored him. 'And we're just giving them Chink gangs a living. It's them we should be gunning for. Not all these posh nancies.'

'Let's not talk shop, hey?' said Tozer. 'I want to get drunk. Only two weeks left and then I'm gone.'

Two weeks, thought Breen, and then she'd be gone.

He turned to Carmichael. 'So how would I go about finding out who was selling Pugh drugs?'

Marilyn barged in and leaned over to give Breen a kiss on the cheek. 'We missed you, Paddy.'

'Only been two days,' said Breen.

Marilyn leaned forward with a hanky and started scrubbing at the lipstick she'd just left on Breen's cheek.

Carmichael said to Tozer, 'Let's get a move on then. We'll miss our table.' He lifted his glass and poured the drink down his throat.

Carmichael grabbed Breen's arm as he stood up to leave with Tozer. 'I'll ask around. No promises though.'

'Thanks,' said Breen, and he watched the two of them leave.

By half past eight, Marilyn had drunk four double Bacardi and Cokes on an empty stomach and said she wanted another. She disappeared to the Ladies when Jones sat down next to him and said, 'I think she was hoping it was just the two of you.'

'Don't be nasty.'

'Because she fancies you. Everybody knows that.'

'She doesn't. She's got a boyfriend.'

'All the women like you, Paddy. Just tell me what I should say to my missus. Since she's been pregnant life's been no fun.'

'Jonesy's pissed,' said a copper.

'Good to see you, though. You coping OK?' Jones slung his arm around Breen's shoulder as if they were the oldest friends in the world.

The pub was full. People standing shoulder to shoulder. Pints spilt on the carpet. The publican barged round with a galvanised bucket to empty the ashtrays into, wiping them with a filthy bar cloth.

'You should go home,' said Breen. 'Spend a bit more time with your wife.'

A couple started dancing in the corner, if you could call it dancing. The man was moustachioed and wore a blue jacket that was at least a size too big for him, the woman in a polka-dot dress. He was drunk, dragging her around a small empty space on the floor. She was reluctant, laughing, trying to push him away. A couple of onlookers cheered. 'Go on,' they shouted. 'Give us a twirl.'

Jones was saying, 'I'd like to smash his bloody face in.'

'Who?'

'My dad of course.'

Another of the constables came over and offered Breen a drink. 'Suspended on full pay. That's worth a celebration,' he said.

The constable sat next to Breen. 'Terrible thing about Michael Prosser,' he said. 'I bet it was his missus.'

'Who's saying that?'

'I bet you. That's all. A copper's instinct. I'm not even in bloody CID and I can tell a mile off.'

'You're talking rubbish,' said Breen. 'I know for a fact she can't have done it.' Though he didn't want to explain why he she couldn't have: he'd have had to explain that he was out with her.

'Keep your hair on, Paddy. OK, if it wasn't her, who was it?'

'Bloody hell. Look at the state of her.'

All eyes went to the door from the public bar. A woman from behind the bar had one hand round Marilyn and was guiding her through the crowd.

'She had locked herself in,' said the barmaid. 'I had to break down the door. Landlord is hopping.'

Marilyn's mascara had run down her face and her eyes were puffy. 'I don't feel well,' said Marilyn.

'Almost killed my shoulder doing it. Landlord's calling a taxi.'

'Something I ate,' said Marilyn.

'Wasn't nothing you ate 'cept rum and Coke,' said the constable.

Sorrowful Marilyn, behive crooked, one of her earrings missing.

'You've got something on your top,' said Breen.

The barmaid looked down too. 'God, Marilyn. You sicked on me.'

'Wasn't on purpose,' said Marilyn, flopping down on the bench seat next to Breen. She pressed hard against him. 'I'm sorry,' she said. 'I've spoiled it all.'

'Doesn't matter,' said Breen.

'Do you mean that, though?'

'Yes. Why not?'

'You're really nice,' said Marilyn. She wrapped herself around his right arm.

The copper who he'd been speaking to said, 'Oi, oi,' and winked.

'She's just a bit drunk, that's all,' said Breen.

'Really nice,' she said.

'We'll put you in a taxi and take you home to your boyfriend,' said Breen.

'What you want to do that for?' slurred Marilyn. Then, 'He says he wants to marry me.' She leaned in closer, leaning her head against his arm.

'You're well in there, mate,' mouthed the copper, winking.

'I don't love him.' She smiled lopsidedly.

'Come on. We've got to get you home.'

Outside the air was cold. A frost was settling across the street. The taxi driver was an elderly man with big ears and a flat cap who said, 'I'm not taking her in my cab. She'll throw up in it and then I'll be off half the night cleaning it.'

Breen held up his warrant card and said, 'You'll take her or there'll be trouble.'

TWENTY-TWO

'What's he do?' They were walking from the station in Borehamwood. The town sat on the edges of London, like a timid rabbit waiting to be swallowed whole.

'Quantity surveyor. Works for the GLC and stuff.'

'Quantity what?'

'It's like an accountant for builders.'

The pavement was half built, disappearing into mud. A road still in the making.

'Any idea why this quantity whatsit is not answering his phone?'

'Holiday, perhaps.'

'Nobody goes on holiday this time of year.'

'I tried.'

'Exactly.'

They had to ask directions three times to find the house. The new streets didn't have signs yet. It was a place that didn't know what it was. Johnny Knight's home turned out to be a new house about ten minutes' walk from the station. Modern, flat roof and white wood fascia boarding. Big glass windows and sliding doors. Very cool. Very with it.

'Who'd want to live here?' said Tozer. 'The suburbs. It's not here and it's not there either.'

'I don't know,' said Breen. 'A bit of peace and quiet.'

'Don't,' she said. 'You just sound even older than you are when you say things like that.'

'*Even* older?'

A short gravel driveway, just enough to park a car on, but no car.

Breen rang the bell. A new electric chime. Two notes. Nobody answered.

Breen called, 'Hello? Mr Knight?'

'Maybe he's with his sister. Wherever she's gone.'

'Maybe.'

A rambling rose, dark with blackspot, snagged on his jacket as he pushed past. He stopped to disentangle himself. Tozer squatted at the letterbox.

'Wherever he's gone, he's been away a while. There's a pile of post a mile high,' she said.

Breen struggled on through to the back of the house. A row of cypresses had been planted at the back, presumably to hide the houses behind when they grew.

There were no nets on the window and a large picture window looked out onto the overgrown lawn. Breen put his forehead against the cool glass. It was a neat living room with new G Plan furniture, a revolving chair and a cream rug. A hi-fi with a Jazz Messengers disc leaning against it. A bachelor's house. Breen imagined living in a place like this. Leaving the darkness of his basement behind.

'There's not been anybody in for weeks by the look of it,' said Tozer. She joined him, head against the glass. On a coffee table there was a pile of books about art and architecture. The one at the top was called *Streets in the Sky*.

'Very contemporary,' said Tozer. 'Not sure about the white carpet. I'd spill tea on it in five minutes.'

The sofa was brown with orange cushions. There was a pouffe and a big 22-inch colour TV.

Breen noticed the flies first, all huddled up in the top corner of the window. There must have been thousands of them, crammed on top of one another. His heart started to jump around in his chest.

'So cool and light, mind you,' Tozer was saying.

The feeling of clamminess when you know something is wrong but before you know what it is.

'I bet he's good-looking too. Broad shoulders. Maybe a little moustache.'

Tozer hadn't noticed the black mass of insects yet. She was still saying, 'The farmhouse I grew up in is like, two hundred and fifty years old. It's so dark and poky. This is beautiful . . . Hey! What's that brown thing on the carpet down there?'

Breen peered closer.

'Oh God,' said Tozer. 'Is it?'

Breen said, 'I think it is.'

'Shit. The flies,' she said.

In the shadow of the sofa, the body of a cat lay curled on the carpet, just skin and bones. There was a dark pool of seepage around it where the body had rotted.

Breen banged the window and the flies exploded into motion, fizzing into the air and clattering pointlessly against the glass.

Tozer jumped back, startled.

'I hate flies,' said Breen.

Breen found a hammer in a toolbox in the garden shed.

'Careful, Paddy,' said Tozer.

The glass panel in the house's back door gave way easily and he reached inside to find the back of the Yale, snagging the sleeve of his jacket and feeling the cloth rip. Flies buzzed past him into the clean air.

'Damn,' he said, looking at another torn sleeve.

But the door was locked with a mortice too, so he raised his foot and kicked at the door a few times.

'Want me to have a go?'

'I'm fine.' He thumped again.

'Only saying,' she said. 'Do you think it's just the cat?'

'How many weeks you think the letters have been piling up?'

'God.'

He pushed his shoulder against the door and felt a sting of pain down his arm. He gave the door one last thump and heard the jamb start to splinter. A second thump and the wood started to shift. A third and it finally swung open.

The house smelt thick and sweet, the stench of putrefying meat. They went in cautiously. Breen took a handkerchief from his pocket and held it over his nose, but it didn't do much to stop the smell.

The ground floor was three rooms and a kitchen.

'Posh,' said Tozer. 'Downstairs lav.'

But apart from the rotting cat and the pile of letters there was nothing out of the ordinary there.

Breen led the way up the stairs. Two bedrooms, a bathroom and a study, all empty. The main bed was neatly made. There was an electric alarm clock by the bed and a book of naval history sat on the bedside table, a leather bookmark poking out of it. Not a single picture on the walls save for a pair of Churchill crown coins mounted in blue velvet. A couple of incongruous horse brasses.

Breen exhaled. 'I thought . . .'

'So did I. You wouldn't have thought a dead cat could make such a stink.'

'Central heating,' said Breen. 'That will do it, with a dead animal, I suppose.'

'All mod cons,' said Tozer.

They opened the cupboards. Breen took a chair and stood under the loft hatch, peering around. Flies in every window buzzing to get out, but nothing else.

He was relieved and simultaneously disappointed.

Tozer put it into words. 'But if he's not here, where the bogging hell is he?'

The low hum of electricity filled the study. The slick new electric typewriter was switched off but an adding machine had been left on. A fancy German model with grey and red keys. There was a large white planning chest. When Breen opened it up it was full of drawings of flats and high-rises. Breen leafed through them. There were maps of roads too. Big curving roads on stilts that were bedded deep into the ground. One drawer was full of stationery. Breen took a couple of unused notebooks out of it.

Downstairs, Tozer had opened the picture window to let the flies and the stink of dead cat out.

'He lived here alone, then?'

There was a silver-framed picture on the sideboard in the living room. Breen recognised Shirley Prosser in it, though she was only a girl, standing in front of a car with her parents. She was pretty, confident, untroubled. There was a younger boy standing next to her, solemn-faced and tall. Breen guessed it must be Knight. He slid the photo out of the frame.

There were a few maggots still writhing on the cat, but mostly it had been picked dry, ribs showing beneath fur. Tozer found a tea towel in the kitchen and placed it over the remains.

'How awful. Poor little cat.'

'I thought you were a farmer's girl. Used to dead animals.'

'Don't mean people should leave them to starve. Whoever did that should be put away.'

'I somehow think he's beyond that.'

'Oh,' said Tozer. 'I got you.'

Breen went to the hallway, picked up the post and took it into the kitchen.

'You think he's dead too?'

There was a single dirty cornflake bowl in the sink, a spoon and an empty mug. It was the only thing out of place in the entire house. He had had breakfast and left, leaving the washing-up until he came home. Except he hadn't.

He opened a cutlery drawer, found a sharp knife and set about slicing open the pile of letters.

'What are you doing?'

He tore open a letter and slipped out the contents. 'Why don't you go and knock on the neighbours' doors and ask if they know anything about him and where he is?'

'Scotland Yard are going to be hopping if they find out we've been through it all first.'

She watched him making piles on the table. Bank statements. Bills. Personal correspondence. 'I'll go then,' she said.

The December days were short. It was dark outside by the time she returned.

'Next-door neighbours say they haven't seen him for weeks. Apparently they didn't see much of him, best of times. Didn't say boo to a goose.'

The bank statements looked very ordinary. Much like his own. The personal letters were dull, mostly cheerily stiff news from ex-army friends Knight had done National Service with. There was a single postcard from his sister Shirley, passing him her address above the record shop: 'Been trying to call. Where are you, Johnny? I'd come and visit but you know what Charlie's like with buses. Everything OK??? Miss you. Big sis.'

He took a cigarette, notched the packet and lit it. There was no ashtray so he put the dead match back in the box. She sat on the kitchen table kicking her legs backwards and forwards like a bored child as he patiently copied details from all of the letters into the notebooks he had taken from Knight's drawer.

'So,' she said.

Breen ignored her, still writing.

'I wonder how bored I'm going to be back on the farm. Scale of one to ten. A ten, I reckon.'

'Can I just finish this?'

'Sor-ry,' she said. 'Only it's supposed to be my day off, remember? Not the best day out with a boy I've had.'

'I'll be done in a minute.' He looked at a company name on a letterhead. The company Johnny Knight had been working with at the time he disappeared. Noted the date.

'You just take me out to a dead cat's house.'

'On the way back she said, 'Are you limping?'

'I think I've done something to my foot.' His right foot hurt when he put weight on it.

'What? Kicking in that door?'

'Don't laugh,' he said.

'Christ, Paddy. You really think this one is dead?' She was smoking a cigarette in the darkness. The red end glowed as she walked.

'Maybe. I think so.'

'I mean . . . This is something, isn't it? So someone's gone and killed Michael Prosser and maybe his brother-in-law too? What's it about?'

'I don't know.'

'You've got to tell Scotland Yard about this. I mean, it's got to be connected,' she said.

He reached into his pocket and handed her the address book he had taken from Shirley Prosser. 'You tell them. Call them up tomorrow. Give them this and tell them you had a hunch.'

She snorted. 'They're not going to believe me,' she said. ' I'm just a Temporary DC.'

'I can't tell them, can I?'

'I'm a girl, so I couldn't be expected to do any of this on my own. God's sake.'

'It doesn't really matter if they believe you or not. Say you came down here on your day off . . .'

She dropped her cigarette and paused to grind it into the pavement.

'That's why you asked me along, isn't it? Because if you found anything you wouldn't be able to tell anyone.'

'No,' he said. 'I just wanted company. Honestly.'

'Say what you like about Carmichael,' she said, 'but at least he takes me out for a Chinese meal.'

By the time they got to the station his foot was hurting like hell. He went to the men's toilets and rolled up his trouser leg and pulled down his sock. There was blood, plenty of it. His big toe looked pink and swollen.

TWENTY-THREE

He was exhausted by the time he made it home. He ran a bath and lay in it, hoping that warm water would soothe the swelling in his foot.

His body lay pale in the warm water.

Once he'd been muscular and lean. Sitting at a desk all day meant his body was softer now, less well defined. Like life, really. He picked up the soap and washed until the water was milky and he could no longer see his limbs.

From above, the thumping of rock music started again.

In the morning, taking the milk bottle off the step, he noticed the black car sitting in front of his window. Breen tried to ignore it. It was just a car. Other tenants had come and gone.

He limped back down the steps. This morning he cooked himself porridge, adding a pinch of salt. He stewed some hard plums that would never ripen. Bowl in hand, he pinned two sheets of paper to the back of the bedroom door, one with Michael Prosser's name on it, the other with Johnny Knight's. Under Michael Prosser he wrote, 'Shot.' On Knight's page he wrote a large question mark.

He took a roll of old wallpaper and sat down at the kitchen table with a cup of coffee and transcribed lists from the notebooks onto the paper. Addresses of people who'd written to Knight. Dates when the letters had been sent. He was just trying to put the dates into some kind of order when the doorbell rang.

It was the postman with a box, wrapped up in brown paper. 'Bloody Christmas. Does my back in,' he said as he handed it over.

Back inside, Breen opened the parcel. A bottle of single malt whisky with a note written in neat italic. 'Rhodri Pugh asked me to send you this, with sincere thanks for all your work.' It was signed, 'Oliver Tarpey.'

Breen considered pouring it straight down the sink, but didn't.

He crunched up the notepaper and threw it into the bin, then went to staring at the figures he'd written on the wallpaper, lists of numbers and addresses, willing them to reveal something, but they didn't.

Walking was good. It loosened up his bruised foot. And it felt good to get away from the black car and the rock music.

His father had liked to walk. Some Sundays they had packed cheese sandwiches and caught trains to Buckinghamshire, Hertfordshire and Surrey, his father holding an Ordnance Survey map in one hand and a stick to push back brambles in the other, Cathal trailing yards behind, claiming his legs were tired. Always seeming to be disappointed by the English countryside, his father muttered about the way the farmers here kept their cattle, or the way the fields were too flat.

Breen walked down to Kingsland Basin and on to the Regent's Canal heading west. The path was narrow and muddy. At times it seemed to disappear entirely into dead weeds. There had been boats working the canal when he had been a child, dark-skinned men at the tiller, but they were all gone now. But at Camden Lock a few canal boats sat on the black water, smoke rising from chimneys. He hadn't realised people still lived on the water. But when he saw the people in them they were long-haired and bearded. One boat was painted with mad swirls in red and green.

The old buildings alongside the canal were dirty and rotten. A few machine shops, a laundry, a garage. Bricks with failing mortar. Gutters hanging off walls. Slime from where the water dripped down the render.

All the pale concrete the GLC were laying down didn't seem enough to hide the wreckage of the city.

A mile later he emerged into Regent's Park near the zoo and continued over towards Francis Pugh's house. A pointless itch he couldn't resist scratching. He walked up and down the street a couple of times, looking around, waiting for something to strike him. Winter had made the site where his house had stood look desolate.

Dead men were forgotten. London was obsessed with what was happening.

He noticed the next-door neighbour's curtains move. The elderly actor who had lived next door to Pugh was peering out at him. Breen waved at the man, and he retreated letting the curtains fall back, as if embarrassed to be mistaken for a nosy parker.

He should go home, Breen thought. He should take advantage of the time and redecorate his flat. Or maybe move out and find somewhere new. Somewhere bright and fresh, like Johnny Knight's house.

He found himself walking down the old man's footpath, knocking on his door. 'Is it the policeman again?' he said. 'Come inside. It's so cold out there.'

Even inside, he was wearing an overcoat. His glasses were smeary with grease. 'Have you found the man who killed Mr Pugh?' he asked.

'No,' Breen said, avoiding explanation. 'I wanted to ask about the squatters behind his house.'

'Awful,' he said.

'What do you mean?'

'I don't mind the noise. I don't sleep much anyway. It's just the general lowering of the tone. And they dress so very badly. It's as if they're contemptuous of quality,' he said. The living room was warmed by an electric fire in the fireplace. Breen looked at the crack in the wall; it looked bigger than he remembered it.

'Noise?'

'They play guitars. They chant oriental mumbo-jumbo at all hours. Absurd. I mean they're not Hindus, are they? They're English. They really shouldn't be there, should they? Your lot were going to evict them and then nothing happened.'

'What?'

'The squatters. They were supposed to be evicted back in July, so the bailiffs said. And then nothing at all. It's all going to the dogs.'

'Do you know who owns the house?' said Breen.

'Why should I?' he said. 'Do you have any cigarettes, dear? I'm right out.'

Breen had only smoked two from his packet, but he gave the man the whole box.

'You're a godsend,' he said. 'An angel of mercy.'

Back out on the road he wished he had not given the whole packet away.

He was standing at the corner, where Marlborough Place met Abbey Road, hands in his pockets, when he saw the girl he had seen at the squat walk past. The one who called herself Hibou, according to Tozer. The one he had spied on in the garden. She was wearing a long Afghan coat and a knitted hat.

He wondered if he should talk to her. He could easily catch up. She was moving slowly. In a world of her own. He started following her.

She loped south, steadily, hair swinging with each step. At almost six foot tall, she was easy to follow. Breen stayed a decent distance behind.

At Hall Road she turned west, past the red-brick mansion houses. It was a quiet street, so Breen dropped even further behind. She stopped to lean down and stroke a tabby cat, but only for a second, as if she could not spare the time.

At Maida Vale she turned south again and, as the pavements became busier, Breen risked walking ten yards behind, though she didn't stop to look behind her.

She reached a bus stop and stood there, waiting, occasionally checking her watch. Breen stood a little way off until the bus came, then boarded it only as it was about to move off.

She took a seat upstairs, so Breen stood at the front of the lower level looking backwards so he could see when she descended again.

It meant he was facing all the passengers. 'Buy Kellogg's Sugar-Sweet Cereals Today!' read the advert above their heads. As the bus turned into Euston Road, Breen flashed his warrant card at the bus conductor, who nodded back at him.

She got off at Warren Street and walked to University College Hospital. He followed, still a few paces behind, to the Out-Patients department. The rows of chairs were filling with young people, some long-haired. Some looked as if they must be sleeping in squats, like Hibou. Some looked anxious. None were talking to each other.

The young woman spoke to a nurse on a desk for a minute. As she turned away, Breen lowered his head and pretended to tie a shoelace. By the time he straightened up again, she was sitting a few rows in front, her back towards him. Breen wished he had brought a paper or a book. Something to hide behind, at least.

Breen watched. One by one, the nurse called out names and the people disappeared into a room to the left of the desk. One by one they emerged after a couple of minutes, clutching small white paper bags. Eventually the nurse called, 'Miss Curtis?' Hibou stood and walked into the consulting room.

When she was safely inside, door closed behind her, Breen marched over to the nurse's station. 'Miss Curtis?' he asked, holding up his warrant card for her to see. The nurse looked wary. 'The woman who just went in?'

'Yes?'

'What's her first name?'

The nurse said, 'You can't just walk in like this . . . These people are patients. It's confidential. If they see the police just barging in here, what do you think—'

'It's important,' said Breen.

'No.'

Her phone rang. Her eyes were turned away only for a second, but for long enough to get a good look at the ledger. When she saw what he was looking at she slammed it shut.

'You are not allowed to see that,' the nurse said shrilly.

'OK,' said Breen. 'I was just asking.'

Hibou wasn't in the consulting room long. She emerged and when she saw Breen still standing in front of the nurse's station, her eyes widened. She must have recognised him from the day he and Jones had tried to talk to the people at the squat.

She turned and walked away rapidly. Approaching the exit, she broke into a trot.

Outside the hospital, it was already growing dark. He felt a little better. He had enjoyed the chase, however pointless. Breen reached into his mackintosh, took out a notebook and wrote: 'Curtis?' He had not been able to see the name properly. But he had seen her date of birth. He wrote '17/1/52'. He did the maths and realised with a shock that Hibou was only sixteen years old.

He remembered the way he had looked at the curve of her breast. She was a child, he thought. Half his age. Someone who should still be at school.

He returned the notebook to his pocket. That was worst of it in some ways. They had taken so many of his notebooks. He was worried he was missing something. Facts needed context. They were useless on their own.

On the long walk home he stopped in at Connor's Hardware and bought a pack of five reporter's notebooks.

He woke early on Tuesday and spent an hour at his kitchen table with a mug of coffee trying to recreate the notes they had taken. Pointless, really.

Before breakfast he did press-ups in the living room. He had never taken much exercise before, but maybe now was the time to start. He felt pale and flabby, and the winter had barely started. After fifteen press-ups, he flopped down onto the living-room carpet, panting.

His father had had a builder's arms. Thick and muscular. Liver-spotted from working outdoors. Maybe he should get a bicycle, he thought, still prostrate on the floor. That's when he noticed the balls of dust. He had used a dustpan and brush to clear up after the fire, but the carpet under his bookshelf was still filthy. How long had it been like that?

He spent the next half-hour hoovering the house. His Hoover was one of those with a light at the front. After the living room he had to empty the bag, dropping the dust into the bin outside. When he clanged the bin lid back on, the curtains upstairs opened. A man's face peered out, pointed at his watch.

Breen checked his wrist. It was still only 7.30 in the morning. Breen smiled back at him. A small wave.

Cleaning under his father's bed, the machine clunked into something. Kneeling down he saw something reflecting in the Hoover's light. An ancient biscuit tin. He hooked it out with one of his father's old walking sticks. The red Huntley & Palmers tin was crammed with old notes: ten-shillings, pounds, fivers and even a few tenners. He counted the money out on the kitchen table. It came to three hundred and eleven pounds.

As his father's brain had gone he had become a hoarder. He had tucked this stash away for years and forgotten about it. Breen put the tin in the kitchen cupboard, behind cans of tomatoes.

Bored. Nothing to do.

How could people bear not working? The empty hours. The lack of purpose. The sheer blandness of the everyday. He missed his job. It was what he did. What he was.

He thought of Danny, Marilyn's feckless boyfriend. Danny hadn't worked in months. Spent his day sitting around her flat and still expected her to cook for him in the evenings. He thought of Shirley. Where had she gone? She had no way of contacting him, he realised.

He went back to the kitchen table and found the photograph of Johnny Knight and his sister that he'd taken from the house full of flies. He stared at them both. On the fresh page of a notebook, he started to sketch him. Added a moustache. Changed the length of his hair. Turned another page. Did it over again. And again. He drew Shirley. More vivid than her brother. Hair up and hair down. Profile and then from an angle, with bare shoulders and a small smile on her face.

Then, from memory, he drew the man from the burnt house. His memory of the photographs that had been taken from his in-tray along with everything else. The exposed teeth. The curve of the hairless head. The blackened skin.

Drawing was strange. Sometimes the pencil breathed life into a picture without you even realising it. He tore out the page and held it up, his head on one side. Not bad.

He pinned it next to Pugh's print. The dots. If he had a house like Johnny Knight's, all glass and cool white paint, the Bridget Riley print would look right in it. Here it just looked stupid.

That afternoon, kicking his heels, he went up to the library and asked if they knew of any life-drawing classes. He considered borrowing some books, but he didn't. Unlike his father, he had never enjoyed reading.

He walked round Abney Park Cemetery for a while as the winter light thinned. Then along to Clissold Park. He didn't want to go home. Home reminded him there was nothing to do. Why hadn't Scotland Yard been in touch? They had not returned to check his alibi: did they have another suspect in the Prosser murder? Were they getting anywhere? Or were they just dragging their feet, waiting for Christmas?

When he got back to the cul-de-sac he could hear his phone ringing inside the flat. It took him a while to get the keys from his trouser pocket, and then the lock in his new front door wouldn't open. When he finally got in, he snatched up the telephone. 'Cathal Breen,' he said.

But the person on the other end of the line had already hung up.

He called up Deason at Scotland Yard CID. 'It's Sergeant Breen. Were you trying to get hold of me just now?'

Sergeant Deason's reply — a no — was muffled. He sounded as if he were eating something.

'And why would I be trying to get hold of you?' asked Deason.

'No reason,' said Breen, and put the phone down.

A long sigh. He stood up. Walked around the living room. Sat down again.

Later that afternoon he was polishing shoes when the phone rang again.

'Paddy. Where you been?' It was Tozer.

'Has anything happened?' he asked. The sweet, ordinary sound of typewriters and telephones in the background.

'I was just checking you were still on for tomorrow?'

'Tomorrow?'

'The Royal Albert Hall.'

'Oh.' He said. 'Right. Of course.'

'Be there on time.'

'Tomorrow, then.'

He wasn't looking forward to it. There would be rock music. He didn't like it much. He wondered what he should wear so he didn't stand out too much. A thirty-two-year-old man at a pop concert. Or 'happening'. Or whatever they were calling it.

Ridiculous.

TWENTY-FOUR

'Is that Donovan?' said Tozer, nudging him in the ribs.

'Where?'

'In the funny jacket. There.'

Breen looked, trying to understand what a funny jacket would be in this context.

'I'm not sure I know what Donovan looks like anyway.'

'Course you do.'

Breen looked into the crowd. They all looked the same to him. Young men with long hair, milling around.

The Royal Albert Hall's uniformed staff stood against the corridor walls, nervously. The place was half full. London's underground had come out in force. All the hippie poets and revolutionaries, and the rock musicians and spaced-out girls with dopey faces. He had the idea that if a bomb fell on this place right now, London would sink back gratefully into the same state it had been in in, say, 1962.

Breen still didn't understand what was supposed to be 'happening' tonight, but then he wasn't sure anyone was. So far, they had been here an hour and nothing had taken place. People were milling around, waiting for it to start, whatever it was.

'What was it you wanted to tell me?' he said.

'In a sec,' said Tozer.

Breen had grown up in a Britain where everyone looked the same. Men wore jackets, women wore skirts and dresses. Here, people came in infinite varieties – denim and suede, pink and green, short skirts and long kaftans. Hair down to shoulders and beyond. A girl here with a painted face. Another wearing an old jacket sewn with coloured buttons. A girl wearing a First World War German helmet sat cross-legged on the carpet holding a sign saying 'Stop The War Now'.

'Which war?' asked Breen.

She looked at him as if he were an idiot. She could only have been about fifteen.

The air was thick with a herbal smell Breen didn't recognise.

Tozer was dressed in a miniskirt and a khaki military jacket. She fitted right in. Breen hadn't worn a tie.

'What is this anyway?'

'It's a benefit, supposedly.'

'Benefiting who?'

A woman in a long skirt handed Tozer a bracelet made from thread. 'I made you this,' she said. 'It's a gift.'

'Arts Lab and the Alternative Information Centre,' said Tozer, holding out her arm.

'I heard the Stones were going to be here,' the woman in the skirt said. 'Somebody said that Dylan was going to come.' The woman was tying the bracelet onto Tozer's arm as if she had known her all her life.

'What's "alternative information"?' asked Breen.

'If you knew, it wouldn't be alternative,' said Tozer.

'Free crash pads, what to do if you're arrested by the fuzz, that kind of thing,' said the woman, finishing her knot.

'Right,' said Breen.

The woman in the cotton skirt said, 'My old man says when they get enough money they're going to build a giant computer where all this information is held so anyone can get it at any time.'

'Wow,' said Breen. 'A giant computer.'

'*Wow*?' said Tozer. 'Did you say that?'

'I don't know,' said Breen. 'It just came out.'

'Are you a cop?' said the woman, looking Breen up and down.

'Yes,' said Breen.

'Is *she*?'

'Yes,' said Tozer.

The girl started untying the thread. 'I can't believe I was going to give the fuzz one of my bracelets,' she said.

'Are you going to say "Cool" next?' she asked Breen, when the girl in the long skirt had scurried off down the curving corridor.

'I'm sorry,' said Breen.

They pushed their way through the crowd. Someone had set up an impromptu cake stall in one of the lobbies, laying out plates of cakes on a white sheet. A sign read 'Macrobiotic gingerbread and banana tea, 1/-'.

'You like macrobiotic, don't you, Paddy?'

'That's not allowed,' one of the ushers was trying to argue. 'This is the Royal Albert Hall.'

'Everything's allowed,' said the man.

Breen asked Tozer, 'Did you tell Scotland Yard about Johnny Knight's house like I said?'

'Yes.'

'Did they believe you?'

'To be honest, they didn't seem particularly bothered. They said nobody had reported him as a missing person anyway.'

'Well, well. It's the policeman, isn't it?' Breen turned. It was Suzi, the revolutionary from Kasmin's gallery. 'What are *you* doing here?'

She was with a young, long-haired man in a grey suit who wore a red star on his lapel.

'Just come to watch,' said Breen.

Suzi looked Tozer up and down, then said to her, 'Did you know he's a cop? Is he bothering you?'

Tozer said, 'I know. You can spot him a mile off.'

The man said, 'We heard there's going to be a raid. Is that why you're here, man?'

Breen said, 'A raid on the Royal Albert Hall?'

'You fuzz are surrounding the building.'

Breen held his hands up. 'Nothing I know anything about,' he said. 'I'm not working.'

The revolutionary girl said, 'So why are you really here? Don't tell me you're here for the poetry.'

'Maybe I like poetry,' said Breen.

Suzi snorted and tugged at the arm of the man in the suit. 'Why can't you just leave us alone, Mr Jones?' she said.

'I'm not doing anything.'

Come on,' Suzi said. 'We should find our seats.'

'God. Where did you meet her? What an arse,' said Tozer.

'Why did she call me Mr Jones?'

' "Something is happening, but you don't know what it is, do you, Mr Jones?" '

'What?'

'Never mind.'

Breen sniffed the air. 'Is that what I think it is?' he asked.

At around nine a bearded man with long hair and thick glasses came on stage and stood on a white sheet laid out on the stage, and mumbled some words into a microphone. There was a squawk of feedback.

'Is that John Lennon?' She pointed at a figure in a brown jacket sitting on a chair at the side of the stage. 'It looks like him.'

The sound from the stage buzzed and squealed. Breen said, 'What is that man saying?'

'He's asking us to listen to the sound of our own silence. It *is* John Lennon. I could swear.'

'What?' said Breen. But the hubbub of the giant hall quietened for a second.

Breen looked around. They were in balcony seats, above the mass of heads below. 'There is work to be done,' the bearded man was saying in an American accent. 'We need to create a silence that will fill this hall itself.'

'For God's sake,' said Tozer.

'Look at the person you came with,' said the man on the centre of the stage.

'There!' Tozer pointed down at the crowd below.

The microphone hummed. 'Now look at someone you didn't come with.' People turned, chattering, laughing, embarrassed.

'What are you pointing at?' asked Breen.

'It's the people from the squat.' Breen looked. He recognised one of the men from the squat. And beside him, the woman he had spied on in the garden: Hibou. The woman he had last seen the day before yesterday.

'Look at your past life,' said the bearded man. 'Now look at your future life.'

People were nodding. Others rolled their eyes: Like, what is this crap?

Tozer stood, took Breen's hand and said, 'Come with me.' She led him back up the steep aisle. 'I want you to get a closer look at them,' she said.

'Is that why we're here?'

'Kind of,' said Tozer. 'I wouldn't mind seeing Leonard Cohen too.'

They were back in the corridor now, circling round to find a staircase that led downstairs.

'You said the squatters were something to do with this event?'

'That's what they told me. They're going to do a chant.'

'A *chant*?'

'On stage. It's a religious thing. Hare Krishna. You know?'

Breen said, 'I don't know what you're talking about.'

'It frees your soul, kind of thing.'

They stopped in one of the long, curved corridors.

'You don't believe that, do you?'

'Don't be an ass, Paddy,' she said. 'I don't believe in anything.'

By the time they reached the stalls, a man was on the stage reading a long, repetitive poem. The audience were mostly ignoring him and chattering. Some were already wandering around, looking for something better to listen to or do, ignoring the ushers who were trying to keep the crowd seated.

Tozer stood on her toes, looking around. 'There they are.'

They stood at the back of the hall. By now a throng of men dressed in orange robes was walking onto the stage, some of them holding drums and bells. They started banging the drums and chanting quietly.

People turned again to look at them.

'Hare Krishna, Hare Krishna, Krishna Krishna, Hare Hare,' they sang. The men had shaved their heads. Some wore painted marks on their faces.

People in the crowd started to sway. Some held their hands up and waved them gently in the air.

Tozer said, 'It's like things have changed so much, no one knows what's good any more. Everyone's terrified they're missing something. They're clutching at anything that comes along. I mean, look them. Hare bloody Krishna!'

The funny thing was that while most of the young people here were all struggling to look different, to be different, on stage there was a big gang of men and women all dressed in the same orange, all trying to be the same. The men had shaved off their long hair into uniform nothingness. The women wore scarves over their heads. A rebellion against rebellion.

'Hare Rama, Hare Rama, Rama Rama, Hare Hare.'

'It's like the emperor's old clothes,' said Tozer.

'New clothes,' said Breen.

'That's what I said.' She took Breen by the hand again and started to push onwards down the aisle. Now others were joining the Hare Krishnas on stage, joining in the chant.

'Look,' she said, pointing ahead.

A chosen few were joining the orange men on stage. And there, with women on either side of him, was the the man from the squat. The man who had called himself Jayakrishna. Breen spotted Hibou again. The women were swaying from side to side, slightly self-conscious about being on stage. Jayakrishna, dressed in a long white collarless shirt, with beads draped around his neck, was at home there, being stared at by the crowd, a small smile on his face as the women danced on either side.

'I had a dream about Hibou,' said Tozer. 'I dreamed she was my sister.'

Tozer had told Breen about her sister only once. Two years younger than herself. She would have been sixteen, then.

'I didn't realise until I dreamed her how much she looked like Alexandra.'

He wondered if he should tell her that Hibou was the same age as Alexandra when she had been killed, too. 'What's he like – that one?' Breen pointed at Jayakrishna.

'He's sexy. Loads of charisma. He could have been a pop star or something. Apparently he used to be in the army.'

'Have you been going there a lot?' Breen said.

'I've been going there most evenings.'

Breen looked at her, puzzled.

The chanting was getting louder and faster. People were dancing more wildly now. Breen watched Hibou: nervous, eyes flicking from side to side, looking uncomfortable, embarrassed, but still swaying from side to side.

'You really learning to play guitar from them?'

'Sort of,' said Tozer. 'I was curious. Look at her.'

'Who?'

'Hibou. She's having sex with him.' She was looking straight ahead of her at the stage.

'Really?'

'Not just her. Other women too. It's a weird place. It's like they've got to fuck each other all the time, otherwise they're not, you know, free.' She made a face.

'She has sex with him? And she knows that the other women who go there have sex with him too?'

'Yes.'

The idea of it made him nauseous. Confused.

'You're sure.'

'Yes.'

'And have you had . . . ?'

'Fuck sake, Paddy.'

'You're just spying on the place?'

'Yes.'

'I thought you were really learning the guitar. I was worried there, for a sec.'

'I *am* actually learning the guitar. For your information. What's wrong with me playing guitar?'

'Krishna krishna, hare hare . . .' chanted the crowd.

Breen said, 'All I mean is that people are allowed to . . . have sex with whoever they like. I suppose it's none of our business.'

Tozer was getting agitated now. Shouting to make herself heard above the chanting. 'That's not what I'm on about.'

'What, then?'

They watched Hibou up on stage, a rabbit in the spotlight, trying to smile as one of the other men Breen recognised from the squat stood behind her and placed his hands on her hips as she danced.

'I think it's creepy, you know,' Tozer said. 'It's not because they want to. Not for the girls. It's that they bloody have to. Or they're *square*. Know what I mean? I couldn't do that. I couldn't think so little of myself.'

And Hibou danced, smiling nervously, looking down at the floor in front of her as the man behind her moved his hands up and down her body.

'The scary thing is they all think they're changing the world. They talk and argue all the time. They sit round till two o'clock in the morning talking crap. Capitalism. Jean-Luc Goddard. Stokely Carmichael. All that stuff. They're so idealistic. The Paradise Hotel is supposed to be like, I don't know, Shangri-La or something.'

Her eyes were fixed on Hibou up on stage.

'She's gorgeous, isn't she?' she said. 'I like her. She's really shy.'

'And you join in? The talking, I mean.'

The chanting was getting louder. More and more people were joining in.

'Kind of. I mean . . . it's not like I don't want the world to be different. They're just so stupid. Like, you and me, we know there are evil, twisted people out there. They think if you smoke loads of pot and fuck a lot all that will disappear. They're like . . . children.'

'Do they smoke drugs?'

Tozer rolled her eyes. 'God, Paddy. What do you think?'

Breen looked at her. 'Helen. If they're doing illegal things you shouldn't be there. It's crossing a line.'

Tozer kept her eyes on the stage. 'I'm not even going to be in the police anymore in, like, less than two weeks.'

A girl took her clothes off.

Right there, on the far side of the auditorium, she stood from her seat and pulled down her jeans, then lifted her black jumper over her head, then unbuttoned a shirt.

Why, Breen didn't know. A spontaneous, exultant gesture? A symbol of being free. A reaction in sympathy with the atavistic drumming and the chanting.

At first only a few people noticed, but soon the whole hall seemed to realise what was taking place. Men stood to get a better view.

'Did she take it all off?'

'Oh my God.'

All eyes had left the Hare Krishnas and the hippies now, and were looking at the girl. Pretty. Red-haired. An oddly unembarrassed smile on her face.

Somebody wolf-whistled.

'I love you,' shouted a man sitting behind them.

The girl beamed and waved. Free yourself and everything will be OK.

'Put your eyes back in your head,' said Tozer.

Breen sat down. 'She's not bad-looking, I'll grant her that,' he said.

'God's sake.'

It took the police less than a minute to start flooding into the hall, about eight or nine of them pushing past the people crowding in the aisles.

'Pigs!' someone shouted.

Was this the raid the revolutionary had been talking about? As they rushed down the aisle, people stood. The policemen hesitated, outnumbered, but only for a second. They pressed forward again.

Two rows behind the naked girl, another woman stood and started to pull a polo-neck over her head. Breen watched, bemused. Then a third started to undress. 'Arrest all of us!' she shouted. More women stood.

'Get 'em off!' shouted the man behind Breen.

Up on stage, Breen noticed the man who called himself Jayakrishna turning to Hibou and the other women. He was telling them something.

Hibou shook her head vigorously, but the other woman from the squat seemed to be less shy. She undid her wraparound skirt and dropped it to the stage, then pulled back her shirt and reached behind to remove her bra.

About half a dozen women were naked now – or naked from the waist up.

'Fascists!'

Now the policemen were at the first naked woman, trying to pull her out of her seat.

'Get lost, fuzz.'

A huge man in a denim jacket forced himself between the policeman and the naked woman.

'Hell's Angels,' someone said. 'They'll stop the pigs.'

'Fuck the police!'

Breen watched Hibou, fascinated. It was clear what was going on. Jayakrishna was ordering her to undress. Was she going to do it? Head down, blushing, Hibou hesitated for a second, then stepped out of her long cotton dress. Her legs were long and pale. Her head seemed to sink even further as she removed her shirt, then her bra, crossing her arms across her naked breasts. Some of the women were exultant, throwing their arms up, showing their bodies to the crowd. For Hibou it was almost an act of public humiliation.

'You going to get naked too, love?' A man in a green shirt leaned forward towards Tozer.

'Bog off,' said Tozer. 'What I want to know is why it's only the girls who are getting their clothes off.'

Next to Hibou, the other girl from the squat was smiling, breasts moving as she swayed from side to side. Hibou was trying to wipe her eyes with the back of her hand, not daring to move her arm too far from her bosom.

It had worked. People were cheering this spontaneous gesture of solidarity. The police had given up trying to arrest the naked woman now. They looked around. There were at least fifteen women now, mostly completely undressed, some in their knickers, others bare-chested. The policemen looked around, confused, waiting for instructions. They were lost. Uniformed men, faced with uniform undress. Their sense of order was melting. They had never had to deal with anything like this ever before.

'Get lost, Nazi stooges!'

'Pigs out!'

'Christ,' said Breen. 'This is hopeless.'

From the stage, Jayakrishna stood grinning at the police with contempt. Among the throng of Hare Krishnas and hippies, he was holding his arms, palms out, in front of him in a messianic gesture. See what power I have over you? And Hibou, standing miserably in only her knickers, socks and shoes, behind him.

'See?' said Tozer. 'Something's not right.'

'I don't know . . .' said Breen.

'That was so awful,' she said.

'Wasn't it?' said Breen. 'I feel sorry for those coppers . . .'

Tozer turned to him. 'Not for them, you twat!' she snapped. 'For her. For Hibou.'

After the chanting there was an interval. People milled around, a little disappointed.

'What if everyone did that when you were about to arrest them?' said Breen.

'You'd like that, wouldn't you?' said Tozer. 'I saw you looking at them.'

Breen looked around him and said, 'I don't see the point of all this. It's just embarrassing. Nothing's really going on, is it?'

But then a buzz went through the crowd. People began barging past to find their seats again. Breen and Tozer returned to the auditorium. People were craning their heads. At the back, people were standing to see what was going on.

'Who is it?'

Somebody said, 'It's the Beatles.'

A smattering of applause.

'Only John Lennon. Not the others.'

'Can you see him?' said Tozer.

Breen found himself trying to see what was going on. People at the back of the hall were standing up so they could get a clear view.

Far away, at the centre of the auditorium, a couple, holding hands, were walking to the stage.

'It's John and his Japanese bird,' said someone.

Breen had no idea at all what was going on. The Japanese woman was saying something into the microphone but her voice was very quiet and Breen couldn't hear it. And then she and John Lennon got under the large white sheet and sat there, out of view.

'What are they doing?'

'They're in a bag.'

'Why?'

'It's a protest.'

'How can you protest in a bag?'

'It's art.'

Breen watched the stage. A few people stood around the sheet that Lennon and the woman were under, but nothing was happening.

'I bet they're fucking,' a man said.

'I don't think so. It's not moving.'

'They might be. You don't know.'

Trying to see what was going on, Breen caught a glimpse of Hibou, now dressed again, pushing her way up the aisle towards them. A few wolf-whistles. 'You're beautiful,' someone shouted.

'Nice boobs.'

'Get them out again, darling.'

Hibou's face was still puffy with shame. Breen nudged Tozer and pointed.

'Hibou!' Tozer called.

The hippie girl looked around to see who was calling her name. She spotted Tozer and smiled shyly. 'Oh, God. Did you see me?'

Tozer said, 'Yes.'

'I was so embarrassed,' she said. 'Was everybody watching?'

Tozer stood and put her arm around her, 'Why did you do it, then?'

'Because . . .' began Hibou. 'Because otherwise that woman would have been arrested.'

'Did Jayakrishna tell you to do it?' asked Tozer.

'No,' she said. 'I did it because . . .'

'It looked like he told you to do it,' said Tozer.

'I mean, it was his idea,' Hibou said. 'He said I should do it. But I wanted to. God, I hope nobody took any photographs. I mean, what if my parents saw?'

'You don't have to do things just because he tells you to,' Tozer said.

Hibou blushed again, yanking herself away. 'It's not like that. I should go.' She turned, and for the first time saw Breen.

'Is he with you?' she said, shocked.

Tozer nodded.

'But he's a policeman. I saw him, on Monday. He was . . . Were you following me?'

Tozer looked at Breen with a frown on her face. 'Were you following her?'

'Kind of,' he said. 'I just noticed you, that's all.'

Tozer turned back to Hibou and said, 'Thing is, Hibou, I'm a police officer too.'

Hibou's eyes were wide again. Maybe that's why they named her after an owl. 'Are you lot spying on us?'

'It's not like that,' said Tozer. 'I'm just concerned.'

'I liked you,' she said, tears in her eyes.

'Hibou?'

The girl had turned and was pushing away from them, through the crowd.

'Hibou!' Tozer called again, and started forcing her way after her.

'Oi!' a man called out. 'Was you that girl with your thingies out up on stage? Let's have another gander.'

People laughed.

'Fuck off,' said Tozer.

'Chill out, lady,' said one man. 'We were only having fun.'

Tozer was faster than Hibou, not afraid of shoving hippies aside to get to her. Breen followed behind.

'Stop, Hibou!' Tozer's voice was sounding more desperate now. 'Please.'

She caught up, finally.

'You're not in any trouble. It's nothing bad. We just want to help.'

'I don't need help,' said Hibou.

'Wait,' said Tozer. 'I saw a guy selling some cakes just now. I'm starving. Aren't you?'

Hibou hesitated.

'They're macrobiotic. Paddy here's a big fan, aren't you? Come on.' Tozer took Hibou's arm and led her through the crowd.

Hibou followed, still looking wary. The man with the ginger cakes was still there.

Breen took out his wallet and found a ten-shilling note. 'Cool,' said the man. 'Only I haven't got any change.'

They sat cross-legged on the carpet, watching Hibou greedily stuff the cake into her face.

'It's cheek,' said Breen. 'Ten shillings for that.'

'Don't they feed you?' Tozer laughed, looking at the crumbs falling to Hibou's lap. 'You're eating like a refugee.'

'You know —' Breen squatted down next to Hibou — 'I've been thinking. Do your parents know where you are?'

The girl frowned.

'They probably want to know you're OK.'

Hibou hesitated. Then took another bite of cake.

'My parents don't love me,' she said.

'Don't they?' said Tozer.

'If they loved me they'd let me be me.'

'Did Jayakrishna tell you that, too?' said Breen. Hibou ignored him and carried on eating.

Tozer said, 'If I was a mother I'd want to know my daughter was OK. That's all. Just a message would do. She wouldn't have to know where I am.'

Hibou nodded. 'Jayakrishna says that they're dead to me. We shouldn't have nuclear families any more. That's bourgeois. We share the kids in our house. Padma has two children, but I look after them too.'

'Dead to you?' said Breen.

Tozer said, 'I argue with my parents sometimes. But they're still my mum and dad, know what I mean?'

Hibou started crying. 'But I don't want my mum and dad to know about me,' she said.

'She all right?' said the man behind the cake stall. 'Bad drugs?'

Breen glared at him and he backed off.

Tozer shuffled over across the carpet and put her arm around the girl. 'What's wrong?'

'Just don't.'

'Is it that you don't want them to know where you are? Or are you worried they'll be angry if they see you like this? That you've let them down in some way?'

The crying got worse.

Tozer said, 'You don't have to call them. I could call them for you. It's easy. Or write. Jayakrishna wouldn't have to know, either.'

Hibou looked up and said, 'Could I have another cake?'

Tozer laughed. 'Jesus. You're starving, aren't you?'

Breen said, 'Just give Helen their address. She'll drop them a postcard. No address or nothing.'

Tozer said, 'I had a sister who disappeared once, and my mum and dad were sick with worry.'

'Really?' said Hibou.

'They didn't sleep.' Raped and murdered. Left in a cold muddy ditch. Body gnawed by rats and foxes.

Hibou was crying again now, wiping her hands on her cheesecloth blouse. 'Will you write to them, then? Like you said.'

'Of course,' said Tozer. 'I'd be happy to.'

'Only promise . . .'

'I won't say anything about where you are.'

Breen butted in. 'Did a guy called Frankie ever come to the squat?'

'Frankie?'

'He lived in the house behind you.'

'You asked about him before.'

'He didn't come to the squat. You're sure about that?'

She shook her head. 'He might have done. All sorts of people come. You came.'

Breen said, 'Were you living there in July, when the police came to evict you?'

Hibou nodded.

'I don't understand. Why weren't you evicted?' Tozer asked.

'Jayakrishna used his special energy. That stopped them.'

'What?' said Breen. 'Special energy?'

'He has special energy. He channels it. He's an ascended being.'

'What's that?'

'Hibou!'

They turned. Jayakrishna was standing by the door to the stalls. 'What's this?'

'I'm eating cake,' she said, looking at the carpet.

'Who's he?' Jayakrishna was tall and muscular. Handsome and thick-jawed in a kind of Viking way. Tied around his wrist were different coloured pieces of cotton like the ones the woman had tried to tie onto Tozer.

'A friend of Helen's,' said Hibou.

'He's a bloody policeman, you idiot.' He strode over and yanked Hibou up by the arm.

'Don't hurt her,' said Tozer.

'Is this why you've been coming to the squat?' he demanded of Tozer. 'To spy on us?'

'You got something to hide?' said Tozer, standing.

'You can't touch us,' said Jayakrishna.

Tozer was standing nose to nose with him, eyes narrowed. Breen looked around. A crowd was gathering.

'Don't,' Breen told Tozer.

'What did the pigs want?' Jayakrishna said, glaring at Breen. 'What was he asking about?'

'Nothing. He wanted to buy me some cake. It's OK. It's macro-biotic,' Hibou said, holding it up. Jayakrishna put his arm around her.

'It's OK now,' he said. 'I'm here. No need to cry, babe.'

'She was fine,' said Tozer. 'We were just talking, OK?'

'You fucking people. Can't you see you've upset her?'

'I'm sorry,' said Hibou, crying again. 'I'm so sorry.'

'Come on.' He put his arm around her. 'We'll take care of you.'

'Course you will,' said Tozer. 'Remember what we said, Hibou.'

'Look out, everyone,' Jayakrishna was saying as he walked away, one arm round Hibou. 'They're undercover pigs. Those two there.'

And the crowd gaped at Breen and Tozer, muttering, with loathing in their eyes.

'Pigs.'

'Go home, fascists. This is our scene.'

'I didn't mean that to happen,' said Tozer. 'He'll take it out on her. I'm sure of it. She's scared of him.'

'She didn't look scared of him,' said Breen.

'Don't you know anything? Women are like that. They're scared of people and they love them at the same time.'

'Really?' said Breen.

'What's she doing that she's too ashamed to go home? You were following her, God's sake, Paddy.' Then, 'You been thinking there's a connection between the squat and Pugh?'

Breen said, 'Possibly. She's only sixteen, you know.'

Tozer said, 'Really? She told me she was eighteen.'

'Sixteen.'

Same as her sister was. 'How do you know that?'

Breen shook his head. 'It's true. I *was* following her. I saw her near the squat, and followed her to some clinic at University College. I got a glimpse of her records.'

'You're not supposed to be doing any of this.'

There were people glaring at them still. 'Pigs.'

Breen tried to ignore them.

Tozer said, 'What was she going to a clinic for? You think she's pregnant?'

He shook his head. 'I don't think so. There were more men there than girls.'

Tozer said, 'Oh, God. There's a dope clinic at University College. One of those drug clinics. You know. For junkies. Did she walk away with anything?'

'A paper bag.'

They looked at each other.

'No wonder she's ashamed of going home.'

'You can't go back there now, you know,' said Breen. 'Jayakrishna knows you're police.'

Tozer didn't say anything.

'Promise me you won't go back there.' said Breen.

By the time they returned to the stalls, the crowd were looking bored. The couple under the sheet still weren't doing anything.

In the upper circle, someone was starting a slow handclap.

'Bring back the naked girls!' a man shouted.

'Play some music.'

'Give us a bloody song. We paid.'

'What do you think they're doing under there?'

'Let's go. I've had enough,' said Tozer. 'This is shite. I'm in a really bad mood now.'

John Lennon and his Japanese girlfriend weren't even doing anything. Somebody booed, but was instantly silenced by a louder reply of hisses.

As they stood to leave, the man they'd seen with the revolutionary girl called Suzi jumped on stage next to Lennon and Yoko and held up a sign saying 'THE END OF THE WORLD IS AT HAND FOR SEVEN MILLION IN BIAFRA'. He started shouting, 'Do you care, John Lennon? Do you care?'

None of the people on stage knew what to do next. Like the police, everyone was confused about what was the right thing to do in a situation like this. Blind. Empty. Meaningless. Pointless. Unsure which way to go next. So they did nothing.

'Do you care?' shouted the protester.

The event was a shambles. People were hissing the protester: 'Shut up and sit down!'

'And a Merry Christmas to you,' said Tozer as they walked out into the drizzle.

He got off the bus at Kingsland High Street, glad to be back in east London. The kindness and cruelty were familiar. At least you knew where you stood.

He stopped in the doorway of an ironmonger to tie a loose shoelace. When he stood and moved on again, he was conscious of another person several doorways down the street. A policeman's instincts.

He carried on walking. Was someone following him?

At his flat, he hesitated before putting the key in the door. With no street lights the cul-de-sac was black, but he thought he heard something moving among the rubbish that was piled up there. Heart thumping now. Should have done more press-ups.

'Who's there?' he said, holding his key in one hand. He peered into the blackness, trying to accustom his eyes to it.

Nobody moved.

'I can see you,' he said. 'Come out of there.'

This time there was a rustling. Just cats? Or rats?

Keeping one eye on the black space, he felt for the keyhole and found it. The moment he opened the door he put the light on, expecting to see at least the outline of some lurking man, but there was nobody there at all. The same leafless buddleia bushes growing out of a crack in the tarmac. The same rusting motorbike engine. A black MG. The same pile of rubbish swept into the corner by the wind.

He took a torch and walked out to where he had seen, or imagined, the man. There was what could have been a footprint in the dirt by the far wall. Or maybe it was just his head playing stupid tricks.

He went inside, closed the front door and leaned back against it.

The bizarre circus at the Albert Hall, and the sense that he was still being pursued, left him rattled. Instead of going to bed, he sat back at the kitchen table to look through the notebooks yet again. Turning pages.

At around two in the morning he was running his index finger down the page of notes he had made at Johnny Knight's house.

A list of dates when each of his letters had been sent.

He stared at the numbers on the paper.

Christ.

How had he missed that? He checked again.

Christ.

Jesus, Jesus, Jesus, Jesus Christ.

He took the sketch of the burnt man off the wall and laid it next to the photograph of Johnny Knight. How had he not seen that before? If he still had his original notes he would have checked the date, but he knew it well enough.

He leaned down and banged his head against the small kitchen table, then lifted it again and looked at his watch. Twelve minutes past two. He wished he could tell someone.

He wanted to talk to Tozer, but she would be asleep in a single bed in a shared room in the women's section house. His mind whirred.

TWENTY-FIVE

Last night, when he had finally gone to bed, Breen had dreamed of
naked women. An army of them removing their clothes in front
of him, exposing naked flesh. Bosoms of all sizes and shapes. Their
bareness terrifying.

He had woken in the small hours, aroused and disturbed, unable to
return to sleep. Though he had been in bed only a couple of hours,
he had dressed and come to the police station early to meet Inspector
Bailey. He had to talk to him now.

When he arrived at the station, the front desk was deserted. A phone
ringing, unanswered. Undrunk tea still steaming on the desk.

Something was wrong. The entire ground floor was empty.

'Hello?' called Breen.

No answer. Then he heard murmuring voices.

He walked down the corridor until he came to the stairs down to the
cells. He descended. A small crowd of coppers was standing outside
one of the cells.

'What happened?' asked Breen.

'I just came in and found him like that,' said the constable.

The man laid out on the cold floor could have been only about
eighteen or nineteen years old. He had on a check flannel shirt, with
a small gold crucifix around his neck, and his thin, dark, scrawny hair
had been brushed down over his forehead.

'What was he in for?'

'Drunk and dis.'

The constable was kneeling beside the dead man. Drunk and disorderlies often got into punch-ups with coppers. Breen noticed the damp flannel in the constable's hand.

'What the hell are you doing?' asked Breen.

The constable was one of the old-school men, about ten years older than Breen, lined face and a bruiser's hands. 'Bit of spit and polish. You wouldn't want his relatives having to see him looking bad.'

'What do you mean, "bad"?' Breen said, striding forward and yanking the flannel out of the constable's hand.

'Steady on,' said the constable.

'That's tampering.'

Breen knelt too and reached out his hand. The chill of skin was always a shock. The man had been dead for hours. Breen pushed back the long dark hair and saw the thick line of colour under his hairline.

'Drunk, you say?'

'Mad,' said the constable.

'And so a couple of coppers gave him a going over?'

'Course not,' said the copper.

'And didn't anybody check on him?'

He looked around. There were at least ten constables now looking back down at him.

'What are you doing, Paddy? Leave him alone.'

'What happened when he was brought in?' There was a pile of cold sick in the corner of the room.

'This isn't your business, Paddy. It's nothing to do with you.'

Breen was undoing the man's check shirt.

'You're not even supposed to be in here. I heard you were suspended.'

There were more bruises on the man's chest.

'He was just drunk, that's all. Leave it to us, Paddy.' Breen heard a note of hostility creeping into the voices around him.

'Paddy?'

Breen turned. Jones was standing at the door of the cell.

'Paddy? What the fuck are you doing?'

'There's a dead man, Jonesy. We're supposed to investigate when that happens.'

'Not you, Paddy. You're not even on the force right now, remember?'

Breen started to loosen the man's trousers.

'I was there, Paddy,' said Jones. 'He was roaring. Probably fell over and banged his head.'

Breen stopped and turned. 'You? You were there?' His voice too loud.

People started chipping in their own opinions. 'He took a slug at us, didn't he?'

'Out of order.'

Breen picked up the boy's right hand. The fingers lay in odd directions, as if they had been broken.

Jones came and grabbed Breen's shoulder, tugging him backwards. 'Leave this alone, Paddy. You're making a mistake.'

Other men were around Breen now. He felt hands grabbing him under his armpits, ready to yank him upwards.

Abruptly, the voices went quiet.

'Let me through.'

Inspector Bailey.

'Shit,' someone muttered behind Breen. The hands under Breen's armpits relaxed.

'What's going on?' Bailey demanded.

Breen turned to see the inspector pushing through the crowd at the doorway of the cell. He too looked down at the dead man.

'Dear God,' he said. There was silence. A shuffling of feet. 'Who brought this man in?'

There was silence.

'Who arrested this man?'

'Don't know, sir,' somebody muttered. 'It'll be in the book.'

'What happened to him?'

Again silence.

'Nothing, sir.'

Bailey's face reddened. 'Don't give me that. I asked a question and I expect a bloody answer!'

'He was drunk. Maybe he just fell over, sir?'

'What are you doing here, Sergeant Breen? You're not even supposed to be in this building.'

'I just arrived, sir,' said Breen. 'A minute before you. I came in to have a word with you, sir.'

'What happened to this man, Paddy?'

'He has a bruise here, sir,' Breen said pointing to his head. 'And he was sick at some point during the night.'

There was a quiet hissing in the room.

'Silence!' shouted Bailey angrily. 'I won't have this. A man is dead. In our police station. I want to know why.'

Somebody muttered, 'One less bugger to worry about.'

'What?' demanded Bailey. 'Who said that?'

Breen had never seen Bailey this angry. A man usually cool under fire. A veteran of worse than this. But his face was crimson, his eyes wide. He twitched his head sideways. 'A man is dead. You are not a bunch of schoolboys caught smoking behind the sheds. I want to know what happened here!'

People at the back of the throng he'd pushed through started to drift away.

'Jones?' said Bailey. 'What do you know?'

'Me, sir? I just got here. Like Paddy.'

Breen stood. Bailey looked suddenly tired. He sat down heavily onto the small cell bed.

'You OK, sir?'

Bailey nodded. 'Could you fetch me a glass of water?'

The crowd that had come down to see the dead body had more or less vanished back upstairs.

'This violence . . .' said Bailey.

'I'll get you some water,' Breen said. He followed the retreating policemen up to the pantry on the ground floor behind the front desk. Looking around for a clean glass he heard someone muttering, 'Stupid cunt. None of Bailey's beeswax anyway.'

By the time he made it back down to the cells with the glass of water, Bailey was lying on the cell bed, his face white and sweaty.

'Sir? What's wrong?' said Breen.

'Chest,' he said. He closed his eyes.

Breen watched the inspector's eyelids flicker, his mouth twitched.

'Get a bloody ambulance!' shouted Breen.

A young constable said, '. . . Else there'll be two stiffs down here.'

'Procedures . . .' Bailey whispered.

'What, sir?'

Bailey breathed slowly in and out, his skin like paper. 'It'll pass,' he said.

Breen sat by Bailey until the ambulance men arrived, looking from one man to the next. One of them was breathing, anyway. Was it a heart attack? What were you supposed to do when this happened?

A sergeant stared round the door. 'He going to be OK?'

Bailey's face was grey now.

The ambulance was quick, at least. The stretcher-men came clattering down the steps. 'Blimey,' said one of them, peering into the cell. 'Two for the price of one. What's been going on down here?'

'Don't ask,' said one of the coppers.

A pair of them took a corner of the stretcher with the ambulance men, keen to see Bailey out of the building. Breen followed their slow progress up the stone stairs and out.

That would be the end of Bailey's career, he thought. Carried out of the building on his back. What a way to go. Twenty-two years on the force and you leave on a stretcher.

★

Breen went upstairs to the CID office.

Jones was alone there. The office was gloomy. One of the neon tubes had finally gone. Jones had made himself a cup of tea and now sat at his desk holding it, staring Breen in the eye as he crossed the room.

'Write it down,' Breen told him.

'You shouldn't even be here, Paddy. You're not supposed to even come to the station any more.'

'Write down exactly what happened last night.'

Jones said, 'Not much point. It happens sometimes, don't it? Besides, I don't really remember. I'd had a few in the Louise.' He looked nervy, shaking slightly.

Breen said, 'For your own good, let alone anyone else's.'

Marilyn arrived, taking off her scarf. 'Oh, Paddy.' She smiled. 'What's going on? There's an ambulance outside.'

Breen said to Jones, 'Write it down. Call Wellington. Make sure a doctor sees him before anybody moves him.'

'You can't tell me what to do,' said Jones. 'You don't even work here right now.' And he took a sip from his tea, still staring at Breen.

'What's wrong?' said Marilyn. 'Why's everybody down in the basement? What did you come in for anyway, Paddy?'

Jones forced a smile and said, 'Bloody hell, Marilyn. Is that actually a skirt?'

'Why? What do you think it is?'

Jones said, 'More of a necktie that slipped down a bit. Not that I mind a bit of leg. Bailey wouldn't like it though. Not that he'll be that bothered now.' A giggle.

Marilyn hung her coat on a hook.

'I'll kill you one of these days, Jonesy.' She stopped. 'What do you mean, all that about Bailey? Where is he, anyway?'

'Haven't you heard? I think he just took early retirement. That was him in the ambulance.'

Marilyn thumped down in her chair, mouth open. 'Oh my God.'

'Heart attack,' said Jones.

'We don't know if it's a heart attack yet,' said Breen.

'That's awful,' said Marilyn.

'Isn't it?' said Jones.

Marilyn frowned. 'You shouldn't sound so bloody pleased about it.'

'Who said I was pleased?'

Breen looked at him. 'Call Wellington. Now.'

'That's the duty officer's job, not mine,' said Jones.

Breen went up to him and stood nose to nose. 'You were there when the dead man was brought in. You've got to make sure it's done by the book.'

'He was steamboats. Fighting drunk. Everyone saw. We got nothing to worry about.'

'What dead man?' said Marilyn. 'My God! Come on, you two. Break it up.'

Breen said, 'Otherwise people will start to think you're trying to cover something up.'

Jones stood. 'You don't want to come in here accusing me of stuff like that. You weren't even there.' He sat down in his chair. 'I tell you what I *am* going to write down. That you're here right now against orders.'

'Boys,' said Marilyn. 'Come on. What's all this about a dead man?'

'A drunk in the cells, that's all,' said Jones.

Breen turned away from Jones and said, 'Is Constable Tozer coming in?'

'Poor old Bailey,' she said. 'Here at the station?'

'Just now. Keeled right over.'

'What about Tozer?' asked Breen again.

'She's in late. Told me she had an appointment at the doctor's this morning,' said Marilyn. 'Has anybody called Bailey's wife yet?'

Breen looked at Jones. 'No,' he said.

'Typical,' said Marilyn. And she started looking through her index cards for Bailey's home number.

Breen said, 'What's Tozer doing at the doctor's, anyway?'

'Bet she's up the duff,' said Jones.

'Keep your dirty thoughts to yourself,' said Marilyn. 'Don't talk about stuff like that.'

'God's sake, woman. I was only joking.'

'Well, it's not funny. Nothing you ever say is bloody funny.'

'What's got into everybody?' said Jones.

'Bailey's had a bloody heart attack and you're acting like a bloody pillock.'

'Think about it, though,' said Jones. 'I mean, she's leaving the force, in't she? Bet she's knocked up.'

Breen said, 'She's leaving the force to look after the family farm.'

'That's what she says,' said Jones. 'She would, wouldn't she?'

'I mean . . . Could be anyone's, the way she puts it about,' muttered Marilyn. 'Not that I'm saying anything. What do you want to see her for anyway, Paddy?' She picked up the telephone.

'Oh, Paddy,' said Jones. 'You should see your face. Is there something you should be telling us?'

'Will you shut up for once in your life, Jonesy,' said Marilyn. 'I'm about to phone Bailey's wife.'

And Jones was finally silent.

Breen picked up his coat. As he left, he heard Marilyn say, 'Mrs Bailey?' And Breen was thinking: They had only spent one night together, but what if . . . ? They had been drunk. They hadn't used anything.

He walked away from the station. Jones had been right. He was not supposed to be there. He had come to the station to talk to Bailey; Bailey was in hospital now, possibly fighting for his life. He would not be back.

The cold wind blew into Breen's bones. His feet were ice. He stamped to keep the blood flowing to his toes, thinking of the man in the cells, cold on concrete, and Bailey turning pale in the cell below the pavements. Then stopped stamping because his right foot was sore again.

People were going to work, heads down into the wind. The last few worn-down days before the Christmas holidays. A man at the bus stop struggled with a copy of the *Express*. 'SOVIETS TEST NEW NUCLEAR DEVICE'. Breen's eyes were on the entrance to the police station, watching the last of the late-night shift leave, and the morning latecomers ambling in. A man in overalls was slowly wheeling a bicycle up to the front door. He seemed to be struggling with it. After a couple of seconds, Breen figured out why: the front wheel was buckled into a heart shape. A broken wheel. Breen guessed he was coming to the station to report some kind of accident. The usual to-and-fro of an ordinary morning.

There would be a broken mother: 'My boy wouldn't do that. Liked a drink, maybe, but wouldn't do that . . .' Suspecting the worst, police closing ranks to look after their own. Like Jones said, it happened all the time.

Abandoning the doorway he had been standing in, he went to a phone box around the corner and fed in a threepenny bit.

'Marilyn? Is Tozer there yet?'

'Paddy? Where did you go to?'

'I'm not supposed to be in the office. I had to get out. Is Tozer back?'

'Not a whiff of her. She should have been in yonks ago. If she's going to be out all morning she should bloody call, shouldn't she?' Marilyn lowered her voice. 'I spoke to Bailey's wife. She cried and everything. What happened, Paddy? Bloody hell.'

'Maybe you should ask Jones about that.'

'I know he's a bit difficult, Bailey, but he's a good man. No one here seems that bothered about it, though.' She was whispering now. 'It's almost as if they're glad it happened. And that bloke who died. I mean . . . Right here. Where I work. That shakes you up a bit.'

A schoolboy in cap and shorts, knees red from the cold, was being dragged along the pavement by a heavily pregnant woman. He was scuffing his shoes, snivelling about something. Breen watched the woman struggling with the child and with the weight in her belly.

'I mean,' Marilyn was saying, 'everyone knows we rough people up a bit. It's only to be expected . . .'

It would be typical of Tozer to have kept it to herself. Breen thought about being a father. What it would be like to be a father? His own father. Distant. Well-meaning. Stuffy. A formal handshake at the school gates in front of all the giggling boys. The smell of shaving soap.

She would probably want an abortion, he supposed. Like Pugh's women. They were legal now, after all. How did it work? How did they kill it? Men knew so little. He imagined shiny surgical instruments. Huge syringes sucking blood and membrane. He was engulfed by a very Catholic sense of horror that he did not even know he was capable of until that moment.

'Paddy?' said Marilyn. 'You still there? I worry about you, Paddy. Are you coping on your own? You didn't look so good this morning.'

But the pips went.

'No more change,' said Breen, though he still had more in his pocket.

After he'd replaced the receiver he watched the pregnant woman and her boy through the dirty glass of the phone box. They were standing on the edge of the pavement, still searching for a gap in the morning traffic.

He watched them cross the road, the mother still pulling the boy along behind her. When they reached the opposite pavement he spotted Tozer, just a few yards away from them, striding towards the police station.

He called her name across the busy road.

She paused. Looked around a second, then walked on, as if thinking she must have imagined it.

Breen ran into the road. A man on a motorbike swerved, swearing at him. A coach, coming slowly the other way, blocked his view of her. By the time it had gone she had disappeared.

He stood on the pavement, looking left and right. She finally emerged from a newsagent, unwrapping a new packet of Juicy Fruit.

'Paddy?' She smiled. 'What are you doing here?'

'I think I figured out what happened to Johnny Knight,' he said.

'Come to the canteen,' she said. 'I'll get you a coffee. You look frozen.'

'I can't,' he said. 'I'm not supposed to be there. I need to talk. You got a minute?'

'I'm doing naff all,' she said. 'They don't give me anything worth doing.'

They walked to Manchester Square, grey but for the lights from the modern office block on the north-east corner.

'See that?' She nodded towards the north-west side of the square. 'That's the Beatles' record company.' There was a commissionaire standing on the door to shoo out any fans who tried to get in. 'I used to dream of seeing that,' she said.

Moving through the square, they headed towards a large red house at the north side of the square, a dusty public art gallery that had survived from the last century. All the time he'd worked in Marylebone, Breen had never even realised it was here. They found the warmest room, huge, with faded red silk wallpaper and dozens of paintings in curly gilt frames. Heat pouring from the big cast-iron radiators.

'What?' said Tozer.

It took a while for Breen to stop shivering. 'You remember when we broke into Johnny Knight's house?'

He held up a notebook and pointed to a date in it – '11 September 1968' – and a note: 'Second class'.

'See?'

She looked at him. 'No.'

He rubbed his stiff fingers on the metal of the radiator. 'It was the oldest postmark on the letters.'

'So?'

'The eleventh is two days before my father died. Don't you get it?'

She frowned. 'I don't see what this has got to do with your father, Paddy.'

He was not explaining things properly. He tried again. 'The oldest letter tells us when Johnny Knight was last at his house.'

'I'm lost, Paddy.'

A woman attendant came into the gallery and glared at them, then sat in a small wooden chair against the opposite wall.

'If a second-class letter was posted on the eleventh, it would have arrived on the thirteenth, right? The day my father died.'

Breen's fingers were aching now. He pulled them away and blew on them.

'So Johnny Knight didn't come home on the thirteenth?'

'That's it.'

The woman opposite them reached below and pulled knitting out of a bag.

'The dead man in Carlton Vale,' said Breen.

It took three or four seconds. 'God,' said Tozer. The burnt man.

The woman with the knitting tutted. Her needles started to flick from side to side. Click-clack, click-clack.

'But that's just coincidence. I mean . . . You can't know it was Johnny Knight. He just disappeared on the same day.'

A party of schoolchildren burst into the room in blazers and grey cloth caps, nattering to each other.

'No talking.' The teacher, a thin woman in tweed, scolded her charges. They fell silent. '*The Laughing Cavalier* by Frans Hals,' she announced. 'See how his eyes follow you around the room?'

'Three things,' Breen told Tozer. 'One. Wellington said there was concrete dust on the man's trousers. I'd always assumed he was a labourer. But quantity surveyors work on building sites, don't they?'

'Miss?' said one of the children. 'That man in the picture is wearing a dress.'

'Silence,' ordered the teacher.

'Two,' said Breen. 'I was put on the case with Prosser. But Prosser warned me off it. He told me not to waste my time on it. Whenever I tried to investigate it he nudged me away.'

'Everyone told you to let it go, Paddy. Not just Prosser. We were worried you were going mental about the case 'cause of your dad.'

The schoolchildren were sitting cross-legged on the floor with their exercise books and pencils now.

'I know, and that's true, but Prosser was really angry. And then there's the third thing. If you were a copper and you killed someone, what would be the easiest way to get rid of a body?'

'Bloody hell.'

The schoolchildren looked up. One pointed at Tozer and said, 'Miss, she did a bad word.'

'I said, silence!'

Tozer hunched across and whispered, 'You think he killed Johnny Knight on D Division turf so he could make sure the investigation got nowhere?'

Breen nodded.

Tozer reached into her handbag and scrambled around for a packet of cigarettes. 'You have a light?'

Breen shook his head.

'This is mad,' said Tozer. 'So Prosser killed him and burned him so bad maybe no one would know. And we were working alongside him all that time?'

'I don't know. It's a theory, that's all.'

Tozer held up a cigarette and said to the teacher, 'Excuse me? Do you have a light?'

The teacher frowned and said, 'Absolutely not. One minute to finish your drawings.' The sound of pencils.

Tozer called to the attendant across the heads of the children. 'How about you?'

The attendant scowled. 'No smoking,' she said.

'Jesus.'

Breen watched one of the boys scritching the pencil across the page, angrily crossing out his drawing. He had loved drawing as a boy. He had spent hours sketching comics in his room, or doing portraits of his friends in return for sweets.

'Stand,' ordered the teacher. The children stood. 'Follow me.'

And they were gone. The room was quiet again, except for the clicking of the attendant's needles.

'What are we going to do about it?' said Tozer.

Breen liked the 'we'. 'I had been going to tell Bailey. That way, at least, there would have been a record. But he's just been taken to hospital. He had a heart attack this morning.'

'Christ. He ok?'

'I don't know.'

'Great timing,' she said.

'As usual.'

Tozer said, 'Bailey wouldn't have done anything, mind. He wouldn't touch anything that made the police look bad.'

'I think you underestimate him.'

'It's kind of beside the point, now, anyway.'

'From the letters we found at the house, Johnny Knight had worked for Morton, Stiles and Prentice. I know the man he was working for,' said Breen. 'I met him at a party once.'

'You go to parties?'

'I was thinking of going to talk to him.'

'This is all for Scotland Yard. You've got to tell them.'

'I know. I'm going to,' he said.

He read the black-and-gilt painted label on a frame. *The Adoration of the Shepherds*. Jesus lying on straw. The shepherds around him, big-eyed and awestruck. A baby and a mother.

Tozer said, 'Something else. I think I know where Shirley Prosser is.'

'How?'

'I thought you'd be interested,' she said. 'I was thinking, What if Charlie has to see a doctor on account of his spastic thing? So I checked the numbers from that address book you gave me. And I was right.'

'God,' said Breen. 'That's why you went to see a doctor this morning?'

'How did you know?' she said.

'Marilyn said. I thought . . .'

'What?'

'Nothing.'

'No. Go on. You're looking weird.'

Breen said, 'Jones thought you were pregnant.'

'What?'

'That's why you were at the doctor.'

Tozer's eyes widened. 'Oh my God. They said that? I'm so embarrassed. Just Jones?'

'Marilyn was there too. I shouldn't have said anything to you about it.'

'And so you thought . . . ?'

'Yes. I'm sorry.'

'Jesus, Paddy. I mean. Bloody hell! How humiliating. Everybody talking about me like that.'

Breen apologised again.

'That's horrible.'

Tozer squinted back at him for a second, then explained. Two days ago Shirley Prosser had rung up her old doctor to ask to transfer to a new GP. 'The doctor hadn't wanted to tell me at first, but I told his secretary it was a murder investigation. It is, isn't it?'

Breen nodded. Was he actually disappointed that she wasn't pregnant? He had the obscure feeling that something had been taken from him that he hadn't known he'd even had.

'So she gave me her new GP's address,' said Tozer.

'Did you call him?'

She shook her head. 'I was worried about scaring Shirley off. If she knows we're looking for her, she might scarper again.'

'You shouldn't leave, you know,' he said. 'You're too good at this.'

She smiled. 'What's up with you?'

'Nothing,' he said. 'Where is it? The place where she's gone.'

'Margate. That's Kent, isn't it? I was thinking I could give the local coppers a call. They could get the address off the GP, without letting her know. They won't have to know what it's about. I'll just say it's a routine family thing. Women Police stuff. Policemen would never ask what. They hate Women Police work.'

'Good,' said Breen. 'Really good.'

'I've never been to Margate. I hear it's nice. What are you looking at?'

He was looking at the painting. Sentimental crap, really. Old men looking weepy and awestruck at the baby. He looked closer.

'The brushwork,' he said. 'It's amazing.' And now he looked closer, he realised it was. Gorgeous. Uninhibited. Free strokes of a hand that worked on this, what, four hundred years ago?

She squinted at it. 'That sheep looks like a Cheviot to me,' she leaned forward. 'I always fancied Cheviots. Well? What about it then? I got the day off on Saturday. We could go. Both of us.'

Click-clack, click-clack, went the knitting needles.

'Saturday is the Christmas Ball,' he said.

'Well, I wasn't thinking of staying overnight,' she said, grinning. 'I'm not that kind of girl.'

TWENTY-SIX

The sign was working again now, though jerkily. Breen could hear the machinery creaking.

Breen walked past the big revolving triangle, through the revolving door, into the lobby of New Scotland Yard. He never liked this place. It made him feel anxious just being here. The front desk was run by three women wearing telephone headsets who sat in a line at a desk, all staring at him as he approached.

Unsure of which of them he was supposed to be talking to, he picked one and said, 'I need to see Detective Sergeant Deason, CID.'

The woman ignored him. The one on her left picked up a telephone and dialled. 'Name?'

Breen waited, standing by the desk. Men, some in uniform, others in plain clothes, emerged from lifts, walking with a sense of purpose, talking loudly, laughing. Breen checked his watch.

'Will he be long?' he asked.

'Don't know,' said the receptionist.

He took out a cigarette. Put it back in the packet. Bent down, tied his shoelaces a little tighter. As he was bending, someone thumped him on the back.

'Paddy? You finally coming to join us here?' Big John Carmichael, slim panatella in hand, with another member of the Drug Squad. 'I just heard about Bailey. Bloody hell.'

Breen, smiled, straightened up, shook Carmichael's hand. 'I don't think he'll be coming back in a hurry.'

'Poor bastard.'

'You never liked him in the first place.'

Carmichael's companion headed towards the lift, leaving the two of them together.

'I never said that, Paddy. Jesus. Can't I just feel sorry for him? You heard the latest? Rumour is, they already marked Creamer down as your new boss. From Maida Vale.'

Breen said, 'Inspector Creamer?' A Rotarian. Probably a Freemason too. Liked a tidy desk. There were stories he liked to make his bobbies Turtle Wax his car during their shifts.

'You're best out of it,' said Carmichael. 'What are you doing here anyway?'

Breen explained, without saying too much, that he had come to meet the detective in charge of Prosser's murder. He had what he thought was new evidence.

Breen said, 'While you're there I have something for you, John. A squat in Abbey Gardens. I think maybe it was them who got the drugs to Francis Pugh. I think they may be selling on prescriptions there.'

'Pugh. The dead bloke?'

'Something else. The squat was about to be evicted in the summer. Guess what? Out of the blue, the eviction was called off.'

'You need to go a bit slower, Paddy. You're talking too fast.'

'I just think somebody is pulling strings, somehow. There's more to it . . .'

A long pull on the mini-cigar. Carmichael, oldest friend and playground pal, said nothing, just watched Breen with a frown on his face.

Breen said, 'So you'll check into the house? Just take a look? You know what to look for. I can't do this myself. I'm suspended.'

Carmichael curled his lip. He looked older, thought Breen. His face fatter than it had been, eyes redder. Maybe it was just seeing him in daylight. Maybe the pints and chasers for lunch.

Carmichael carefully stubbed out the panatella in an ashtray on a stand by the lift doors and put the unsmoked half back in the tin. 'I can't make any promises, Paddy. I'm the new boy in the Drug Squad. I have to check with my superiors first.'

'But it's worth a look, isn't it?'

Carmichael said, 'You should be putting your feet up. This isn't even your responsibility anymore. What you doing for Christmas anyway?'

Before Breen had a chance to answer, the receptionist called out loudly, 'Breen? Someone from Detective Sergeant Deason's team will see you now. Third floor, turn left out of the lift.'

'Do you know Deason?' Breen asked.

Carmichael shook his head. 'Never heard of him. Are you all right?'

'I'm fine, John. Fine.'

'I'll see what I can do. One day we'll catch up properly, yes?'

'Yes. We should do that.'

Carmichael turned up the collar of his coat. 'What about you and me go out one evening? Find a couple of birds. Not that scrawny one, Tozer. Some really nice ones. I know a couple.'

'I thought you liked Tozer?'

'Deal then? You and me? Night on the town?'

Neither of them named a date though.

'I have to go,' Breen said, and walked quickly away from his friend.

Deason's desk was in a large open-plan room. Breen sat on a plastic chair, opposite a police constable with a notebook. It turned out that Deason was away. He had been off sick for a week. 'Hong Kong flu,' said the constable. 'Loads of us have had it. Going down like bloody skittles.'

The constable held a cigarette and a pencil in the same hand, alternately making notes and smoking. Breen kept thinking he was going to poke the pencil into his eye every time he took a pull. 'So you're saying you think Shirley Knight's brother-in-law disappeared the same day as this body appeared on your turf?'

Breen nodded. 'So who's running the investigation while Sergeant Deason's absent?'

The constable ignored him. 'And you're guessing that Sergeant Prosser had something to do with it?'

'Yes,' said Breen. 'It's a guess.'

The constable said, 'What if the dead body's not him? You checked?'

'You need to find Johnny Knight's dental records. You need to request our police surgeon to do that. I can't. I'm suspended. The sooner you do that, the sooner we can rule that out.'

The constable nodded. Pursed his lips. 'You are admitting you broke into a house without a warrant while you were supposed to be suspended?'

The constable was pudgy and expressionless. He took another puff from his cigarette.

'I don't like sitting on my hands,' said Breen.

'I wouldn't mind sitting on my hands for a bit. Chance would be a bloody fine thing round here. We're rushed off our feet. Shouldn't have been doing that, though.' The constable leaned across the desk and winked. 'Tell you what, though, I won't tell if you won't,' he said, and burst out laughing.

Breen said, 'So what are you going to do?'

The constable smiled. 'We'll look into it.'

'Today?'

'Right away. Leave it to us.' Breen watched him open a drawer and put the sheet of paper he'd been writing on into it. 'Don't you worry. Go back and put your feet up, lucky bugger.'

The lift squealed as it descended, but nobody seemed to notice how bad the noise was.

Breen woke up and wrote the details of his nightmare in his police notebook. This time the naked women had knives.

Breen hated knives. He had seen men sliced up after fights so badly their organs showed, vague and pale beneath the skin. He had seen the blood pumping out of men on pub floors. Once, not so long ago, a Chinese burglar he'd disturbed had pulled a huge kitchen knife on him and Breen had turned and fled, hiding outside, shaking like a baby. 'Breen is windy,' people had said.

The details of the dream evaporated as he wrote them down. He couldn't remember if he'd escaped or not.

He caught the bus out west. Morton, Stiles & Prentice's offices were just north of Oxford Street. A sleek, newly built modern block.

There was a Christmas tree in reception. Beneath, neatly wrapped, were piles of boxes, all the same size, all neatly wrapped in red foil paper.

'Who are they for?' asked Breen.

'No one. They're all empty.'

'What's the point of that?' asked Breen.

'Do you have an appointment?' said the woman on the reception desk. In her late twenties, she sat beneath an enormous beehive hairdo.

'No,' said Breen. He handed over his warrant card. The reception room was surrounded by big glass walls. An enormous orange lampshade hung from a wire in the middle of the lobby.

'Oooh,' said the woman. 'I hope Mr Cox hasn't been naughty.'

'I hope so too,' said Breen. The woman's eyes grew bigger.

She dialled a number and spoke for a minute. 'He can spare ten minutes in about an hour,' said the Beehive.

If he'd been doing a legitimate investigation, Breen would have insisted on seeing him now. But he was chancing it just coming here. So he looked at his watch and said, 'OK.' Nothing better to do.

He had done what he was supposed to do: told Scotland Yard what he knew. Or rather, what he thought he knew.

He killed time walking up and down Oxford Street, dawdling by shop windows. He had been a teenager in the 1950s. In those days there had been nothing in shops. Now they were full of the latest fads and fashions. Eight-track cassette player for Dad. Airfix model aeroplanes for boys. Miners, the make-up for girls. So much stuff. Down past Gamages. Outside, a couple of coppers were stopping the traffic while a team of men from the council climbed the lamp posts to fix the Christmas lights. A big model railway train in the department store window weaving in and out of tunnels in some imaginary Alpine scene.

The wind was bitter. After half an hour wandering the streets he returned to the lobby. The Beehive regarded him with a curious look. 'You're early, Sergeant,' she said.

There was a coffee table with magazines and newspapers. *Architects' Journal.* A copy of *Nova* with a woman showing bare breasts through a gauze top. He picked it up and looked at it until he realised that Beehive Woman was looking at him with a small smirk on her face.

Breen turned the magazine over.

A minute later her phone rang. 'He'll see you now,' she said.

Harry Cox had an office on the third floor; the desk was a little too large for it. A bookshelf full of bound copies of *Architectural Review*. Today Harry Cox wore a blue suit with a bright orange tie.

'Do I know you?' said the man nervously. He seemed to be trying to place Breen. 'You're with the police?'

'I met you at a party, once,' said Breen. 'At Kasmin's gallery. You bought a picture.'

There was a Roy Lichtenstein print on the office wall and opposite, on a wall that was almost too small to hold it, one of the geometric paintings he had seen at Kasmin's.

'The art critic.' Harry Cox smiled, leaning forward to shake Breen's hand, confident now he knew they knew each other. Everything would be fine. 'I remember. Which force are you from? Remind me?'

'Marylebone CID.' Breen sat down in a modern plastic chair. 'Have you bought any more art?'

'Just starting out.' He laughed. 'I remember now. You're a pal of Robert Fraser's, aren't you? He thought highly of your opinions. Hope

you don't mind me saying, but his stuff's a little too out there for me.'
He opened a drawer, pulled out a cigar box on his desk, and held it out.
'I invited you to the rugby. Couldn't you make it?'

'Sorry,' said Breen.

Harry Cox waved his hand. 'I have bought a few pictures. You
should see my collection. You'll probably think it's rubbish. Interested
to know what you think. See if I was right buying them. Perhaps you
should come round to my place. Do you like that fellow Hockney? I'm
extremely keen. Are you? Lovely sense of colour. Really fresh. Ever
met him? Just back from a spell in Los Angeles. I would like to meet
him if you ever—'

Breen interrupted. 'Do you know a quantity surveyor called Johnny
Knight?'

Cox's head twitched sideways, just a fraction of an inch. 'What is
this about?'

'Mr Knight has gone missing. We are anxious to talk to him.'

Harry Cox blinked. 'Knight? Yes. He has done work for us over the
years. Why? Is anything wrong?'

Breen said, 'I'm not sure. Is there?'

'I can't say I've seen him for a while,' said Cox. He snapped the cigar
box shut.

'How long ago is that?' asked Breen.

Cox picked up his red telephone. 'Look through my diary, dear,'
he told a secretary, 'and find out when I last saw John Knight.' He put
down the phone and said, 'Why are you here, Sergeant?'

'What work does Mr Knight do for you?'

'We employ him sometimes. He's an independent quantity surveyor.'

'What was the last job he did?'

'He's worked on the West Cross Route of Ringway One. The road
project.'

'The Westway?'

Cox nodded.

'Big project,' said Breen.

'Immense.' Cox grinned. 'Tremendously exciting. It's a large project and obviously we need good oversight on it. The materials bill alone runs into hundreds of thousands.'

'And Knight would be in charge of that money?'

'Lord, no.' Another smile. Cox felt more confident on this ground. 'He's just an abacus-wallah. We need people to estimate how much material is needed for any project. And to supervise its delivery. Don't get me wrong, he's very good. An über-abacus-wallah, if you like. But he's a cog in the machine.' Then, 'Please tell me why you're here, Sergeant. You're making me nervous.'

'Do you know any reason why Johnny Knight would be in any trouble?' said Breen.

The smile dropped. 'Please. As a friend. What's all this about? Has Johnny Knight been doing something he shouldn't? This is a serious business. We have significant government contracts. We can't afford any scandal. If anything was to damage our reputation . . .'

'Do you have any reason to know why he would have gone abroad or left home?'

'Christ. Has he?'

'He appears to have been missing from his house since mid-September.'

The phone rang. A woman's voice crackled on the line. Cox nodded. He replaced the receiver and said, 'Well, as it happens, I was right. Mr Knight hasn't worked with us since September. That was the last time I saw him, according to my secretary.' He frowned. 'Apparently he hasn't cashed his last pay cheque, either.'

'And you don't know of anyone who would have wished him any harm?'

'Harm?' said Cox. 'What sort of harm? Please don't keep me in the dark like this. It's not fair.'

Breen opened his notebook.

'No. No idea at all,' said Cox. 'Marylebone, you said?'

'Yes.'

'Correct me if I'm wrong,' said Cox, 'but your boss just had the misfortune of a heart attack, is that right?'

Breen stopped writing. 'How did you know that?'

'Like I say, I'm friends with loads of coppers. Rugby. Remember?'

'I do.'

'My company donated their services to building a new club room at Imber Court, the Police Rugby Club. I've stayed friends with the committee ever since.'

Breen nodded. The scratching of backs. The way this world worked. Cox was one of those Londoners who lived on his connections.

'Good people,' said Cox. 'Salt of the earth. And I believe I know who your new boss is going to be. I was out with him last night. Jack Creamer? He's an old pal from the club. A lovely fellow. Solid. Do you mind awfully if I call him? I need to get to the bottom of this. And I'm sure he'll be pleased to hear his men are out and about.'

'Good,' said Breen. Fixed smile. 'Make sure and do that.'

He closed his notebook. There was an awkward pause.

'Is that everything?' And Cox got up, opened the door of his office into the wide corridor beyond, and stood there waiting for Breen to leave. 'And please do come round some time for dinner. I'd love to talk art with you. Perhaps you could bring your friend, Mr Fraser. I've got my eyes on a John Plumb. I expect you lot think that's rather old hat. I'll get my secretary to call.'

At home, the music was thumping from behind the front door of the rooms above his.

He went downstairs to his flat, to his father's old room, and pulled out the tin from the kitchen cupboard. He took out the folded money and put it in a brown envelope for the morning.

Then he went back upstairs and thumped on the door with the side of his fist.

A woman in a man's dressing gown opened the door. She looked about nineteen. 'Who is it?' called a man's voice from behind her.

Breen smelt the same smell that had filled the air at the Albert Hall wafting from behind her.

'Please,' he said. 'Turn the music down. I need to sleep.'

'Sure, man,' said the man.

Back downstairs, he lay on his bed, the music just as loud as it had been before.

TWENTY-SEVEN

Tozer had made cheese sandwiches from Wonderloaf. The cheese was almost as pale as the bread. Breen had bought two bagels from Joe's All Night Cafe and filled them with smoked salmon, cream cheese, pickled cucumber and fresh black pepper. He had also got another bag with some dill pickles and blinis. Tozer had what looked like orange squash in an old Tizer bottle; Breen had a thermos of fresh black coffee.

Tozer looked at her paper bag, to the brown paper parcel Breen was unwrapping, and back again.

They had found an empty compartment in Second Class. It was a Saturday morning, so the train was pretty quiet. There was chewing gum on one of the seats, but apart from that it was clean.

She held out one of her sandwiches. 'I'll swap you one of yours for one of mine,' she said.

'I'm OK, thanks,' said Breen. But he handed her one of his bagels and offered her a coffee.

'Don't you have milk?' Tozer asked peering at the paper cup he'd handed her.

Breen shook his head. 'I prefer it black.'

She took a sip and made a face. 'That's horrible,' she said. 'It's too bitter. No one in their right mind is going to drink that.'

He took it back and poured it into his own cup as she dug into the bagel.

'This's delicious, mind,' she said. 'You make that yourself? My dad can't even boil an egg.'

'I'm twenty years younger than your dad.'

'Fifteen,' she said, taking another bite out of his bagel.

Then she kicked off her shoes and put her stockinged feet on the seat next to Breen. He looked at her feet, painted toenails dark beneath the nylon, then looked away out of the window.

Breen stared at the north Kent countryside. A flat and muddy land, brown winter fields and grey estuary light. The tide was out and the coast smelt rotten and muddy. A flock of small gulls rose above them, startled by the noise of the train. He thought about Harry Cox. Calling up his pal, Inspector Creamer. You know a detective called Breen?

He watched Tozer's reflection in the carriage window. She had taken out a paperback and started reading. After only a page she dropped the book onto the seat and closed her eyes to sleep. Breen watched her head against the side of the carriage, mouth open, skinny chest rising and falling with each breath.

When she woke she said, 'Hibou,' then blinked as if surprised she had spoken aloud.

'What made you think of her?' said Breen.

'I went there, last night.'

'To the squat? I thought you promised to never go back there?'

She looked towards the the window. 'I never promised.'

'What happened?'

'They wouldn't let me in. They wouldn't let me see her. They called me names.' She chewed on her lip slowly.

'Didn't I say?'

'I could kill him, you know?' she said. 'Jayakrishna. He's such a smug arse. He called me a pig. You know what they call him? A guru. What is that?'

'It's like a priest or something.'

Still looking out the window she said, 'Perv, more like. You think she was even on drugs before she got there?'

'I told you not to go.' It was all he could think to say.

'Fab, Paddy. Bloody fab.'

★

It was midday in the afternoon by the time the train reached Margate. A dirty postcard of a town. In winter, these gleeful seaside towns looked doubly bleak. A fierce north wind blew straight off the sea at them as they left the station. Kent Police had visited the GP and had phoned Tozer with the address at which Charlie Prosser was registered. Breen had bought a map of Margate at W.H. Smith's in Charing Cross and was now holding its flapping sheet into the wind.

'That way,' he said, pointing.

It took only two minutes to walk to the Mooring Guest House. It looked out onto a deserted concrete crazy golf course and beyond that the North Sea. A four-storey Victorian terrace, paint peeling from the salt wind, curtains closed against the cold. An old wrought-iron balcony sent pink rust stains down the pale paint.

A hand-written sign in the window: 'VACANCIES'.

Breen rang on the bell. The short woman who answered it looked from Breen to Tozer disapprovingly.

'Is there a Shirley Prosser staying here?'

'Are you looking for a room?' She frowned.

'We're looking for a woman called Shirley Prosser,' said Tozer. 'She's a woman of about thirty with a boy. He's a spastic. Prosser was her married name.'

One hand holding her hair to stop the wind blowing it, the other holding the top of her dark cardigan closed, the landlady narrowed her eyes and said, 'Who wants to know?'

'We want to give her some news,' said Tozer.

The landlady looked Tozer up and down. 'She in't here,' she said and went to close the door.

Tozer stepped forward. 'Can we wait for her?'

'Go away,' she said. 'I don't like the look of you.'

'Do you know when she'll be back?'

'I don't like people nosing around my guests,' she said, and closed the door in their faces.

Breen looked up and down the street. The B & B was halfway down a row of a dozen houses all lined up to face the sea, but there was no cafe or other shelter they could stay in to watch for Shirley Prosser's return. In her miniskirt and jacket, Tozer was already shivering.

The front-room curtain twitched and the woman peered out, waiting for them to leave. 'Get off!' She banged on the glass. 'Or I'll call the police.'

Breen said, 'Let's take a look at the town and come back later.'

'Can we find somewhere warm?' said Tozer.

To the east, the seafront was a wide curve of yellow sand. They walked along the road alongside the beach, past the big amusement park with the sign that read 'DREAMLAND'. The rollercoaster rising slowly, all giggles and shouts. Then the sudden descent of underdressed teenage girls screaming into the wind as it clattered round the wooden tracks. Beyond it was a parade of shops. They found a cafe in an arcade, filled with the clatter of pinball machines and the wail of pop music. A couple of lads were sitting drinking tea at a yellow Formica table. Both had identical short hair and long sideboards. Trousers that ended an inch above their boots. One of them wore braces over a check shirt, sleeves rolled up despite the cold.

'What you looking at?' he said.

Breen ordered two hot chocolates and sipped his, slowly looking out of the window at the wind whipping foam off the cold sand.

'It's a bit like Torquay,' said Tozer. 'Only worse.' She dug around in her bag for a cigarette, pulling out the novel she'd been reading on the train. 'Why would she have come to a dump like this? I mean . . . It would be OK in summer.'

'She's frightened of something.' Breen picked up the book. *Valley of the Dolls.* 'Any good?' he asked.

'Not really. Only bought it because all the girls in the section house are reading it. It's about sex and drugs,' she said.

'Really?'

'But mostly sex.'

She found the packet of cigarettes and lit one.

'When you went to the doctor yesterday,' said Breen, 'and Jonesy . . . said he thought you were pregnant.'

Tozer's face stiffened. 'What?'

'I was thinking: what if you were? I mean, we did it, didn't we?'

'It? What's "it"?'

'You know. And we were both a bit drunk.'

'Made love?' she said.

The two bootboys looked interested for the first time.

'Yes.'

'So you thought I was pregnant too?'

Breen glared back at the two lads until they looked away, embarrassed. 'I didn't know what I thought,' said Breen. 'That's the point.'

'I bloody hate that,' said Tozer. 'All you lot talking about me behind my back.'

'I didn't say anything,' protested Breen.

'Precisely. Maybe you bloody should have,' said Tozer. 'I'm going for a walk.'

'I'll come too,' said Breen.

She stood. 'I want to be on my own for ten minutes, OK?' said Tozer. 'Stretch my legs.'

'Right,' said Breen, sitting back down again.

The two bootboys had their heads together, whispering, glancing at Breen. A third lad came in and joined them briefly to cadge a cigarette. He was dressed similarly, though his trousers were turned up even higher, showing a pair of red socks above a pair of second-hand army boots. Comical and scary at the same time.

Since when did every young working-class man have to belong to a tribe? Breen finished his sickly hot chocolate and went to play at one of the pinball machines. It was called 'Football Fun' and Breen didn't have much idea what he was doing with the flippers. Five balls disappeared down the hole in no time. He put in another shilling and tried it again, learning to press the flippers just as the balls were about to land on them, sending the ball bearing careening back up the machine into the bumpers. On his third shilling he realised there was a girl standing behind him.

This time he kept the first ball bouncing up in the machine for at least a minute before it disappeared between the flippers.

'You're useless,' said the girl. She looked about twelve. Dumpy, greasy hair, jeans and a baggy red jumper, smoking a cigarette and chewing gum at the same time.

'No I'm not,' said Breen.

'Give me your next ball and I'll get you a replay.'

'Get your own machine,' said Breen, and released another ball. The silver ball sailed up, hit one of the bumpers and spat straight back towards him before he could reach it with his flippers, disappearing back into the machine.

'Completely crap,' said the girl to herself. Then, louder: 'Never done it before, have you?'

Breen said, 'Go on then. Show me how it's done if you think you're better.' And he let her have his next ball.

She took a puff of her cigarette and handed him the stub. 'You can have the rest if you like,' she said.

He looked at the fag-end in his hand and said, 'Thanks.'

''s OK.' As soon as he was sure she was concentrating on the machine, he dropped the cigarette end on the floor.

Her focus was totally on the ball, watching it zing around the machine. Click, bleep, ching, bleep. GOAL. GOAL. GOAL. A pink bubble of gum escaped her lips. He watched the bubble growing as her fingers twitched on either side of the machine, lights flashing, numbers clicking round on the dials.

'Fanny's got a new boyfriend.'

Breen looked around. The two bootboys were looking at them, laughing.

'Flap off,' said the girl.

'Oi, mister! We'll tell her brother you're trying to cop off with Fanny.'

'My name's not Fanny,' said the girl.

'Yes it is, Fanny. Fanny Flap-Off.'

'Watch it, mister. Her brother's a wrestler. He's fought Mick McManus. He'll come and rip your ears off.'

'How old are you?' Breen asked the girl they were calling Fanny.

'I'm fourteen,' said the girl. She was still concentrating on the machine.

'I bet you're here every day, aren't you?'

'See? He's trying to pick you up, Fanny.'

'Most days.'

'I'm looking for someone. Have you seen a spastic boy around town this last week or so?'

She turned her head. 'Them two –' she jerked it at the two boys – 'they're spazzers.' A moment's lack of concentration. The ball spun and was gone. Game over. 'You bloody messed up my bloody game,' she said.

'You chucking him already, Fanny?'

'Lover's tiff.'

'It was my game, if you remember,' said Breen.

'Got another shilling, mister?' asked the girl. 'I'll play doubles with you.'

'Oooh. Playing doubles with Fanny now. Know what that means?'

'Flap off, you morons.' She stuck her tongue behind her bottom gums.

Breen said, 'The boy's about ten years old. You'd know him if you saw him.'

'Give me a shilling and I'll tell you.'

Breen handed over a shilling. 'Well?' he said.

She pushed him aside, took the shilling, put it in the machine again and started to play. 'No. Never seen him. You his dad?'

'No.'

'Why you looking for him then?' And she pressed the button marked 'Single Play' and was lost in the machine again.

'Yeah. Why you looking for a spaz, anyway?'

Breen turned. It was one of the boys.

'This dump is dead in winter. Nobody comes here in their right mind. Only spazzers. Shouldn't be hard to find him.'

The other one – check shirt and braces – said, 'He walk like this?' And started to hobble round, toe of right boot on the floor, dragging it behind him. He stuck his tongue behind his lower lip and opened his eyes wide.

'Why?' said Breen.

The other one was doubled up. 'Is that your dad when he's on the whisky?' He laughed. He began flapping his limbs about too.

'Only there's a lad like that I seen walking on the beach with his mam just now.'

He pointed north, out to sea.

Outside, a gust of wind sent an old newspaper page flying up above his head. It circled, then hung in the air before another blasted it away over the roofs. Breen clutched at the collar of his coat and wished he'd brought a scarf.

He walked across the sand. It was damp from the rain. The beach was wide and empty. When had he last walked on a beach? His father had taken him to Brighton once. They had stood on the shingle in bare feet eating ice creams and looking at the crashing waves. He had wanted to swim, but his father had forgotten to bring any trunks. 'Go in in your pants,' said his father in his thick Kerry brogue. 'Nobody will mind.'

Breen had sat throwing stones, ashamed his country-born father would even suggest such a thing.

The wind tasted of salt. Beyond the tideline the sand changed from from irregular mounds to smooth, dark ripples. There were few footprints. It was too cold for most walkers.

Large indentations made by heavy boots. Smaller ones nearby – a woman's presumably. Then another woman's, with a dog's paw prints alongside. Had that been the woman he had just seen out walking her dog?

He made his way closer to the light line of spume.

He didn't find them until he reached the water's edge, but the prints were clear. A woman walking next to a boy. His right foot dragged, creating a pattern that looked like a line of shallow 'm's. The pair had been walking east, away from the boarding house. The waves of the incoming tide were already rippling over the marks on the flat sand.

He scanned the beach, but the only people he could see were an old couple walking hand in hand towards the Harbour Arm. Looking back towards the town, he scanned the pavements for any sign of Tozer.

A wave splashed against his feet. Cold water filled his left shoe.

'Damn,' he said loudly.

Where would you go in a seaside town if you had little money and a boy you had to look after all day? The footsteps were leading towards the old town.

Breen found the library in a red-brick building in the old streets.

The librarian was in her mid-sixties, hair pulled into a tight bun on the back of her head. She held a red biro in one hand and said, in a hushed voice, 'I don't let them in here. They came once.'

'Why not?'

'They made too much noise.'

An elderly man brought a pair of books and placed them on the desk in front of her. The librarian pulled the cards out of the books, stamped them, then handed them back.

Breen said, 'Too much noise?'

'Well, I suppose you have to feel sorry for him. It's not his fault. He doesn't know how to talk quietly,' she said. 'But you can't have it, can you?'

Her pink lipstick had leaked into the creases around her mouth. 'He should be in a home, really. It's not fair on the poor lad.' She strode away from the desk, calling loudly, 'Closing in five minutes.'

Breen turned to go. 'I seen him a couple of times,' said the elderly man.

'The boy?'

'That woman's a cow,' said the man, nodding at the librarian.

'I heard you,' said the librarian. 'I'm not having that in my library.'

'Poor lad,' said the man. 'He was no trouble.'

'You know him?' said Breen.

'No talking.'

'It's not your ruddy library anyway,' said the man.

'I can ban you too, you know.'

'Hard to miss him, really.' He looked at his watch. 'Matinee at two,' he said. 'It's warm in there. He's there some days with his mum.'

Breen looked at his watch. It was twenty to two now. 'Where's the cinema?' he asked.

'Shh,' said the librarian.

Carry On Up the Khyber and *King Kong Escapes*. Double bill. 'Enlist in a World of Laughter', said the poster. Cheap British pap padded out with some dubbed Japanese flick. Now they were putting films on TV on Saturday afternoons, cinemas were dying on their feet.

Breen stood in the lobby behind a pillar, watching the audience file in. As a boy, he had sneaked coins out of his father's milk-money tin to watch thrillers in the Hammersmith Odeon. It was a brash, loud place, compared to the infuriating quietness of the house he shared with his father. He'd loved it. His father had been disappointed by a boy who showed little interest in books.

The two skinheads came past, all smiles. 'You found him?'

'No,' said Breen.

'We saw that cripple just now. He was in the queue outside. We told his ma you was looking for him. Should have seen the look she give us. Do we get a reward or something?'

But Breen was already pushing past them. A mum was making her way slowly through the swing door with two small children, each sucking on a lollipop. He had to wait while the boys dawdled in the doorway before he could make it outside. There was a box office in the wall of the cinema. The queue was about twenty people long, but by the time he reached it there was no sign of Shirley or Charlie.

Breen started to run. Which way though? How fast could Charlie Prosser move with his gammy leg? He reached the end of the street, but there was no sign of them, so he turned and ran back the other way.

The small streets of the old fishing town confused him. Which was south?

Dodging between pedestrians, he tripped over a wicker shopping trolley, sending cans rolling into the road. 'Watch where you're ruddy going!' a woman shouted.

A couple of boys came clattering down the pavement on roller skates, forcing Breen into the road. A car honked.

Round the corner.

Look left and right. No sign. And where was bloody Tozer when he needed her?

Breen stood there, panting.

And noticed heads turning up ahead. People laughing.

Breen ran towards them.

He could see from twenty yards away that Charlie was on the ground – panting, eyes wild. He must have tripped. 'Shirley!' shouted Breen.

She didn't turn; she was lifting her son. 'Help!' she shouted.

'Shirley!'

People stood around, not knowing what to do.

TWENTY-EIGHT

'Oh,' said Shirley Prosser. 'It's you. I thought . . .'

Charlie was crying, trying not to, wiping his eyes with the back of his hand.

'Who did you think I was?'

'How was I to bloody know?' said Shirley.

The crowd of shoppers paused, stared a little more, muttered, then moved on.

And suddenly Tozer was there too, arm around Charlie. 'You OK? I saw you running. You can't half shift.'

'Where were you?' said Breen. He hadn't seen her appearing out of the crowd.

'I was looking for you, weren't I? Say sorry to Charlie, Paddy,' said Tozer. 'You frightened him.'

'What?' said Breen. 'I needed you and you disappeared.'

'No need to be shirty. Say sorry. He thought you were someone bad, didn't you, Charlie? That's why they ran. He was scared.'

Breen looked from Tozer to Charlie. 'Sorry, Charlie. It was a misunderstanding. I just need to talk to your mother, that's all.'

Charlie shook his head from side to side, a gob of dribble on his chin.

'He doesn't like you,' his mother said. She stood there, arms folded, looking at Breen suspiciously, still not convinced. 'What do you need to talk to me about?' She was different. Stiffer. More cautious.

'I meant it. I'm sorry we gave you a fright,' said Breen.

Shirley nodded. Her skin was grey; she was thinner than she had been last time he had seen her. Her hair was greasy and unwashed.

'You found out where I was?'

'Yes. Helen did.'

'Why?'

'You were going to the cinema, weren't you?'

Charlie glared.

'So why doesn't Helen here take you to see the film? That way I can talk to your mum.'

Charlie looked at Tozer suspiciously.

'I'd like that, Charlie,' Tozer said. 'And you could get your breath back.'

'What about?' said Shirley.

Breen paused. A plastic windmill fluttered in the wind outside a newsagent. Here on the street, with her son next to her, he couldn't explain why he thought her brother was dead. 'Something important,' said Breen.

Shirley bit her lip. 'OK. Fancy that, Charlie? Going to the flicks with Helen? It might be nice, mightn't it?' She leaned forward and kissed her son gently on the forehead. 'I'm sorry, lovely. Didn't mean to scare you.'

'Get off,' Charlie mumbled. 'Not scared,' he said.

After Tozer and Charlie had disappeared into the auditorium, he and Shirley found a bench in the foyer. There were sweet wrappers all over the floor. A dollop of dropped ice cream.

'I'm sorry about your husband,' said Breen. 'It must have been a terrible shock.'

She nodded.

'It's probably not the right time to say it, but I enjoyed going out with you. It was good.'

'Yes,' she said.

They sat awkwardly, side by side. 'You should have got in touch with me, at least. Let me know where you were. I've been worried.'

She gave a small, sad laugh. 'You've been worried? I'm sorry! I've been scared out of my wits.'

'Because you know who killed him?'

She shook her head. No words.

'No idea at all?'

'The other police asked me that. Over and over,' she said.

'No suspicion of anyone?'

She looked at him fiercely. 'What about you, Paddy? Did you kill him?'

Breen shook his head. 'No. God, no. I was with you when he was shot.'

She nodded again, as if she accepted this.

'I want to find out who did. After he left the police he didn't tell anyone where he went. Why was he hiding? Was he scared of something?'

She looked away.

'I think he must have been frightened,' she said. 'If you're a policeman, no one can touch you. But once you're on your own, it's different.'

Breen frowned. Leaving the police meant that Prosser had no longer been safe. So had he, in some way, been responsible for Prosser's death by forcing him to leave the police force? Did she hold him responsible for that?

'The police who interviewed me said you were suspended. How come you're doing this?'

'Until I can show that it wasn't me that killed your husband, I'm still a suspect.'

A small, tired laugh. 'So this is all about you, then?'

'I know you're scared. But if we find who killed your husband, then you can be safe. You and Charlie won't have to keep running away. Do you want to spend your life like this?'

She looked down, shook her head. 'I couldn't even trust my own husband.' Then she reached out and put her hand on his. 'I'm sorry,' she said. 'I didn't mean to be like this. I don't think you did it. I'm scared, that's all. I'm tired.'

He looked down. The contact of a woman's hand. Breen said, 'Whatever your husband was up to, I need you to believe that I am not involved.' He was going to say he was 'not that sort of copper', but he stopped himself. 'I only found out your husband was on the take by accident. I wasn't involved in any of that. I had no idea until a few days ago, until I talked to you, that he was into anything bigger than that. You have to believe me. The only way we can stop this is by figuring out what was really going on.' He took a breath and said, 'I'm worried about your brother, too. Do you know where he is?'

She didn't answer.

'It's important.' He paused. He didn't want to be the one who said this to her, but there was no one else. 'I think something has happened to him.'

When he looked back up he saw that tears were streaming down her face. Awkward, Breen offered her his handkerchief.

Behind the sweets stand, a moon-faced teenage girl in a brown nylon uniform watched her impassively, as if this kind of thing happened all the time in Margate. Maybe it did, Breen wondered.

She looked away and said, 'I think he's dead.'

'Johnny, you mean? Your brother?'

She nodded, and began to cry again. 'I haven't had anyone to talk to about this for so long,' she said.

'Tell me.'

She looked up at the ceiling. 'Johnny disappeared. Vanished. Back in September. He just stopped answering calls and letters. I've been to his house, but there's no one there. He just vanished.'

He felt that guilty thrill of being on the right track. Facts were finally starting to come into focus.

'Your brother . . .'

She looked him straight in the eye. 'You think he's dead too . . . isn't he?'

'I think so.' Breen nodded. 'And I think your husband might have had something to do with his death.'

It was not even a human noise that came out of her. A feral howl, almost. Breen wished Tozer was here too. She would be able to handle this better. Women knew this territory.

The woman at the sweet counter glared at Breen. 'If you two are arguing, I'll call the manager,' she said.

Breen ignored her.

'What do you think the connection is between your husband's death and your brother's?' he pressed her.

She took a deep breath. 'I'm sorry,' she said. 'I'm tired. We don't get much sleep in that boarding house.'

'You have to think,' he said.

'I can't.' She was crying again.

'I'm sorry,' he said. He offered her a cigarette, which she took without saying anything. She took two large quick puffs on it and wiped her eyes on the back of her hand before she started talking. 'This all started with Johnny. Johnny got himself mixed up in something way out his depth.'

'And your husband was in on it too?'

'Not at the start. All this is my fault. All of this wouldn't have happened . . .'

The lights came on outside the cinema. Through the doors, Breen could see the shine of neon on the pavement.

'My younger brother. The successful one of the family,' she said. 'He went to college. None of our family had ever gone to college before. Had his own house at twenty-eight, and everything. We were all so proud of him. Poor little Johnny.'

'What happened?' said Breen.

'About six months ago, Johnny came to me for help. Knocking on my door. He was drunk. And he was just talking all this stuff about the cost of materials. Steel and concrete. My little brother.'

'He had got involved in something illegal?'

She nodded.

'He'd been false-accounting?'

'I'm not sure. Some kind of fraud. One of the companies he worked for.'

'Morton, Stiles and Prentice?'

She looked shocked. 'So you do know, then? You're just stringing me along, pretending?'

'I looked through your brother's letters. It was a guess,' said Breen. 'I know he had been working for them.'

Her eyes were wider now.

'What about a man called Harry Cox? Your brother was working for him.'

She frowned, looked at him, then shook her head. 'I never heard him say any names,' she said.

'He's a large man. Flashy.'

'No.'

'Was Michael interested in rugby, then?'

'Rugby? Not really. He preferred football. Crystal Palace.' She put the hand with the cigarette in it to her mouth, eyes big. 'Christ sake. You've been investigating these people? Do they know you're looking for Johnny?'

'What?' said Breen.

'Nothing. Only . . .' The hand was shaking, ash dropping onto the dirty floor. 'If you found out where I am, they could too. Michael, Johnny: if they're both dead . . .'

'Nobody needs to know where you are,' he said.

'How did you find out? It's Charlie, isn't it?'

He nodded. Hard to hide when you have a son like Charlie.

She looked away, towards the doors of the cinema where her son was with Tozer. She chewed her bottom lip for a few seconds. Took a last tug from the cig.

'Tell me about your brother Johnny. You said he came to you asking for help.'

'It happened a few times after that. He'd get drunk and tearful and come around mine. I tried to get it out of him. What was wrong? One day he told me. Some people in that company – he never told me who – had put pressure on him to overestimate materials for jobs. Just a little bit here and there. No harm done. The councils never check properly. Happens on every building site. Only with some of the jobs they do now, that starts to add up to a lot of money. And they were putting pressure on him to get more and more money out of it. So he said.'

'Never any names?'

She looked at him briefly, then shook her head. 'No. He never said anyone's name.'

'Your brother came to you because your husband was a policeman?'

'Good old Michael.' She nodded. 'Good old fucking Michael.'

'He wanted to find a way to end it?'

'Johnny thought if he went to the police they could tidy it all up and he'd be OK.'

'Only your husband wanted in on it?'

'I don't know. Michael said he'd handle it. That's all.'

Breen nodded. She reached out and laid his hand on his again.

'Thing about Michael was, he loves Charlie – loved Charlie. I suppose he wanted to show he could look after him. If he could get money, he thought I'd love him. Or at least stay with him. He knew I didn't love him. I never did. I just got pregnant by him.'

'So instead of helping your brother take his story to the police he blackmailed him?'

'I don't know,' she said. 'Yes, maybe.'

Breen had to sit and think about this. Johnny Knight had been part of some syndicate skimming money off the top of building projects in London. With so much construction going on in the city, there was always scope for fraud. He tried to imagine what had gone on. At first it would have been small amounts – fifty pounds here and there – but with that much money being paid out, there was always potential for someone to get greedy. As the sums increased and the total grew larger, Johnny had started to panic. The figures were becoming too significant not to be noticed, perhaps. And he was the first person they would come to for an explanation. He could lose his lovely house, his lovely life. He was a star pupil. An achiever. He would have tried to find a way out. He imagined him thinking about his sister's husband, a policeman. He would have approached him, asked him if he could investigate it, perhaps even get a reward for letting the police know. Golden boys like Johnny always imagined there was some way they could come up smelling nice. But Michael Prosser wasn't that sort of policeman. He would have seen it as an opportunity. He would have wanted a cut, maybe, for adding his own police protection to the racket.

'What are you thinking?'

'Why didn't you report him missing? Why didn't you tell me about this last time I came to see you?'

A gulp of air. 'I loved him,' she said. 'He was my brother. He'd been planning to run away to Spain. He'd talked to me about it. Said he'd be in touch when he found a place. I thought maybe he had. See, if I'd gone and told the police he was missing people would start looking for him.'

She took her hand away from Breen's. 'But I'm starting to think,' she said, looking at Breen, 'that he didn't. You know. Get away.'

'I don't think so either,' said Breen. A long pause. The quiet popping of corn in the machine. A wave of muffled laughter from the cinema. 'Who do you think killed him?'

She didn't answer. That's when the crying started again. She leaned forward, put her face in her hands and cried, shoulders trembling. Still unsure, Breen reached out a hand and laid it carefully on her shoulder.

When the sobbing had stopped, she said, 'I'm scared.'

Breen looked at her. She looked half exhausted, half starved. Her husband was dead. Her brother was probably dead too. They had both been involved in the same scam. She had reason to be frightened. If her

288 • WILLIAM SHAW

brother had been killed for threatening to tell the police about it, she had just done exactly what he had been killed for.

He said, 'If it was just you maybe you could run away from whoever has done all this. But it's not just you, is it?'

She shook her head, smiled a little, and laughed. 'No. It's not just me. Sometimes, I wish to God it was. That sounds awful, doesn't it?'

'No. Not really.'

'You know what? This is the first time I've not been with Charlie since we went out for dinner. That was the first time I've had a break from him in almost two months. I've been with him every minute of the day. Every hour. You're not a father, are you?'

'No,' said Breen.

'Since we left Michael he's had no school. No nothing. Every minute of the day. Just me. And that's what makes me cry.'

Breen said, 'I understand.'

'No you don't,' she said. 'You have no bloody idea. At night it gets to the point where I wish Charlie was dead too. Can you imagine what it's like, thinking that?'

Breen took out a cigarette for himself and offered her another.

'My father took a long time to die,' Breen said. 'I used to wish he would hurry up.' He felt in his pocket for a box of matches. 'It's probably not the same,' he said.

The door to the cinema stalls opened just as the audience inside burst into laughter again.

'I'm sorry,' she said. She took a drag on her cigarette.

'You're doing a great job with Charlie. It can't be easy.'

'It's bloody not. I'd do anything for him though,' she said. 'That's just how it is.' She blew out smoke. 'I'd go through hell.'

The film was over. People started streaming out into the lobby.

They had talked for over an hour. Breen pulled out the envelope, wrote his address on it and gave it to her. 'It'll keep you going,' he said. 'Don't open it here.'

She felt the thickness of the paper inside.

Breen said, 'Use it to move somewhere else. Don't talk to anyone. Don't see anyone. Just keep your head down. Stay safe. I've written down my address. In a week or so, send me a postcard. Don't write anything. Don't sign it. Just let me know the place. I'll come and find you. Everything will be fine.'

She smiled and said, 'Promise?'

Tozer was among the last to emerge from the cinema, with Charlie Prosser hanging on to her arm. Breen watched the audience members staring at him as he waddled across the worn red carpet. Some avoided him, pressing themselves against the walls as he squeezed past. A couple of lads pushed into him, giggling. Charlie didn't seem to notice. Breen wasn't sure whether they were laughing at Charlie or at something they were remembering from the film.

Shirley Prosser smiled at her son. 'What was it like, Charlie?'

'Budd' ru'ish.' He grinned.

'What have I told you about swearing, Charlie?' said Shirley. 'You're always together. Are you two an item?' she asked, looking from Tozer to Breen.

'No,' said Tozer.

'I just thought . . .' said Shirley.

'No,' she said again.

When they were going, Shirley shook Tozer's hand, then lunged out and kissed Breen on the cheek. 'Thank you,' she said quietly, into his ear. 'For the money.'

'What was all that about?' said Tozer.

'She was just saying thank you,' said Breen.

'It looked like more than that,' said Tozer.

'Well it wasn't,' said Breen.

'Sorry I spoke,' said Tozer.

'Charlie was right though,' said Tozer as they ran to the station to try and make the five o'clock train. 'The film was bloody rubbish.'

The lights were on in Dreamland. They could hear the clatter of winnings from the fruit machines and the screams from the rollercoaster faded behind them, as they reached the dullness of the station, quiet on a Saturday afternoon.

The train back to London was empty. Breen and Tozer sat in the buffet car. The carriage smelt of dust and cooking grease.

Breen said, 'Her brother Johnny was on the take.'

'She said that?'

'Yes.'

'How does that work?'

'He was a quantity surveyor. Say they need twenty thousand tons of concrete for a tower block,' said Breen. 'He and his pals say twenty-*five* thousand and pocket the difference. The Greater London Council spends millions on buildings. Easy to miss the odd twenty grand here and there.'

Tozer whistled. 'A little bit here and there.'

Breen nodded.

'How did she find out? Was she in on it?'

Breen shook his head. 'She says her brother got drunk a lot. More as he got deeper into it. One night he told her. He was ashamed, she said. He wanted to come clean and thought Michael Prosser could help him.'

'That's like asking an alky to help you go on the wagon.' Tozer called out to the barman, 'Can I have a drink?'

'Not till Faversham,' said the man. 'Bar don't open till then.'

He was sitting on a stool behind the bar checking his pools coupon.

'How long's that?'

'Forty minutes.'

'Bloody hell. You could serve us one now,' she said. 'You're not doing anything else.'

'Rules,' said the man, and he went back to his pools coupon.

'Win anything?' said Tozer.

The man crumpled up the paper and threw it behind him. 'Nope.'

'Good,' said Tozer. Then, more quietly to Breen, 'Why didn't she tell us about this earlier?'

'She thought he might have escaped to Spain or somewhere. He'd been talking about it. If he had, she didn't want us investigating his disappearance.'

'So why is Johnny Knight dead? If he is.'

'Perhaps they were worried he would spill the beans.' He pulled out a notebook and showed her the name of the building contractors Prosser was working for. 'Morton, Stiles and Prentice.' Breen said, 'Big company. They do loads of stuff. My dad worked for them.'

'Really?'

'He worked for a few in his time.'

'What if there were people on the council who were getting kickbacks too, to turn a blind eye?'

Breen nodded. 'Yes.'

Tozer said, 'So he did this cheating thing even though he said he didn't want to? And he took the money anyway?'

'Yes.'

'I know his sort. So what about Michael Prosser? They kill him too?'

'I don't know,' said Breen.

She was thinking it through. 'Johnny Knight had gone to Michael Prosser because he wanted to come clean. They both knew about this scam and they're both dead.'

'Maybe they killed them just because they knew about it. Whoever they are.'

'Maybe.'

'No wonder she's scared shitty,' said Tozer. ''Cause they must know she knew too. And they killed her brother and her ex.'

'Precisely.'

'Poor cow,' said Tozer. 'What's she going to do?'

'I told her to stay put. I told her we wouldn't tell anyone where she was.'

'Did she believe you?'

Breen looked out of the window. It was black outside now. Only the occasional lights of a farmhouse or a ship in the estuary.

He asked, 'What about the boy? Charlie?'

'He's all right. Just have to figure out what he's trying to say, that's all. He ate ice cream just like any other ten-year-old. You still going to the party?'

'Oh,' said Breen. 'The Christmas party? I don't know.'

'I bought the ticket. Might as well go. There'll be food, won't there? I'm ruddy starving.'

He said, 'Must be hard for her, all alone.'

'You fancy her, don't you?'

'I feel sorry for her, that's all.'

'Vulnerable woman – brings out all your instincts, don't it?'

'Lay off,' said Breen.

'One thing. Why did she run off like that?' asked Tozer.

The window of the carriage suddenly thumped. Lighted windows shot past. Another train passing. 'Like you said,' said Breen. 'She's scared. She heard someone was following her.'

'Only she knew it was you. Why was she so scared of you?'

Breen looked at her. 'She didn't know it was me.'

Tozer looked at Breen and said, 'Yes she did. I'd been following them for about twenty minutes.'

'You were following them?'

'Don't look so surprised. I saw them buying sweets in Woolies. I followed them to the cinema. Some boys talked to them outside and pointed in the cinema. She crept up to the door and peered in. Long enough to see it was you. Then she grabbed Charlie's hand and they legged it.'

Breen thought. 'Why should she trust me, I suppose? She doesn't trust anyone. Her husband was bent. Why shouldn't I be?'

The train had passed. The night outside was dark again.

She said, 'It's not going to look good though. With a copper being involved.'

'No,' said Breen.

'I could kill for a gin and orange. You open yet?'

The British Rail man opened one eye, looked at his watch and shook his head.

TWENTY-NINE

The horse didn't seem to mind the noise. It stood on the edge of the dance floor chewing oats from a bag hung around its head. Somebody had decorated the strap with tinsel.

'You missed everything,' said Marilyn.

'What was it?' asked Tozer.

'Roast,' said Jones.

'I'm bloody starving,' said Tozer. 'You think they've got anything left in the kitchen?'

'Main course was delicious, weren't it?' Marilyn poked her boyfriend.

Danny, Marilyn's boyfriend, said, 'My potatoes was burnt.'

'I wish I hadn't invited you,' said Marilyn. 'Moan, moan, moan.'

Normally it was strictly husbands and wives only but Marilyn had organised the invites so she could do what she liked.

'Turkey and all the trimmings,' said Jones. 'Superb it was. You should learn to cook like that,' he said to his wife.

'You look lovely,' Tozer told Mrs Jones. Jones's wife was wearing a pink dress with beads sewn in around the top half but which didn't quite hide the bump of her belly. 'Doesn't she?'

'A picture,' said Jones. 'Should do. Took her bloody ages to choose which one to put on.'

The young Mrs Jones glared at her husband. 'I wasn't sure it was right, you know? It's so easy for the fellers. All they do is put on a dress suit. And what with this . . .' She placed her hands on her bump and smiled shyly.

The wives all had their best dresses on. Wigs were in this year. Big earrings. They had spent time in front of the mirrors, knowing they were on show to their husbands' bosses. And to all the other wives.

Streamers hung from the chandeliers. Paper chains hung from the walls. Glitterball light spun around the room.

People were drunk already. Loudly, goofily, hurrah-for-us drunk.

Breen was thinking that he should have stayed in Margate. He shouldn't have left Shirley Prosser on her own. She was scared.

'Why is the horse here, anyway?' asked Breen.

'I already asked that,' said Tozer. There was a bottle of whisky, a bottle of brandy and a soda siphon sitting in the middle of each table. She leaned forward and poured herself some brandy and then passed the bottle to Marilyn. 'It brought in the sleigh.'

'A cart, really,' said Marilyn.

'You've had enough, sweetie,' said Danny.

'No I haven't,' said Marilyn, and she poured a wine glass full and gave him a fixed smile.

'Did we miss a sleigh?'

'Santa Claus came just after the main course.'

'Should have been a reindeer then, shouldn't it?' said Tozer. 'If it was pulling a sleigh.'

Jones said, 'Isn't this the best bloody Christmas party ever? D Division. 1968. Kings of bloody London, we are.'

'Kings of London,' people cheered.

'Is the dancing going to start soon?' said Mrs Jones. 'Only I get tired early now. With the baby.'

'I want my pudding first,' said Marilyn.

'Let's all do the conga, let's all do the conga!' The real dancing hadn't started, but some constables were snaking around the tables in a line. 'Don't be boring, come on.'

Inspector Creamer came over with a pint of bitter in his hand. 'And how are all my new CID pals enjoying themselves?'

'Best party yet, sir,' said Jones.

'Bum lick,' muttered Marilyn a little too loudly.

Bailey's replacement, straw-coloured hair above a red face, shirt buttons ready to burst, was holding the handle of his pint as if it were some kind of statement.

Mrs Jones said, 'Somebody told me the horse was deaf. That's why it's not bothered. I didn't know you could get deaf horses.'

'I know you lot have been through some pretty tough times,' said Creamer. 'But I know that basically you're pretty good men.'

Tozer coughed loudly, but Creamer didn't notice.

'You need some leadership. Some new blood.'

Sitting facing away from him, Marilyn was making faces. Breen tried not to smile.

'Come Monday you'll be seeing some new faces in CID, don't you worry,' he said.

'What's he on about?' said Marilyn.

'Shh,' said Jones.

'Righto,' said Inspector Creamer. 'You lot enjoy yourselves. You deserve it.'

'Prat,' said Marilyn, when he'd turned away.

'He could bloody hear you,' said Jones.

'So?' said Marilyn and she reached for the brandy again even though her glass was still full.

Danny hissed, 'Stop it.'

Breen stood and followed Creamer. 'Sir?'

He was standing with his wife, a short, plump woman who wore make-up that stopped at the sides of her face and who held a wide champagne glass in one hand and a long cigarette in the other. 'Paddy, isn't it? What is it, Paddy?'

'I want to talk to you about the Prosser case.'

Creamer frowned. 'I heard you were suspended.'

'It's important.'

Creamer paused.

'This isn't the time to talk shop, Paddy. Marilyn will make an appointment.'

'Yes sir.' A brush-off. Breen made it back to the table just as the lights went down. The hubbub of conversation died.

A silver trolley came through the double doors. On it was an immense Christmas pudding. It was alight, blue flames flickering in the darkness.

'Magical,' said Mrs Jones.

'Isn't it?' said Tozer.

Someone started clapping. Then the whole room.

'Waste of good brandy,' Marilyn said lighting up a cigarette.

Carmichael had come along for old times' sake, though strictly speaking he wasn't in D Division. He arrived at their table with a pretty, fair-haired typist from the Drug Squad. She was wearing a long sequinned dress and he kept squeezing her bum. She kept pushing his hand away.

'I love your accent,' she told Tozer. 'It's so sweet. Where's it from?'

Tozer smiled. 'My mum and dad,' she said.

The woman's laugh was a high-pitched squeak. Breen watched Carmichael flinching.

'How goes it, Paddy?' Carmichael asked.

'So-so,' he said. 'You?'

'So-so.'

'Your meeting with Deason OK?'

Breen shrugged. 'They're not telling me anything. To be honest, I think they're dragging their feet. I could be stuck out here in the cold for ever.'

'Why don't you just relax? It's fine. It'll all blow over soon. Tough luck on Bailey. Still in hospital? I'm getting a pint,' Carmichael said. 'Want one?'

After the pudding they moved the horse out through the double doors and Kenny Ball and his Jazzmen started playing 'Swanee River', all banjos and trumpets. Marilyn grabbed his arm and said, 'Come on. Let's dance.'

Breen said, 'What about you, Danny? Don't you want to dance with your girlfriend?'

Danny sat with his arms crossed. 'Why should I care?' He was as drunk as she was.

Marilyn said, 'I told you you'd only get sulky if you came.'

'Just don't like to see you making a tit of yourself, Marilyn.'

'I'll sit this one out,' said Breen.

But Marilyn laughed and yanked on his arm until he stood. The dance floor had filled quickly. Officers showing off their pretty wives and girlfriends. Men in black dress suits, women in colours. Breen hated dancing. He hated the music. His suit felt too big, his clothes too sweaty and crumpled from chasing around in Margate, his Oxfords too small, pinching his toes. Uncertainly stepping this way and that, hobbled by a sense of horror. Shirley Prosser waiting, terrified that they would come for her and Charlie, in a small cold room in a boarding house; her brother, burnt and cold in the basement of the hospital; his colleague Michael Prosser trying to crawl away from the gunman who killed him; and a young man whose father didn't want to acknowledge him, dying of a heroin overdose in NW8.

Happy Christmas to everyone.

'D Division. The best in London,' read the banner that hung on the stage behind Kenny Ball. The seven-piece band were dressed in pale-blue jackets with pink shirts and black trousers. Must have cost a fortune to book them.

Tozer had started dancing with one of the constables, a young man with hair longer than it should have been. He had his hand on her bottom. As she passed, she stuck her tongue out at Breen. He watched the younger man's hands.

Jones was up now too, with his wife. She looked uncomfortable in heels, her face red from the heat.

'Kenny Ball,' Jones shouted. 'I bloody love him. Proper music, that is.'

The band played one song after another. Marilyn clung on to him harder with each dance.

'Don't you want a break?' Breen said.

'No,' Marilyn said and she squeezed even closer. He could feel the press of her large breasts against his chest. She wobbled as if some string that was holding her up was giving way. He tried to push away, but she was grasping him tightly.

Marilyn was saying something above the music.

'What?'

'I said you're different, Paddy. Not like the other men. You're sensitive. Do you like me, Paddy?' said Marilyn. 'Sometimes I think you don't like me at all.'

Her fingers dug into the shoulder of his jacket.

'Everybody likes you, Marilyn.'

'That's not what I meant,' she said.

Jones swept past again, and wriggled his eyebrows.

'You must get lonely,' she said. 'Living on your own. You should have a girl. To look after you.'

'I need to pee,' Breen said, and he pressed her away from him.

'You're coming back, aren't you?'

Someone had already thrown up on the floor in the Gents. Breen backed out again and tried to find another toilet. Opening doors, he found a small yard at the back of the hotel behind the ballroom.

The air was cold and fresh. Breen sucked in a lungful.

The horse was standing in the middle of the yard behind where the stage was, its harness tied to the bars on a window. There were crates full of empty beer bottles piled up along the wall. Someone had put a blanket over the horse but it stood trembling in the cold. The band sounded just as loud here as they had in the ballroom. They had been paid to play until midnight.

'Count yourself lucky you're deaf,' said Breen and he unzipped his flies and urinated into a drain.

When he'd finished, he pulled out his packet of cigarettes and checked the side of it. He made marks with his thumbnail to count how many he'd had each day. But it was dark in the yard, and he couldn't see how many he'd had. He pulled one out and lit it anyway and laid his head against the horse's neck.

The hair was coarse, but he could feel the warmth of the blood pumping under the hide. He took a pull on the cigarette and closed his eyes. Kenny Ball making 'Beale Street Blues' sound tacky and maudlin. He should go to his empty home and leave Helen Tozer to be kissed by young constables. He should have rented a hotel room in Margate. Two rooms. That way he could have made sure Shirley Prosser was OK.

Tomorrow was Sunday. Nothing to do except tidy up his flat and sit on his own. The terrifying loneliness of a day with no place to go, no work to do, nobody to talk to. A day wasted on nothing when the person who killed Sergeant Prosser could get away.

He felt the horse tense suddenly. He looked and saw the horse's eyes widen. He turned in time to see Marilyn's boyfriend.

'I thought it was you,' he said.

'The toilets were full,' said Breen. 'I came out here instead.'

Danny nodded. 'I heard you been suspended.'

Breen said, 'I should go back in.'

Danny said, 'I'm glad. It keeps you out of Marilyn's way.'

'You should go back in too. Marilyn's a bit tipsy.'

Danny laughed. 'Pissed, you mean.'

'So are you.'

Breen tried to push past him, but Danny stood firm. 'She talks about you all the time.'

The horse shivered, ripples of muscle moving under the hair. Breen stood back.

A sudden moment of realisation. It might have been the lager going to his head after an exhausting day. But it suddenly seemed so obvious and so absurd. 'It was you, wasn't it?'

'Are you laughing at me?'

Breen couldn't help it. He couldn't stop himself.

'It was just you, wasn't it?' he said again.

'Me what?'

Breen had to shout to make himself heard above the band. 'Who set fire to my door. Who sent all those notes. Who took a shit in my drawer. All the time I thought it was someone serious.'

Danny seemed to shrink. He said, 'Don't bloody laugh at me.' He lifted up his fists. 'Let's have it out now. You and me.'

'Don't be ridiculous, Danny. You're drunk. I'm bigger than you.'

'Fuck you. Fucking Irish twat.'

'Everybody thought it was Prosser, but he's not that stupid,' said Breen. 'I'm sorry. I don't mean to laugh. But it's so bloody ridiculous. You got into the office and left those notes. You were outside my house the other night, weren't you?'

Danny was almost a foot shorter than Breen. He held up a fist in front of Breen's face, jabbing at him. 'OK. Come on then.'

'Don't be an idiot,' said Breen. 'I could knock your head right off. Go in and have a drink of water.'

'I should stove your face in. Maybe she'd shut up about you, then.' His lips curled, lower teeth showing.

Breen tried to turn away. 'I'm not doing this here,' he said.

'You're a coward, that's why,' said Danny. 'When that guy pulled a knife on you a few weeks back, you legged it, didn't you?'

And, from the pocket of his suit, he pulled out a knife, clicked open the blade and held it up in front of his face.

'Don't be stupid,' said Breen, brain suddenly working again. How drunk was he? He had misread the situation completely. He had not thought about Danny being a real threat. He had treated him as a joke. Yet he had almost killed him once before.

Breen looked at the knife and felt sick. It was true. He had run from one once, leaving another policeman to do the fighting.

He had stopped laughing now.

'Put it away. I'll pretend you never did that.'

Danny started laughing. 'You're bloody windy, aren't you? I knew it.'

Breen backed up until he was against the horse. The warm skin against the back of his neck.

Danny came towards him, holding the knife up to his face.

'Don't be stupid. They'll put you away for life.'

One push and it would be in him.

'I can see you shaking. You're trembling like a baby.'

Breen kept his eyes fixed on the blade, watching it for any sign of sudden motion.

'Please,' said Breen.

The door swung open and the music was louder, and the horse tugged at its short leash.

'Paddy?' said a voice. 'You all right?'

At his back, Breen felt the horse balk, spooked. As it kicked out, the full weight of its quarters slammed into his shoulders, catapulting him straight at the knife. He skittled straight into Danny, knocking him to the ground and tumbling down on top of him. A crack as Danny's head hit the hard step.

A glimpse of the horse, still jerking at its halter, legs still kicking out dangerously, shoes clacking on the yard floor. Danny was struggling to get to his feet to avoid being trampled.

Above Breen, Jones pulling back a fist, and thumping it into the side of Danny's head. Danny crashed down again, knife skeetering onto the cobbles.

Danny went down hard, face first this time, on the pavement. The horse, still wheeling left and right above him, whinnying. Jones dragged Danny away by the sleeve, but only so he could get enough space to start kicking him, once, twice, again and again.

Breen checked his body. No wound. No blood. He had missed the knife.

Danny curled on the floor, twitching and groaning. Jones trying to aim his boot to best effect. 'Keep still, you bastard.'

When Marilyn came out of the back door, everyone stopped and stared at her. For a minute she seemed to be struggling to understand what was going on. A horse. Breen. Her boyfriend with his eye pouring blood, snivelling.

Breen had pulled Jones off Danny, but the boy would need an ambulance.

And then she turned and swung her handbag so hard at Danny's head he didn't have a chance to duck, slapping him right on the temple with a noise that could be heard above the band.

'You're bloody chucked,' she said.

'Terrific,' said Jones rubbing his hands together. 'Enjoyed that. Best party yet. Shall I take him down the station then?'

'Don't you dare,' said Breen. 'We know what happens to people you get down the cells.'

'I just saved your life,' muttered Jones. 'Ungrateful cunt.'

'Him and a fucking horse,' said another copper.

And the band carried on playing 'Sweet Georgia Brown' as Danny sat on the step laughing and crying, waiting for the ambulance to arrive.

Tozer said, 'So it was Danny that tried to kill you?'

Back in the dance hall everyone was staring at Breen.

'That time at your flat?'

'What did I do to him?'

'Oh, Paddy, you're such a twat.'

Marilyn was back at their table downing brandy and crying onto the tablecloth. Breen and Tozer stayed well away, found a pair of stools at the bar. Tozer had taken off her shoes because her feet hurt. Inspector

Creamer and his wife approached. She still had a cigarette in one hand and a champagne glass in the other.

'Did I hear right? You were attacked?'

'Not really, sir.'

'I won't have fighting,' he said. 'You lot are going to have to bloody shape up. There are ladies here.'

He walked away, his wife waddling after him.

Tozer said, 'Marilyn's as mad as he is, you ask me. They deserve each other. Shall we get really drunk?'. 'Really, really drunk.'

'You look like you are already.'

She smiled slightly crookedly. 'I haven't even started. That poor bloody woman in Margate though. I keep thinking about her. She's so scared, but I keep thinking she was just as frightened of us as the bad people.'

'Maybe we are the bad people,' said Breen. 'I mean, not us. But the police.'

'Yep,' she said. 'Maybe you are.'

Carmichael came up with his dolly bird on his arm. 'Aye, aye,' he said. 'I missed all the excitement. Who'd have thought he was jealous of you, Paddy.'

'Can we go?' said Sequin Girl. 'I'm bored.'

Carmichael said, 'Don't you want to have another dance?'

'Not really,' she said. 'The band's square. Can we leave now?'

'There's a couple of tossers from Paddington Green going at it in the lobby,' said Carmichael. 'Normally they'd have drawn a crowd by now but nobody's bothered tonight. The main event's already happened.' Sequin Girl was dragging him away. '1968 is the year you were saved by a deaf horse, Paddy Breen.'

'I need to speak to you, John,' said Breen. 'About those squatters.'

'Next week,' Carmichael said.

Tozer said, 'You look pale. Have another drink.'

'Of course I'm pale,' said Breen. 'Bloody hell.'

'At least you know now . . . who it was, trying to do you in.'

Breen nodded. His head hurt.

'Poor Paddy. I should take you home and look after you.' She leaned forward and kissed him gently. 'No funny stuff, mind you.'

'I thought you wanted to stay and get drunk on the free booze.'

'I'll manage.' While the barman wasn't looking she reached over the bar. Breen looked at her bony, awkward body, stretched across the width of the counter. Her skirt rode up, showing her bare legs. All the other women in the room were wearing tights.

And as he looked away from her bare skin he caught Marilyn's eye. She was looking at him and Tozer with pure, sodden hatred.

When Tozer sat back on her bar stool she was holding something which she stuffed into her handbag before Breen could get a good look at it.

'If we leave together there's going to be gossip whether you sleep in my dad's bed or not.'

'I'm only here a couple of days more. Let's get a taxi,' Tozer said. 'Can you afford it?'

Out on the street, while Breen was looking for a passing cab to hail she pulled the bottle she'd stolen out of her handbag and said, 'Chivas Regal? Is that any good?'

'Is that all?' said Breen as the taxi rattled across the London potholes, 'Just a couple of days?'

THIRTY

Breen lay in his narrow bed, with Tozer taking more than her fair share of the space. She was snoring.

The luminous hands of his travel clock said it was gone eight in the morning. He needed to pee and his head hurt. They had drunk too much.

Tozer had crawled into his bed at around four-ish, and had fallen straight to sleep. They had not had sex. His father's bed lay empty in the small room next door. No one had slept there since his father had died.

He was conscious that he had his pyjamas on, but that she was dressed in a pair of cotton knickers and nothing else. The closeness of her skin. The rise and fall of her shoulders. Even the smell of cigarettes in her hair smelt good. He tried not to think too hard about it. He prayed she would not wake and notice his erection.

He was not used to this. He had grown up in a woman-less house; yes, he had slept around a little in his teenage years and a few times in his early twenties, but that seemed like a long time ago. Looking after his father had left him little time for women. A few weeks ago he and Tozer had had sex and it had been good. But she was young; it hadn't meant anything to her.

He thought about Shirley Prosser instead. A woman his age. A more responsible woman who knew, like him, what it was to have to care for someone. She was more his type, wasn't she?

At around half past eight he couldn't take the pressure on his bladder any longer, so he edged out of bed slowly, springs creaking. He grabbed his clothes off the chair and tiptoed away.

The flat was freezing. He switched on the electric bar fire in his living room, put another couple of half-crowns in the meter, went to the kitchen and filled the kettle with water, then put it on the hob.

There was a hard frost outside. Black stalks of dead plants rimmed with white outside the window. It was the last Sunday before Christmas.

The newsagent's stall by the police station was busy. 'Sunday Times,' he said, handing over a shilling. Moon rocket launches. Peace talks in Vietnam. Civil Rights march in Londonderry.

He walked down to Joe's cafe and bought fresh bagels and smoked salmon.

Back at the flat, he peeked in on Tozer. She was laid across the bed now, arms splayed out, a single nipple poking out above the blankets. He looked at her a little too long, then retreated to the kitchen to put the coffee on and to look for a bottle of aspirin.

She appeared at the kitchen doorway looking white. 'That coffee smells off,' she said. 'You don't have any ordinary, do you?'

'I feel rubbish,' she said, lying on the sofa.

He handed her a cup of Nescafé and two aspirin. She had found his dressing gown and was wearing it. It looked huge on her, bare feet poking out of the bottom.

'Are you hungry?'

She scowled at him. Best to leave her alone. He would have liked the chance to talk to her about where they stood, but the time never seemed right. He fetched a blanket and laid it over her, then sat in his father's chair reading the paper with the bagel sitting on a sideplate on one side of him and his coffee on the other. Tozer left hers to grow cold.

'I think I'm going to be sick,' she said.

He fetched the washing-up bowl from the sink and laid it next to her on the sofa.

'What's that smell?'

'Smoked salmon,' he said.

'Can you eat it somewhere else?'

He sighed, stood up and took his half-finished bagel and put it in the fridge, then returned to his coffee and paper. 'I told Creamer I wanted to speak to him. I should tell him what I know. What I think I know.'

'He's an arse,' she said. 'First day in, he pinched my bum.'

'What did you do?'

She shrugged as if it happened all the time.

Breen looked at her. 'Aren't you going to miss all this?'

'I love London,' she said. 'I'll go crazy down in Devon. But I've no choice. You looked after your dad, didn't you? I'm the only one, now. You know what it's like. I have to go back.'

Breen nodded.

Breen kept his father's address book in his father's bedside table. He went to get it, then flicked through and found John Nolan's name written in his father's spidery hand.

He dialled him.

'Who are you calling?' asked Tozer.

'A friend of my father's.'

The phone rang and rang. Breen was about to put the phone down when it finally picked up.

'Hello?'

'John? It's Cathal Breen.'

'We were just coming in from Mass,' said Nolan.

Breen heard the sound of children shouting in the background. A house full of people. He felt envious of the warmth of it. The opposite of his silent flat.

'John, you were working for Morton, Stiles and Prentice, weren't you?'

'That's right.'

'I'm looking for some background into a case that may involve the building trade.'

Breen could hear Nolan calling, 'Mary? Can we fit in another for lunch?'

Breen said, 'I don't know, John . . . That's kind but I'm with someone right now.'

'A girlfriend?'

'Not exactly.'

'Not exactly?' Nolan was laughing. 'Mary, what about an extra two? Bring her along as well.'

'She may not want to come with me . . .'

'What's that?' said Tozer.

Breen put his phone over the receiver and said, 'An old friend of my father's. Remember? We met him on a building site. He's inviting me for lunch and—'

'Like, a Sunday lunch?'

'Yes.

'Oh, God. I didn't think anyone in London ate Sunday lunch. I'd kill for a bit of roast.'

'I thought you were feeling sick?' said Breen.

'Is that a yes?' said Nolan. 'Splendid.'

A boy in shorts opened the door. 'Grandad. Two people at the door,' he shouted. A house in Fulham, bursting with people and noise.

'Bring him in,' shouted a voice from inside the house. Breen recognised it as Nolan's.

'That smell,' said Tozer. 'I feel better already.'

Most of the men were in the living room drinking from a keg of beer. The women were in the kitchen, helping with the Sunday dinner. Loud, warm, enveloping. Nolan emerged from the kitchen, wiping his hands on a tea towel. 'I was just press-ganged to dry up some more glasses. We don't have enough.'

'If you *will* spring guests on me at the last minute, what do you expect?' A bird-like woman, her Irish accent even stronger than Nolan's.

'This is Cathal Breen, son of Tomas Breen,' said Nolan. He pronounced his name the way his father had used to, with no 'th' sound in the middle, not the way the English did. 'The young policeman I told you about. And his friend, Miss . . . ?'

'Call me Helen,' said Tozer, holding out her hand.

'She works with me in CID,' said Breen.

The women looked saucer-eyed. 'A woman in the police? You imagine that in the Garda Síochána? What next?'

'What's the gardy whatsit?' said Tozer.

'Would you have a whiskey?' asked Mrs Nolan.

'My . . . isn't that a pretty dress,' said one of the women, looking at Tozer, eyebrows raised.

'Very fashionable, I would say,' said Mrs Nolan.

'I was at a party last night,' said Tozer. 'I haven't had a chance to change.'

And the noise in the kitchen stopped dead for just a second as the full thump of what Tozer had said was taken on board. They looked from Breen to Tozer and back again. Tozer seemed not to notice the sidelong glances of the women.

'A good party?' asked Nolan, breaking the awkward silence.

'Not bad, if you weren't a horse,' said Tozer, taking a glass of whiskey from Mrs Nolan. She looked at the glass for a second. 'Kill or cure,' she said.

'I could give you a drop of American Dry in that if you'd prefer,' said Mrs Nolan.

'I'll be fine,' said Tozer, and she took a hearty gulp from the glass.

'Great girl,' said Nolan, smiling.

The walls of the dining room were bare except for a brass Jesus impaled on a wooden crucifix, a framed picture of John F. Kennedy and a single postcard from Ireland.

'Cathal Breen is the only son of Tomas Breen of Tralee, God rest his soul, who used to be known as the best foreman in London.'

'Your father is dead, Cathal?' said one of the women.

'He died in September.'

Murmurs of sympathy passed around the room. Nolan set about introducing them to the dozen or so men, women and children milling in the room and in the tiny kitchen behind it. They all seemed to be aunts or uncles or cousins.

'I wanted to pick your brain,' said Breen holding a massive glass of whiskey that Nolan had given him.

'There will be time for that after lunch. These women cook the best roast dinner in West London,' said Nolan.

Breen's father had arrived in London a generation before this wave of immigrants, driven out of Kerry by the scandal of his eloping with a married woman. He had wanted Cathal to have nothing to do with these uneducated families who crowded into London slums. And yet, Breen thought, he and his father would have been made so welcome. His father had kept all this from him. All this companionship lost.

When they discovered Tozer's family were farmers, her stock rose a little. They quizzed her about what cows they had, about how many they had, how many they sent for slaughter each year, and seemed impressed by her answers.

'My father's not well. I'm going back to run the farm in January.'

'Giving up the police?' said one thin, sharp-nosed woman. 'No job for a woman anyway, I would say.'

'Why not?' said Tozer.

The whiskey was kicking in already.

Breen drew the conversation away from her, 'You're still working on the Westway?'

Nolan nodded. 'Years of work in that still,' he said.

Breen wandered into the kitchen. 'Can I give you a hand with anything?' he offered Mrs Nolan. He peered into the pot on the hob and said, 'Shall I drain those potatoes for you?'

The women turned and looked puzzled.

'I cook,' said Breen, watching one of them pouring away the water from the carrots down the plughole, thinking, That would have gone well in a gravy.

'I'm sure we'll manage perfectly well,' the woman said, as if offended by the enquiry.

They ate with little ceremony, starting as soon as the plates were on the table, so that by the time Mrs Nolan sat down, after filling the men's glasses with beer, most people's plates were already almost empty. And before she had had a chance to finish her own she was standing again, offering seconds and not taking no for an answer when Breen protested that he could eat no more. Even Tozer refused a second plateful.

Apple pie for pudding. Afterwards the men went out into the garden and stood in the cold air and Nolan handed around cheap cigars. 'She won't have them in the house,' he complained. 'Imagine having to smoke outdoors. It's not civilised.'

'That was delicious,' said Breen. 'Thank you.' Though the meat had been gristly and the vegetables boiled to death, it had somehow tasted good. A taste of home that never was. Perhaps it was the unfamiliar feeling of sitting at a big family table. For Breen, it had always just been himself and his father, sitting in their plain kitchen, his father complaining that the mash had bits in it.

Nolan led Breen to one side and said, 'What was it you wanted to ask me about? Another missing man?'

'In a kind of way,' said Breen. 'Have you ever heard of a man called Johnny Knight?' he asked.

Nolan shook his head.

'He worked for Morton, Stiles and Prentice. He's a quantity surveyor — *was*.'

'Dead?'

'I think.'

'Plenty of pen pushers around building sites these days. I never heard of him though.' He took a puff on his cigar and blew out smoke. The men sat at garden chairs on a large concrete patio.

'It's nice what you've done here,' said Breen.

Nolan shrugged. 'My wife wanted it. She says the garden gets too much mud in the house. She'd like the whole thing covered over in concrete if she had her way.'

'And there's always a little spare concrete on a building site,' said Breen.

Nolan looked mock-outraged. 'Is that what you came here for? To accuse me of stealing from my own building sites?'

Breen said, 'It's my job.'

'Maybe the odd bag does go missing now and then,' said Nolan.

Breen looked at the concrete. It had been painted green.

'You could hide a few bodies under that,' said Tozer.

'Maybe I have,' said Nolan.

'What about Harry Cox? Do you know him?'

'Harry Cox? Fat bugger with less hair than a billiard ball?'

'That's him.'

'Met him a couple of times. Senior fellow. Working on the Westway. A smooth bastard. Doesn't show his face down our way much. Why do you ask?'

'I'm not sure,' said Breen. 'A contract like the Westway, though. It would be worth a lot of money.'

'Sure,' said Nolan. 'Hundreds of thousands. And the Westway is just a little part of it. That's just the first of the ringways. There are supposed to be a bunch of them.'

'Will you do me a favour, John? I want to find out about him. Do you know where he lives?'

'Why? Has he done something wrong?'

'I'd appreciate it if you didn't ask.'

'No problem, Cathal. I'll nose around.'

Breen said, 'I like your family. They're nice people.'

'You're almost family to me,' said Nolan. 'Think of it that way.' They sat in silence for a little while longer, until Nolan asked, 'You still going back to Ireland, you think?'

'I'd like to.'

'Don't expect too much, Cathal. We've had the bollocks ripped out of us.'

They walked as far as Hammersmith to catch the tube train. There were only a few running on a Sunday.

Breen went up to the ticket booth and dug in his pocket for change, but there was no one at the counter.

Tozer asked, 'When you thought I was pregnant, what were you going to do?'

'I don't know. Ask you to marry me, I suppose.'

Tozer burst out into laughter.

'What's wrong with that?'

'Sorry,' she said. 'You're sweet.' She leaned forward and kissed him on the cheek.

A man with a nicotine-stained moustache appeared at the window of the ticket office.

'I have to pack. I'm going down to Devon after work tomorrow. For Christmas Eve,' she said.

'Oh,' said Breen. 'Of course.' Breen put fivepence down on the counter for her ticket.

In the empty tube compartment, rattling round the District Line, she said, 'I hate Christmas.' He nodded. He thought of her dead sister. All families with murdered children hated Christmas.

They both stood as the train approached Notting Hill Gate. They would go their own ways. He would carry on to Paddington and change there to head home; she would take the Central Line back to the section house. She got out and stood on the platform facing him in the doorway of the Underground train. She gave a small smile and waved at him as the doors closed and his train jerked away from her, eastwards. He sat back down, alone in the compartment, still irritated at how she'd laughed at him.

THIRTY-ONE

On Monday he woke up with the beginning of something. A cold or worse.

Too much to drink over the weekend.

Frustrated. Angry. Too many loose ends. He looked around the living room. Where had all the pieces of paper scattered around the floor come from? Lists of names. Diagrams. He had been writing them late into the night.

There was a pile of pages for Frankie Pugh, another for Sergeant Michael Prosser, and a third for Johnny Knight. Times of death. Dates. Associates. Theories.

Three dead men. Two murders and a death by misadventure.

Two of the deaths, at least, were inconvenient. The sons of ministers were not supposed to be drug addicts. Policemen were not supposed to be bent.

At 9.30 the phone rang. So loud that Breen jumped.

'Yes?'

'Morning, Paddy. How's the Christmas wrapping going?' Marilyn's voice. Sing-song cheery, as if nothing at all had happened on Saturday night.

'How's your fiancé?' Breen asked.

'Don't be like that,' she said. 'I've chucked him out. Honestly, Paddy. I didn't know he was so haywire.'

Breen said, 'He tried to kill me.'

'He ruined everything between us,' she said miserably. 'I'm so ashamed. I almost didn't make it to work today.'

'What do you mean, "between us"? There was never anything between us.'

Was it the crackle on the telephone, or was she just pretending not to hear?

'Paddy? You still there? Inspector Creamer says you should come in. You wanted to see him, he said. Know what?' She lowered her voice. 'He just told Jones he should go for Sergeant.'

'Jones? You're joking. You think he's getting me back to work?'

'Maybe.'

That would be something at least.

'When?'

'This afternoon. Four o'clock.'

'Four?' That was hours away. 'Tell him I'll be there. That all?'

'Paddy? Don't be like that. It wasn't my fault. I don't think Creamer likes me much. He's talking about bringing in his own typist.'

She was still talking when Breen put down the phone on her.

'Turn down that moronic racket,' he shouted through the letterbox of the flat upstairs.

He went into town early and tried Christmas shopping instead. An unfamiliar experience.

At Macari's on Charing Cross Road he bought a steel-string guitar for twenty-five guineas and carried it away in a big cardboard box, all tied up with string. He walked through to Hamleys to see if he could find anything for Charlie Prosser, but the shop was packed and his parcel kept hitting small kiddies, plus he couldn't find anything he thought Charlie would like. Besides, he and Shirley were travelling light.

First thing Jones said to him was, 'What the hell are you doing here?' Then: 'What's in the cardboard box?'

'Creamer expecting me?' said Breen. The office. Monday afternoon. The dull, delicious familiarity of it. He wished he were back.

There was a man sitting at Breen's desk, in front of a large bacon sandwich and a cup of tea. Young to be so bald, thin lines of hair combed across his scalp.

'Who are you?' asked Breen. 'And why are you sitting at my desk?'

But the man had just taken a bite out of the sandwich and his mouth was full, so he couldn't answer.

'Ain't your desk,' said Jones.

'Where's Marilyn?'

'Gone to the Ladies. She's a bit upset. Creamer's told her she's getting the boot, he says.'

'Marilyn?'

Jones nodded.

'He can't give Marilyn the sack.'

'Her boyfriend just tried to remove your liver.'

'Marilyn is the only thing that holds this stupid place together. And where am I supposed to sit when I come back?' said Breen. Bad-tempered. Head starting to swim. This morning's cold wasn't going away. Now he was feeling bad for being so spiky to Marilyn on the phone this morning.

Creamer opened the door and smiled. 'Ah, Paddy Breen,' he said. 'Do come in.'

The African violets were gone. Bailey's shelves had been emptied. The desk was clear, apart from a single cream telephone. New pictures on the wall. New comfy chair behind the desk.

'So. Am I back?'

'Dear, no.' Creamer smiled. 'That's not in my jurisdiction, I'm afraid. But I'm glad you came in. I wanted a word.'

Inspector Creamer's room smelt fusty. Of armpits and cigarettes. A new photograph on the wall. The Met First XV Rugby Team, all thick armed and cauliflower-eared.

'Close the door, there's a good lad.'

Oh.

'I had a call from a friend of mine. Harry Cox. He said you came to him asking questions about a man from his company who's gone missing.'

'Johnny Knight, sir. Sergeant Prosser's brother-in-law. He worked for Harry Cox's company—'

'Harry Cox was under the impression you were working for Marylebone CID.'

'I met with Scotland Yard CID. I told them all this, sir. I thought it was important they knew.'

Creamer smiled. 'I'm not as stupid as you must think I am, Sergeant Breen. You're suspended, yet you still went to Cox and questioned him. You had no right to go bothering the man. You are not a policeman right now. You are a civilian. Go home and stay there until you hear from me. Don't even pick up the phone. I don't want to see you here. You're fortunate I don't discipline you for what you've done.'

'Sir.'

The lips twitched slightly. 'You were in a bit of a fight on Saturday night, weren't you?'

'I was attacked, sir.'

Creamer hummed to himself, then said, 'I'm looking to make some changes here. I think it's fair to say that I'm not sure I'll be needing you, when your suspension is over. Don't think this is personal. Bailey thought very highly of you, I understand.' His smile became a smirk. Anyone Bailey thought highly of . . . 'But I want officers I can rely on. It's no secret this CID division has been letting the side down. If I can't trust officers, I don't want to have them as part of my team. It would be a good time to look into a transfer. I'm only trying to be fair.'

'But Constable Jones is staying?'

Creamer smiled again. 'Don't look so shocked. This whole department was due for a shake-up. We need young blood to come through. Jones is keen. Does what he's bloody told.'

He picked up some papers and tapped them straight on his desktop. Three times. Tack, tack, tack.

*

'Where you going?' said Jones.

'Have you seen Tozer?'

'No. What's wrong? You look rubbish, Paddy. What's that in the box?'

He sat at Marilyn's empty desk. 'Have you got any Sellotape?'

'Marilyn will.' Breen pulled open the drawers and pulled out a big heavy metal dispenser and set about wrapping the box the guitar was in with gaudy red-and-green Christmas paper.

Nobody said anything.

'There,' he said, when he was finished, standing back to look. A bit messy. There were still patches of cardboard showing through the wrapping, but he had run out of paper. He picked it up and put it on Jones's desk.

'Make sure Helen gets it,' he said. 'It's a goodbye present.'

'Oooh,' said Jones. 'She's Helen now, is she?'

Breen was already pushing his way out of the CID room door to make his way out of the building.

He woke on Christmas Eve. Even under his blankets he could tell that the weather had turned bitter.

And he was coming down with a cold. His head ached and his sinuses felt thick with mucus.

In the morning on BBC 2 they showed grainy pictures of the moon taken from Apollo 8. In a London studio they were talking about the great adventure of the human spirit. From across the Atlantic came the chatter of men in the vast NASA mission control office. 230,000 miles away, men had disappeared behind the moon. They were waiting for them to re-emerge.

While men in suits at Jodrell Bank speculated about how close the Soviets were to a moon landing, the minutes ticked by. Everyone waited, not completely convinced that the spacecraft would emerge again.

Breen watched, feverish, feeling for a while that he was witnessing an adventure as great as Captain Cook's voyages. Not just witnessing it. By watching, he was part of it. Connected by the television. The newness of the world seemed amazing.

But when he switched the television off to go to the kitchen to make some soup from a piece of chicken and some vegetables, the feeling of the big connectedness vanished just as quickly as the dot on his TV screen. The ordinary mid-winter greyness of London reasserted itself. He went to the drawer in his bedroom and fetched himself a clean handkerchief.

He slept through the afternoon and woke to the sound of bells. A midnight Mass somewhere.

He looked at his watch. Just past midnight. Happy Christmas. His first alone, without his father. He crawled into bed and lay there thinking about the strangeness of this year. He could not bring it into focus. Increasingly it seemed like a series of bizarre events that had whirled around him like a storm, fragments passing in the air.

At eleven in the morning, the next day, he woke to the smell of cooking turkey, drifting down from the flats above. He was shivering and drenched in sweat.

He pulled his dressing gown around him and went to the front room. The smell of his neighbours' cooking made him feel nauseous.

He switched on the TV and sat there, wondering what Shirley Prosser was doing. Were she and Charlie unwrapping presents?

He phoned Directory Enquiries to find the number for the Mooring Guest House in Margate, but the line was engaged. As he put the phone down, it rang, making him jump.

'Listen,' a voice said.

And there was a strum of music.

'Hear that?'

'I heard it,' said Breen.

'It's fab. It must have cost millions.'

'Millions,' said Breen. 'How are your mum and dad?'

'You OK? You sound funny.'

'A cold,' he said.

'My dad, he's not so good.' Another strum of the guitar. 'My mum is great, though. It brings up stuff being back here. Crazy stuff.'

'Your sister?'

Strum. He imagined her holding the receiver with her shoulder, guitar on her lap.

'I was her older sister. I should have looked after her better.' Strum. 'Hibou too. I shouldn't have left her.'

'Have you been drinking?'

'The odd sherry,' said Tozer. 'I keep thinking about Hibou. I can't help it.'

'She'll be OK.'

'I don't think so. Women like that get fucked. Sorry. A bit drunk.'

'It's OK.'

Breen could hear Tozer's mother in the background. 'Helen. You OK in there?'

'I'm on the phone, Mum.' Then, 'I've got to go and do the milking in a minute. Takes twice as long when you've had a skinful. Bloody freezing out there.'

He woke up in his father's armchair later in the evening with the sense that he had dreamed the phone conversation with Tozer. The TV was showing *Christmas Night with Stars*. He switched it off and went back to bed.

By Friday, the day after Boxing Day, his cold was no worse.

He took the Bridget Riley off the wall and wrapped it in brown paper, caught a bus to the West End, and walked to Mount Street. It was a working day, one of the the last of the year.

The musician with the longish hair and the silver rings came to the door.

'All right?' he said. Breen thought, Tozer would probably know who this man is. Was he a pop star of some kind? She said Fraser hung out with them.

'Who is it?' The foreign-sounding woman called from behind him.

'That plod pal of Fraser's. Robert's at the gallery, I think, man.'

'Ah. The art police,' said Fraser, when he opened the glass gallery door to Breen.

He was packing boxes from a desk.

'Moving out?' said Breen.

'No. But I think I will soon. Had enough of this bloody city. Swinging London, m-my arse. London is never going to enter the twentieth century.'

Fraser looked tired. Breen guessed he'd lost whatever money the gallery had ever made. On drugs probably. He didn't look well to Breen. He looked pale and his skin was dry and flaky.

'That's a shame,' said Breen. 'People will miss you.'

'Truth?' said Fraser. 'I need to get away. Only way I can kick my habit. My flat is full of bloody junkies. Hate them. Had enough. Keep it under your hat though.'

'Is it hard, kicking a habit?'

'Staying off it. That's the hard part.'

'How was your controversial piece of work?' The work with the two St Martin's students Fraser had talked about.

'Not controversial enough, clearly. Barely raised a ripple. I can't even get arrested any more. Soon you'll be able to have sex in Trafalgar Square and call it art and nobody will bat an eyelid.'

Breen held out the wrapped print. 'I brought this back for you. I didn't want it.'

Fraser took the paper off. 'Why?'

'I didn't really like it enough. I thought you could find someone who did.'

Fraser smiled. 'OK.'

'I meant to ask. You said you knew Oliver Tarpey.'

'Yes.'

'Tell me what you know.'

Fraser took a small picture off the wall. Uncharacteristically un-modern. The moon above a dark field. 'He's everything that's despicable about England.'

'How was he with Francis Pugh?'

Fraser smiled. 'He was his babysitter. His father sent him to look after Frankie. Keep him under observation. Why are you still interested in all this?'

'He was there to keep him out of trouble?'

'Nobody from that family gave a monkey's prick for Frankie,' said Fraser. 'It was about the reputation of the Party. If Frankie made headlines for doing something stupid, for getting a girl knocked up, it would reflect badly on the dear Labour Party. The lovely working-class men who have pulled themselves up by their bootstraps. Don't get me wrong. I like working-class men. I met a lot of them in prison. I had a delightful time with them. But Tarpey was there to make sure that none of this came out.'

'You know about the abortions, then?'

Fraser nodded.

'I wanted to ask: how far do you think Tarpey would go?'

Fraser said, 'What do you mean?'

Breen said, 'How far do you think he would go to cover up whatever Francis was getting himself into.'

'The moon and back,' said Fraser. He held up the small painting.

Breen looked around at the empty art gallery. 'What'll you do next?' he asked.

'I want to learn to dance,' said Fraser.

'Seriously?'

'Absolutely. Something completely different. Contemporary dance. Don't you ever want to do something completely different?'

Tozer was off to become a farmer. Fraser was going to learn to dance. Breen just wanted to find out where he was before he went anywhere else.

'I've been thinking of doing life-drawing classes,' offered Breen.

Fraser snorted. 'I suppose, on the scale of things, that's different. For a policeman, at least.'

'What would you advise? Heroin?'

'Why not? At least you'd know what it's like then.'

'I really don't think so,' said Breen.

London was quiet. He caught a bus along Oxford Street and got off by Centre Point and walked the long way home from there.

On Saturday, restless, lonely, frustrated by being on the outside of everything, he tried Directory Enquiries again. They gave him a number for the guest house.

A man with a Scottish accent answered. 'Who?'

'Shirley.'

'Don't know.'

'She's there with a son called Charlie. He's a boy. A spastic.'

The man sounded drunk. 'The cripple lad.'

'Yes.'

'They left days ago. Just cleared out.'

The man belched loudly down the phone. Breen put the receiver down.

Breen wondered if she had gone abroad. She had at least taken his money to hide somewhere. Like the last time, it would be unlikely she would have left a forwarding address. There was no way of knowing, probably. She hadn't sent him a card letting him know where she'd gone like he'd asked her to. Too frightened, maybe. Or perhaps it was just delayed in the Christmas post. Still, another loose end.

He paced around the living room. When he found he was walking in rhythm to the rock music from the flat above he tried to vary his pace, but he kept falling back into the same rhythm.

★

That evening, Breen was sitting drawing the almost-empty bottle of Chivas Regal that Tozer had stolen from the Christmas party, sitting in his father's chair with a sketch pad on his lap when Carmichael called.

It was ten o'clock. Carmichael had been drinking and smoking. His voice was always deeper after three or four pints.

'Paddy? You were bloody right,' he said. 'The address in Abbey Gardens? Back in the summer we were watching the place. We had a tip-off they were selling drugs.'

'The squat?'

Carmichael began coughing into the phone.

'Where are you, John?'

'Some private members' club in Victoria. A few of the lads go there. It's our place.'

'You watched the squat. But you never raided the place? Was the place clean, then?'

'No. The opposite,' said Carmichael. There was the sound of a fruit machine paying out, coins pouring into the tray. 'I only found this out from talking to a couple of the old guys here. One of them was watching the place for us. But there's nothing in the files at all. Not a mention of it. I already looked.'

Breen said, 'Nothing on the files?'

Carmichael was coughing again. A rich, forty-a-day cough. 'Not surprising, given the way the Drug Squad operates. But this feller I just been buying drinks for says there he remembered writing up reports about it.'

'And no raid or anything?'

Carmichael said something he couldn't hear.

'Speak up,' said Breen. He put his finger in his ear to try to drown out the rock music.

'Listen. He says the word came from on top. Lay off them. One day they were about to raid it. Next, nothing. And somebody must have got rid of the files. The reports he wrote are gone.'

Breen said, 'What do you mean, "from on top"?'

'I don't know. I asked but he didn't know either. The Inspector? Commissioner? The Pope? Harold ruddy Wilson? I don't know. But serious. Because there's no record of us ever watching it, and there should be.'

'You sure?'

The pips went on the phone.

'Bollocks,' said Carmichael.

'Give me a number and I'll call you back.'

Breen heard the sound of more coins clunking into the phone box.

'It's OK. I got . . . I got it.'

'You drunk, John?'

'Clobbered, Paddy. All sails hoisted. But I'm sure. This guy is OK.'

'You should go home.'

'Who wants to go home?' said Carmichael. 'You should come out. I bet you're sitting at home on your own, aren't you? Come and I'll buy you a drink. Two drinks. We used to be mates, you and me.'

'We still are mates.'

'Good mates, though. Remember?'

'I've just been preoccupied, John.'

'Yeah. Well.'

The pips went again. He could hear Carmichael swearing, trying to find change, before the long beep disconnected them.

Breen sat back in the chair for a while after that, thinking. Then he went to the phone again, picked it up and dialled.

'Jones?' he said.

'What's wrong?' said Jones.

'Were you asleep?'

'No.'

Breen could hear Jones's wife in the background: 'Who's that?' The sound of pop music on the radio.

'It's Paddy Breen,' Jones said.

'What's he doing calling at this time of night?'

'I want a favour,' said Breen.

That night he went for a walk around Stoke Newington. The streets were dark and colourless. On Kingsland Road he startled a stray dog rummaging at an overturned rubbish bin. He thought he should go and see if they were showing the Buster Keaton movie, the one his father had liked, but when he reached the cinema he discovered it had been replaced by a Hammer horror movie.

He thought about Shirley and hoped she had found a place somewhere far away. Somewhere with bright white houses and blue water, with a beach so Charlie could drop into the sea and swim, free of London's awkward gravity.

THIRTY-TWO

On the last Monday of the year Jones met Breen outside the Home Office building in Petty France, the same building where Breen had gone a month earlier to meet Pugh's father.

'What are we doing here?' asked Jones. He was holding an umbrella that flapped in the wind.

'Thanks for coming. How's your wife?'

'I have to be back at my desk in half an hour. Will this take long? What's going on?'

'Better if you don't know.'

'What?'

As they were standing there, a black Rover drew up outside the main doors. Now someone was holding the door open. A familiar-looking man with grey hair and spectacles came out of the doors of the building, an aide on either side.

'Bloody hell. Is that . . . ? He looks ordinary in real life.' The Home Secretary got into the car and drove away.

'I'm just meeting someone. I want it to look good,' said Breen.

'Look good? What do you mean?'

'Don't worry about it. It'll be fine.'

Jones was all nerves. 'Paddy, we can't come here. The bloody Home Office. What are you getting me into? You're suspended. I'm going for Sergeant. I can't cock that up.'

Breen said, 'It's OK, I promise. You won't get into trouble.' He hoped. 'Just come with me and say nothing.'

'Why?'

'I just need someone to look scary.'

'Do I look scary?' said Jones, brightening.

'Whatever this man says, don't react. OK? Just keep your eyes on him.'

'Just saying. I can't afford trouble, Paddy. I got a baby coming and all.'

Again they waited in the lobby, Jones like a pupil waiting to see the headmaster.

'Don't act nervous.'

'What are you getting me into, Paddy? Who is this bloke?'

Breen said, 'A favour. It's all I ask.'

Phones rang. People trotted here and there, clutching folders and newspapers. Civil servants in pinstripes laughed loudly and called each other by nicknames that all ended in 'y'.

Fifteen minutes passed. Twenty.

'I've got to go in a second. I've got stuff to do.'

'Just five more minutes,' said Breen.

Eventually the young man at the desk said, 'Mr Tarpey will be with you shortly.'

Tarpey had commandeered a desk in an office at the top of the stairs, in what might once have been the servants' quarters of this old building. Tarpey opened the door, as ironed and crisp as ever. There was a red carnation in a small glass vase on his desk.

'Good to see you, Mr Breen,' he said, holding out his big hand. 'And this is?'

'Constable Jones. Marylebone CID.'

Tarpey frowned, skipped a beat. 'But the investigation is done? I think the Home Office should have made that absolutely clear.'

Without being asked, Breen sat down. Jones remained standing behind him.

'This is another investigation, Mr Tarpey.'

Tarpey stared at Breen for a second.

'I'm not one hundred per cent sure I understand you,' he said. He pulled his chair closer to his desk.

Breen took a moment to look around the office. The room was full of grey filing cabinets and piles of yellowing papers. On the one vertical wall hung a watercolour of a country house and an oil painting of a prize cow.

'Twenty-one, Abbey Gardens.' Breen took an *A–Z* out of his coat pocket and pointed at the page. 'We believe drugs were being dealt from that address.'

Tarpey looked briefly at the map, then straight at Breen, and said, 'And your question is?'

'Do you know anything about drugs being dealt from that house?'

Tarpey paused, screwed up his eyes. 'Why are you asking me that?'

Breen looked at his face, hoping for a sign of nerves. But there was nothing. Had he guessed wrongly? Or was he underestimating Tarpey?

Breen tried again. 'I asked whether you knew anything.'

'Again, I admit, I am baffled by your question, Mr Breen. This sort of investigation is not exactly in the remit of your department, is it? You lot are in the business of death, not drugs.' The smile again.

'Twenty-one, Abbey Gardens,' said Breen again.

Tarpey looked from Breen to Jones, then leaned forward and picked up the phone. 'I'll need to speak to your superior officer.'

Breen smiled. It would always be Tarpey's reflex to hide behind authority, he guessed. Breen leaned forward and pressed down the stubs on the telephone's cradle. 'That's not necessary,' said Breen. 'Or even advisable.'

For the first time, it was Tarpey looking confused. 'What do you think you're doing?'

'It was you that called off the investigation by the Drug Squad into people in that house dealing drugs, wasn't it?'

Tarpey's smile was a little more fixed now. He pulled the cuff on his right-hand sleeve straight. 'Of course not. I'm not even a civil servant. I wouldn't have the power to do anything of the sort.'

'I don't believe that for a second,' said Breen.

'I'm certainly not going to discuss any of this with a junior officer. Please remove your hand or I will have you thrown out of here.'

Behind Breen, Jones fidgeted. Nerves.

Had he overplayed the few cards he had? Breen pressed on. 'You used the Home Office's authority to stop a police investigation.'

Tarpey said nothing. He was looking beyond Breen, at the wall behind his head. A first sign of anger, perhaps?

Breen said, 'How did you find out that Francis Pugh was buying heroin from the squatters in Abbey Gardens?'

'As I said, I am not going to discuss this with junior officers.'

'I think you'll find it in your best interest to tell me,' said Breen. 'Did Rhodri Pugh know that you prevented the Drug Squad from doing their job? Or was it him that ordered you to make them stop the investigation into drug dealing from the squat?'

Tarpey stayed quiet. He was thinking.

Breen went on. 'Because if it was known that a minister had interfered with the business of the Metropolitan Police to protect his son, who was addicted to heroin, that would be quite a scandal.'

'There's no way of proving that.'

'I don't have to prove it. I just need to suggest it.'

Tarpey put down the handset finally. He sucked his lower lip.

'If you're trying to threaten me, it won't work.'

Breen said, 'With the government cracking down on drugs, Francis Pugh would be an embarrassment. It wouldn't do if the son of a senior Home Office minister turned out to be a drug addict.'

Tarpey looked sideways at the filing cabinet. He would be calculating the risk. The options.

'The Drug Squad were going to raid Abbey Gardens. You found out about it. Or maybe Francis's father did. You put a stop to it to protect Rhodri Pugh from scandal.'

Breen could hear Jones shuffling uneasily behind him.

'But that didn't get rid of the problem, did it? I'm sure you tried to persuade Francis to stop taking heroin, but it's not as easy as that, is it?'

Tarpey was still looking away, his face unreadable.

Breen continued, 'What I'm not sure about is whether Francis was simply found dead from an overdose, and you persuaded someone to try and cover it up, or whether it's something much worse than that.'

'I sincerely hope you know what you're doing,' said Tarpey very quietly.

'As you say, newspapers can get the wrong end of the stick,' said Breen.

Tarpey looked down at the paper on his desk and, finally, met Breen's eyes. 'Yes, you're right. They can.'

'Good,' said Breen. 'Now we've got that out of the way, we can talk?'

Tarpey nodded. 'We had better.'

Breen turned in his chair. 'It's OK, Jones. You can go now.'

Jones looked puzzled. 'Go?'

'Yes,' said Breen. 'Back to the station.'

Jones hesitated for a second. 'You sure?'

Breen nodded, heard Jones clear his throat. Confused about what he'd been doing there. He scratched his head a couple of times and then said, 'See you, Paddy. I mean, Sergeant.'

'Very clever,' said Tarpey, when he was gone. 'Very well played, got to admit. Now. There is a point to this exercise, I presume?'

Breen said, 'I need you to do something for me.'

'Perhaps,' said Tarpey, standing, 'we should continue this discussion elsewhere.'

They left the building and walked through Parliament Square. Westminster was looking grey and tired. Gothic verticals disappearing into foggy sky. Only the odd red bus or black taxi sweeping through.

They sat on a bench behind the black statue of the Burghers of Calais; men with rope around their necks. Side by side, Breen and

Tarpey talked, not looking at each other, instead both gazing out over the pigeon shit-spattered wall to the river beyond, towards Lambeth. The tide was high. Tugs chugged upriver, pulling barges.

A thin drizzle was falling but it wasn't enough to disturb them. They negotiated. This was the way Tarpey did things. Breen had come to understand that. Small deals here and there. A whisper. A nudge. After around twenty minutes Tarpey stood and shook Breen's hand.

It was dark when he got home. There was an envelope on the doormat. A late Christmas card. With fingers stiff from the late December cold, he opened it. A mawkish picture of baby Jesus, laid on straw, a shiny halo above his head and a knowing smile on his face. The card was from John Nolan. 'Happy Christmas from John and all of the family.' Breen put it on the kitchen table.

In the evening he made leek and potato soup, and while it was cooking, phoned Tozer at the farm. Her mother said she was out.

He imagined her in some cider bar in the local town.

'One of the byres has a leaky roof. She's fixing it up.'

'Oh,' said Breen.

'Any message?'

He told Tozer's mother he would call again in the morning. 'It's very important I talk to her,' he said.

He was disappointed. He couldn't help it, but he felt proud of himself. Something he had not felt in a long time. In years, maybe. He had wanted to tell Tozer what he'd done. What he was about to do.

THIRTY-THREE

Upstairs there was a New Year's Eve party.

Tozer called that evening.

'I'm shagged out,' she said. 'And we're short of hay already 'cause it was such a rubbish summer. I can play "Sunshine Superman" on the guitar though. Driving my dad mad.'

'How is he?' asked Breen. 'Your father?'

'The farm is worse than I thought. The cows are in a bad state. He kept them out in the pasture too long in the autumn and they suffered. Yield is way down. He doesn't even talk much. What was it you wanted?'

Then he told her about the meeting with Tarpey. Tarpey had told him how Rhodri Pugh had tried to get his son off heroin. He had paid for blood transfusions and other quack cures. None of them had worked. And then about how they had become increasingly worried he was going to be arrested, exposed in the papers as an addict. For the last year, Pugh's department had been taking a new hard line on drug taking. Lock up the addicts. Cut off the demand.

Then Tarpey had discovered that the Drug Squad were watching the squat, getting ready to raid it. Tarpey realised that if they were raided they would almost certainly start to shout about the cabinet minister's son they had been suppling with drugs. It would not look good for the ministry. He went to Pugh; told him what was going on. Pleaded with him to act. For the good of the Party. Reluctantly, Pugh pulled strings. The investigation was dropped. Effectively from that point onwards, the Paradise Hotel was now dealing drugs under police protection.

'Bloody hell,' said Tozer.

'Don't you swear in this house,' said someone in the background. Tozer's mum.

'Then Tarpey says he got a phone call from Jayakrishna one night saying that Francis Pugh had overdosed on heroin. Jayakrishna knew that if it came out in the papers he'd lose everything. They only had protection as long as they were keeping Frankie Pugh's addiction a secret. So he suggested they cover it up.'

'So the stupid hippie buggers blew the whole lot up?'

'Helen. I told you!'

'And stripped his arms and legs of skin to hide the heroin tracks.'

'And did their best to empty him of blood in an attempt to stop them being able to test the body for opiates.'

'My God.'

Breen told Tozer about the deal they'd made, sitting in the park overlooking the Thames. Breen said he would keep Tarpey's secret as long he promised to make Jayakrishna set up a meeting between Tozer and Hibou. If Hibou wanted to go, Jayakrishna would have to let her.

'Or I said I'd go to the papers. That way the whole deal would come down.' Pugh would be exposed, not only as the father of a drug addict but as a minister who abused his power to protect his reputation. Jayakrishna would lose the house. 'Tarpey rang me today. It's all set up.'

'Bloody, bloody hell.'

'Helen. I'm not having that.'

He could hear Tozer shouting, 'Shut up, Mum. For once. This is bloody important!' Then she spoke into the handset again. 'But if you went to the papers, that would have been your career over.'

'Possibly,' said Breen.

They talked a little longer until Tozer said she had to run. There was a problem with the milking machine.

'Happy New Year, Paddy. You deserve one.'

He sat without moving for a long time after the call. Upstairs somebody broke something. A glass or a bottle. She was right. He did deserve a good one.

Dangerous to be so pleased with himself. His father had always taught him never to be sure of anything. At any moment the rug could be pulled from under you. But his father had been a bitter and disappointed man. Maybe he didn't have to be one himself.

The party carried on late into the morning. Maybe two or three o'clock. There had been dancing in the room above his head. Thumping on the floorboards. Cheers. Loud singing of 'Auld Lang Syne'.

It was dark when Breen woke.

Welcome to 1969.

Seven in the morning. Cold and dark. It didn't feel like a good one. He turned up the wireless, loud as it would go, in the hope that they would hear it above. The race was on to get the first supersonic airliner into the air.

He did sit-ups. He had made a resolution to himself at midnight. He would get fitter this year.

After twenty-three, his stomach hurt too much. He rolled over onto his front to try some press-ups. That was when he noticed a small piece of paper on the floor just under the bookshelf. A rectangle, maybe two inches by three. He stood and scooped it up. It was a handwritten address. He looked at it, eyes wide.

Unbelievable.

The name said Harry Cox, but the careful italic handwriting was his father's.

For a mad second, tired from lack of sleep, he wondered how it could be there. His father had come back from the dead somehow to leave him a note?

Dad?

His eyes went to the corridor, the room where his father had lived. He spilt coffee down his dressing gown, onto the carpet. Impossible. Unreal.

Ghosts.

Then he remembered the card from John Nolan.

They were men of a similar age, raised in the same country schools. Everybody's handwriting was the same in those days. The piece of paper must have been tucked inside there and fallen out the day before when he opened it.

Calmer now, he turned the paper over. 'This is where he lives,' written in the same fine hand. The address was Heathside in Hampstead.

Breen sat finishing his coffee, waiting for the shakes to subside. It was New Year's Day. There would be few buses running today. Taxis scarce. He would walk. Only seven or eight miles. He ate biscuits and cheddar with a second coffee and planned his route on an *A–Z*.

Harry Cox. He had mentioned Prosser's name at the party at Kasmin's gallery. But Prosser was not one of his Met Rugby Club contacts. The connection was through Knight. Breen was sure of it now.

Clissold Park was dark and wet, water slushing under his feet on the pavements. The streets were quieter than he had ever seen them at this time of day.

As he pressed towards Finsbury Park, London was waking to a grey New Year's Day morning. He had the feeling that his presence was bringing the city to life as he moved through it. Children waking early behind closed doors. Lights came on in living rooms.

On the Seven Sisters Road a beardy tramp sat next to a brazier drinking brandy. 'Happy Christmas,' said the man, watery-eyed from drink.

'Happy New Year,' said Breen.

The Holloway Road was full of rubbish, sodden by the drizzle, the shops all bolted and shuttered. He trudged onwards, climbing up the slow hill towards Highgate.

He found a petrol station open near Whittington Park and bought a packet of cigarettes from a man in blue overalls, huddled by a paraffin heater. He never usually smoked this early in the morning but nicotine might clear his head.

The Holloway Road was so quiet he could hear his own footsteps. This was a London he had never visited. A dead zone. Only the occasional car swishing up the wet tarmac.

Marching now, body warming against the cold.

As he moved westwards towards Dartmouth Park, he noticed how the middle classes didn't have lace on the windows. They dared you to look in to see what they had.

They were switching on lights. Some still had Christmas trees in the windows so you could see how well they had decorated them.

He had been walking an hour and a half now. He felt he was getting closer. A feeling that each step was making sense of the world.

Breen stepped rapidly into the gateway of a garden. A child on a new bike was hurtling down the pavement towards him, chased by an anxious parent. A sudden interruption in the calm of the dead morning.

'Stop him!' the father cried. But it was too late. The boy was already far ahead.

'You stupid, stupid child,' shouted the chasing father. Breen looked down the hill after them, but they had rounded a corner. He walked on.

The pavements started to fill with men in tweeds with dogs, women in stout footwear. New Year's Day walks. He must be getting near to the Heath.

It was a big house, just off the Heath. A holly tree in the driveway, still covered in red berries. Two cars parked on the gravel outside. Breen was not a car person. Carmichael loved cars; he dreamed of a Lotus Cortina. Fast, masculine and flashy. Breen had never been bothered. But this time Breen noticed the cars.

Breen thought of the rollercoaster ride he'd seen at Margate. The slow rise to the top and then the crashing descent.

The man at Jumbo Records had mentioned a man in a Bristol. They were not common cars. Carmichael would know about them. There was one parked here, a big shiny grey slug on the gravel.

Breen walked up to the car, peered into the driver's window. Leather seats. Walnut fascia punctured by dials and a car radio. A pair of kid driving gloves dangling over the steering wheel. A man's car.

'Hey, you.' A voice came from the direction of the house. 'What do you think you are doing?'

Breen looked. Damn. Harry Cox, slacks and white shirt, was standing at the front door. Way out of his area, Breen had no right to be here.

'It's that bloody policeman, isn't it?'

Though it was only ten in the morning, Cox held a cut-glass tumbler with some kind of spirit in it. A puzzled look on his face. He looked from left to right behind Breen to see if there was anyone else there with him.

'What the fuck are you doing here?' Cox said. A twitch of his pale eyebrows. 'I told Inspector Creamer about you. He said you were suspended. He'll have you bloody cashiered.'

'I think we need to have a chat,' said Breen.

'I have nothing to say to you. I'm going to phone your boss. Are you mad? Just coming up here to me and my family. This is a bloody outrage.'

'Shirley Prosser,' said Breen. Just her name.

Cox hesitated long enough.

'You know her, don't you?' Until then he had not realised it. She had said she didn't know him. She had lied.

'What do you want?' He looked around. 'Just you? No other police?'

'Just me.'

Quieter now. 'Is it money?' A slight sneer to the voice.

'I'm not like Sergeant Prosser, if that's what you mean. I just want to talk.'

Cox said, 'You're right. We should talk,' He looked behind him for a moment. 'I'm not having you come in the house,' he said. 'My family are here. Come around the side.'

Cox was the sort of man who had a tradesman's entrance. He closed the front door quietly behind him. Breen followed him to the side of the house, past a grey wooden door, down an alleyway.

If Shirley had lied about Cox, what else had she lied about?

At the other end of the path he found himself standing in front of a huge, carefully clipped garden. A lawn mown in stripes. Not a weed in it. Neat beds, full of brown perennials waiting their turn. A child's swing hung from the branch of a huge cedar tree.

'It's beautiful,' Breen said and turned.

Just in time to see Cox swinging a spade at his head.

He had been an idiot.

He wasn't aware of the spade hitting him, just that he had lost consciousness for a second. He came to on the ground, struggling on hands and knees. He started crawling. There was blood on his face.

Cox was coming to hit him again. All the energy in his fat frame was straining upwards ready to bring the spade down on him. Luckily the alleyway was narrow. There was not much room to swing the tool in. It clanged off the wall and cracked half-heartedly into Breen's shoulder.

He was on all fours now. If he could stand, he could run, Breen thought sluggishly. If he didn't run, Cox would kill him.

He had killed before. He was sure of it now. But Cox was raising the spade a third time, ready to smash it down onto him.

And Breen saw movement at the end of the alleyway.

Outlined by the light at the end of the pathway, a girl in a blue best dress, blue ribbons in her hair, mouth wide.

Almost ridiculously English. A daddy's girl, all made from sugar and spice.

'Daddy?'

A second's hesitation. Enough for Breen to recover a little.

She was staring at a man on his knees, blood coming from the wound on Breen's head. Her father, open-mouthed, holding a spade.

The girl started bawling.

He shouldn't have come here alone. He shouldn't have come here at all. He should have run the moment he saw the Bristol.

As he was sluggishly struggling to his knees, the girl still screaming, a woman appeared. She was in her forties, elegant even in a striped apron, a smudge of flour on her chin.

Breen finally made it to his feet. Looked quickly behind him. Harry had run. Disappeared. Gate wide open behind him.

'Where's Harry?' Breen shouted. He was standing now, swaying.

The woman – Cox's wife? – was open-mouthed. Dumbstruck and horrified. A stranger in her garden, screaming at her, head covered in blood.

'Where did he go?' shouted Breen.

She found her voice. 'Help, help, help!'

Breen wiped the wetness from his eyes. He stumbled back down the alleyway to the driveway in time to see the Bristol disappearing through the gate, spitting gravel behind it.

The woman had followed him and was standing behind him screaming, 'Get out! Get out of here.'

She had picked up the discarded spade and was waving it at him.

'Where's the phone?' he shouted.

Another child, a boy this time, in corduroy shorts and a blazer, appeared at the front door.

Breen pushed past him.

'Get out of my house!' screamed the woman. She looked terrified.

Breen looked around for the telephone, but it wasn't in the hallway.

'Phone,' he said again.

The woman just stood there, horrified.

'I'm a policeman. Where's the phone?'

But the woman was beyond speaking. He ran down the corridor

into the kitchen. A big room. Pots of peeled vegetables on the hob. The smell of pork. Spices.

No phone though. From there into the living room. Huge. Harry Cox's taste in art came home with him. A big Patrick Caulfield painting above the fireplace. A neat Christmas tree with electric lights. The startled little girl and boy looking at him, eyes like pennies.

And a cream-coloured telephone on a small regency table.

He picked it up and dialled. 'CID duty officer,' he said to the woman who answered the phone. She put him through to another extension. A phone somewhere in Scotland Yard, ringing.

Mrs Cox was in the living room now. 'Can someone please tell me what the hell is going on?' she said.

Receiver still ringing in his ear, Breen said, 'What's the registration of the Bristol? The number plate?'

'What?'

'The number plate,' he shouted. The boy in shorts started to cry.

'XKX 754 F,' the girl in the blue dress said.

'Write it down. Give it to me on a bit of paper.'

Shocked, she did exactly what he asked.

'Please. What are you doing?' the mother said.

A voice answered the phone. 'CID?'

'I'm Detective Sergeant Cathal Breen, D Division. Take this down. I have a suspect for the murder of former Detective Sergeant Michael Prosser. His name is Harold Cox.'

When he put the phone down there was a sticky red handprint on the ivory-coloured handset.

Afterwards, having held his head under the cold tap, watching the red circle down the plug hole, he held a tea towel that he'd taken from the kitchen to his head, waiting for the police cars to arrive.

Mrs Cox was in shock. She didn't know what to do. She had guests to entertain.

'Perhaps he's gone to fetch his mother?' she said. 'She comes to us for lunch.'

'I don't think so,' said Breen. He looked at the tea towel. His head was still bleeding, but slower now.

The boy was still crying. 'Daddy promised to help me with my aeroplane.'

'Go away,' shouted Mrs Cox.

The boy cried louder. Sobbing. Gulping air. His sister, blue ribbons swinging in the air, punched him hard on the arm. 'Shut up,' she screamed. 'Shut up, shut up, shut up.'

The boy cried louder still.

Breen stood in the hallway, waiting. Dozens of Christmas cards, hung on loops of string.

Mrs Cox didn't know what to do. The table was half laid for lunch. A Labrador scritched at the door waiting to be let out.

'Would you like a cup of tea?' she said, unsure of what else to do.

Breen shook his head. 'Have you ever heard your husband talking about a man called Michael Prosser?'

She frowned. 'I don't think so,' she said. The crying boy came and wiped his nose on her apron. She pushed him away. 'That's horrid,' she said.

'What about Shirley Prosser?'

'Shirley?'

'Yes.'

'I think there was a woman called Shirley called a few times. He said it was work. Or was it Sally? I'm not sure. Something like that.'

Breen fingered a notebook in his pocket. 'Shirley or Sally? Which?'

'What's this about a murder?' she said. 'Please tell me.'

'Which name? You have to remember.'

'I can't bloody remember,' she shouted, too loudly. 'For Christ's sake. I don't understand.' Then: 'Sorry. I really don't know. I have a lot to do today.'

The men would arrive soon and start searching the house, looking for anything that could connect Harry Cox to Michael Prosser, turning this nice family house upside down.

They would not be long. The streets would be empty of traffic today.

In the oven, something neglected was starting to burn.

After having his head bandaged at the hospital, there was an hour of questions and explanations at New Scotland Yard. Finally, a police car dropped him back home in Stoke Newington.

The man from upstairs was just letting himself in with a pint of milk. 'Was that a police car I saw dropping you off?'

'Yes,' said Breen.

The man smiled. 'You been up to no good?'

'Kind of,' said Breen.

'Bloody hell. What happened to your head?'

Inside, he took off his suit. It was ruined. The knees were torn and the blood had dried into the jacket. He rolled it up and put it in a paper bag, ready to put into a bin.

He looked at the bottle of whisky that Oliver Tarpey had bought him and decided he should open it. He took the bottle and a glass to the bathroom, ran the bath and lay in it, exhausted.

His brain was fizzing. He needed to calm down. To stop. To relax.

The hot had run out too early. He wondered if he should go to the kitchen and boil a kettle, but he didn't. He just lay in the cooling water.

He had thought he had it all figured out. He had felt so clever after confronting Tarpey.

Now he was much less sure of himself. He started to shiver in the cold bath.

THIRTY-FOUR

On Thursday Breen put on a suit, covered his bandage with a cloth cap of his father's and travelled to work as if it were a normal day.

He took the tube. No jesters or buskers. Everything was perfectly ordinary. The same fug of cigarette smoke in the compartment. The same puddles on the pavement. The same worn stone steps up to the front of the police station.

Inside, on the first floor, Marilyn was not at her desk. Another woman, much older, was sitting there. The office looked oddly different. Breen noticed Carmichael's old pictures of film stars had finally been taken down.

'Yes?' she said. The woman at Marilyn's desk had a cream cardigan on and wore her hair in a bun.

'Where's Marilyn?'

'She no longer works in this particular office,' said the woman.

'And you do instead?'

'I am Inspector Creamer's assistant,' she said, looking up at him.

'Good. I want to see Inspector Creamer.'

She smiled. 'And you are?'

'Detective Sergeant Cathal Breen. I work here.'

'Do you?' she looked puzzled. 'I'm sorry. I'm new.' She banged a staple into the corner of a sheaf of papers. 'I think he's busy, but I'll check,' she said, and dialled the phone even though Creamer was only fifteen feet away in his office.

Jones was head down at his desk, as if pretending not to have noticed Breen was in. The balding man who had taken over Breen's desk looked over the top of his typewriter at him.

It was different, but the same.

'He'll see you now,' chirped the woman, smiling.

Creamer's top button was undone. He looked hot, or flustered, or both. There was a sheet of paper crumpled up into a ball on the blotting paper in front of him. 'Breen. How's your head? Took a nasty knock then?'

Without being asked, Breen sat down opposite him.

'Perhaps you can tell me what's going on? Scotland Yard want to interview me about Harry Cox.'

Breen ignored the question. 'Do you know where Cox is?' he asked.

Creamer squinted. 'That's what Scotland Yard wanted to know.' He looked nervous. 'Christ's sake, please, tell me. What has happened?'

For the next ten minutes, Breen talked and Creamer listened. He started from Sergeant Prosser being caught out for taking money to help local gangs rob shops. He moved on to how a body had been discovered in a burnt-out empty house, how Prosser had discouraged him from investigating the case. He talked about how he'd discovered Prosser was bent and how he'd forced him to resign. From there he talked about Prosser's disappearance and then his murder. Then about discovering Johnny Knight's house empty. And the links between Prosser, Cox and Knight. He explained how Harry Cox had come to be a suspect in the Prosser murder case and how he was also apparently connected to the death of Michael Prosser's brother-in-law.

He left Shirley Prosser's name out of it. Less out of any gallantry than knowing he had been wrong.

Throughout all this Creamer stayed silent, nodding, fiddling with the crumpled paper on his desk.

Finally he spoke. 'I would never have believed it of Harry Cox. He seemed such a respectable man.'

'He was a close friend of yours,' said Breen.

'Not close, really,' said Creamer, looking away.

'Really? That's what he said to me.' Breen stood. He peered at the photographs of the rugby teams on Creamer's wall.

'Did he?'

'Mentioned you by name several times. In fact, isn't that him?' he said, pointing to a short man in a blazer standing next to one of the teams.

'No,' said Creamer. 'I don't think so.' He stood. Tugged at his shirtsleeves. 'It does look a little like him, I suppose. But it's definitely not.'

'You probably know him from the Freemasons as well, don't you?'

Creamer coloured. 'Is he a Mason? I had no idea.'

'Of course not.' Breen had spotted the Masonic ring on Cox's pudgy finger the first time he'd seen him. He had asked around a little. His hunch that Creamer too, was a Freemason had been right. He sat down again and smiled. 'So. Here we are then.'

'Yes,' said Creamer.

Creamer had looked anxious before, but he looked worse now: his face redder, his lips tighter.

'Just now, did Scotland Yard have any idea where Cox had gone to?'

'No. None at all. He's disappeared. His wife has no idea. Poor girl. Nice woman,' Creamer mumbled.

'Anyway, as I'm sure you're aware, Scotland Yard no longer regard me as a suspect. I presume that means I can return to work.'

'Right away.' Creamer attempted a smile. 'I should apologise. I spoke to you harshly the other week.'

'I didn't mention to Scotland Yard that you and Cox had spoken. That he used his connection to you to try and close down the investigation into Johnny Knight.'

Creamer looked clammier. 'I wouldn't put it like that,' said Creamer. 'Just because he used my name . . .'

'As I said. I didn't mention it to Scotland Yard.' But he could at any point.

You never knew where these things would lead. There might be an investigation. Some jumped-up inspector from the provinces coming in to poke their nose into Metropolitan Police business. How they would love that.

A part of Breen was shocked at how easy he found it to do this. The look of fright in Creamer's eyes. The sense of power he wielded over him. He should be disgusted at himself. This is the kind of thing Oliver Tarpey did. Using people's secrets against them.

He wasn't too different. Dealing with bad people, his father had said, the stink of the sewer will rub off on you.

'Same desk?' Breen asked.

'If you like.'

They sat in silence for a minute, until Creamer said, 'Well then, Paddy. I'm sure you have a lot to do.'

Breen didn't move. 'A birdie told me you were telling Constable Jones he should go for Sergeant.'

An uncertain smile. 'Yes. Good man.'

'Do you think he'll make Sergeant if he's the subject of an internal investigation?'

Creamer looked puzzled. 'What investigation?'

Breen leaned forward and wrote the name of the man who had died in the cells on Creamer's blotting paper. 'The investigation into a recent death in the cells that you might wish to initiate.' He added the date the man died and underlined it.

Creamer peered at the paper. 'Death in the cells? I've not heard anything about that.'

'You should start asking a few questions then.'

Creamer looked puzzled but said, 'Yes. I will. Of course.'

Breen nodded. 'I was wondering. Will later this afternoon be OK for me to return to work, sir? Only I've got something I've got to finish first.'

He was fifteen minutes early for the 11.52 at Paddington. He stood on the platform end. He was back at work. He was a policeman again. He had something to do. But he was also a little appalled at himself. First Tarpey, now Creamer. This was the way it started. A slow corruption.

And scared, too, about the way so much had spiralled out of control.

Tozer got off the diesel train wearing a duffel coat and black boots. He spotted her strolling down the long platform towards him, pushing past families with trunks and bags. He waved. She didn't wave back even though she wasn't carrying any bags; she was planning to catch the train back to Devon that evening.

'You look different,' he said when she arrived.

She said, 'I'm not a copper anymore.'

'Good trip?' he asked.

'I'm nervous,' she said. 'She may not want to leave.'

Breen nodded. 'It's very possible,' he said.

'Your head?' she said.

White bandage showed from under the cap.

'Long story,' he said.

She didn't ask.

They made their way through the filthy station. The steam trains had stopped a few years ago, but the place still stank of coal and smut. As they waited for a taxi in the queue at the side of the station, Breen tried small talk but Tozer was only giving one-word answers, so he stopped.

She didn't ask anymore about how he was. She didn't ask about the Prosser case, or give him a chance to tell her that his suspension was over. Or explain what had happened in Hampstead with Harry Cox trying to kill him.

She was only thinking about Hibou. She stood, craning her neck to the front of the taxi queue, biting her nails.

Abbey Gardens looked the same as when he had last seen it. A little more dilapidated, perhaps. When they knocked, one of the men from the commune opened the door.

'Shoes off, please,' he said. He wore some kind of African sandals.

Breen bent to unlace his brogues, but the man said, 'Not you. Just her.'

'But—'

'I'll be fine, Paddy. Thanks.' Tozer stepped inside and started taking her big brown boots off.

Breen peered inside. The hallway had been painted a deep, dark green that sucked the light out of the place. It was lit by a single bare bulb hanging from a flaking ceiling. A girl Breen didn't recognise peered out of a doorway at them. In this house lived the people who had taken knives and skinned Frankie Pugh, cut his dead throat and wrists and hung him till he was dry.

'This way,' the man said.

The people in the house pressed their backs against the walls as Tozer passed, as if she were the carrier of some disease.

As she turned the corner and disappeared out of sight, someone closed the door on Breen, leaving him standing on the doorstep.

He took his handkerchief out of his pocket, laid it on the step and sat down, facing away from the front door.

The street was busy. A vicar pushing a bicycle. A black man with a suitcase. Two women laughing about some man.

Like Tozer, Breen wasn't sure if Hibou would want to leave the commune. These people had enfolded her. Without them she would just be a sixteen-year-old, alone in the world.

Tozer had her own reasons for wanting to save this girl. They were complex and dark, Breen was starting to realise. When someone close to you is killed, you start to calculate relationships differently. You lose a sense of proportion; or maybe gain one. Older sisters were supposed to look after their younger siblings, but Tozer had not been able to save hers. She had been killed, and in the worst possible way. And the killer had never been found. Breen wondered if getting Hibou away from these men was a way of trying to put something right. She would always be trying to save her sister. And she would never be able to. She must have seen something of her sister in Hibou: a lost girl, the same age.

But just because Tozer wanted to save Hibou didn't mean she wanted to be saved.

They were talking inside. Negotiating. How did you negotiate with a man who would strip the skin and drain the blood from another in order to protect himself? Jayakrishna was determined. He would not want to lose face. Men like that did not like to be challenged.

But when the door opened, Tozer was standing there with Hibou.

Hibou was dressed in a grubby men's army coat. It looked ridiculous on her. She carried a small cloth bag with a few possessions.

'Is that all she's got?' Breen asked.

'Here, nobody owns anything,' said Jayakrishna from inside.

'What did she come with?'

'It doesn't matter,' whispered Hibou. She looked her age now. A scared teenager not sure of what she was doing.

'Come on,' said Tozer, holding out her hand to the girl.

Jayakrishna looked angry. He glared at Hibou and said, 'Go. We took you in and looked after you and this is the way you treat us.'

Tozer was shaking. She said, 'Looked after her? You got her on drugs . . . and you—'

'Not here,' said Breen.

'You're only trouble now, you bitch,' Jayakrishna was saying. 'You're poison. You'll bring down the whole beautiful thing.'

Tozer said, 'So much for love.'

'Don't ever threaten us again,' said Jayakrishna, nose to nose with Breen. 'You are filth. Excrescence. Putrefaction.'

'Let's go,' said Tozer, tugging at Breen's sleeve, taking Hibou's hand. 'He's not worth it.'

And she pulled them both away from the door, towards the street.

In the taxi back to the station, Tozer said, 'Are you going to be all right?'

Hibou moved her head in the tiniest of nods. Tozer looked grim, focused.

'How long before you start to feel bad?'

'Three, four hours, maybe,' said Hibou.

'You want to find a doctor?'

Hibou shook her head.

'Doctor?' asked Breen.

'She's going to start going cold turkey,' said Tozer. 'She's an addict. Without heroin, she'll be sick. Sooner we get her to the farm, sooner we can look after her.'

It was just gone two o'clock. There was a train in half an hour.

'You'll love my mum,' Tozer said. 'She'll take care of you. Feed you up. You'd like that, wouldn't you?'

Hibou nodded. She was snuffling tears now. She leaned towards Tozer who closed her eyes and hugged her close.

Tozer said, 'So you threatened to expose everything if they didn't let her go?'

'I told Tarpey that if he didn't persuade Jayakrishna to let her go, I'd go to the papers. If Rhodri Pugh was exposed for perverting the course of justice, the commune would lose its protection. They'd be evicted.'

Tozer nodded and said, 'Fab.'

And the taxi driver turned into Eastbourne Terrace, pressing hard on the horn to scare some pedestrians who were dawdling in the road.

They put Hibou in an empty second-class compartment. There were a few minutes before the train had to leave. Breen got off and stood on the platform. Tozer leaned out of the carriage door window.

'Is she going to be OK?' asked Breen.

'I don't know. I think so. She's out of that place anyway.'

'And what about you?'

'I'll be fine.' The guard was walking up and down the platform slamming the doors shut.

'Something you should know,' said Tozer. 'Something Jayakrishna said.'

Breen looked at her, small in the doorway of the train.

'Jayakrishna said it was Chinese junk that killed him. All the new Chinese heroin that's coming in. It's dirty. Apparently you don't know how much to take any more. Some is strong, some is weak. When it was from the doctors you knew what you were getting. Now you don't know any more. That's what happened.'

Breen said, 'It was stronger than he realised?'

'The squat sold good heroin. They got it from the clinics. That was what Hibou was doing. All of them in the Paradise Hotel. They're registered addicts. They were getting prescriptions and selling some of it to fund the squat.'

'He was getting them addicted so he could sell their heroin?'

'Maybe. Only the clinics were giving them less and less, I suppose. So they started getting it from the gangs.'

The porter was blowing a whistle, walking down the platform towards them.

'Another thing. Frankie Pugh was still alive when Jayakrishna called Tarpey. He had overdosed, but he was still alive. They told Tarpey to send a doctor. But he never did. Jayakrishna says he was too scared of a scandal.' The carriage jolted. 'He let him die instead. Then they panicked, I reckon. Tried to cover it all up.'

Breen's desk had been cleared by the time he returned to the office. The balding man had moved to a desk facing the wall. He didn't say a word about it.

Wellington called at around three.

'I'll put you through to Detective Sergeant Breen directly, Dr Wellington,' said the new woman, all hoity-toity.

He missed Marilyn, in spite of everything.

'I just called to say you were right, Breen,' said Wellington. 'The body from the fire was John Knight.'

'You're sure?'

'Of course I'm bloody sure. I have Knight's dental records.' Maybe he was still angry at Breen for proving him wrong about Francis Pugh.

Breen sat down and called up Deason at Scotland Yard.

'You heard?'

'Yes. You were right. It was Knight.'

'Any news of Harry Cox?'

'Not a rustle. We're keeping an eye on the ports. He may have changed cars. The Bristol would be pretty conspicuous.'

'What about Shirley Prosser?'

'Long gone. Last seen before Christmas in a boarding house in Margate,' said Deason. 'We talked to the landlady. She left in a taxi heading for Dover.'

'What date was that?'

'Why?'

'Just curious.'

Deason hesitated as if he was unsure he wanted to share this bit of information with Breen. A man from a different department, who had been a suspect in this investigation. 'Four days before Christmas,' he said eventually.

'Spain,' Breen said. 'Johnny Knight had talked about escaping there. Perhaps she's there too. Or Greece.'

Franco's Spain was a mess. It was easy enough for criminals and runaways to hide there. Greece was no better, both countries run by dictators.

After he put the phone down, Breen did the calculation. Four days before Christmas. That was the day he and Tozer had visited them. She had taken his money and left just as soon as she could. He had given her the means.

Breen went home after work, but when he got there he could hear the rock music coming from the flat above. It wasn't just the volume. It was the deliberate moronic thump of it. The artificiality of the electric music.

He went straight to the front door and knocked on it. A woman with short hair opened the door. She smiled at him. 'It's the man from downstairs,' she called above the music.

The man stuck his head out of the living-room door.

'What is it?'

Breen said, 'Your music is too loud. Turn it down.'

'Sure, man.' And he turned away, probably intending to ignore Breen as he had always done before.

'No,' said Breen. 'Really.' And he pulled out his warrant card and showed them that he was a policeman.

The man looked at the card for a second, then said, 'Bloody hell.'

The woman's smile vanished. Breen was shocked to see how scared she looked.

Afterwards he felt a little ashamed of what he had done, using his power as a policeman this way. Flashing a warrant card.

But the music was much quieter after that. They were afraid of him now. He would sleep, at least.

THIRTY-FIVE

On Friday a cardboard box addressed to Breen arrived at Marylebone. It was from Scotland Yard and contained all the notebooks and papers they had taken from him.

It included the photographs of the burnt man. Breen laid them out on his desk for one last time, side by side.

For over three months he had puzzled over the identity of the man who had died the night his father went into hospital.

The puzzle of who he was had been solved, but nothing was fixed. Nothing had been made better. He had thought that the identity of the dead man would mean something bigger, but it didn't. It meant something small and mean and greedy. A man who died over money. And whoever it was that had killed Knight had not been caught. And he had still let his father down. He had failed to love the man who had raised him alone.

Creamer assigned him a new case that morning. Nothing complicated. Two men had got into a fist fight over a taxi outside Madame Tussaud's. They were both drunk. One had punched the other on the side of the head and he had gone down hard. The winner of the fight had then disappeared in the taxi.

The beaten man had not got up from the ground. He had been a costermonger from Covent Garden. He died from bleeding on the brain in hospital at around four in the morning.

The dead man's girlfriend had been more sober than either of the men. She had seen everything. Sitting in the front room of her parents' house in Finsbury Park, she gave Breen a good description of the other man. It would be an easy case, Breen reckoned. Not the sort of case they would even be bothering CID with at other times of year. The girlfriend didn't cry once. Sometimes she even giggled. It hadn't sunk in yet.

After interviewing her, Breen drove back up to Hampstead in the CID car, peering into driveways and garages, looking for any glimpse of Harry Cox's car. The *Standard* and the *Evening News* had both carried photographs of Harry Cox and the missing vehicle. 'London Man Sought Over Police Murder'. Few details though.

Back at his desk that afternoon he tried to get used to the new room. It felt unfamiliar and cold. The new typist's voice annoyed him. After lunch he called Scotland Yard again. Deason told them they had impounded all the files in Morton, Stiles & Prentice's office to start figuring out where the money had been going missing.

'That's going to take a while, going through the books,' Deason said. 'He hid it well.'

'That would have been Johnny Knight. Making the figures look good,' said Breen. 'Any news about Cox?'

'Nothing,' said Deason. 'We got the airports and ports covered. He's vanished. You any ideas?'

Breen wondered if he had escaped. Were he and Shirley in this together? The thought made him nauseous.

'No,' said Breen. 'Nothing.'

In the afternoon he went to visit Marilyn. She had been transferred to Paddington Green where she was working out her notice.

Nobody knew where she was. He wandered through the big old station, knocking on doors, poking his head around them, looking for her. He found her, eventually, in a small office at the back of the station.

'I came to see how you are. If you're OK.'

She thumped a pile of files down onto her desk and said, 'What do you care?'

She looked different. 'You've had a haircut,' he said. It was short.

She put one hand up and touched it. 'It's supposed to be Mia Farrow,' she said.

'I just wanted to ask if there's anything I can do.'

She closed her eyes and said, 'Just go away.'

'What happened to your boyfriend?'

'They let him go. Don't know where he is. Don't care. I'm giving up on men.'

'I just wanted to say, if you want your old job back, I can put in a word.'

'Leave me alone,' she said, turning away. 'I'm busy.'

She opened a folder and poured the contents into a bin.

The night was silent. The flat above had been cowed into submission. He should have been able to sleep now, but instead he lay awake, aware of the silence.

Saturday was worse. The whole cul-de-sac seemed unnaturally empty and still. He did his shopping quickly in case the phone rang. The moment he was back he called Scotland Yard.

'Calm down, Breen. We'll call you.'

He soaked the bandage on his head with a sponge, then gingerly took the dressing off the scab, scowling at himself in the bathroom mirror. The man upstairs had stopped parking his car in front of Breen's window. Now the silence was starting to irritate him as much as the noise had. He imagined the man in his socks, tiptoeing around the flat.

In the end he decided to take his mind off waiting. He wanted to finish clearing out his father's room. It would give him something else to think about.

Though he had already taken most of his father's clothes and books to the Salvation Army, a few belongings remained. There wasn't much. On the small iron mantel of the fireplace, an ugly carriage clock he had been given as a thank-you from one of the building firms he had worked for. A small lamp with a red-fringed shade which had come from his father's house. Plays and poetry, mostly by Irish writers. In the small bedside cabinet a penknife which he had always carried with him. His mother's ring, which Breen took, wrapped in cotton wool and placed in the drawer of his dresser.

There was a rag-and-bone man who came past on Sundays, cart pulled by a horse. He was putting things in a cardboard box when the phone rang.

Breen dropped the carriage clock, breaking the glass, scrabbling for the phone.

'We thought you'd want to know. We found the car,' said a man's voice.

'Deason? Is that you?'

'Stay where you are. We'll come and pick you up.'

'Not him though?'

'No. Not him. Arsenal. That's not so far from you, is it?'

A flicker of paranoia. Had Cox been coming for him? The car arrived five minutes later, blue light flashing, a constable driving.

The man from upstairs watching from the window.

The Bristol 404 was parked in a side street just off the Hornsey Road. Locals came out of their front doors into the cold afternoon air to mutter and nudge each other and to watch the coppers as they searched the car and questioned people. The police had broken into a sidelight window but there was nothing inside. Sergeant Deason was looking at a map of the area.

'Nice car,' he said to Breen.

'How long has it been there?'

'A couple of days,' said Deason. He wrinkled his nose. 'Maybe three.'

The driving gloves were on the steering wheel, just as he had seen them before. 'You asked his wife if she knows why he'd be coming here?' Breen asked him.

Deason nodded. 'She had no idea. We've sent a car for her.'

It was cold. A pale frost had formed on the Bristol's windscreen.

'He might have just dumped it. Swapped it for something less conspicuous.'

Breen left Deason and the car, walking around the streets to try and get a feel for the neighbourhood. What would have brought Cox here? Had there been another car parked somewhere? He doubted it. He would have taken the driving gloves.

Or someone to pick him up? Possible. But why would they have met here? There was a small furniture factory close to where the car had been found. Run-down Victorian houses. Hopscotch in chalk on the pavements. Also in chalk: 'KILL ALL THE NIGGS'. There were new tower blocks to the east, still unoccupied. Huge, ugly things, black outlines in the sky.

A huge roar came from the east.

'Highbury,' said a constable. 'Arsenal playing Sheffield.'

Breen looked at his watch. The football must have just started. How long would the match last? The streets were empty now. When the match finished they would be packed.

'Is there a phone anywhere?' he asked the sergeant.

'Main road,' said the copper.

He walked to the road and dialled John Nolan's number.

'Cathal? Coming around for lunch again this Sunday?'

'Harry Cox was bent,' Breen said. 'On the take. Double-counting for materials.'

'No surprise. They're all bent, far as I'm concerned,' said Nolan. 'Are you OK?'

'Not so bad,' said Breen. 'Not so good either. I'm surprised how much I'm missing my father. We didn't even like each other that much.'

Another roar from the crowd. Nolan said, 'Sorry? I couldn't hear you. There's an awful noise on the line.'

'Cox has done a runner. Any idea where he's gone?'

'Barely knew the man, Cathal. Are you OK? Christmas on your own. It's hard.'

'They found his car on Hornsey Road,' said Breen.

A pause. 'Where, exactly?' Nolan pronounced the last word as if it had an extra syllable.

'Annette Road. By Tollington Road.'

'The Citizen Estate,' said Nolan. 'We built that one. Four fucking big boxes. Been empty all this time. Nobody wants high rise since Ronan Point.' Ronan Point. Those twenty-two storeys of tower block that had partially collapsed in that gas explosion last May. 'Can't say I blame them,' Nolan said. 'So now the council are stripping out all the gas fittings and replacing them with the electric to say the place is safe.'

In the phone box, Breen turned, trying to see the tower blocks he had been looking at earlier. 'And Morton, Stiles and Prentice are doing the work?' he said.

'Right,' Nolan said. 'Tying a pretty bow on a pig.'

'So Harry Cox would know the place?'

'Sure of it,' said Nolan.

Breen put the phone down, then went back to the sergeant and pointed to the tower blocks. Four large dark rectangles. Ugly, black-windowed and dead.

'In there?' said the sergeant.

'Maybe,' said Breen. 'His company built the place.'

'Wouldn't be very smart, would it? Leave your car right next to where you're hiding.'

'He's desperate' said Breen. 'Smart has nothing to do with it.'

There was a caretaker's hut. Deason pressed the 'In case of emergency' button and eventually a jobsworth appeared with bunches of keys. He had beer on his breath.

'Have you seen anybody in any of the buildings?'

The man took offence. 'No. 'Cause there isn't nobody there.'

'So you say,' said Breen.

'You telling me I don't know my job?'

The sergeant looked at the buildings. 'How many floors?'

'Nineteen. All of them.'

'I've only got three men. This could take us the whole bollocking day,' said Deason.

'Any chance we can get more local men on this?' said Breen.

'With the footie? You have to be pulling my leg.'

They stood on raw earth by the side of the empty buildings.

'How long they been finished?' Deason asked the caretaker.

'The last one, three months. No bugger wants them now,' he said. 'Scared to move in. They're having to strengthen them all. Bloody mess.'

Breen craned his neck back. Dark clouds moved across the top of them, making the buildings seem to topple slowly backwards.

The four buildings were identical. Anyone's guess which he might be in, if he was in any.

'Lifts working?' said the copper.

The caretaker shook his head. 'No electric,' he said.

'Fuck that for a game of whatsit,' Deason said.

Another tidal roar from the stadium.

'You wait here. I'll go up,' said Breen.

Deason looked uncertain. 'We reckon he's a killer.'

'If he's up there, he's seen the police cars. He'll try to disappear unless we nail him now. Once the match is finished we'll have no chance catching him.'

'Be my guest.' Breen had been right. A plodder.

Breen craned his neck upwards. This is where the rich had decided poor people should live. 'I'll take one of your men. One young enough to climb eighteen flights of stairs. The rest stay here to make sure he doesn't run.'

Deason nodded. 'I got all night,' he said. He shouted to a constable, told him to accompany Breen up the towers.

364 · WILLIAM SHAW

There was a torch in Deason's car. Breen borrowed another one from the caretaker.

'Which one first?' said the caretaker.

'Eeny meeny,' said the constable.

'That one,' said Breen, pointing. 'What about the doors to the flats?'

'All unlocked inside,' said the caretaker. 'Just the main doors.'

The constable walked with a stoop. Six foot six or more. Huge. Didn't seem to tire though. Breen's legs were singing with pain by the tenth floor of the first tower. There were two staircases, presumably for safety. They split up and took a staircase each, meeting on each floor as they arrived. Looking into each flat, then spiralling on up the concrete stairs. Precisely seventeen steps for each floor.

Four o'clock and the light was almost gone. They had borrowed a torch but hadn't switched it on yet. By the time they reached the top of the first tower Breen was panting for breath.

On the landing outside the lift Breen opened a metal window and looked out. Sunlight in a pale-yellow line below a grey sky. The floodlights shone over Highbury stadium.

'Fag?' said the lanky policeman, taking one out. He talked slowly, smiled a lot. His hair was longer than it should have been, curling over the top of his ears. The sort of copper Tozer would have gone for.

Breen shook his head. 'I don't think my lungs are up to it.' He could make out the outline of King's Cross station on the skyline to the south.

'Tell you what, though. Bit bloody high up here. I wouldn't like it.'

'I'd prefer it if there was a lift,' said Breen.

'Vertigo,' said the copper. 'Got it terrible.'

'Six foot something and you're scared of heights?' said Breen.

'Further to fall,' said the copper, dropping a half-smoked ciggie onto bare concrete. 'Race you down then.'

And he set off, bootnails clacking on the concrete stairs.

★

At the eighth floor of the second tower they paused for breath again.

'Almost halfway now,' said the constable.

Breen was conscious of the fact that the constable was now always first up the stairs to the next floor. Breen arrived, panting for breath, to find the policeman already searching the rooms.

'I don't know if I'll make all four,' said Breen. 'My chest is going to explode.'

He looked down at the ground below. No more police had arrived yet to assist them.

'Come on,' the constable said, but Breen didn't move for another minute. They had stopped trying to take the steps two at a time. Now it was just one foot after another.

Breen looked in each flat. They were bare. All identical. Plain walls waiting to be decorated. A bath. A toilet. A kitchen sink.

It was not so much a building as a manifesto: 'Everyone will be given an opportunity, and that opportunity will be the same shape and colour as everyone else's.'

Except for those who lived in posh houses in Hampstead. Who steal from everyone else's opportunity, who buy art and hang it on their walls.

Breen and the constable rested in one of the flats. Another fag break. The copper stood, first with his back to the wall, then edged forward slowly towards the windows. Cautiously, as if the floor were going to give way beneath him.

It was dark now. They looked out at the other three blocks, black against the dark blue of the winter evening.

'There!' he said.

'What?'

'Thought I saw a light.' He pointed upwards at one of the two blocks they had not been in yet.

Breen peered up. 'I don't see anything.'

'Maybe it was just the reflection of my fag.'

Breen peered and saw nothing. 'Reflections don't work like that. You're looking up.'

'Maybe I was imagining it. Let's go.'

'No,' said Breen, and continued looking. Maybe because it was easier than pounding on up the stairs. He stared into the blackness until he thought his eyes were playing tricks on him. But there was nothing there. It could have been a reflection of an aeroplane, or just imagination.

After a few minutes he gave up. They went on up to the top, searching each room.

By the third block, Breen was exhausted. He had to pause on every landing, legs cramping, waiting in the darkness as the copper looked around with his torch.

'I think my battery's going,' said Breen. The constable's torch seemed much brighter than his own.

'He's not going to be here, is he?' said the copper.

Fifteenth floor.

'I wonder who's winning?' said the copper. 'Hope it's Sheffield. Bloody hate Arsenal. I hope they're having the shite kicked out of them.'

Sixteenth floor.

'I mean, we don't know for sure he's anywhere near here. They reckon Ronnie Biggs is in Australia, don't they?'

Seventeenth floor.

'Do you reckon we'll be finished by five? I'm supposed to be going to the dog track this evening with the wife.'

Eighteenth floor. Even the lanky copper was panting now.

Breen noticed that the young man took a few seconds longer inside the top flat than he had on all the others.

'Constable?'

'Sir. I think you should come in here. I've found something.'

★

The policeman shone his torch around the room. A blanket. Two empty tins of mulligatawny soup. No sign of a fire. He would have had to eat them cold. A pile of cigarettes stubbed out on the floor. Some cigars too. Four Gordon's gin bottles, three empty, one half full.

'How do we know it's him?' whispered the copper. 'I mean, we can't be a hundred per cent, can we?'

'I'm sure,' said Breen. A smell of cigarettes still in the air.

Breen opened the window. Wind pushed back at him. There was rain coming. The weather was getting wilder.

'He was here!' Breen shouted down. But it was dark and it was a long way down. The roar of the city was too loud for him to know if they'd heard. He could see Deason's car but no sign of the sergeant himself. And no other officers yet.

'Here!' he shouted. But no one seemed to hear him.

The match would be finishing any minute. The streets would be thronged with people. It would be difficult to drive any vehicle through them, even a police car.

'Stay by the doors!' he called again. But he couldn't see anyone below.

If Cox hadn't made it out of the building already, somehow. Was there some service exit only he knew? He was an architect, after all. He would have seen them coming, seen the torchlight.

They had checked each floor, though, as they had gone up, and there were two staircases. Could he have somehow remained hidden and descended after they had passed?

It was hard to know. The two men were exhausted now from climbing. They could have made a mistake.

He ran his torch around the flat. Into the bath. Into the empty kitchen. No sign. He had been here, and not long ago.

'Roof?' said the policeman.

'Christ!' said Breen.

They both dashed back out of the room.

'You stay here,' shouted the copper.

'Let me go,' said Breen.

'You're tired. I'll go – keep an eye. He might be using the roof as a way to get to the other staircase and get down.'

The stairs continued up another floor onto the roof. The constable dashed up them, banging back the door at the top.

Breen waited in the corridor, heart thumping.

Without the other copper there he realised how little light his own torch was giving off. Nearly dead. He switched it off to preserve the batteries.

Pure darkness. With the flat doors closed there were no windows onto the connecting corridor. The shapes of the building disappeared into nothingness. Breen pressed against the wall to reassure himself it was there.

'All right?' he shouted.

The constable would be searching the roof. But how long did it take?

'Any sign of him?'

No answer. He strained to hear footsteps. Anything at all. But there was nothing. It was as if the man had evaporated.

'Hello?' shouted Breen.

He switched on his torch again. At first the beam seemed brighter than it had before. Was that because his eyes had become used to the blackness? But the light dimmed rapidly, lighting less and less of the corridor he was standing in. He switched it off again. It was his only source of light. He should save it.

The blackness inside the building was thick and crushing.

'Constable?' He shouted as loudly as he could. He didn't even know the man's name.

Scared now, he switched the torch back on. Nothing. Totally dead. He was alone. It was dark.

THIRTY-SIX

Breen felt his way back to the staircase, listening for any sign of movement.

With his hands on the metal banister, he inched his way up the final floor, following where the constable had disappeared.

The door at the top was swinging open. It was a relief to make out the dull light of a night sky beyond.

The wind up here was wild. It felt as if a single gust could blow you off. Breen spread his legs wide to anchor himself to the roof. The roof was flat, apart from two large shed-like rectangles which Breen guessed had been built to house the lift apparatuses.

Far above, the lights of a jet airliner, moving west to Heathrow.

He looked left and right. The roof appeared to be empty. He walked slowly towards the edge and peered over.

He could make out Deason now, clearly. Tiny, far below, sitting on the bonnet of his car, smoking a cigarette. If the constable had fallen there would be a commotion, at least.

But he had not come down the other stairs, so he must be here, somewhere.

'Hello!' Breen shouted down to Deason, but his voice was carried away. Deason didn't even move. There seemed to be no chance of being heard up here above the roar of the city and the rush of the wind. With no light at the top of the building, Breen was in darkness, invisible.

Breen looked around for a stone to throw to attract his attention, but the roof was bare.

A noise behind him.

Breen turned, rapidly. He thought he had seen something ducking behind one of the lift housings. He ran slowly, careful not to trip on unseen obstacles in the blackness.

His foot hit something soft. At first he thought it was a pile of rags or workmen's tools. Then he realised with a lurch it was the constable.

The man lay face up on the flat black roof. Breen knelt, looking around him.

He felt the man's uniform. It was warm, wet, soaked.

He held his hand up. Dark with blood.

Head thumping suddenly, Breen went to feel for a pulse on the man's neck. Instead his finger dipped into a wide warm wound. Right into bone and blood.

He yanked back his hand, horrified. The constable's head had been blasted apart. Shocked, Breen jumped up to his feet, urgently wiping his hand on his suit jacket, trying to get the dead man's blood off him.

He could see nothing in the blackness, but it must have been a bullet. Yet he had heard nothing in the darkness and the wind.

He screwed up his eyes and tried to make out his surroundings. He had miscalculated badly. Cox had already tried to kill him. Stupid. Now another man was dead. It was his fault.

'Cox!' he shouted, looking around him. 'I know you're here.'

But he didn't know it for certain. Had he taken the chance to run back down the other stairs? Breen had not heard him do it. But the darkness, the wind, the unfamiliarity with the place, made it hard to know anything for certain.

But there. Again. A noise.

Breen went to run, slipped in something – the constable's blood – and crashed downwards.

He was up on his knees when the torch came on, blinding him.

'Cox?' said Breen, holding his bloodied hand up in front of his eyes.

'Oh, fucking hell. It's you again.'

★

Breen managed to stand. He walked towards the torch. 'It's finished, Harry.'

'Stop. I'll kill you properly this time.' A laugh.

'No point. You shouldn't have killed that man. It's stupid. It's over.'

'I'll decide when it's fucking over, thank you very much.'

Breen could only hear him. The brightness was blinding. He held his hands in front of his eyes to shield them. 'Want a cigarette, Harry?'

Breen reached inside his jacket, but continued tiptoeing.

'Don't move. I've got a fucking gun,' said Cox. He was drunk. Breen could hear it in his voice.

Breen stopped. Took his hand slowly out of his jacket.

The light hurt his eyeballs.

'Fuck off, copper. Go away. I've already seen to your friend.'

The wind was cool. Deliciously cool. Drying the sweat on Breen's face.

'I wish everybody would fuck off and leave me alone.' He lowered the torch onto the ground in front of them. For the first time he caught sight of Harry Cox. He was dressed in the same slacks he had been wearing on New Year's Day. In his other hand was what looked like a .38.

'Is that the gun you shot Michael Prosser with?' asked Breen.

Keep him talking at least.

'I said stop right there. Don't come any closer.' The torch came back up. Breen blinked in the light.

'Fire that and everyone will hear.'

'Not up here.'

'There are hundreds of police arriving down there. They'll be up here soon.'

'You're lying.'

Breen said, 'Your wife is on the way, too.'

A pause. 'Are you fucking joking? Don't let her come here. You cretins. Oh, Christ. What a bloody mess. I'm so pissed off with you all.'

Breen inched forward again.

'What about that cigarette?' said Breen.

'Fuck off. Just fuck off.'

They were two hundred feet up in the air. Above London in their own world. Just him and the man who had killed Michael Prosser and who had just murdered another policeman. Would the other coppers be wondering what was taking them so long yet?

'Why don't you just give yourself up?'

'Bugger that. Prison. Actually, I had meant to kill myself, but it's harder than I imagined.' A laugh.

Breen edged in, cautious. What could he talk about to keep him calm?

'Is this one of your buildings?' said Breen.

'Shit, isn't it?' said Cox. Another laugh. 'Imagine living in a place like this.'

Cox switched off the torch. Breen could see him now, outlined against the starless sky. His jacket flapping in the breeze. He bent down and picked up the bottle, not taking his eyes off Breen.

'Give us a gasper then,' he said. 'Left mine downstairs. All this place is good for is jumping off it. But I can't do it. I'm a bit of a cowardy custard.'

'I don't think I would be able to, either,' said Breen.

'What if you pushed me? No one would see.'

Breen moved forward, holding out the pack.

'I didn't mean it, you moron!' screeched Cox.

'I was just bringing you a cigarette,' said Breen.

Cox was pointing the gun right at Breen. 'Just put them down on the ground.'

Breen stopped and bent down to leave the packet on the roof, then backed off.

Cox stuck the gun in his jacket pocket, approached, picked up the packet, then started tapping his pockets.

'Do you want a light?'

'Fuck off. Got some.' And he pulled out a box of matches from his inside pocket. It took two hands to light the cigarette, gun waving in the air. Breen watched him wobble as he struck the match. He was definitely drunk. Not so drunk that he hadn't been able to kill the policeman though.

The first match went straight out. And the second.

'Bastard,' said Cox.

'Come inside. It'll be easier to light in here.'

'Fuck off. I know what you're trying to do.'

Breen watched him strike another match.

'Why don't we at least sit down?' said Breen.

'Prefer to stand,' said Cox.

A man who liked to control things, even when drunk. A man who turned into a vicious child when control was taken away from him. Breen looked around, trying to get his bearings. The immensity of London, spread out around them, sodium lights as far as the eye could see.

'Tell me a few things,' Breen said.

'Fuck off.'

'There are things I need to know. Names. Johnny Knight.'

'Great with numbers, Johnny. Smart man.'

'You persuaded him to cook the books for you.'

'And bloody good at it he was.'

'So you used him to cream money off the top of your contracts with the GLC.'

Cox didn't say anything for a minute. Then he spoke. 'Wish I'd never made him do it. Johnny never really wanted to do it. But it was too bloody easy. Honestly. They didn't deserve to have the money it was so easy. And I'm no good with numbers. Johnny was good. It was all pretty harmless. Just a little bit here and there.'

'What about Michael Prosser?'

'Cunt,' said Cox.

'Johnny Knight went to Prosser. Said he wanted out. But when

Prosser found out about the scam you were running, he wanted money. He blackmailed you.'

'Not at first. Poor Johnny. Poor foolish Johnny. He blackmailed Johnny. I had no idea. My fault he's dead.' That laugh again.

'So Prosser just forced him to cut him in on the deal?'

'Horrible man, Michael Prosser.'

'And when Johnny couldn't take any more and threatened to go to the police and shop Prosser as well . . . ?'

Cox took out yet another match and lit it. It lasted long enough to touch the end of the cigarette, but not long enough for the cigarette to catch fire.

'Prosser couldn't afford that?'

'Prosser was a bastard.'

They were standing about ten feet away from each other. The wind was colder now.

'I mean . . . I never meant it to go this far,' said Cox. 'I'm not somebody who goes around killing people, fuck's sake. Just a little bit here and a little bit there. Where's the harm in that? Nobody would have noticed. Got into the art racket. Buy a few paintings. Sell a few paintings. Easy to hide a bit of money that way. Lovely stuff too. You should see my collection some time. And then poor Johnny cracks and says he's not going to do it anymore . . . Jesus. Won't this fucking wind stop?'

'We could go inside.'

'I'd never met Michael Prosser. And then he comes up one day to my house. To my fucking house. And he tells me he knows everything. And he's killed poor Johnny. And if he doesn't get money, he'll kill me too. Keep everything quiet. He has the power because he's a copper. He got away with killing Johnny and he's going to kill me too. I was scared.'

Breen said, 'Let me light a cigarette. Throw me the pack. You can light yours off mine.'

'Good plan.' He dug in his pocket and picked out Breen's packet.

Threw it. The wind carried it too far, to within a couple of feet of the edge of the building. Breen went to pick it up, hunkering down as he approached the edge, keeping his eyes on Cox all the time.

'So Prosser blackmailed you instead?' he shouted above the noise of the wind.

'Yes.'

'So you decided to kill him.'

Cox started to laugh. 'I decided? Not really. Not my idea at all.'

'Shirley Prosser,' said Breen.

'Poor bloody Shirley Prosser,' he said. 'A murderer for a husband and a cripple for a child. She's a clever girl,' he said.

'She and you . . . ?'

'She first came to my house one night in November. My wife was out. I had no idea who she was. Then she told me how her husband had killed her brother. Started crying. She loved her brother. Imagine what it's like, suspecting your own husband of killing him. God, she hated her husband. So one thing leads to another. I put my arm round her. There, there. Poor girl. Not a bad body. Knew a thing or two in bed. Made me feel like I could save her. Fell in love. I've had sex with loads of people. Pretty wife. But I have urges, like any man. Always other women you want to fuck. But Shirley was different. Made me think I really had to save her, know what I mean? Any man can fuck a woman. But saving a woman . . . that's special.'

'Yes,' said Breen. 'I know.'

Cox snorted. 'Poor little dark-eyed woman with the cripple. I wanted to be her fucking warrior. Her white knight. And fuck her too, of course. I used to go to her little flat above the record shop late at night. I offered her money but she wouldn't take it. Dirty money. She didn't like it. Funny thing was, I was having to give it to her cunt of a husband and he was passing it to her anyway. So I don't know why she wouldn't take it from me. That was peculiar, don't you think?'

He was tiring, Breen thought. Speaking more slowly. Perhaps he should try to overpower him.

'Then one night she told me the only way to stop this was to kill her husband. We could run away together. Place by the sea. You know, that sort of bullshit. Christ, I thought. She wants me to kill him. I thought, she can't be serious. Until she pulled open a drawer. Gave me this gun.'

'It was all her idea?'

He snorted. 'Completely. I didn't bloody want to do it. Squeamish. But she said it was the only way. And that way she could have revenge on the man who killed her brother. I didn't actually think she meant it. It was a game. Saving the princess from the dragon.'

A thick gust of wind made Cox wobble. For a second Breen thought he would fall, but he didn't.

'Then about three weeks ago she called me up and said you have to do it tonight. She gave me the address and told me exactly what to do. How to pull the trigger. Everything.'

Breen could see him starting to sag. Keep him talking. The longer he could keep him going, the less focused he would be. The easier it would be to take him on.

'I tried to put her off. Maybe tomorrow. Maybe the next day. "I don't actually fancy killing your husband tonight." No, she said. It has to be tonight. We have the perfect alibi.' Cox started laughing.

'What?'

' "Some policeman has invited me for dinner," she said.' He giggled. 'Me.'

'You. You were the chump,' he said. 'Her get-out-of-jail card.'

She had taken revenge on her husband by getting Cox to kill him. And she had used Breen to cover it up.

'First shot, I cocked it up. Just wounded him. He came crawling over towards me, trying to get the gun. I was so angry at him for not being dead I shot him right in the head that time.'

Would the other police be here soon? Surely they would have noticed how long they had been away by now?

'And you know what? It felt bloody good. I walked out of that horrid boarding house like I was on a bloody cloud. I wanted to fuck Shirley again right then. But she had told me to stay out of touch for a week. Otherwise people might suspect. She'd call me when it was safe. Then we could be together. And of course she vanished. Last I heard of her. Clever bitch,' he said. 'She had it all planned out.'

'Because it wasn't just Prosser she wanted to nail. It was you too,' said Breen. 'She wanted to destroy you because you were the one who corrupted her brother.'

He could just make out Cox nodding in the darkness.

Breen opened his jacket and used it to shield the match. His cigarette lit. He held it up, tip glowing brightly in the wind.

'I'm coming over to you.'

Breen made his way slowly across the roof.

'Beautiful eyes,' he said. 'Beautiful tits.'

'Shirley?'

'Gorgeous. And so bloody helpless. "Help poor little me and my crippled child." What a performance.'

'Maybe it wasn't a performance.'

'Oh, please. You fancied her too. Pretty girl. Looking after a poor kid. Monster for a husband. She knew what tune to play on all of us. Bloody genius.'

Breen held out the cigarette.

'Did she let you fuck her? No?' Cox laughed. 'At least I got to fuck her. Poor fuckless policeman. But she still had you running round after her, didn't she?'

The longer he kept Cox talking, the more chance there was that Deason would send somebody up to find out what was happening. Keep it going.

'Is that man dead?' Cox asked. He nodded at the constable's body.

'I think so.'

Cox said, 'I wasn't sure it was two of you. I thought it was just him. But then I heard you too.'

'Are you going to kill me too?'

Cox hesitated. 'I don't know. Probably. If I fancy it. I thought we were going to be friends, when we first met.'

'Here,' said Breen. The wind was burning it fast. He stepped forward. Cox took a step backwards, towards the edge of the building. 'Take the cigarette.'

'Don't fuck about with me.'

'Here,' said Breen.

Cox held out his hand for the cigarette. Breen lunged to grab his hand. Cox lurched back, out of reach, hands tightening on the .38. Breen had thought he would have time to grab at it, but Cox was faster than he'd imagined he would be. The gun was pointing straight at him.

And there was a massive roar from the stadium. And Breen caught a second's glimpse of Cox losing his balance, falling backwards, arms waving desperately, towards the edge of the building.

But Breen was flying through the air too, in the opposite direction. He thumped backwards, flat onto concrete. At first he imagined he must have tripped somehow himself, because nothing hurt. Not at first, anyway. But you don't trip backwards. Then he felt blood. And when tried to sit up, his shoulder was on fire.

He couldn't figure it out.

Then it came to him, looking up at the darkness, that Cox must have shot him. That's what must have sent Cox reeling backwards too, drunk, unprepared for the recoil. Breen hadn't even registered the shot. He had heard people say that you don't hear the bullet that hits you, but never quite believed it.

He had been shot. Yet he was curiously calm. He had to get up before Cox had a chance to fire again.

Slowly Breen tried to stand, first making the mistake of trying to use his left arm to push him upwards. It didn't seem to be working properly. Or even at all.

He was taking too long. His movements were too slow. It was as if the air had thickened around him, turning to honey.

He figured out that if he rolled onto his front he could use his good arm to push him upwards.

Where was Cox? Finally upright, he looked around him. Cox was nowhere.

He remembered the sight of him falling backwards and inched towards the edge of the building. Not too close because he was starting to feel dizzy now, unsteady on his feet.

Leaned forward as far as he dared. Looked down.

There was no sign at all of Cox in the darkness on the ground below.

Gone.

He had been inches from the edge when he'd fired.

Breen leaned forward a little further. No noise. Nothing. Until a huge groan rose from the stadium behind the block.

He looked around again. No one except for the shape of the dead constable. Had Cox escaped down the stairs?

Breen had the strange sense that Cox had never been there. He had completely disappeared.

THIRTY-SEVEN

It seemed to take an age, descending the stairs in the darkness.

One step at a time. Going a little slower each floor. Light-headed. Knowing he had to make it downstairs soon or they might not find him before it was too late.

Had Cox fallen? Breen had seen bodies of those who had jumped before. If they landed cleanly it was not so bad. If they hit anything on the way down the bodies were smashed to pieces: they became blood, guts, bone and meat.

Somewhere around the fifth floor his legs gave way under him. He sank slowly to the ground.

Damn. He lay on the stairs, wondering if they would come for him in time, and he thought about how Shirley Prosser had manipulated Cox to become a killer. Her weapon of vengeance. Maybe she was in Spain, or South America now. Life would not be easy for her in a new country, with Charlie to look after. A beach somewhere.

He listened. It was still quiet. Nobody was coming for him yet.

Slowly he stood again, panting. He was shivering now too. The blood on his back was like ice.

He moved more slowly now, counting stairs, feeling his way down in the dark. He was losing too much blood.

He sank down onto the floor again. Exhausted. It would be nice to sleep. If only this floor were more comfortable. He must have passed out for a second. When he opened his eyes, Tozer was standing above him, inviting him to some pop concert. At first he was pleased to see her. Her smile looked so beautiful, he thought. How had she known to find him here? Then he remembered that he had been shot and was irritated that she could be talking about something so trivial as bloody pop music. But when she held out her hand to him, he tried to raise himself up to go with her. Then he jerked awake. Nobody was there.

If he died, who was going to come to his funeral? he wondered. Pathetic, really. Stupid way for it all to end.

Tozer had been right all along. He had been a sucker for a woman in distress. He had never understood women at all. Perhaps she could come to the funeral.

The pain was growing now. He wished it would stop.

And then there was a voice shouting at him. It was Deason.

'Help me,' he was shouting to someone.

The pain of being lifted, someone on each side, was excruciating. Whiteness filled his whole skull, obliterating his vision. They dragged him down the stairs, feet slapping against the steps. Two floors of pain so wild and vicious that Breen was pleading for them just to drop him on the ground.

Eventually they dragged him to the cold flat tarmac outside, laying him flat.

'Where's Cox?' they were shouting.

Somebody was shouting. 'Call an ambulance now. This man's been shot.'

'Jesus. Is he dead?'

'Not yet.'

They hadn't heard the gunshot either, Breen realised.

'Where's Cox?' Deason was shouting at him.

Breen said, 'He killed the constable.'

Deason leaned in to hear what he was saying. Breen realised his voice was weak. He must have lost a lot of blood. But he rolled his head from side to side on the tarmac. There was no body he could see that had fallen from the building.

This was strange. This was where he should have fallen, wasn't it? Was he on the right side of the building?

He was looking up at the huge monolith above him. Oddly beautiful in the orange light against the blue-black sky. Perhaps he had lost his sense of direction. Maybe he had fallen another way.

'He fell,' said Breen. 'I couldn't stop him.'

They shone the torch all around where they were, but the ground was empty. Then upwards, but the torch was too weak to show anything above the seventh or eighth floor.

'Nobody fell.'

'I saw him. I think I saw him.'

There was a pause.

'Should we check the other side?' suggested a young constable.

They went to look, sweeping the torch left and right. Nowhere to be seen.

Deason knelt beside Breen.

'There's an ambulance coming. Keep awake.'

'He was there. And then he wasn't.'

He lay on his back on the cold ground, looking up at the building, its long lines reaching upwards into the blackness.

'I mean,' Deason was saying, 'he can't just vanish. He was a fat little bastard.'

A car was driving onto the site, rumbling over the uneven track that led up to the buildings.

'Who's that?'

'His wife, I expect.'

'What if he got down the other stairs?'

The car was driving closer.

'Door's still locked, in't it?'

'He fell,' said Breen again. 'I saw him.'

There seemed to be people everywhere running around them.

Cox had flown away, maybe. Why did Breen find that funny?

★

But then, from far above them, a brief scream.

Breen had a glimpse of Cox's face, head down, eyes white, sailing towards him. It took only two or three seconds for his body to fall from the top of the building to the bottom.

Then he felt the tarmac tremble as Cox hit.

And just as the headlights from an approaching car lit the spot, Cox's body was there, splayed out on the tarmac, just a foot from where one of the constables stood. Eyes staring at Breen still.

And the woman in the car, behind the headlights, was open-mouthed at the sight of her husband's body, head cracked open, brains leaking onto the blackness of the ground.

'Fucking hell!' He had missed the young policeman by inches. He was blubbering in shock.

Gravity had been suspended. Usual rules don't apply. This was a dream, anyway, probably. Sleep.

But people kept shouting. Cox's wife got out of the car. 'It's not . . .' she said. 'It's not him.'

'He almost bloody hit me,' said the constable who'd been standing there, his voice high.

'Sit down,' someone was saying. 'You've had a shock.'

Cox's half-head, crumpled, but eyes still wide. Less than a yard away.

'What happened?'

'That's not him,' said the woman, a little louder this time.

'Oh, for God's sake,' shouted the constable.

Breen whispered, 'No. It really is him.'

Cox: lying next to him like a badly folded suit. Dropped from the night sky.

The pain had lessened for a while when they'd laid him on the ground, but now his shoulder was starting to sing. Was the bullet still in him, or had it emerged out the other side?

'He must have been bloody up there all this time, clinging on to something with his fingers.'

'Christ.'

'Maybe he got caught on something.'

The window Breen had opened, maybe. Clothing snagged until it gave way.

Mrs Cox was crying, he realised, through the haze that was starting to wrap around him.

The constable who had been missed by inches was weeping too.

It felt a human thing to do. He was crying too now, he realised. He thought he was, at least. It was hard to tell. He wished he had cried all those weeks ago when his father died.

There was an ambulance coming soon. He thought he could hear it. The oddly beautiful sound of a bell ringing, a long way away.

'Stay awake, Sergeant. Please, stay awake.'

But he was not sure he could be bothered to. He felt so exhausted. He'd had so much to think about. And now he didn't have to, anymore. And the tarmac around him seemed to melt and swallow him whole.

THIRTY-EIGHT

The room above the kitchen is warm. The Aga is on below. He finds he sleeps a lot in the heat.

The bed is old and comfortable. The doctor says he should stay in bed a few more days, at least.

Sometimes Hibou comes in with tea she has made from rosehips and honey. It's not as bad as it sounds. She is being treated by the same doctor as Breen is, Tozer says.

Helen Tozer's mother brings more conventional cups of tea, refusing to believe that Breen doesn't like them. 'Drink it and you'll feel better,' she says.

He would love a real coffee but thinks it probably doesn't exist this far west of London.

The doctor says his arm will be OK. The bullet smashed his collarbone, shattering it, sending fragments of bone down into his shoulder. But they've put metal in there instead, joining two bits of broken bone.

Tozer knocks on his door sometimes to ask if he is all right. He screams often in his sleep, they tell him. He dreams about Cox on the tarmac beside him. In some dreams he lies there. In others he stands up again.

It is Tozer's sister's room. Her dead sister. Nightmares are to be expected.

Tozer often looks tired. She has lost weight, if that's possible. The farm is a lot of work. Her father has given up on everything. He's never recovered. It's all down to her now to keep it going. A young woman running a whole dairy farm, keeping the family going.

Breen was driven down here in the back of an ambulance after a few days in hospital in London. Tozer had insisted on it. There was no one else to look after him, she said. And no one to object to her insisting, either.

They say his left arm will not move that well for a while.

Today he gets up in his pyjamas and goes slowly downstairs. Mrs Tozer is cooking lunch. Beef stew and dumplings.

'Oh,' she says, surprised to see him up. She runs round, moving chairs, fetching a blanket for him. 'Joining us for lunch, are you?'

It's a first. Breen apologises for causing so much trouble.

She laughs. 'No trouble.'

'Extra mouths to feed,' he says.

'No trouble at all,' she says, and looks out of the small square window into the farmyard.

'It's good to have the girl here,' she says.

She means Hibou. The same age as Tozer's sister was. Like someone falling out of the sky unexpectedly. Breen wonders whether it's Tozer who's bringing the farm back to life with her energy and work, or Hibou, by filling the space left behind by a dead girl. Even Tozer's father talks to her, sometimes. He taught her how to change a spark plug in the tractor the other day.

Hibou is doing well, apparently. She doesn't talk much, but she's over the worst. There is some colour in her skin now, at least. Tozer asked her if she wanted them to call her anything different. Her real name, perhaps? But she prefers to be known as Hibou. Tozer tells her she's a dab hand with the milking machine. A real help.

At night you can hear real owls round here, too.

The food smells rich. Almost too rich. Breen doesn't want to disappoint her by not eating, but he's not sure he can face it.

'It's good of you, Mrs Tozer, to put up with me.'

'You miss your father, I expect,' she says.

She ladles the stew into a bowl. Before he can stop himself, he says, 'I wasn't there, the day he died. I feel bad about that.'

Mrs Tozer drops gravy onto the top of the cooker. It bubbles and steams in the heat.

'You can't always be there,' she says. 'That's the sad thing.'

To change the subject, Breen asks if he can use the phone after lunch. He wants to call London to see if there is any news of Shirley Prosser.

He doubts there will be. She used him. Not as badly as she'd used Harry Cox though.

'She's lucky,' Helen Tozer said yesterday as they walked by the estuary. 'And smart. She got her revenge on the people who killed the one she loved. I admire her.'

Breen does not want to think about her too much. She got away.

He will be off work for weeks, though he's not sure how long he can stay down here. It's not that he's not welcome. But he is not a country person. He misses the city his father raised him in. He's bored already. This is not where he is from. Hibou fits in here, but he doesn't. He peers out of the window at the browns of winter. The leafless trees full of rooks.

The quiet complacency of everyday life. He knows it is not really like this. In this house they all secretly know it too. He can't live here. He's not sure Tozer can either, but she has to try.

She will be coming in soon, talking too loudly, smelling of sour milk and dung.

Few figures have had a bigger influence on the British art scene than Robert Fraser. He was the man who linked the art world of Peter Blake and Richard Hamilton to the Beatles, and the man who gave the Rolling Stones their bohemian credibility through his ultimately destructive relationship with Keith Richards and Anita Pallenberg, who were sharing his flat at the time this book is set. He was also the man who hosted Yoko Ono and John Lennon's joint exhibition 'You Are Here' and who gave Gilbert and George their first exhibition. His life is explored in Harriet Vyner's brilliant aural history *Groovy Bob*. I was delighted to discover that book was edited by Jon Riley, who also edited the book you've just read.

Rhodri Pugh is an entirely imagined character, though he would have served under James Callaghan, Labour Home Secretary at the time this book is set. Before becoming Prime Minister in 1976, Callaghan was a key figure in pushing back the so-called British model of drug treatment, in which drug use was regarded as principally a medical problem. In 1971, when James Callaghan introduced the Misuse of Drugs Act, there were fewer than five thousand problematic drug users in the UK. There are now over a quarter of a million, mostly using heroin or cocaine. I owe thanks to Caroline Coon, co-founder of Release, for taking time to talk to me about drug abuse and the state's response to it in the period the book is set.

The shambolic 'Alchemical Wedding' at the Royal Albert Hall was the first time John Lennon and Yoko Ono performed their 'Bagism' artwork. The episode in which the police attempted to prevent women taking their clothes off is taken from a contemporary account in *International Times*. The Hell's Angel who stood up to the police that day is identified as Billy Tumbleweed, aka 'Sweet William' Fritsch, the San Francisco Hell's Angel leader, poet and occasional lover of Janis Joplin. He was also the man employed to organise the Rolling Stones' lethally slipshod security at Altamont in December 1969.

Huge thanks to Roz Brody, Mike Holmes, Janet King and Chris Sansom for their continued advice and encouragement (particularly Chris, this time, for helping turn the impossible into the plausible); to Laura Wilson, Professor Bernard Knight and Carol Bridgestock for their expert help, and to Jon Riley, Rose Tomaszewska and Nick de Somogyi at Quercus, as well as Joshua Kendall at Mulholland for all their many smart comments. Thanks also, finally, to Jane McMorrow.

ABOUT THE AUTHOR

WILLIAM SHAW is an award-winning pop-culture journalist who has written for *The Observer* (London), *The Independent*, and *The Telegraph*, as well as the *New York Times*, *Wired*, and *Details*, and he is the author of the novel *She's Leaving Home*. He lives in Sussex, England.

MULHOLLAND BOOKS

You won't be able to put down these Mulholland books.

BROKEN MONSTERS *by Lauren Beukes*

BROOD *by Chase Novak*

GENOCIDE OF ONE *by Kazuaki Takano*

THE CONVERT'S SONG *by Sebastian Rotella*

SERPENTS IN THE COLD *by Thomas O'Malley and Douglas Graham Purdy*

THE KINGS OF LONDON *by William Shaw*

SWEET NOTHING *by Richard Lange*

LAMENTATION *by C. J. Sansom*

CANARY *by Duane Swierczynski*

LIFE OR DEATH *by Michael Robotham*

INSPECTOR OF THE DEAD *by David Morrell*

COMA *by Robin Cook*

HARDCASE *by Dan Simmons*

THE THICKET *by Joe R. Lansdale*

DOMINION *by C. J. Sansom*

THE STRING DIARIES *by Stephen Lloyd Jones*

SHE'S LEAVING HOME *by William Shaw*

WATCHING YOU *by Michael Robotham*

SEAL TEAM SIX: HUNT THE JACKAL *by Don Mann with Ralph Pezzullo*

BRAVO *by Greg Rucka*

THE COMPETITION *by Marcia Clark*

Visit mulhollandbooks.com for
your daily suspense fiction fix.

Download the FREE Mulholland Books app.